THE LONG WAY HOME

THE LONG WAY HOME

stories by
RICHARD CHIZMAR

CEMETERY DANCE PUBLICATIONS

Baltimore

 2019

shiny layers, revealing the rot that lies underneath. His stories feel like so many teeth: short and sharp and ready to draw blood."

— Scott Smith

"Richard Chizmar's voice is authentic and powerful, and the stories he tells in *A Long December* are a joy, by turns dark and darkly funny, always compelling, always evocative. He hooks you fast and his words will linger in your mind long after you've finished reading, the mark of a special talent."

—Michael Koryta

"Exceptional stories that lay our hearts, lives and fears bare with brutal, beautiful economy."

—Michael Marshall Smith

"Richard Chizmar's talent is a fierce, poignant marvel. His exquisite stories shatter."

—Richard Christian Matheson

"Richard Chizmar is the kind of writer I love—his prose is sharp, simple, and to the point. He grabs your attention in the first paragraph, and never lets go, and, even better, his writing never gets in the way of his story. It flows so smoothly it's as if you're experiencing it rather than reading it. Another writer told me years ago that whenever he wrote what he thought was a showstopper of a sentence or paragraph, he would stop writing, admire his work, then immediately cut it. 'The last thing you want the reader to do is stop to admire the writing,' he said. 'All that does is pull them out of the story you're trying to tell.' This, of course, is not advice you'll ever hear from MFA writing programs, but for those of us battling in the trenches every day, it was great advice. Chizmar is a master of this form, and hats off to him!"

—John Saul

"Chilling and thought-provoking tales that quietly uncover horror in the most ordinary of lives."

—Kelley Armstrong

"Richard Chizmar has a very special talent for creating a homely, believable world — the kind of world that you and I live in every day. But he gradually invests that world with a creeping sense of unease, and then he throws open those suburban front doors and brings us face to face with all the unthinkable horrors that have been hiding behind them."

—Graham Masterton

"Richard Chizmar is a master delineator of two phenomena – the human condition and the inhuman condition. Some of his people may be monsters, but Chizmar has the rare talent to make you see his monsters as people. His work eloquently and expertly expands the dimensions of the genre…and should concern anyone interested in exceptional writing talent."

— **Robert Bloch**

"…a writer of great accomplishment. His work, always effective, is notable for its clarity and originality of concept. Chizmar has a great gift for the sinister."

— **Peter Straub**

"Richard Chizmar will soon distinguish himself as a major writer of American suspense fiction."

— **Ed Gorman**

"Richard Chizmar is the kind of writer who gives the genre of dark fiction the dignity it deserves. He is not only a superb writer, but a seductive storyteller as well. He dangles hidden secrets in front of our faces, and then dares us not to follow him as he pulls away. We do follow, we *have* to follow. With vivid characters, confident prose, dialogue so realistic that the pages nearly speak it *aloud*, and carefully constructed plots, Chizmar *makes* us follow those hidden secrets he dangles before us, just out of reach, and at the end of the journey, we are always amply rewarded."

— **Ray Garton**

"Richard Chizmar is one of the great, unsung short story writers in the horror genre. His work is powerful, bruising and often emotionally devastating. His new novella, *A Long December,* which closes this collection, is a towering achievement in an already impressive career."

— **Josh Boone**

"Richard Chizmar's stories are brisk but thoughtful, sometimes tender and sometimes baring their teeth…and occasionally at the same time. His work has a distinctive and human—and eminently readable—voice."

— **Mick Garris**

"Tight, imaginative and totally engaging writing make this a must have book. Grab a copy of *A Long December.* It's fantastic."

— **Joe R. Lansdale**

"In *A Long December*, Richard Chizmar reminds us all that not only is he an accomplished editor and publisher, he is also one hell of a writer. This is something most of us have known forever, but given Rich's preoccupation with launching the careers of a thousand other writers via *Cemetery Dance*, fresh examples were few and far between. Thankfully we now have a season's worth of treasures to savor, and given the breadth and scope of the nightmares contained within this massive tome, and the sure hand with which they have been created, Chizmar's enormous talent as a writer is something we're unlikely to forget anytime soon. In all respects, he is one of the best in the business, and this book is a veritable feast for horror fans."

— **Kealan Patrick Burke**

"There's a nostalgic pulp sensibility to the stories in Richard Chizmar's *A Long December*, and it is neatly rendered in a way as to be refreshing and deeply disturbing. These stories are about our secrets, and our darkest and deepest desires. Full of heart and nasty shocks in equal doses."

— **Paul Tremblay**

"Comparisons to Ray Bradbury and Stephen King come to mind first, but as you journey through Richard Chizmar's stories – peopled with the ordinary, dark and dangerous – you begin to realize this is purely Chizmar territory and there is no escape. The prose is taut, the insights surprising. *A Long December* is a vivid, disturbing, darkly humorous work by a writer at the top of his game."

— **Douglas Clegg**

"*A Long December* is horror fiction at its very best, and at its most frightening. Chizmar is a deceptive, masterful writer. His prose is so clean and direct, you don't realize just how macabre and terrifying each story is until you've devoured a half dozen in one fevered sitting and suddenly realize your blood is cold, nerves wrecked, and adrenaline screaming. By then, it's too late. You're trapped. Chizmar has lured you into his mad, warped world of horror and psychological depravity, and there is nothing for you to do but see it to the end. Masterful, classic, stay-up-all-night stories that should not be missed."

— **Eric Rickstad**

"Man, these are great stories. One can't help but wonder if the souls of Ray Bradbury, O Henry and Rod Serling have taken up residence in Richard Chizmar's noggin."

— **Linwood Barclay**

For Mary Wilson and Nancy Chizmar,
sisters and Guardian Angels

THE LONG WAY HOME

"The human face is, after all, nothing more nor less than a mask."

—AGATHA CHRISTIE

"Monsters are real, and ghosts are real too. They live inside us, and sometimes, they win."

—STEPHEN KING

"Man is the cruelest animal."

—FRIEDRICH NIETZSCHE

THE MAN BEHIND THE MASK

She steers the car to the curb, fumbles her cellphone out of her purse and calls her husband.

He answers after the first ring. "Having second thoughts?"

"Yes…no…I don't know." Her hand is trembling.

"Want me to come get you?"

"No," she says quickly. "I just…I just needed to hear your voice I think."

"Where are you?"

"Parked down the street from her house. I've already driven past once."

"Honey, you know you don't have to do this. You can change your mind. You can postpone."

"I know."

"Are you sure you don't want me to—"

"Brad?"

"Yeah, honey?"

"It's been fifteen years. I have to do this."

Deep sigh. "I just wish you had let me come with you."

"And I love you for wanting that, I do, but you've done enough."

"You'll call me the minute you're finished?"

"Promise." She glances in the rearview mirror, takes some Kleenex from her purse and dabs at her eyes.

"Okay…I love you, Jenn. I hope you find what you're looking for."

"Me too, baby. Me too."

JENNIFER SHEA, thirty-five-year-old mother of two little girls, second grade teacher, and recreation league soccer coach, was The Boogeyman's fifth victim.

Between the years of 1999 and 2006, The Boogeyman (deemed so by both local and national press) kidnapped, tortured and killed at least sixteen young women ranging from the ages of seventeen to twenty-three.

Jennifer was nineteen when she was taken. A sophomore journalism major at the University of Maryland, she was walking to her car alone after a night class when she was knocked unconscious from behind in the parking lot. When she regained consciousness, she was naked and shackled to a wall in a damp cellar. The cellar floor was dirt and the walls were constructed of blocks of stone. The room was lit by a single naked light bulb. She had no idea how long she had been unconscious or how far they had traveled.

Jennifer estimated it was at least twelve hours before her captor made his first appearance in the cellar. He was tall and thick-bodied and wore jeans, a flannel shirt and black work boots. He also wore a mask. She struggled to accurately describe it to the police detectives later, but the closest comparison she could make was the Michael Myers mask from the *Halloween* movies. It was ghostly pale and almost shapeless, and she still had nightmares about it fifteen years later.

The Boogeyman had brought her a glass of warm water on that first visit. He hadn't spoken a word. Just stood there and watched her drink and took the glass from her when she was finished. As he reached for it, his fingers brushed against Jennifer's trembling hand, and she couldn't stop herself from crying out in revulsion. Terrified that he was going to punish her, Jennifer cowered against the rough stone wall and prepared to be beaten. But the man only continued watching her for another silent moment before walking away.

The beatings—and much worse—would come soon enough.

Jennifer's family and the police worked hard to keep the details of her thirteen-day captivity and eventual escape out of the press, but as is often the case, someone inside the department leaked confidential files. Probably for a nice, five-figure payday. Serial killer stories were always big sellers.

In the weeks that followed, the entire country learned about Jennifer's ordeal. *The Baltimore Sun* ran a three-part series that dominated the front page on three consecutive Sundays. *People* magazine put Jennifer's student ID photo on the front cover with a blood-red headline that read: 13 DAYS OF TORTURE AND TERROR. The accompanying article went into tabloid levels of graphic detail about The Boogeyman and his preferred methods of torture: the cigarette burns, the scalpels, the nail gun, and even the hedge clippers. There was also a police photograph of Jennifer's grime-covered right hand, badly infected and missing the pinky finger.

Even worse, if that were possible, was the blurry—and highly illegal—scan of Jennifer's medical report that appeared as a sidebar in the *People* article, which not only confirmed that she had been repeatedly raped and sodomized by The Boogeyman, but stated the doctors felt her mental state was borderline close to suffering permanent damage. In other words, they were afraid that she had been driven crazy by the ordeal.

Jennifer's parents threatened to sue the hospital and *People* and even went so far as to hire a team of lawyers, but in the days following her release, Jennifer realized that the doctors were right. The Boogeyman hadn't merely taken her body; he had stolen her soul.

JENNIFER ISN'T religious by nature. She believes in a higher power of some sort, but doesn't read the bible or attend church, and isn't entirely sold on Heaven or Hell. Still, she crosses herself before getting out of the car. "Here goes nothing."

The house is a neat two-story with a dark blue door and shutters and a tidy lawn split down the middle by a winding brick walkway leading up to a wide front porch. The veranda is lined with a bed of tulips. Jennifer notices them and thinks: *Anyone with tulips has to be a nice person, right?*

She limps slightly as she makes her way up the sidewalk because of the missing toes on her right foot, but she doesn't think anyone watching her will notice. She's had years of practice now.

She reaches the porch and while deciding whether to ring the bell or knock on the door, a horrible thought occurs to her: *What if she doesn't answer? What if I worked up my courage and came all this way and she changed her mind and isn't home? Or even worse, she's home and refuses to come to the door?*

She glances over her shoulder at her car parked at the curb. *I could just leave. It's not too late.* She vigorously shakes her head, scolding herself, and squeezes her hands together. *You can do this. You* need *to do this.*

She steadies herself and rings the doorbell—and immediately hears muffled footsteps from inside the house and the unlocking of a deadbolt.

The door opens and she is standing there, the woman Jennifer knows from so many photographs and television news reports: Mrs. Joanne Cavanaugh.

Jennifer thinks she might actually faint, right there on the front porch, but then Mrs. Cavanaugh smiles and it's a warm smile that reaches all the way up to her tired green eyes—and the kindness Jennifer sees in that smile makes her want to cry.

"Mrs. Cavanaugh," she says, her voice not much more than a whisper.

The older woman surprises her—no, shocks her—by opening her arms. "Jennifer, come here."

And Jennifer does. She steps forward and lets Mrs. Cavanaugh hug her tight, and then she's hugging back, and it's all she can do to choke back her sobs.

Mrs. Cavanaugh pulls away first, breaking the long, silent embrace, her hands still on Jennifer's shoulders. Jennifer uses the back of her hand to wipe at the tears and snot on her face. "I'm sorry, I'm a mess."

"Come in, come in," the older woman says, and steps back into the house to allow Jennifer entry.

Jennifer walks into the foyer, thinking: *Everything is going to be okay now.*

But then she sees the carpeted stairway leading up to the second floor and all along the wall there are framed school pictures of Cassidy Cavanaugh. They are perfectly spaced in ascending order, the little blonde girl with the pretty smile growing a year older with each subsequent photo.

Jennifer tries to look away, tries to recapture the good feeling she just experienced, but she can't.

TIME WAS impossible to track in the cellar. There were no windows, so Jennifer never knew if it was night or day. For a while, she'd tried to keep track by estimating each hour's passage, stacking them up inside her head, but that only served to make her thoughts more confused and jumbled. She was always hungry and thirsty and her body ached.

The Boogeyman came to the cellar more frequently now. Sometimes he brought her a glass or a bottle of water. Other times, a cold hamburger from McDonald's or Burger King. Once, he came with a small Coke with ice and a chicken sandwich, and Jennifer thought she had to be dreaming.

But it wasn't a dream. It wasn't even a nightmare.

The Boogeyman raped her. He burned her nipples with cigarettes. He carved random patterns into her stomach and thighs with a scalpel, the blood hot and sticky on her flesh. And he did other things, unspeakable things.

He always wore the mask and rarely talked, and when he did, it was only to make demands of her. His voice was rough and raspy, his laughter cruel. Jennifer hated him more than she had ever hated anything else in the world and prayed that she would die soon.

Then, after what Jennifer guessed was a week of this madness—and a guess was all it really was—The Boogeyman walked down the wooden stairs to the cellar carrying another girl in his arms.

She was naked and unconscious and had long blonde hair that covered her face. Jennifer watched as he dropped the girl roughly to the dirt floor and chained her to the opposite wall of the cellar. Jennifer had never even noticed the shackles on the other side of the room.

When he was finished, the Boogeyman knelt down and double-checked each of the locks. Then he leaned over and pressed his face close to the woman's neck and face. Jennifer shuddered at the sight and her own recent memories. She knew what the Boogeyman was doing: he was smelling her.

Hours later, long after the Boogeyman had left without a word, the blonde girl regained consciousness with a groan. The moans soon turned to tears and her sobs to screams. Jennifer sat against the far wall and watched and listened to all of it.

When the screams finally stopped, Jennifer asked quietly, "What's your name?"

The blonde girl flinched and looked up at her with wide crazy eyes, and Jennifer realized that the girl hadn't noticed she wasn't alone. "Cass…Cassidy," she said. "How did I get here?"

JENNIFER SITS on the sofa in Mrs. Cavanaugh's living room and tries to push the memories away. The older woman has retreated to the kitchen to fix them tea and Jennifer is alone in the room.

She looks around. *Reader's Digest* condensed volumes line two tall bookshelves. A curio cabinet filled with tiny crystal figurines stands in one corner. An enormous cat-tree dominates another corner, but there are no cats anywhere in sight. An old-fashioned tube television is centered along the far wall. A large family portrait hangs above it: Mrs. Cavanaugh standing next to her late husband, with a pig-tailed, braces-wearing Cassidy in front of them.

"Here we go," Mrs. Cavanaugh says, walking into the room carrying a tray with matching teapot and cups and a small plate stacked with cookies.

She places the tray on the glass coffee table in front of the sofa, pours both cups, and takes her tea with her as she sits in a well-used reading chair.

Jennifer knows from all the articles that Mrs. Cavanaugh is about the same age as her own mother, but she looks at least ten years older. There are streaks of gray in her hair and dark circles beneath her eyes.

"Okay, first things first," the older woman says after sipping her tea. "Now that we've finally met, I'm Joanne. No more Mrs. Cavanaugh."

Jennifer nods. "Okay…Joanne."

"That's better. Next thing: no more apologies from either one of us. I know I wasn't the kindest person back when all this happened. I was angry and bitter and a first-class bitch, but that's all in the past. And I know we've had a few false starts with this meeting of ours, but that's understandable. I always said it would happen when the time was right."

"That's the same thing my counselor always said."

"Smart lady." Joanne hesitates. "Your counselor *is* a woman?"

"Yes."

"Makes sense that it would be." Joanne takes another sip of tea and then a bite of a cookie, and Jennifer realizes the woman is waiting for her to start. She takes a deep breath and begins:

"I've wanted to talk to you for so long. I know you've read the police reports and my letters, but there were some things I needed to say face-to-face."

Jennifer forces herself to stop fidgeting with a seam in the sofa cushion. She clasps her hands together in her lap and goes on.

"Your daughter...Cassidy...and I were only together for a short period of time, not even a week, but we grew very close. All we had in that horrible place was each other."

Her voice cracks and tears begin to stream down Jennifer's face. Joanne gets up and takes a box of tissue from a nearby end table and hands it to her.

"Thank you," Jennifer says, wiping her eyes.

"Just take your time. I know this is difficult."

Jennifer blows her nose and continues. "We talked about *everything*. Growing up. School. Boyfriends. Pets. Vacations. Books and movies. Friends. Our parents. We shared what little food we were given. We watched over each other when one of us fell asleep. He...he tried to make us hurt each other, for fun, but we refused. It was the one thing we wouldn't do, no matter how much he hit us or threatened us. We wouldn't hurt each other."

"Thank you, Jesus, for that," Joanne says, and now her eyes are a little shiny.

"The worst part was watching…and listening…to him hurt her. I wanted to close my eyes and disappear, but I couldn't leave her alone with him. Instead, I would yell to her that it was going to be okay, that it would be over soon. He would tell me to shut up, to be quiet, but I wouldn't listen. I kept on yelling. She would do the same thing when it was my turn. We held on tight to each other's voices. We took care of each other the best we could. It wasn't much, but it was all we had."

"The things he did to her…the bad stuff…did you leave anything out in your letters? Did you tell me everything or did you leave some things out to spare me?"

Jennifer shakes her head. "No. I couldn't do that. I told you everything I could remember."

"You're sure?"

"I'm sure. My counselor had me keep a journal and any-time I remembered something new I would write it down—for myself and the police. The press never got a hold of most of the things I remembered later on. But I always told the detectives and I always told you in my letters."

"Cassidy…she talked about us?"

"Oh, yes," Jennifer says, surprising herself with the slight-est of smiles. "She adored you both. She told me all about the movie nights you and her had from the time she was a little girl right up until college. Double features with popcorn and pizza and blankets on the sofa. She told me that you were the one who taught her her love of books. And I heard all about how her father was the worrier in the family. How he was too nervous to teach her to ride a bike, so you had to do it. How he didn't want her to play soccer or ride a skateboard because he was afraid she'd break a bone. She told me how it was you who taught her to climb trees and that, the first time she fell, you bandaged her knee and took her to get a milkshake and made her promise not to tell her father how it happened."

Joanne laughs and it's a wonderful sound to hear in the quiet living room. "That man could worry the bark off a tree, I swear to you." She stares out the big bay window overlooking the front yard, remembering, dust motes dancing in the rays of sunshine slanting into the room. "He was a good man, a good father." She looks back at Jennifer. "And she was the best daughter in the whole world."

ON JUNE 20, 2001, Jennifer Shea became the first—and only—person to escape from the serial killer known as The Boogeyman.

This is how it happened:

One day The Boogeyman simply made a mistake and failed to properly lock Jennifer's shackles. She claimed that this occurred after a rather violent episode and that The Boogeyman seemed to be unusually angry and out of control that day. No matter the cause, once she was certain he was gone from the house, Jennifer was able to thread the heavy chains through the rungs in her shackles and get her arms and legs free.

She slowly crossed the cellar on legs that could barely walk and tried to free Cassidy. She tried everything she could think of, but was unsuccessful. Next, she decided to sneak upstairs and search the house for a key or a tool to help free her friend, or for a telephone to summon help. Unable to locate any of these items, she had begun to return to the basement when headlights from outside swept over the dark kitchen she was standing in. The Boogeyman was back.

She hurried best she could down the stairs, easing closed the cellar door behind her, and pretended to lock herself up again. She prayed he wouldn't notice anything out of place inside the house or anything different with her chains. She prayed he was spent from the earlier episode and wouldn't come for her.

Instead, he came for Cassidy.

Practically growling at her, The Boogeyman battered her with his fists, again and again, striking her in the stomach and face until, exhausted, he dropped to a knee in front of her, gasping for breath.

That was the moment a bleeding Cassidy had been waiting for. She lifted her arms overhead with all the strength remaining inside her petite body and brought the heavy metal shackle around her wrists directly down on top of The Boogeyman's bowed head. There was a loud *thunk* as steel met flesh and he collapsed hard to the ground, dazed and mumbling and on the cusp of unconsciousness.

Cassidy looked up at Jennifer and screamed, "Run!"

Jennifer hurriedly unthreaded the chains again and started across the room toward her friend.

"Just run," Cassidy yelled at her. "He's gonna wake up. You can't help me. Just GO!"

Jennifer ran. Stumbling upstairs. Across the kitchen. Out the door and into an uncut grassy field where a red pick-up truck was parked. She didn't stop to check for keys. She kept running across the field and into the woods beyond. She kept going once she broke free of the tree-line and came upon a seldom-traveled dirt back road. She didn't stop until nearly an hour later when she was found by a pair of teenaged brothers out hunting for squirrels on the northern edge of their family property.

The police were called and Jennifer was helicoptered to the hospital where she was combed over for evidence and given an IV with fluids to combat dehydration and something to help her anxiety. Her family rushed to the hospital and members of the police detective squad bustled in and out of the room with question after question. There was even a sketch artist, but all Jennifer could describe was The Boogeyman's mask.

Three-and-a-half hours later, with Jennifer's help, the police located the farm where The Boogeyman had been taking his victims. There, they found the dirt cellar with the shackles, just as Jennifer had described.

They also found the lifeless body of Cassidy Cavanaugh still chained to the wall. Her heart had been removed from her chest.

The next day, during excavation of a suspicious-looking section of the yard, the police discovered the remains of four more missing women. The bodies were quickly identified and the next of kin notified.

Of course, the Boogeyman was long gone by the time the police and SWAT teams reached the secluded farm. Forensic experts pored over the house, lifting prints and fabric and hair samples, but they found little of any use. The Boogeyman was a genuine mystery. He went by the name of Jackson Greene—not his real name, the police would soon discover—and had rented the house over the telephone some two years earlier. He paid his rent on time each month, mailing a money order to the landlord, and there had never been any problems with his occupancy. Mr. Greene owned no credit cards, didn't work anywhere within three hundred miles of the town, and had never been in trouble with local law enforcement.

The landlord, a real estate agent by the name of Bryan Kennedy, claimed to have met Mr. Greene once, when he'd handed over the keys to the house at his real estate office two years earlier. His description of the man as "white and tall and kinda chunky" did little to aid the police in their pursuit of The Boogeyman.

Mr. Kennedy did, however, remember one important character trait about the man: he was able to recall from that one meeting and several subsequent phone calls that Mr. Greene's voice was particularly memorable. He described it as "kinda rough and raspy, like maybe he was a longtime smoker." This observation—based on Jennifer's testimony—reinforced for detectives that Mr. Greene and The Boogeyman were indeed one and the same man.

The sensationalistic Boogeyman article appeared in *People* magazine one week later and additional feature stories soon popped up in several other high-circulation periodicals, including *Time* magazine and the *New York Times*. Book and movie agents called the house. Reporters camped out in the front yard hoping for a thirty-second clip for the evening news. Police even arrested a local photographer who had hidden in the bushes in the back yard to try and take pictures through a window.

Jennifer Shea, Cassidy Cavanaugh, and The Boogeyman were national news for much of the remainder of the summer—until a bigger, gaudier story came along. Then they slowly slipped to the back pages and were eventually all but forgotten…

Until nearly a year later, when to the police and public's horror, the killings started again a few hundred miles south in central Virginia. That it was the same Jackson Greene, the same Boogeyman, committing these atrocities was never in question to the detectives investigating the disappearances. Everything was exactly the same: the type of victims, the method with which they were taken, even the timing of the disappearances.

The Boogeyman had simply relocated to another state and, once he had settled in, started killing again.

Until, one day, four years later, he finally stopped for good.

The last known victim of The Boogeyman was a nurse by the name of Ashley Francenti. Miss Francenti was taken from a hospital parking lot on the night of October 3, 2006 and remained missing for almost two weeks, until her mutilated body was discovered by a road crew in a drainage ditch running alongside I-95 not a half-mile away from her apartment. Miss Francenti was missing two fingers from her right hand and her heart had been carved from her chest. It remains to this day the only time The Boogeyman returned one of his victims.

Jennifer Shea lived those years in a perpetual state of fear and anxiety and guilt. Fear and apprehension that The Boogeyman would hunt her down and find her again. Guilt that she had abandoned Cassidy in that filthy cellar and was ultimately responsible for her death.

When the disappearances eventually stopped, it did little to ease her troubled mind. As one of the detectives who originally investigated Jennifer's case told her one afternoon on the telephone: "We have to hope that the son-of-a-bitch died or was picked up for another crime and is rotting away inside a prison cell somewhere. Otherwise, people like him don't just stop. Sometimes, they move on to other places. Sometimes, they take a break. But they don't just stop. Ever."

"I TRIED so hard to free her…"

Jennifer stops to catch her breath. The sun from the bay window has crept across the living room and is shining on her back now. She wishes she had a glass of cold water.

"…but it was hopeless. When she yelled for me to run, I took off on instinct. We were so used to listening to each other. Later, I wondered why I had run at all and thought…hoped… she had found the key in one of his pockets and was able to free herself."

She struggles to get the next part out of her mouth.

"Not a day has gone by that I haven't felt regret. Not a day that I haven't felt guilt. I loved your daughter, Mrs. Cavanaugh. We only knew each other for six days, but I loved Cassidy like a sister."

Jennifer is crying again, her words rendered almost unintelligible, and she is startled to see fresh tears coursing down the older woman's cheeks. She realizes Joanne is choking back sobs of her own and Jennifer sees something else in her expression that causes a sensation of almost joyous relief to wash over her: the woman is looking at Jennifer with forgiveness in her eyes.

Jennifer wipes at the tears on her cheeks and opens her mouth to continue, but she stops when a shadow falls over her from behind the sofa and Joanne's eyes flash wide.

Jennifer realizes in that moment, too late, that it's not forgiveness she sees in the old woman's eyes. It's *regret*.

"I'm sorry," Joanne sobs, shrinking back into the reading chair. "I'm so sorry. He…tricked me."

Jennifer feels a brush of air as the shadow behind her moves closer and a hand touches her shoulder.

"It's so very lovely to see you again after all these years," a familiar raspy voice whispers just inches from her ear.

Jennifer Shea wants to get up from the sofa and run. She wants to run far away and never stop running, but she can't. Not this time. Instead, she slowly turns around and, for the first and final time, looks at the man behind the mask.

THE BAD GUYS

"I'm scared," the dying cop said.

"You're gonna be okay. Help'll be here soon."

"I'm dying."

I shook my head. "No, you're not. You're gonna be okay."

My partner of fifteen years coughed and blood bubbled from between his lips. I lifted his head higher, my fingers slick with sweat. My other hand remained pressed against the bullet wound in his chest, a warm scarlet glove.

"You get him, Ken? You get the bad guy?"

I nodded, glancing at the crumpled figure lying on the other side of the dark parking lot. "I got him."

He coughed again. A mist of blood sprayed my face.

I didn't know what else to do. Head up so he doesn't choke. Pressure on the wound to control the bleeding. I keyed the radio unit hanging on my vest. "Dispatch, where the hell's my ambulance?"

"Accident on 22. ETA six minutes."

I didn't know if he had six minutes.

As if he were reading my mind, he closed his eyes and his head went heavy in my hand. "Hang on, buddy. Ambulance on the way."

I looked up at the deserted road leading into the warehouse parking lot. I knew my 10-00 would be answered by every officer in the area, but we were way out in the middle of nowhere. In another ten minutes, this place would be a circus. I just prayed it wouldn't be too late.

"I took...it."

His voice caught me by surprise, and I wasn't sure I'd heard him right. I looked down and his eyes were open—wide open and fierce. "What? What'd you—"

"I...took the money."

My entire body went numb. My stomach clenched.

"The money and..." He started to cough again, and then he was moaning in pain. An awful sound.

"Don't talk, buddy. It's okay. Don't—"

"Have...to."

I didn't want to hear it. Not another damn word.

"The money...the guns," he whispered, his eyes closing again. "I took. Parker's...innocent."

Rookie Donald Parker. Home on administrative leave these past three weeks pending investigation.

Sirens now in the distance.

He heard them, too. He opened his eyes, and my heart broke. My partner. My best friend.

I couldn't help it. I thought of his wife asleep at home. Jillian. Now that the kids were old enough, she'd just gone back to work at the elementary school. She was excited to teach again. Aaron, his ten-year-old son. His old man had been showing him how to throw a curve ball. Kayla, his eight-year-old daughter. He'd just built her a two-story play-house in the back yard. He'd painted it pink, and she called it her castle. I never once wondered where the money had come from.

The sirens were louder now. Closer.

"It doesn't matter," I said, knowing even then it was a lie. "Don't say a word to anyone."

He surprised me by lifting his head. His lips moved, but I couldn't hear what he was saying. I bent closer.

He reached up with a blood-streaked hand and grabbed my arm. "I...I'm sorry."

He held my gaze, tears spilling from his eyes and running down his cheeks. I started crying then, too. Silently, the way men like us are supposed to cry.

I heard the wail of sirens and the screech of tires on gravel behind me. I looked over my shoulder and saw a trio of patrol cars. More on the way in the distance. Still no ambulance.

I looked back at my partner and knew it would be too late. His eyes were open and sightless. His body limp. I watched as his lifeless hand slipped from my arm to the gravel below.

I heard the slam of car doors and rising voices.

I took his hand in mine and squeezed it.

I thought of his wife and kids at home and the knock on their door that was coming later that night.

I thought of the funeral service. The dress blues and white gloves. The news helicopters and procession to the cemetery.

And then I thought of the body camera I was wearing—and how I would have to find a way to disable it. Damaged in the exchange of gunfire. When I dove behind the car.

I glanced at the bad guy lying dead across the parking lot. It would be ruled a good shooting. I would be okay.

I would be okay.

THE MEEK SHALL INHERIT...

"Would you eat a dog turd for a hundred bucks?"

Brian stopped mid-shot, the basketball poised above his head. He looked over at his friend standing in the driveway. "Dry turd or fresh and wet?"

Jimmy considered the question and answered with a crooked smile, "Moist. Couple hours old."

Brian dribbled to the baseline and shot. *Swish.* He gathered the loose ball and drilled a pass into Jimmy's scrawny chest. "Make it or you're the horse. Again."

Jimmy dribbled awkwardly to the baseline. Started to shoot.

"Back up, you little cheater."

Jimmy flipped his best friend the finger and backed up a few steps. Took the shot. *Airball.*

Brian threw his arms in the air and ran around the court, hooting, "Brian Anderson! Champion of the worldddd!"

Jimmy shook his head and kicked the ball into the front yard. "Dick sucking champion of the world."

Out on the street, a muscular, bare-chested teenager cruised by on a skateboard. He glanced at the two boys standing in the driveway and smirked. "You girls having fun playing kickball?"

Jimmy took a step toward the road. "Your mom had fun playing with my—"

Brian came up behind him, clamped a hand over his friend's mouth, silencing him in mid-insult.

But it was too late.

The muscle-head on the skateboard grinded to a stop. "What was that?"

"He was talking to me," Brian said. "Not you, Billy."

Brian squeezed Jimmy's shoulder, and Jimmy got the hint. "Oww. Yeah, I wasn't talking to you."

Billy glared at the two boys for a moment, deciding whether they were worth the trouble. He looked up and down the street—most bullies, Brian believed, had a kind of grown-up radar—and then he gave them the double-bird and pushed off, disappearing around the corner.

Brian sat down in the grassy front yard and let out a deep breath. "Jesus, Jimmy, you and your big mouth."

Jimmy plopped down next to him. "I think we could take him."

"I think you're wrong."

"He's not that tough."

"He's fifteen. We're twelve. He smokes and has arms the size of our legs. We still have sleepovers."

Jimmy shrugged. "Nothing wrong with sleepovers. They're fun."

Brian couldn't argue with that, so he laid back and stared at the passing clouds overhead. Jimmy plucked blades of grass and flicked them into the air, one after the other. Somewhere down the street, a dog barked.

Jimmy finally broke the silence. "This sucks. Second week of summer vacation and we're already bored."

"At least you were at the lake all last week," Brian said, squinting at a cloud that resembled an alligator.

"Yeah, with my mom and dad. Like that's any fun. You have any idea how much sunscreen my Mom makes me wear?"

Brian laughed. He did have an idea. He had seen it many times firsthand at the neighborhood swimming pool. When Jimmy's mom was finished with him, Jimmy looked like a skinny, little Yeti ready to prowl a snowy mountaintop.

"And my Dad…did you know he still wears a Speedo?"

Brian belly-laughed. He couldn't help it.

"Not funny, dude. It's freaking embarrassing. You can practically see his junk."

Thinking about Mr. Gallagher's junk was not a pretty picture. Jimmy's old man weighed about three hundred pounds—and that was naked. How he had produced a beanpole of a son (that's what he always called Jimmy) was a mystery to everyone.

Brian shook away the disturbing image, sat up and patted Jimmy on the back. "C'mon, let's play another game of Horse."

Jimmy groaned and pushed himself to his feet just as a van slowed out on the road and swung into the driveway next door. The boys watched a middle-aged man, tall and thin, bald and wearing thick glasses, get out of the van and walk toward the house.

"Hi, Mr. Pruitt," Jimmy yelled, waving.

The man flinched, like he had been woken from a day-dream, and looked over at the boys. He opened his mouth like he was going to say something, then closed it again and gave them a shy wave before disappearing into the front door.

"That was weird," Brian said.

Jimmy nodded, still staring at the closed front door. "He's been like that for awhile now. My mom says it's because he's still in mourning."

"Didn't Mrs. Pruitt die like a year ago?"

Jimmy shrugged. "My mom says it takes a long time, especially when you've been together for so many years." And, just like that, Jimmy was thinking about Mrs. Pruitt's kind face and her sweet voice and her chocolate chip cookies—and he felt his eyes filling up.

"You okay, man?" Brian asked.

Jimmy turned away, wiping at his eyes. "I'm fine. It's just sad, that's all. I feel sorry for him."

"Me, too."

"I don't ever want to get married," Jimmy said.

"No worries there, retard. What chick is gonna be dumb enough to marry your ugly ass?"

Jimmy was bright enough in the ways of childhood to understand the twelve-year-old translation of this insult was: *it's all gonna be okay, buddy*—so he returned the favor.

"Plenty...starting with your naked sister."

Brian tackled him and the two boys rolled around in the front yard, laughing and wrestling, until Jimmy's mom poked her head out the front door a few minutes later and called him inside for dinner.

LATER THAT evening, a June thunderstorm swept in from the north, turning curbside gutters into miniature rapids and knocking out electricity for most of the town, including both sides of Jimmy's street.

By ten o'clock the next morning, the storm had cleared out, the sky was a brilliant, robin-egg blue, and the electric was back up and running at Jimmy's house.

Jimmy and Brian sat across from each other on the front porch. Half-finished glasses of lemonade and stacks of baseball cards covered the small table, which sat between them. After an hour of intense bargaining (arguing) about fair trades, both boys were slumped back in plastic patio chairs, staring at the screens of their cellphones.

"Damn it," Jimmy moaned and tossed his phone onto the table, knocking over a pile of cards. "I'm getting tired of Hearthstone."

Brian looked up from his phone. "That's because you suck at Hearthstone."

Jimmy ignored the dig and sat up in his chair, an uncharacteristically serious look on his face. "Can I tell you something?"

Brian recognized the tone of his friend's voice and knew it was something important. The last time he'd heard that tone of voice was when Jimmy confided in him about seeing Jan Thompson changing into a bathing suit through her bedroom window. He was eleven then.

Brian turned off his game. "Sure, what's up?"

"You promise not to laugh?"

Brian shrugged. "I promise to try not to. What's going on, man?"

Jimmy looked over his left shoulder at the house, and then over his right at the front yard. Seemingly content that no one was eavesdropping, he scooted his chair closer to Brian. Lowered his voice. "You remember what we were talking about yesterday...about Mr. Pruitt?"

"About him being sad?"

Jimmy shook his head. "About him being different, acting weird."

"Okay, yeah."

Jimmy looked over his shoulder again in the direction of his next-door neighbor's house, then back at Brian. "I was thinking about it last night...remembering *things*." He took a deep breath. "I think something bad might be going on over there."

"What exactly does *something bad* mean?" Brian slid his chair a little closer.

Jimmy thought about it for a moment before answering. "You promised you wouldn't laugh."

"Just tell me what you—"

"I think Mr. Pruitt might be a serial killer."

Brian laughed in his friend's face, then immediately regretted it as he watched Jimmy's cheeks flush beet-red in anger and embarrassment.

"You promised!" Jimmy hissed, jumping to his feet and heading off the porch.

Brian chased after him. "I promised to *try* not to laugh, and I couldn't help it. I'm sorry, man, but Mr. Pruitt a serial killer? That's just nutty."

Jimmy spun on him, his eyes darting all around the yard. "Keep your voice down."

Brian whispered, "Okay, okay, I'm sorry."

"C'mon." Jimmy led Brian across the still-soggy front lawn, away from the house, to the curb, where they sat side by side, their bare feet resting in the slow-trickling run-off that still flowed down the street toward a distant sewer grate.

Jimmy sat there silently, pouting, staring down at the ground. He flicked a pebble onto the road with his big toe. Cleared his throat. Coughed. Finally, he looked up at Brian and said, "I've seen things. Heard things."

"*Things...*" Brian said. "Like the time you thought you saw a UFO landing in the woods behind the park? Or the time you thought you saw the librarian from school holding up a bank on the evening news?"

"The lady in the security video looked just like her and—"

Brian put out his hands in surrender. "All I'm saying is that you watch a lot of movies and have a big imagination and tell a lot of crazy stories." He glanced at the house next door. "Mr. Pruitt is a cool guy. Remember when he helped us fix our go-cart? And when he bought all our lemonade when no one else was even slowing down to take a look?"

"I know he's a nice guy, Brian."

"How about when he covered for us to your parents the night we were bombing cars with snowballs? He saved our asses."

"Look, I know Mr. Pruitt has always been nice to us. But my mom is right—he's changed since his wife died."

"So what, he's quiet now, keeps to himself, maybe he's a little weird. Doesn't make him a serial killer."

"I've heard screams over there."

Brian looked closely at his friend. "Screams?"

Jimmy nodded. "Couple of times."

"And you're sure?"

"First time, I was raking grass in the back yard and I wasn't a hundred percent sure what I'd heard. But the next evening, I was back there shooting my BB gun and I heard it again." Jimmy nodded. "I'm sure."

"Okay, what else?"

"The van."

"What about it?"

"What does an old guy like that need with a van? I mean, why trade in a perfectly good Cadillac for a van when you're all alone?"

Brian shrugged. "Maybe the Cadillac reminded him too much of his wife."

"And he's been shopping a lot. Every day he brings home something new."

"So what?"

"What's he need with a video camera and a tripod? I watched him haul in two metal cages another day. What's he need cages for?"

"Maybe he bought a dog."

"Must be the kind of dog that never needs to go outside then."

Brian rolled his eyes. "What else, Sherlock?"

"The other night, I was helping my dad lay down mulch in the front yard when Mr. Pruitt came home. He'd backed the van into the driveway and was unloading something into his carport, so my dad sent me over there to help. But he didn't want my help. He acted all nervous and pretty much shooed my ass outta there. But I saw some of what he was unloading..."

"What was it?"

"I didn't really know at first. It was all these big sheets of insulation and big foam panels and boxes of sealant and glue." Jimmy, dead serious, locked his eyes on his friend's face. "I looked it up on the internet later that night...I had memorized the exact brands I saw on the boxes. It was all material for sound-proofing a room."

Brian looked down at the wet pavement, his mind turning. He knew Jimmy liked to tell stories, he always had, but he also knew Jimmy was the smartest kid in the entire middle school.

"What do you think?" Jimmy prodded.

Brian looked up at his friend. "I think I should spend the night at your house tonight—and we should keep a close eye on Mr. Pruitt."

"BE QUIET or he's gonna hear us," Jimmy whispered.

"He's not even home, dork. How's he gonna hear us?"

"Oh, yeah."

Despite the serious nature of their investigation, both boys giggled as they crawled on their bellies along the side of Mr. Pruitt's house. It was dusk now. Fireflies blinked in the creeping darkness. Crickets chirped their night symphony in the tall grass. A hush lay over the neighborhood.

As the morning had passed into afternoon, and afternoon into evening, the boys' moods had lightened. They'd spent the majority of the day playing whiffle-ball in the park with their friends and watching high school girls in short-shorts and tank-tops playing Frisbee.

They'd been disappointed to discover that Mr. Pruitt hadn't returned home when they'd first come outside after dinner. To pass the time, they'd gone back in the house and watched the first three innings of the Orioles game with Jimmy's father in the den. Once it was dark enough outside, they'd told Jimmy's dad that they were going to the store for ice cream and were once again disappointed to find Mr. Pruitt's driveway and carport still empty.

Instead of waiting any longer, they'd decided to take advantage of his absence and investigate his ground-level basement windows. Brian led the way, slithering flat on his stomach like a snake, just a dozen or so feet away from the first window, with Jimmy right behind him. For both boys, it felt a lot like playing Army when they were younger.

"Ugh...I think I just put my elbow in dog crap," Jimmy whined.

Brian giggled softly. "Maybe Mr. Pruitt got that dog after all."

"Oh, shut up."

They both shut up and kept crawling.

After another minute, Brian looked back over his shoulder and asked, "What're we gonna say if your dad looks out the window and sees us?"

"That's easy. We say we're looking for toads in the window wells. Remember how we used to collect 'em in buckets?"

"Sometimes I actually forget that you're so smart. Almost there..."

Brian crawled another few feet and stopped—and let out a quiet gasp. Jimmy crawled around him and halted at his side, leaning up on his elbows for a better look.

The narrow basement window had been blacked out. It was hard to tell in the shadows, but it looked like someone had taken thick black tape and covered the inside of the glass with it. Whatever it was, you definitely couldn't see through it.

"Believe me now?" Jimmy whispered.

"WAKE UP."

Brian went on snoring. Jimmy poked his friend in the ribs again, harder this time. "C'mon, wake up."

Brian groaned and rolled onto his side. "Lemme alone."

"He's home," Jimmy whispered and crawled to the window.

Brian sat up in his sleeping bag on the floor. "What time is it?"

"Almost midnight. He just pulled in. Hurry up."

Brian kicked his way out of the sleeping bag and, rubbing his eyes, joined his friend at the window. "What's he doing?"

"Nothing yet. He's still in the van."

They watched in silence, their faces pressed close to the window. Mr. Pruitt's lawn and driveway were lost in a spider-web of shadows.

"You sure he's still in there?" Brian asked.

Before Jimmy could answer, the driver's-side door opened, the van's interior light flashed on, and the boys had a clear view of Mr. Pruitt stepping out onto the driveway. He closed the door with a muffled *thud* and the night swallowed him.

Brian shifted for a better look and bumped his head against the window.

"Be careful," Jimmy whispered. "He could hear us."

"I can't see him. Did he go inside?"

"I never saw the front door open. Maybe he went in the side door under the carport."

"Or maybe he's sneaking over here right now for a closer look at us," Brian teased. "And he's wearing a clown mask and carrying a butcher knife."

Jimmy punched his friend in the shoulder. "That's not funny."

"Hey, there he is," Brian whispered, pointing out the window.

A narrow slice of dim light appeared at the back of the van. The boys squinted into the shadows and could just make out the bottom half of Mr. Pruitt's legs; the upper half of his body was blocked by the open rear door.

"What's he doing?" Jimmy asked.

"Getting something out of the back of the van I think."

"I told you, didn't I? I told you—"

The door closed with another *thud* and even though the driveway was thrown back into shadow, the boys' eyes had adjusted to the dark well enough for them to catch a glimpse—

—of Mr. Pruitt disappearing into the carport, carrying a large burlap sack over his shoulder. The sack was moving in jerks and fits, as if whatever was trapped inside were struggling to get out.

"ARE YOU crazy? We can't call the police. Not yet."

It was the next morning, and a sleep-deprived Jimmy was pacing on his front porch. His mother had made the boys a breakfast of scrambled eggs and bacon and toast, and taken off for a day of shopping with one of her girlfriends. Jimmy's father was at work. The boys had the house to themselves for the rest of the morning and afternoon.

"What do you mean, *not yet?*" Brian asked, watching his friend stroll back and forth like one of those lonely tigers you always saw at the zoo. "He could've had a little kid in that sack."

"Do you have any idea what my father will do to me if we call the police on Mr. Pruitt and we're wrong? I'll be grounded for the rest of the summer."

"Now we're *wrong?* You're the one who was so sure. You even have me half-convinced!"

Jimmy stopped pacing. Walked over to his friend. "Listen, we're not wrong. Something weird is going on over there. We just have to figure out what it is before we tell my parents or call the police."

"And how we gonna do that?" Jimmy tilted his head in a way that Brian immediately recognized as trouble.

"Oh, shit, I know that look."

Jimmy smiled. His face was pale and drawn, but his eyes were bright. "Mr. Pruitt never comes home for lunch. Ever. We're in and out in ten minutes."

Brian groaned. "I knew it."

"We empty our pockets beforehand. Take nothing we might leave behind on accident. Yes, I learned that from a movie. I'll set the timer on my watch. Ten minutes and we're gone, no matter what."

"How we getting in? The doors will be locked."

Jimmy pulled two objects out of the back pocket of his jeans: a small screwdriver and a laminated *GameStop* membership card.

"Uncle Manny?" Brian asked, eyebrows raised.

Manny was Jimmy's dad's black-sheep younger brother. He talked too loud, drank too much, and had actually done time when he was barely in his twenties. He was firecrackers and magic tricks and dirty jokes. A big kid with a heart of gold. The boys loved him.

Jimmy smiled that tired smile of his and nodded. "Good old Uncle Manny."

"HE PROMISED to show me how to hot-wire a car one day, too. He said it's a lot harder than in the movies."

Brian stood behind his friend at Mr. Pruitt's back door, glancing anxiously over his shoulder. "Just hurry the hell up, will ya?"

"The key is to not leave any marks on the door frame, in case you have to come back later." Jimmy carefully wedged the screwdriver in a little further and jiggled it up and down.

"We ain't coming back later."

"I know that, just saying." He held the screwdriver in place with his left hand and removed the card from his pocket with his other hand. He aligned the card between the wooden doorframe and the metal latch, then started swiping it up and down. After a moment, he stopped and wiped his hand on his jeans. "Sweaty. Guess I'm nervous."

"That makes two of us," Brian said. "Hey, if we're being so careful, why aren't we wearing gloves or something?"

"Don't need 'em. It gets to the point where cops are over here lifting fingerprints, we're screwed anyway."

The thought made Brian even more nervous. "We should just give it up, man. It's not gonna work."

There was an audible *click*—and the door swung inward a few inches. They caught a glimpse of linoleum floor inside.

Jimmy looked back at his friend. "You were saying?"

"Oh, bite me."

Jimmy stuffed the screwdriver and membership card back into his pocket, carefully nudged the door open, and stepped inside. Brian followed right behind him and started to close the door.

"Leave it cracked open. In case we have to make a quick escape."

"Lemme guess…you saw it in a movie?"

"As a matter of fact, I did."

"Jesus," Brian said, looking around. "What's that smell?"

They were standing in Mr. Pruitt's kitchen, and it was a mess. Dirty dishes were stacked in the sink and on the surrounding countertop. Empty pizza and Chinese food delivery boxes littered the kitchen table and overflowed from the trashcan. There was a leaning tower of old newspapers piled in front of the dishwasher.

"I have a bad feeling about this," Jimmy whispered.

Brian, eyes wide, nodded in agreement.

"The smell is coming from down there," Jimmy said, motioning to a door in the adjoining hallway.

"Basement?"

Jimmy nodded and headed that way.

"I was afraid you were gonna say that," Brian said, following close on his friend's heels.

"I used to come down here every Christmas Eve when I was little to see Mr. Pruitt's train-set. He let me play with it for hours."

Jimmy opened the door into complete darkness. He gathered his courage and slid his hand along the wall just inside the doorway, feeling for the light switch. He found it and flipped it on. The stairway was long and narrow and covered in the same ugly shade of gold carpeting Jimmy remembered from years past.

"After you," Brian said, voice cracking.

They slowly started down the stairs. Both boys heard and smelled the animals before they actually saw them.

"What the hell is that?" Jimmy asked, and then they reached the bottom of the stairway and turned the corner.

The room erupted in a cacophony of frantic barking and growling and whining as soon as the boys walked into view.

The entire length of one wall was lined with small cages. There had to be at least twenty or more of them. Each secured with a heavy padlock. Inside the metal cages were mostly dogs and cats. But there were also squirrels and rabbits and even a raccoon. And positioned along the adjoining wall, underneath one of the blacked-out basement windows, were two large, clear-plastic hutches, each containing a monkey. The wiry monkeys skittered from one side of their enclosures to the other, eyes bugging, clawing madly to get out.

Jimmy stood a few feet from the bottom of the stairway, his mind racing to register what his eyes were seeing. The smell was horrible here in the closed room; a toxic mixture of piss and crap and something chemical he could almost taste on his tongue. The basement walls were soundproofed.

"Some serial killer!" Brian said from behind him in a booming voice. He walked deeper into the room, laughing with relief. "Old Man Pruitt is Doctor Doolittle!"

"Sometimes they start by torturing animals," Jimmy said, his words almost drowned out by the animal screeches. "Then they move on to people."

Brian pointed out a stainless steel table—with leather straps—in the far corner of the basement. Syringes and vials of what looked like medicine were lined up on a nearby shelf. "Looks like he's trying to help them, not torture them."

Jimmy glanced in the opposite corner of the room, noticed a computer, its monitor-screen glowing, sitting on a small desk next to a printer. He headed that way.

Behind him, Brian bent down and reached his hand through one of the cages. A mangy cocker spaniel gently licked his fingers. "Poor little guy. All cramped up in there." He got to his feet and studied several of the other cages. "Helping or not, they shouldn't be locked up like this. Most of them don't even have water."

Jimmy stopped in front of the desk. Reached out and nudged the mouse, and the screen-saver image of a sunny beach disappeared and was replaced by a series of strange letters and numbers. He leaned closer, trying to remember where he had seen something similar.

"Hey, Jimmy," Brian said from behind him. "Wonder what the suit's for."

He looked over and saw Brian struggling to hold up a full-body suit, the heavy-duty kind you see astronauts wearing on television. A helmet with a clear faceplate hung from a hook on the wall next to him.

"Beats me. Just put it back, man." Jimmy returned his attention to the computer screen, once again searching his memory for where he'd seen such writing.

"I bet these keys are for the cages," Brian said, but Jimmy, lost in deep thought, didn't hear him. His eyes and nose stung from the horrible stench; his brain hurt from thinking. He was about to give up when the answer suddenly came to him like a ship sailing free of a fogbank. He snapped his fingers.

"It's Arabic! I remember it from school." He scrolled down, then clicked on a blurry photo at the bottom of the computer screen—and almost screamed when something brushed against his pants leg.

He looked down and saw a flash of black cat. He turned back to his friend and frowned. "What are you doing?"

Loose dogs and cats scampered across the basement and fled up the stairs to freedom. As Jimmy watched, Brian flung open another cage door and lifted a fat rabbit onto the floor below. The rabbit hopped in a drunk circle, then raced away, joining the others. "What's it look like I'm doing?" He laughed and moved on to the next cage.

Jimmy opened his mouth to protest, but before he could, screaming erupted from the computer behind him. Startled, he spun around and realized that a video was playing on the monitor:

A dark-skinned man wearing a filthy robe sat strapped to a chair in the middle of a small room. He screamed and wailed and fought against his restraints to no avail. Harsh voices could be heard off-screen speaking in a foreign language. After another thirty seconds of screaming, a scraggly mutt limped on-screen. The man stopped screaming and started crying. The dog wagged its tail and licked the man's restrained hands. The man started screaming again and tried to jerk away, but before long the screams were drowned out by a deep guttural choking sound. The camera zoomed in on the man's face, and Jimmy could see blood and bile spilling from the man's mouth in a foamy mess. And then his eyes erupted in twin geysers of blood that dribbled down his cheeks, and after a few more seconds, the man went limp and quiet. The foreign voice spoke up again, and then someone shuffled on-screen wearing

a heavy-duty suit eerily similar to the one hanging on the wall right
there in the basement.

The puzzle pieces suddenly snapped into place inside Jimmy's brain and his entire body went rigid with terror. "Brian..." All of a sudden, he wished he had brought his cellphone. He wished it more than anything else in the world. "Brian...STOP!"

Brian was kneeling in front of the second monkey enclosure. The first hutch was empty, the door wide open. "Why? I feel sorry for 'em, Jimmy."

Jimmy's voice was thick with surging fear. "He might not be a serial killer, but I think Mr. Pruitt is working with some very bad people."

Brian pulled the open lock from the latch and tossed it to the floor beside him. "What kind of bad people?"

"Like ISIS-terrorist-bad people."

Brian rolled his eyes. "Dude, you've seen too many movies. Mr. Pruitt's an old man. He's up to some weird shit down here, but he's as American as you and me."

"I don't think so," Jimmy said, his legs feeling like rubber. "Not anymore."

Brian yanked open the glass door and the brown monkey skittered into his arms.

"Brian, don't..."

Brian, still down on a knee in front of the hutch, grinned and cradled the monkey in his arms like a baby. "Look how cute he is!" He pressed his face close to the monkey's tiny head. "You're so cute. Yes, you are. You're so darn..."

The words suddenly stopped—and Brian's voice faded to a wet gargle. The monkey slipped from his arms and scampered happily away. Brian didn't move, just kept staring down at his lap, his long hair obscuring his face.

Jimmy backed up a step. "You okay, man?"

He didn't answer.

Jimmy backed up another step. "Brian…?"

Brian slowly lifted his head, looked up at his friend. His eyes were bleeding. Dark foam bubbled from his gaping mouth. He rose up and reached out for Jimmy, took a zombie-like step forward, and then he collapsed to the ground face-first, convulsing.

Jimmy stood there, frozen, watching his friend die. Everything made sense now—*the animals, the vials, the chemical smell, the Hazmat suit*—and nothing made sense at all. He thought about his mother and father and his Uncle Manny, as he turned and sprinted for the stairs.

He was almost to the top of the staircase when he felt something small and heavy latch onto his back with an ear-piercing screech. Sharp claws tore at his shirt, digging into his flesh, and he felt the brush of bristly fur against his neck.

He staggered into the kitchen, flailing, trying to wrestle the beast off of him. Even in his panic, he noticed the dogs and cats fleeing outside through the open kitchen door, scattering in the yard and running off in all directions. Free again.

His frantic mind chose that moment to flash another scene from a movie and even amidst the chaos, it bothered him that he couldn't remember the title: *Common house-pets carrying a dangerous new strain of rabies. Infected people going violently insane before dying agonizing deaths. And then, finally...the end of the world.*

Jimmy slammed his back against the kitchen wall, trying to shake the beast loose. He knocked piles of dishes to the floor where they shattered into pieces. He kicked over the pile of newspapers. The beast only screeched its awful banshee cry and dug its claws deeper into Jimmy's scalp.

He stumbled out the door into the back yard and felt the sun hit his tear-stained face. Its comforting warmth and blinding brightness filled his final moment of consciousness before the monkey lunged and buried its razor-sharp teeth deep in the flesh of Jimmy's neck.

And then his throat was closing up like a caved-in mineshaft and he couldn't breathe; and his skin felt like it had been set ablaze; and hot blood poured from his eyes in twin rivulets—and then he felt and saw nothing at all.

SILENT
NIGHT

The man sat in his car parked alongside the cemetery and finished his cigarette. The engine was off and the driver's window was down. It was raining, not too hard, not too soft, a steady rain that drummed the man a lonely lullaby on the roof of his car and soaked his left elbow, which was propped out the window.

He reached over with a gloved hand and dropped the butt into an empty water bottle sitting on the passenger seat next to him. He did this by feel, never once taking his eyes off the cemetery grounds. He scanned from left to right, and back again.

The cemetery had been crowded earlier—always was this time of year—but now the grounds were nearly abandoned thanks to the late hour and the cold and rain. His eyes touched an elderly man a few hundred yards to his right. The old-timer had been there for the better part of an hour, standing still and rigid, staring down at a grave marker, lost in thought and memory. A middle-aged couple knelt on the wet ground directly in front of the man's car, maybe a hundred yards out. Had they lost a child, the man wondered? Or were they mourning a mother or father or both? The man thought it could have been all three. The way this world works.

The old-timer left first, weaving his way surprisingly fast between the headstones to a faded red pick-up. The truck started with a backfire that sounded too much like a gunshot and slunk away into the twilight. The man watched the taillights fade to tiny red sparks and imagined a dinner table set for one awaiting the old man at home and wished he hadn't.

Five minutes later, the middle-aged man helped the middle-aged woman to her feet and, with wet knees, they walked hand-in-hand to a gray SUV parked at the opposite end of the road. The middle-aged woman never looked up, but the middle-aged man did. Just before he opened his car door and got inside, he glanced back at the man and nodded.

The man remained perfectly still in his car. He didn't return the nod and he didn't lift a hand to wave. He cast his eyes downward for a moment out of habit, an old trick, but he knew it wasn't necessary. He was being paranoid again. He gauged the distance at sixty yards and it was raining and his wipers weren't on. The middle-aged man was merely nodding at a dark shape behind blurry glass; a polite acknowledgement that he and the man sitting alone in his car both belonged to the same somber fraternity. A moment of kindness shared, and nothing else.

The man watched the middle-aged couple drive away and fought the urge to light up another cigarette. He scanned the cemetery grounds, left to right and back again, waited five more minutes to be sure, and then he got out of the car.

LET'S PRETEND, for just a moment, that Forest Hills Memorial Gardens employs a night watchman. And let's further pretend that, at 6:19pm on December 24, this watchman is lurking in the dark shadows just inside the tree-line of gnarly old pines that marks the cemetery's northernmost property line, perhaps smoking a cigar (which is strictly prohibited by employee rules) or perhaps just trying to keep dry in the rain.

If this scenario is indeed accepted as fact instead of fiction, then this is what our stealthy night watchman might witness at that particular time on that particular night:

A single man exits the lone car that remains parked on cemetery property, a dark sedan with rental license plates. The man is of medium height but broad in his chest and shoulders. He looks around, like he's making sure he's alone, straightens his jacket, lowers his winter hat, and despite walking with a slight limp, he makes his way quickly and confidently to a nearby gravesite. The man's eyes never stop moving beneath that winter hat, and the path he takes is precise and direct. The man has been here before.

Once he reaches his destination, the man bends down and places a single red rose—our night watchman has wickedly sharp eyesight—at the base of a headstone, where it joins several other much fancier flower arrangements and a plastic Santa decoration with a candle inside, its flame long since drenched by the falling December rain. The man traces a finger along the names engraved on the marker, and now the watchman notices that he is wearing gloves on both of his hands, and then he catches a glimpse of something much more interesting: a flash of dark gunmetal at the back of the man's waistband.

The man doesn't linger. He quickly stands up, readjusts his jacket and once again surveys the cemetery, slower this time, as if he somehow senses the watchman's presence there in the trees, and then he heads back to his car without a backward glance.

Within a heartbeat of closing his car door, the man starts the engine and speeds out of the cemetery. Headlights off and nary a tapping of brake lights. A dark shadow swallowed by the night and the approaching storm.

High in the towering pines, the rain changes over to snow and the wind picks up, whispering its secrets.

But the cemetery is deserted now and there is no one left to hear.

The man is gone, and, of course, our night watchman never existed.

"ARE YOU Santa Claus?"

The man stopped in mid-step, one foot in the kitchen, one foot still in the family room, staring over his shoulder at the little boy standing in the glow of the Christmas tree lights. The boy was wearing red-and-white pajamas and blinking sleep from his eyes. The man slowly removed his hand from the gun in his waistband, where it had instinctually moved to at the sound of the boy's voice, turned around, and lifted a finger to his lips. *Sshhh.*

The little boy—nine years old and named Peter, the man knew—wrinkled his nose in confusion, but stayed quiet.

The man slowly stepped back into the family room. His hands held out in front of him. "It's okay," he whispered. "I was just on my way out."

The little boy moved closer, unafraid, and whispered right back: "If you're not Santa, then who are you?"

The man didn't know what to say, so he just stood there, memorizing every inch of the little boy. He had entered the house twenty minutes earlier through the basement door. It had been too easy; he hadn't even needed to use his special tools. He'd crept up the carpeted stairs, silent as a house cat, and eased his way into a dark kitchen, and then the family room, where he'd found a Christmas tree tucked into the corner by the fireplace with dozens of wrapped presents waiting beneath it. The man had stood there in the quiet darkness for a long time, taking it all in. The decorations on the tree, many of which he recognized. The framed pictures on the mantle, several featuring the man's younger, smiling face. He stared at the paintings on the wall, the knickknacks on the shelves, the furniture, even the curtains. This was the man's first—and most likely last—time inside the new house, and he wanted to soak up everything he could into his memory banks…to remember later.

Somehow he had missed the little boy, who'd probably snuck downstairs after his mother had fallen asleep and curled up on the sofa beneath a blanket waiting for Santa. Some agent he was…

"You know what? You look a lot like my Uncle Bobby," the little boy whispered, his cute little nose all wrinkled up again. "Only his hair is a lot longer than yours."

The man felt his eyes grow wet and fought it. His pulse quickened. There was so much he wanted to say. So much he needed to say.

But he knew he couldn't.

The letter and box of money he had placed under the tree would have to be enough.

The man reached out and rested a shaky, gloved hand on the boy's small shoulder.

"Give your mom and Uncle Bobby a hug for me. I bet they're awesome folks." The man bent down and kissed the top of the boy's head—and that was when he smelled her on the little boy. His wife. Even after all those years.

Inhaling deeply, voice shaking now, the man said, "I left you all something under the tree."

The little boy's eyes flashed wide and, with a smile, he looked back at the Christmas tree. "What did you leave us?" he asked.

But when he turned back around, the man was gone.

EVEN WITH the drifting snow and occasional tears blurring his vision, the man traveled back roads to the airport, careful to make certain no one was following him. He hoped he was just being paranoid, but he couldn't be sure. It had been a quiet fifteen months since they had almost found him in Mexico. Two years before that, they had somehow tracked him to the coast of Venezuela, and it was only with God's good grace that he'd remained a free man. They would never stop looking, and he would never stop running. He knew too much, had seen and done too much.

The plows hadn't touched most of the back roads, so the going was slow. That was okay with the man. The airport was only twenty-seven miles away, and he had almost three hours to return the rental car and make his gate for the return flight overseas. Better safe than sorry, he thought, although even if a policeman found him stuck on the side of the road in a ditch, he should be fine. His rental papers were in order, and he carried a legal driver's license, credit cards, social security card and everything else he needed to appear a normal, law-abiding U.S. citizen. If, for any reason, the cop decided to search his rental car, then that would be another story. The man would be forced to resort to other options.

With that thought in mind, the man glanced in the rear-view mirror and dropped his speed another five miles per hour. He turned the windshield wipers up a notch. The man knew he would have to be at his most vigilant at the airport. These days, they watched the international flights with special attention, especially around the holidays. He would dispose of his weapons once he reached the rental car return lot, but not a moment sooner.

Ten minutes later, the winding back road he was traveling on merged with MD Route 40 and soon after he passed an old-fashioned road sign that read: WELCOME TO EDGEWOOD. The man looked at the sign with a sad smile.

Maybe a mile later, he slowed through an intersection beneath a blinking yellow traffic light that was dancing wildly in the whipping wind and snow. There was a strip mall bordering the right side of the road, all the stores gone dark except for a Dunkin' Donuts at the far end of the building. Twin mounds of snow covered two small cars in the parking lot, probably belonging to the unfortunate workers inside.

The man tapped the brakes and steered into the lot, feeling his back tires slide a little in the accumulating slush. He swung around and parked facing the road, away from the Dunkin' Donuts front windows, and turned off the car. His eyes had grown weary, and he knew from experience that strong coffee was the remedy. His stomach was talking to him, too. He thought maybe a couple chocolate donuts or a hot breakfast sandwich, if they served those this time of night.

The man got out of his car and watched as a snowplow loomed out of the darkness like some kind of huge, prehistoric animal, its glowing yellow eyes illuminating the swirling snow. The driver flipped him a wave from inside the warmth of his cab, and this time the man waved back. He was halfway to the front door of Dunkin' Donuts when his wrist began to vibrate. Startled, the man looked down at his arm and thumbed a button on the side of his watch, silencing it.

It was midnight.

Christmas.

The man stopped in the middle of the parking lot, oblivious to the cold and falling snow. It had been ten Christmases since he'd last held her in his arms. Ten impossibly long years. She had been pregnant with his child then—with Peter. They had been so excited that they were going to be parents. They had painted and decorated the nursery together. Shopped for outfits and baby supplies. They had been happy.

Six months later, on a routine assignment in Turkey, the man had found himself in the wrong place at the wrong time— and instead of helping him, his government had tried to solve the problem by erasing his existence. He'd been on the run ever since. Running from dangerous men trained just as he had been trained, from men he'd once called his brothers. They would laugh at him now, the man thought. Tired and hungry and crying, sneaking back home like a scared mouse in the forest. They had taught him better than that. They had taught him to be superhuman. Invisible. Immortal.

The man let out a deep breath and watched the vapor fill the air in front of his face. The night was hushed and serene, not even the falling snow hitting the store's front windows making a sound, and it made the man think of nights like this when he'd been just a kid, sledding down Hanson Hill long after dark with his neighborhood friends, their excited voices echoing across the snowy fields.

The man glanced down Route 40 toward the blinking yellow traffic light. Imagined driving back there and turning left, cruising two miles north on Hanson Road to the house he had grown up in. It had been a happy house. Filled with board games and books and laughter. Filled with the love of his parents and his baby brother and the eternal mysteries of three older sisters.

Then he imagined turning right at the intersection, taking Mountain Road until it spilled into 22, following it for twenty minutes or so until it took him right back to where the night had started.

The cemetery…

…where his mother and father had been buried.

…where the United States Government had claimed to bury him with full military honors.

The man stood there alone in the middle of the strip mall parking lot, his hands beginning to shake despite his gloves, his mind betraying him with visions of empty coffins buried deep in frozen ground and little boys with wide, innocent eyes looking up at him and asking, *"Are you Santa Claus?"*

And this time he couldn't stop the tears from falling. Sloppy cold tears, equal parts shame and regret.

He should have answered him, the man thought in a panic. He should have told him, "That's right, son, I'm Santa. My red suit's in the wash…"

Or at the very least—the truth. He owed him that much: "No, not Santa, son. I'm no one. Just a ghost."

Instead, he'd said nothing and snuck away into the night.

Out on the road, another snowplow roared by, headed in the opposite direction.

The man blinked, as if waking from a dream, turned around and walked back to his car. He got inside and drove away.

Away from the only home he'd ever known.

Away from everything.

"A ghost," the man whispered to himself in the darkness and drove on toward the airport.

The man wasn't tired or hungry anymore.

WIDOW'S POINT

**Video/audio footage #1A
(5:49pm, Friday, July 11, 2017)**

The man holds the video camera in his left hand and grips the steering wheel with his right. The road, and calling it a road is charitable at best, is unpaved dirt and gravel, and the camera POV is unsteady. Mostly we see bouncing images of the interior dashboard and snippets of blue sky through a dirty windshield. The Rolling Stones' "Sympathy for the Devil" plays at low volume on the radio.

After another thirty seconds of this, we hear the squeal of brakes in need of repair and the car swings in a wide circle—giving us a shaky glimpse of a stone lighthouse standing atop a grassy point of land—and comes to a stop facing rocky cliffs that drop perilously to the Atlantic Ocean below. The ocean here is dark and rough and foreboding, even on this clear day.

The man turns off the engine and we immediately hear the whine of the wind through his open window. In the foreground, an old man with thinning gray hair, thick glasses, and a wrinkled apple of a face, shuffles into view.

The man recording exits the car, still pointing the camera at the old man, and we see a hand enter the top corner of the screen as the driver flips a wave.

"Hello," he yells above the wind, walking toward the old man.

Up ahead, we watch the old man shuffling his way toward us through the blowing grass. His body is so frail, it appears as if the wind might steal him away and send him kiting over the distant cliffs. At first, we believe he is smiling. As we draw closer, we realize we are wrong, and the old man is scowling. It's not a pretty sight—like a skeletal corpse grinning from inside a moldy coffin.

"Turn that damn camera off," the old man growls.

The picture is immediately replaced with a blurry patch of brown and green grass as the camera is lowered.

"Okayyy, we'll just edit that out later," the man says to himself off-camera.

And then in a louder voice: "Sorry, I didn't think it would—"

Video/audio footage #2A
(6:01pm, Friday, July 11, 2017)

THE SCREEN comes to life again and we see the stone lighthouse off in the distance and hear the muffled crash of waves pounding the shoreline. It's evident from the swaying view of the lighthouse and the intense howl of the wind that the camera is now affixed to a tripod and positioned somewhere close to the edge of the cliffs.

The man walks on-screen, carrying a knapsack and what looks like a remote control of some sort. He appears to be in his mid-forties, shaggy blonde hair, neat dark-framed glasses, artfully scuffed boots, pressed jeans, and a gray sweatshirt. He stares directly at the camera, green eyes squinting against the wind, and sidesteps back and forth, searching for the proper positioning.

He settles on a spot just in time to witness a particularly violent gust of wind defeat the tripod.

"Shit," the man blurts, and sprints toward the camera—as it leans hard to the left and crashes to the ground.

There is a squawk of static and the screen goes blank.

Video/audio footage #3A
(6:04pm, Friday, July 11, 2017)

THE VIDEO switches on, and we see the man standing in the foreground of the lighthouse, pointing the remote at the camera. The image is steadier this time around. The man slides the remote into the back pocket of his jeans and clears his throat.

"Okay, only have a few minutes, folks. Mr. Parker is in quite the hurry to get out of here. He's either playing the role of hesitant and anxious lighthouse owner to the extreme and faking his discomfort, or he's genuinely unnerved and wants to be pretty much anywhere else but here on the property his family has owned for over a century now."

He leans over, his hands disappearing just off-screen, and returns holding the knapsack, which he places close on the ground at his side. He stands with an erect but relaxed posture and folds his hands together in front of him.

"My name is Thomas Livingston, bestselling author of *Shattered Dreams, Ashes to Ashes,* and eleven other bestselling non-fiction volumes of the supernatural. I'm here today on the windswept coast of Harper's Cove at the far northern tip of Nova Scotia standing at the foot of the legendary Widow's Point Lighthouse.

"According to historical records, the Widow's Point Lighthouse, originally named for the large number of ships that crashed in the rocky shallows below before its existence, was erected in the summer of 1838 by Franklin Washburn II, the proprietor of the largest fishing and gaming company in Nova Scotia."

Livingston's face grows somber.

"There is little doubt that the Widow's Point Lighthouse led to a sharp decrease in the number of nautical accidents off her shoreline—but at what cost? Legend and literally centuries of first-hand accounts seem to reinforce the belief that the Widow's Point Lighthouse is cursed...or perhaps an even more apt description...*haunted.*

"The legend was born when three workers were killed during the lighthouse's construction, including the young nephew of Mr. Washburn II, who plunged to his death from the lighthouse catwalk during the final week of work. The weather was clear that day, the winds offshore and light. All safety precautions were in place. The tragic accident was never explained.

"The dark fortunes continued when the lighthouse's first keeper, a by-all-accounts 'steadfast individual' named Ian Gallagher went inexplicably mad during one historically violent storm and strangled his wife to death before taking his own life by cutting his wrists with a carving knife.

"In the decades that followed, nearly two dozen additional mysterious deaths occurred within the confines—or on the nearby grounds—of the Widow's Point Lighthouse, including cold-blooded murder, suicide, unexplained accidents, the mass-slaughter of an entire family in 1933, and even rumors of devil worship and human sacrifice.

"After the final abomination in 1933, in which the murderer of the Collins' family left behind a letter claiming he was 'instructed' to kill by a ghostly visitor, the most recent owner of the Widow's Point Lighthouse, seafood tycoon Robert James Parker—yes, the grandfather of Mr. Ronald Parker, the camera-shy gentleman you glimpsed earlier—decided to cease operations and shutter the lighthouse permanently.

"Or so he believed…

"Because in 1985, Parker's eldest son, Ronald's father, entered into an agreement with the United Artists film studio from Hollywood, California to allow the studio to film a movie both inside the lighthouse and on the surrounding acreage. The movie, a gothic thriller entitled *Rosemary's Spirit*, was filmed over a period of six weeks from mid-September to the first week of November. Despite the lighthouse's menacing reputation, the filming went off without a hitch…until the final week of shooting, that is…when supporting actress Lydia Pearl hung herself from the polished iron guard railing that encircles the catwalk high atop the lighthouse.

"Trade publications reported that Ms. Pearl was despondent following a recent break-up with her professional baseball-playing fiancé, Roger Barthelme. But locals here believed differently. They believed with great conviction that, after all those long years of silent slumber, the Widow's Point curse had reawakened and claimed another victim.

"Regardless of the reasoning, the lighthouse was once again shuttered tight against the elements three years later in 1988 and for the first time, a security fence was erected around the property, making the lighthouse accessible only by scaling the over one-hundred-and-fifty-foot high cliffs that line its eastern border along the Atlantic.

"So…in other words, no human being has been inside the Widow's Point Lighthouse in nearly thirty years…"

Livingston takes a dramatic pause, then steps closer to the camera, his face clenched and square-jawed.

"…until now. Until *today*.

"That's right—tonight, for the first time in over three decades, someone will spend the night in the dark heart of the Widow's Point Lighthouse. That someone is *me*, Thomas Livingston.

"After months of spirited—pardon the pun—negotiation, I have been able to secure arrangements to spend an entire weekend inside the legendary lighthouse. The ground rules are simple. Today is Friday, July 11, in the year of 2017. It is…"

He checks his wristwatch.

"…6:09pm Eastern Standard Time on Friday evening. In a matter of minutes, Mr. Ronald Parker, current proprietor of the Widow's Point Lighthouse, will escort me through the only entrance or exit to the lighthouse, and once I am safely inside, he will close and lock the door behind me…"

Livingston bends down and comes back fully into view holding a heavy chain and padlock.

"…using these."

He holds the chain and padlock up to the camera for another dramatic beat, then drops them unseen to the ground below.

"I will be permitted to take inside only enough food and water to last me three days and three nights, as well as a lantern, flashlight, sanitary supplies, two notebooks and pens, along with this video camera and tripod, and several extra batteries. In addition, this…"

Livingston backs up a couple steps, reaches down into his knapsack, and quickly comes up with a small machine in his right hand.

"…Sony Digital Voice Recorder, capable of recording over one thousand hours of memory with a battery life of nearly ninety-six hours without a single charging. And, yes, please consider that an official product placement for the Sony Corporation."

He laughs—and we get a glimpse of the handsome and charming author pictured on the dust jacket of one of his books—and then he returns the voice recorder to his knapsack.

"I will not be allowed a cellphone or a computer of any kind. Absolutely no Internet access. No way to communicate, or should anything go wrong, no way to request assistance of any kind. I will be completely cut off from the outside world for three long and hopefully eventful nights."

We hear a car horn blare from off-screen, and a startled Livingston's eyes flash in that direction. He looks back at the camera, shaking his head, a bemused expression on his face.

"Okay, folks, it's time to begin my journey, or shall I say, *our* journey, as I will be recording all of my innermost thoughts and observations in an effort to take you, my readers, along with me. The next time I appear on camera, I will be entering the legendary—some say, *haunted*—Widow's Point Lighthouse. Wish me luck. I may need it.

"And cut…"

Video/audio footage #4A
(6:22pm, Friday, July 11, 2017)

LIVINGSTON IS carrying the video camera in his hand, and we share his shaky POV as he slowly approaches the lighthouse.

Mr. Parker remains off-screen, but we hear his gravelly voice: "Eight o'clock Monday morning. I'll be here not a minute later."

"That will be perfect. Thank you."

The lighthouse door draws nearer, large and weathered and constructed of heavy beams of scarred wood, most likely from an ancient ship, as Livingston had once unearthed in his research. The men stop when they reach the entrance.

"And you're certain you cannot be convinced otherwise?" the old man asks.

Livingston turns to him—and we finally get a close-up of the reclusive Mr. Parker, an antique crone of a man, his knobby head framed by the blue-gray sea behind him—and Livingston laughs. "No, no. Everything will be fine, I promise."

The old man grunts in reply.

The camera swings back toward the lighthouse and is lowered. We catch a fleeting glimpse of Livingston's knapsack hanging from his shoulder and then, resting on the ground at the foot of the entrance, a dirty white cooler with handles by which to carry or drag it. Livingston leans down and takes hold of it by one plastic handle.

"Then I wish you Godspeed," the old man says.

The camera is lifted once again and focused on the heavy wooden door. A wrinkled, liver-spotted hand swims into view holding a key. The key is inserted into an impossible-to-see keyhole directly beneath an oversized, ornate doorknob and, with much effort, turned.

The heavy door opens with a loud *sigh*, and we can practically hear the ancient air escaping.

"Whew, musty," Livingston says with a cough, and we watch his hand reach on-screen and push the door all the way open with a loud *creak*—into total darkness.

"Aye. She's been breathing thirty years of dead air."

Livingston pauses—perhaps it's the mention of "dead air" that slows his pace—before re-gripping the cooler's plastic handle and stepping inside.

At the exact moment that Livingston crosses the threshold into the lighthouse, unbeknownst to him, the video goes blank. Entirely blank—with the exception of a time code in the lower left corner of the screen, which at that moment reads: 6:26pm.

"I'll see you Monday morning," Livingston says.

The old man doesn't respond, simply nods and closes the door in Livingston's face. The screen is already dark, so we do not see this; instead, we hear it with perfect clarity and finality.

Then we listen as the key is once again turned in the lock, and the heavy chain is wrestled into place. After a brief moment of silence, the loud *click* of a padlock being snapped shut is heard, followed by a final tug on the chain.

Then, there is only silence...

...until a rustle of clothing whispers in the darkness and there comes the *thud* of the cooler being set down at Livingston's feet.

"And so it begins, ladies and gentlemen, our journey into the heart of the Widow's Point Lighthouse. I will now climb the two hundred and sixty-eight spiraling stairs to the living quarters of the lighthouse, lantern in one hand, camera in the other. I will return a short time later this evening for food and water supplies, after some initial exploration."

We hear the sound of ascending footsteps.

"Originally built in 1838, the Widow's Point Lighthouse is two hundred and seven feet tall, constructed of stone, mostly granite taken from a nearby quarry, and positioned some seventy-five yards from the sheer cliffs which tower above the stormy Atlantic..."

Video/audio footage #5A
(6:41pm, Friday, July 11, 2017)

WE HEAR Livingston's heavy breathing and notice the time code—6·41pm—appear in the lower left hand corner. Once again, the rest of the screen remains dark.

"Two hundred-sixty-six...two hundred-sixty-seven...two hundred-sixty-*eight*. And with that, we have reached the pinnacle, ladies and gents, and just in time, too. Your faithful host is feeling rather...spent, I have to admit."

Even without a video feed, we can almost picture Livingston dropping his knapsack and holding up the lantern to survey his home for the next three nights.

"Well, as you can certainly see for yourselves, Mr. Parker spoke the truth when he claimed this place was in a state of severe ill repair. In fact, he may have managed to actually underestimate the pathetic condition of the Widow's Point living quarters."

A deep sigh.

"I believe I shall now rest for a moment, and then venture upward and explore the lantern room and perhaps even the catwalk if it appears sturdy enough before returning downstairs for my food and water supplies. Once I've straightened up a bit and established proper housekeeping, I will return to you with a further update.

"I also promise to discuss the mysterious incidents I referenced earlier—and many more—in greater and more graphic detail once I have made myself at home."

The sound of shuffling footsteps.

"But, first, before I go…lord in heaven…just gaze upon this magnificent sight for a moment."

Livingston's voice takes on a tone of genuine awe. The phony theatrics are gone; he means every word he is saying.

"Resplendent mother ocean as far as the eye can see…and beyond. The vision is almost enough to render me speechless." A chuckle. "Almost."

The time code disappears—and the video ends.

**(Voice recorder entry #1B—
7:27pm, Friday, July 11, 2017)**

WELL, THIS is rather strange and unfortunate. After I last left you, I returned downstairs and brought up a day's ration of food and water, then spent considerable time cleaning and straightening in preparation for the weekend. Once these tasks were completed to my satisfaction, I settled down for some rest and to double-check the video footage I had shot earlier.

The first batch of videos was fine, if a little rough around the edges, but then I came to the fourth video…and discovered a problem. I was shocked to find that while the audio portion of the recording worked just fine, the video portion seemed to have somehow malfunctioned once I entered the lighthouse. And I do mean as soon as I stepped inside the lighthouse.

I proceeded to check the camera lens and conduct several test videos, all with the same result—the audio function appears to be operating in perfect order, while video capabilities are disabled. I admit I find the whole matter more puzzling than troubling or unsettling, even with the rather bizarre timing of the issue.

Perhaps, something inside the camera was broken when the wind knocked it down earlier by the cliffs. Or…perhaps the otherworldly influence that dwells here inside the Widow's Point Lighthouse has already made its presence known. I suppose only time will tell.

In the meantime, this Sony—hear that, folks, *Sony*—digital voice recorder will serve my purpose here just fine.

**(Voice recorder entry #2B—
9:03pm, Friday, July 11, 2017)**

GOOD EVENING. I've just taken my first dinner here in Widow's Point—a simple affair; a ham-and-Swiss sandwich slathered with mustard, side of fresh fruit, and for dessert, a thin slice of homemade carrot cake. Next I finished organizing my copious notes.

Now it's time for another brief history lesson.

Earlier, I referenced more than a handful of disturbing incidents that have taken place in and around the Widow's Point Lighthouse. I also promised to discuss in further detail many of the lesser-known tragedies and unexplained occurrences that have become part of the lighthouse's checkered history. In time, I will do exactly that.

However, for the sake of simplicity, I will first discuss the three most recent and widely-known stories involving the Widow's Point Lighthouse. I will do so in chronological order.

I referenced earlier the 1933 mass murder of the entire Collins' family. What I did not mention were the gory details. On the night of September 4, 1933, lighthouse keeper Patrick Collins invited his brother-in-law and three local men to the lighthouse for an evening of card-playing and whiskey. This was a nearly monthly occurrence, so it did not prove particularly troublesome to Patrick's wife, Abigail, or their two children, Stephen, age nine, and Delaney, age six.

One of the men whom Patrick invited was a close friend of his brother-in-law's, a worker from the nearby docks. Joseph O'Leary was, by all accounts, a quiet man. A lifelong bachelor, O'Leary was perhaps best known in town as the man who had once single-handedly foiled a bank robbery when the would-be robber ran out of the bank and directly into O'Leary's formidable chest. O'Leary simply wrapped up the thug in a suffocating bear hug until the authorities arrived.

According to Collins' brother-in-law and the other two surviving card players—Joshua Tempe, bookkeeper and Donald Garland, fisherman—the night of September 4 was fairly typical of one of their get-togethers. Collins and Tempe both drank too much and their games became sloppy and their voices slurred and loud as the night wore on. On the other hand, the brother-in-law ate too many peanuts and strips of spicy jerky, and as usual, there were many complaints voiced about his equally spicy flatulence.

O'Leary was his quiet, affable self throughout the evening, and if any one observation could be made regarding the man, it was agreed by the others that O'Leary experienced a stunning run of good luck throughout the second half of the game.

By evening's end, a short time after midnight, the vast majority of the coins on the table were stacked in front of O'Leary, with a grumbling Donald Garland finishing a distant second. The men shrugged on their coats, bid each other goodnight, descended the winding staircase in a slow, staggered parade, and returned to their respective homes and beds.

All except Joseph O'Leary.

When he reached his rented flat on Westbury Avenue, O'Leary went directly to his kitchen table, where he sat for just over an hour and composed the now-infamous, lengthy, rambling, handwritten letter explaining that earlier in the night while taking a break from card-playing to visit the bathroom, he had experienced an unsettling—though admittedly, thrilling and liberating—supernatural occurrence.

To relieve yourself in 1933 in the Widow's Point Lighthouse, you had to descend to what was commonly (albeit crudely) referred to as the Shit Room. Once you found yourself in this isolated and dimly lit chamber, you tended to do your business as quickly as possible for it was a genuinely eerie setting and not designed for one's comfort.

It was here, inside the Shit Room, that O'Leary claims the ghostly, transparent image of a young beautiful woman wearing a flowing white bed-robe appeared before him—at first frightening him with her spectral whisperings before ultimately seducing him with both words and embrace.

Afterward, O'Leary returned to his friends and the card game in a daze. His letter claimed it felt as if he had dreamt the entire incident.

Dreamlike or not, once O'Leary finished composing his letter, he rose from the kitchen table, took down the heaviest hammer from his workbench, returned to the Widow's Point Lighthouse, where earlier he had purposely failed to lock the door behind him as was usually the custom, ascended the two hundred-and-sixty-eight steps—and bludgeoned the Collins' family to death in their beds.

Once the slaughter was complete, O'Leary strolled outside onto the catwalk—perhaps to rendezvous with his ghostly lover now that the task she had burdened him with was complete—and climbed over the iron railing and simply stepped off into the starless night.

O'Leary's body was found early the next morning by a local fisherman, shattered on the rocky ground below. Shortly after, the authorities arrived and a much more gruesome discovery was made inside the lighthouse.

**(Voice recorder entry #3B—
10:59pm, Friday, July 11, 2017)**

IT'S LATE and I can barely keep my eyes open. I'm rather exhausted from the day's events, so I bid you all a fair good-night and pleasant dreams. I pray my own slumber passes uninterrupted, as I am planning for an early start in the morning. Exciting times lay ahead.

**(Voice recorder entry #4B—
4:51am, Saturday, July 12, 2017)**

(Mumbling)

I can't. I don't want to. They're…my friends.

**(Voice recorder entry #5B—
7:14am, Saturday, July 12, 2017)**

GOOD MORNING and what a splendid morning it is!

If I sound particularly rested and cheerful for a man who has just spent the night in a filthy, abandoned, and reputedly haunted lighthouse, it's because indeed I am. Rested and cheerful, that is.

Trust me, folks, I'm as surprised as you are.

My night didn't begin in very promising fashion. Although I tucked myself into my sleeping bag and dimmed the lantern shortly after eleven o'clock, I found myself still wide-awake at half past midnight. Why? I'm not exactly certain. Perhaps excitement. Perhaps trepidation. Or perhaps simply the surprising coldness of the lighthouse floor, felt deep in my bones even through my overpriced sleeping bag.

I lay there all that time and listened to the lighthouse whisper its secrets to me and a singular thought echoed inside my exhausted brain: *what was I hoping to find here?*

It's a question I had been asked many times in the days leading up to this adventure—by Mr. Ronald Parker and my literary agent and even my ex-wife, just to name a few—and never once had I been able to come up with a response that rang with any measure of authenticity.

Until last night, that is, when—in the midst of my unexpected bout of insomnia, as I lay there on the chilly floor in the shadows, wondering if what I was hearing…the distant hollow clanking of heavy metal chains somewhere below me and the uneven scuffling of stealthy footfalls on the dusty staircase…were reality or imagination—the answer to the question occurred to me with startling clarity.

What was I hoping to find here?

Inarguable proof that the Widow's Point Lighthouse was haunted? Incontrovertible evidence that nothing supernatural had ever dwelled within the structure, all the stories and legends nothing more than centuries-old campfire tales and superstition?

The answer that occurred to me was none of the above—and all of the above.

I realized I didn't care what I found here in the Widow's Point Lighthouse. For once, I wasn't looking for a book deal or a movie option. I wasn't looking for fame or fortune.

I was simply looking for the *truth*.

And with that liberating revelation caressing my conscience, my eyes slid closed and I fell into a deep and peaceful sleep.

**(Voice recorder entry #6B—
8:39am, Saturday, July 12, 2017)**

NOW THAT I've completed my morning exercises and taken a bit of breakfast, it's time for another history lesson.

As I already noted in my opening segment—and I'll try not to repeat myself too much here—Hollywood came calling to the town of Harper's Cove in September of 1985. More specifically, Hollywood came to the Widow's Point Lighthouse.

Although town officials and a handful of local merchants were enthusiastic about the financial rewards Harper's Cove stood to gain from the production, the vast majority of the townspeople expressed extreme unease—and even anger—when they learned that the subject matter of the film so closely paralleled the lighthouse's tragic history. It was one thing to rent out the lighthouse for a motion picture production, but a horror film? And a ghost story at that? It felt morally wrong to the residents of Harper's Cove. It felt *dangerous*. A handful of women from the Harper's Cove Library Association even gathered and picketed outside the movie set, but they gave up after a week of particularly harsh weather drove them inside.

Rosemary's Spirit was budgeted at just over eight million dollars. The film starred Garrett Utley and Britney Longshire, both coming off modest hits for the United Artists studio. Popular daytime television actress, Lydia Pearl, appeared in a supporting role, and by many accounts, stole the movie with her inspired and daring performance.

The film's director, Henry Rothchild, was quoted as saying, "Lydia was such a lovely young woman and she turned in the performance of a lifetime. She showed up on set each day full of energy and wonderfully prepared, and I have no doubt that she would have gone on to amazing things. The whole thing is unimaginable and tragic."

Executive producer, Doug Sharretts, of *Gunsmoke* fame, added: "There were no signs of distress. I had breakfast with Lydia the day it happened. We sat outside and watched the sunlight sparkle across the ocean. She was enchanted. She loved it here. She was in fine spirits and excited to shoot her final scenes later that evening. And she was confident that she and Roger would work out their problems and be married. There were no signs. Nothing."

The rest of the cast and crew are on record with similar statements regarding Miss Pearl and the events of the night of November 3, 1985. Lydia was, by all accounts, in fine spirits, well liked and respected, and her death came as a shock to everyone involved in the film.

However, there was one dissenting voice and it belonged to Carlos Pena, *Rosemary's Spirit's* renowned director of photography. At the time of Lydia Pearl's death, Pena was one of the few members of the crew who refused to comment on record. Most people attributed this to Pena's reticent nature. He was that rare individual in Hollywood: a modest and private man in a very public business.

Fifteen years later, dying of lung cancer at his ranch in Mexico, it was a different story, as Pena told a reporter from

Variety: "I've worked on over a hundred films and I've never witnessed anything like it. It still haunts me to this day.

"The rest of the cast and crew were on lunch break and I thought I was alone in the lighthouse. I was going over the next scene, pacing out camera shots and thinking about changing the angle on camera number two when I heard someone whispering from the level below me. I was surprised but I figured it was just one of the actors running their lines. After a few minutes, the whispering grew in volume and intensity, to the point where I couldn't concentrate any longer, so I went to investigate.

"Some of the crew had constructed a makeshift break room on the next level down. It was cramped quarters but there was enough room for a small refrigerator and a handful of uncomfortable chairs.

"I was surprised to find the room in total darkness when I reached the doorway. The lights had been on not ten minutes earlier when I'd passed it on my way up to the set. I figured once the person heard my footfalls, they would stop running lines and call out to me, but they didn't. The whispering continued unabated. It was a woman's voice, and now that I could make out the words she was saying, it chilled me. Whoever this was, hidden here in the darkness, she wasn't running lines; she was having a conversation—with herself.

"Uneasy, I reached inside the doorway and turned on the light, and I was shocked to see Lydia Pearl standing in the far corner facing the wall. The whispering continued despite my intrusion.

"I called out to her: 'Lydia? I'm sorry to interrupt.'

"She didn't respond. I walked closer, my heart beating faster in my chest.

"'Is everything okay?' I was almost upon her now.

"Again, there was no response. Just that frenzied whispering, almost a hissing, as though she were arguing with herself. She stood with a rigid posture, but with her arms dangling at her sides.

"Once I was close enough, being careful not to startle her, I softly called her name and reached out and placed a hand gently on her shoulder—and she whirled on me, a rattlesnake-quick hand lunging out to claw at my eyes. I back-stepped in shock, blocking her advance.

"Her face is what I best remember, even now in my dreams. It was twisted in rage. Spittle hanging from her drawn lips. Teeth bared. Her eyes were the worst. They were impossibly large and unlike any human eyes I had ever seen. They were feral and burning with unimaginable hatred. This woman I barely knew wanted to kill me, wanted to devour me.

"And then, as quickly as it had begun, it was over. Her face relaxed, arms lowered, and she drew back, blinking rapidly, as if awakening from a dream. Her eyes seemed to regain focus and she saw me standing there in front of her, quite a sight, I am sure. She sobbed, 'I'm…I'm sorry' and ran from the room, brushing against me as she fled. I remember her skin was ice cold where she had touched me.

"Later that evening, when news of her suicide reached me at my hotel, I was not surprised. I was sad, but not surprised.

"I've never spoken of this before and I never will again."

According to William McKay, the reporter from *Variety*, Carlos Pena had grasped his rosary in his hands and crossed himself numerous times while recounting this unsettling story. Six weeks later, he was dead.

**(Voice recorder entry #7B—
11:44am, Saturday, July 12, 2017)**

HELLO THERE, again. I've spent the past hour or so scribbling in my notebook, thoughts and observations to look back upon once this experience is over. I've learned not to rely too heavily on memory. Memory is a tricky beast, as I have learned the hard way over the years. It's not to be trusted.

Lunch soon and then another history lesson, this one even more scandalous than the last.

**(Voice recorder entry #8B—
11:49am, Saturday, July 12, 2017)**

DID I mention that several times now I've heard the echo of footsteps in this lonely place? Last night and twice again this morning. I'm fairly convinced that it's not my imagination, but if that is truly the case, then what is it I'm hearing? The Widow's Point Lighthouse, all these years later, still settling into the rocky earth below? The harsh Atlantic wind searching for entry and creeping its way inside these heavy stone walls? Hungry rats scavenging for food? Restless spirits?

**(Voice recorder entry #9B—
1:01pm, Saturday, July 12, 2017)**

DESPITE THE highly publicized and controversial death of actress Lydia Pearl in the fall of 1985, the Widow's Point Lighthouse—save for a handful of NO TRESPASSING signs set about the perimeter—remained unguarded and largely accessible to the general public. It wasn't until almost three years later, during the late summer of 1988, that the razor-topped security fence was erected and local authorities began patrolling the area.

This is the reason why:

In the spring of 1988, fifteen-year-old Michael Risley had just finished his freshman year at Harper's Cove High School. Michael wasn't considered particularly popular or unpopular. In fact, he wasn't considered much at all. Even in a school as small as Harper's Cove, he was largely invisible.

Because of this, no one knew of Michael Risley's fascination—his outright obsession—with the occult and the Widow's Point Lighthouse. No one knew that he had spent countless hours in the local library doing research and talking to the old-timers down at the docks about the turn-of-the-century legends regarding devil worship taking place in the woods surrounding the lighthouse.

And, because of this, no one knew that Michael Risley had spent much of his freshman year performing his own satanic rituals in those same woods just outside of the Widow's Point Lighthouse, sacrificing dozens of small animals, on several occasions even going so far as to drink their blood.

By the time July rolled around that summer, Michael was ready to graduate from small animals and move on to bigger things. On the night of a Thursday full moon, he snuck out of his house after bedtime, leaving a note for his parents on the foyer table, and met two younger kids—Tabitha Froehling, age 14, and Benjamin Lawrence, age 13—at the end of his street. Earlier in the day, Michael had promised them beer and cigarettes and dared them to accompany him to the old lighthouse at midnight. Every small town has a haunted house and for the children of Harper's Point, it had always been— and always would be—the Widow's Point Lighthouse.

The three of them walked side-by-side down the middle of First Street, their shadows from the bright moonlight trailing behind them. They walked slowly and silently, backpacks slung across their shoulders. It was an idyllic scene, full of youthful promise and innocence.

Early the next morning, Michael Risley's mother read the note her son had left on the foyer table the night before. She managed to call out once to her husband before fainting to the hardwood floor. A frantic Mr. Risley bound down the stairs, carried his wife to the living room sofa, read the note grasped in her right hand, and then immediately called 911.

The police found Michael and the other two children exactly where the note had told them they would be. A break in the thick forest formed a natural, circular clearing. A fire pit ringed in small stones was still smoldering at the center of the clearing. Tabitha and Benjamin lay sprawled on their backs not far from the fire. Strange symbols, matching the symbols adorning many nearby trees, had been carved into their foreheads with a sharp knife. Both of their throats had been cut, their chests sliced open. Their hearts were missing. Deep, ragged bite marks covered their exposed legs.

Michael was discovered several hundred yards away—at the base of the Widow's Point Lighthouse—naked and incoherent. The officer in charge claimed in his written report that it was like looking at a "devil on earth." Michael had used the other children's blood to paint every inch of his body red. Then, he had consumed portions of both hearts.

According to the note he had left, Michael believed that once this final ritual was completed, he would be "taken in by the Dark Lord and spirited away to a better place."

Instead, at some point during the long and bloody night, Michael Risley's sanity had snapped, and the only place he was spirited away to was the mental hospital in nearby Coffman's Corner.

A week later, the security fence was in place.

**(Voice recorder entry #10B—
3:15pm, Saturday, July 12, 2017)**

ON A whim, I took the video camera out onto the catwalk a short time ago and gave it another try. It's such a gorgeous afternoon, the sun high in a cloudless sky, the ocean, unusually calm for this time of year, sparkling like a crush of fine emeralds scattered across a tabletop. I spotted a pair of cruise ships steaming south on the horizon. Later, a parade of fishing vessels hauling the day's catch will journey past on their way home to port.

I filmed the entirety of this spectacle and tested the footage when I returned below. Alas, the screen remained blank.

(Voice recorder entry #11B— 4:56pm, Saturday, July 12, 2017)

YOU'LL HAVE to excuse my labored breathing, as you are kindly accompanying me to the bottom of the Widow's Point Lighthouse to retrieve additional water supplies, traversing the same spiral staircase once climbed by killer and actress alike.

I can feel history here with each step I take. The atmosphere feels similar to a leisurely stroll through the grassy hills of Gettysburg, another haunted place where history and death lock arms and dance for all to see. A spectacle of names and dates flittering through your conscience while you construct a façade of mournful respect, all while secretly wishing to have borne witness to the ancient slaughter. A macabre thought, most certainly, but also an undeniable truth. Interstate rubberneckers don't clog traffic due to frivolous curiosity; rather they can't help themselves, hoping to be fortunate enough to see a splash of scarlet blood on the roadside or a glimpse of mangled flesh. After all, the scores of spectators that crowded into the ancient coliseums didn't come for the popcorn.

Navigating these endless stairs, I must admit I feel a closer kinship with Lydia Pearl and Joseph O'Leary than I ever have with any fallen soldier of the Civil War. Why is this the case?

Perhaps it is simply the nature of time and urban legends…or perhaps it is just the nature of the Widow's Point Lighthouse. Ghosts surround me here.

**(Voice recorder entry #12B—
5:10pm, Saturday, July 12, 2017)**

I'VE JUST tested several bottles of water from the cooler and discovered something mildly alarming. The water has a salty tang to it. Subtle, but present nonetheless. The bottles were purchased from a grocery store just yesterday afternoon, and the water I consumed last night and earlier today suffered no such issue. Perhaps I'm a victim of my own overgrown imagination, or perhaps it's just an unexpected effect of the salty air here on the Nova Scotia coast. Regardless, I can't help but wonder and I can't help but tell you all about it. After all, my own voice is—*(chuckles)* and always has been—my greatest companion.

**(Voice recorder entry #13B—
5:29pm, Saturday, July 12, 2017)**

NINETY-ONE, NINETY-TWO, ninety-three…

**(Voice recorder entry #14B—
5:53pm, Saturday, July 12, 2017)**

MY GOODNESS, I am winded. The journey down these twisting stairs felt endless, but the journey back up feels like forever-and-a-half, as my late father was wont to say. I tried counting the two-hundred-and-sixty-eight steps, as I did during my summit just yesterday, but I kept losing count. I swear to you I have climbed over five hundred stairs by now.

To add to my sense of displacement, I can hear the unmistakable rumblings of a storm approaching outside. Odd, as the skies were crystal clear just hours ago I had been particularly meticulous about checking the local weather reports in the days leading up to this adventure. Each and every online report called for clear days and pleasant nights. Oh, well, no matter, a storm will just add to the mounting atmosphere.

**(Voice recorder entry #15B—
6:01pm, Saturday, July 12, 2017)**

MANY OF the historical volumes I read about the Widow's Point Lighthouse discussed the frequent storms that hit this particular section of the Nova Scotia coastline. More than one author claimed that during the most violent of these storms, you could actually feel the old stone lighthouse trembling on its foundation. I chalked this observation up to showmanship and hyperbole, but boy was I mistaken.

When I finally reached the lantern room after what felt like an eternity of climbing, I was stunned at the vision that greeted me outside. Heavy rain lashed the lighthouse windows. The once-crystal skies were now boiling with fast-moving, dark, roiling clouds. Jagged shards of lightning stabbed at the horizon. Angry whitecaps danced across the churning sea. The wind was howling and I could feel in the very bones of the lighthouse the surging waves crashing onto the rocky shoreline at the base of the cliffs.

I stared in awe—and yes, I admit, a sliver of encroaching fear. I have never witnessed the sea in such a state.

**(Voice recorder entry #16B—
7:15pm, Saturday, July 12, 2017)**

I'VE SOMEHOW managed to lose my flashlight. I carried it with me during my earlier journey down the staircase and I'm certain I brought it back with me upstairs. I clearly recall placing it next to my sleeping bag while I prepared dinner. But now it's gone. I've looked everywhere. Puzzling to say the least.

**(Voice recorder entry #17B—
8:12pm, Saturday, July 12, 2017)**

FIRST MY flashlight, and now I'm hearing things again. Twice in the past hour, I could've sworn I heard the faint strains of a child singing somewhere below me. Each time I moved to the doorway to listen, and each time the singing ceased. Perhaps the ghosts of Widow's Point and the storm are playing tricks on this old boy. Despite my initial sense of unease, I'm grateful for the experience. It will make a fine addition to my notes.

Still no sign of that blasted flashlight.

**(Voice recorder entry #18B—
8:24pm, Saturday, July 12, 2017)**

THERE! CAN you hear it? A banging, like someone knocking on the floor right underneath me, and—

(Loud staccato rapping)

> There it is again!
> I'm not imagining it.
> Can you hear it?

**(Voice recorder entry #19B—
9:57pm, Saturday, July 12, 2017)**

WHAT A night it has been! First, the unexpected arrival of the storm and the disappearance of my flashlight. Then, the mysterious singing and knocking sounds. Perhaps most exciting of all, and I know precisely how trite this sounds, I now feel certain that someone is watching me. Several times I have sensed something…a *presence*…directly behind me. I have *felt* it. Yet each time I've turned to find nothing but shadows. I'm sure my colleagues would find great pleasure at my skittish behavior.

I've lectured and written ad nauseam about the psychic energy that is often trapped inside houses of haunted repute, especially those places where violent crimes have occurred. I now feel that energy here in the Widow's Point Lighthouse. And it's getting stronger.

It's not yet ten o'clock and I'm already tucked inside my sleeping bag, hoping for an early night of it. I can hardly see the floor in front of me. The lantern, although in fine working order last night, has proven a sad replacement for my flashlight, as the flame tends to extinguish within minutes of each lighting. Whether this is the result of a malicious gust or *geist*, I cannot say, but my temporary home certainly has a draft that I hadn't noticed before. And it's a chilly draft at that. I had been told that the summer heat would be retained in this old stone monolith, but it seems as if the ocean winds blow colder inside the lighthouse than outside.

Speaking of outside, the storm continues to rage. If anything, it's grown stronger as the night has progressed. Every few moments, lightning slashes the sky, illuminating the room around me with a startling brilliance before plunging it back into darkness. I can't help but wonder if—

(A long, silent beat followed by a beeping sound)

Well, what do you know, ladies and gentlemen, the video camera appears to have come back to life.

Video/audio footage #6A
(10:06pm, Saturday, July 12, 2017)

AS THE video switches on, the screen is flooded with murky shadows. Only the time-code can be clearly seen. Then we hear a muted crash of thunder and a flash of lightning illuminates the lighthouse living quarters. A few seconds later, the lightning is gone and we are greeted again by mostly darkness.

"Initially, I dismissed what I was seeing as a trick of the lightning, but then I realized that the blinking red light at my feet was coming from the video camera. When I heard the beep of the battery, I immediately retrieved the camera and ran a series of quick tests. For whatever reason, it seems to be working fine now.

"I'm thinking perhaps I jarred something when I moved the camera after dinner or — JESUS, WHAT WAS THAT?!"

The video shifts and we hear heavy breathing growing more rapid by the moment. Then, the rustle of footsteps, moving cautiously at first, but gaining urgency. The echo of boots slapping pavement transitions to boots clanging against metal as Livingston ascends the stairs and ventures outside onto the lighthouse's catwalk.

We hear a door being yanked open and are overpowered by the cacophony of the storm. Wind howls. Rain lashes. Thunder roars. Skeletal fingers of lightning dance across the violent sea.

Livingston moves closer to the iron railing and points the camera at the ocean below. Enormous swells crash on the rocks below, sending sprays of whitewater high into the night. The camera zooms closer—and Livingston gasps.

"My God, do you see it?!" he yells, his voice swallowed by the wind. "Someone needs to help them!"

The screen goes blank.

**Video/audio footage #7A
(10:50pm, Saturday, July 12, 2017)**

WE SEE Thomas Livingston's haggard face staring back at us. His hair is wet and he's shivering. His bloodshot eyes dart nervously around the room. For the moment, the lantern is lit, bathing his skin in an orange glow.

He looks at the camera for maybe thirty seconds but doesn't say anything. We can see him searching for his words. Finally:

"I know what I heard. And I know what I saw."

He sounds as if he might break into tears.

"I heard it crashing upon the rocks."

He glances down at the ground, steels himself, then looks back at the camera and continues.

"It was a massive ship. At least two hundred feet long. And it broke into a thousand pieces. It was an awful sound. Dozens of men...thrashed and tossed upon the rocks...impaled on splintered planks...flailing and drowning in the waves. I can still hear their screams.

"I recorded all of it, I'm certain of that. I knew what I was witnessing wasn't possible, but I saw what I saw and I kept the camera rolling..."

A deep breath.

"But there's nothing there now. I checked the video after I returned inside and changed into dry clothes. I checked it a dozen times. There's nothing there."

He looks up at the camera and the brash showman we saw earlier is gone.

"You can hear the thunder and the crash of the waves. You can see the lightning flash and the ocean illuminated below... but there's no ship anywhere to be seen. No bodies. No screams."

Livingston rubs his eyes with his fists.

"I offer no explanation, ladies and gentlemen, because I have none."

Video/audio footage #8A
(11:16pm, Saturday, July 12, 2017)

THE VIDEO turns on and once again we see a shaky image of the churning ocean at the base of the cliffs. The rain has slowed, but the wind is still gusting and shards of lightning still decorate the sky.

"It's taken me the better part of an hour to summon the courage to come out here again."

The camera zooms in for a closer view. Waves crash onto an empty shoreline.

"The ship is gone."

The camera zooms back out.

"But I know what I saw."

After a moment, the camera lowers and we hear footsteps on the catwalk, and then a loud *clanging*.

"What the…?"

The camera shifts as Livingston bends down and steadies on the object he almost tripped over.

The missing flashlight.

"Jesus."

(Voice recorder entry #20B—
11:33pm, Saturday, July 12, 2017)

I MUST sleep now, if such a thing is possible in my current state. I've had enough adventure—or shall I say misadventure—for one day. Do you remember earlier when I said I was only here for the truth? Well, that was a fucking lie.

**(Voice recorder entry #21B—
1:12am, Sunday, July 13, 2017)**

(The sound of footsteps descending the stairway)

Sixty-eight, sixty-nine, seventy, seventy-one, seventy-two, seventy-three...

**(Voice recorder entry #22B—
1:35am, Sunday, July 13, 2017)**

TWO-SIXTY-six, two-sixty-seven, two-sixty-eight.

(Shuffling of footsteps as Livingston reaches the bottom, turns around, and immediately starts climbing again)

One, two, three, four, five, six, seven, eight, nine, ten, eleven, twelve, thirteen...

**(Voice recorder entry #23B—
2:09am, Sunday, July 13, 2017)**

...TWO-HUNDRED-and-ninety-nine, three-hundred, three-hundred-and-one, three-hundred-and-two, three-hundred-and-three, three-hundred-and-four, three-hundred-and-five...

(Livingston's voice is monotone, deliberate, as if he has been hypnotized)

**(Voice recorder entry #24B—
6:42am, Sunday, July 13, 2017)**

THE NIGHT was endless, a nightmare. If I slept at all, I don't remember. The hours passed in a fever dream. At one point, I heard someone crying, a woman, but was too frightened to get up and investigate. A short time later I thought I saw something moving in the doorway, the pale outline of a person, but it vanished when I fumbled with the lantern. It's so cold in here I can't stop shivering, even inside my sleeping bag. My entire body aches, and my feet are filthy and tattered, as if I've walked a great distance without shoes.

I need to eat and drink, but I'm too exhausted.

**(Voice recorder entry #25B—
7:29am, Sunday, July 13, 2017)**

IT OCCURS to me now that someone might be playing a cruel and elaborate joke. Either that old bastard Parker or perhaps my bitch of an ex-wife. To what end, I haven't the slightest idea, but I don't know what else it could be.

All of the water bottles I brought up with me last night are empty. And I certainly didn't drink them. I was too shaken to even take a sip. And the crackers and the cheese I carried up, all stale. The apples and the one remaining pear, rotten to the core. I need to somehow summon the energy to walk downstairs to the cooler. My mouth is so dry I can barely spit. My stomach is growling.

**(Voice recorder entry #26B—
8:17am, Sunday, July 13, 2017)**

I'VE NEARLY reached the bottom, thank God. Just another couple dozen stairs.

(Labored breathing)

The video camera is once again malfunctioning. It was my intention to bring it with me to chronicle what I found below, but the camera wouldn't even turn on this morning. I tried several times to no avail, leaving me with this crummy voice recorder—sorry, Sony, and go fuck yourself while you're at it.

(A deep breath and the sound of heavy footsteps on the stairway ceases)

Thank God…after everything else that has occurred, I almost expected the cooler to be gone.

(Cooler lid is lifted. A rustling of ice as a plastic bottle is lifted out. The snap of the cap being loosened and a loud gulp of water being swallowed, then—a chorus of violent gagging and vomiting)

**(Voice recorder entry #27B—
9:09am, Sunday, July 13, 2017)**

ALL OF the water is contaminated. Pure salt water. Every goddam bottle. The caps were all sealed tight. This isn't a joke. This isn't a prank. This is…something else.

All of the food has gone bad too. There are maggots in the lunchmeat. The fruit is rotten. The bread is brittle and spotted with mold.

I'm so tired. I feel like I'm losing my mind.

**(Voice recorder entry #28B—
9:48am, Sunday, July 13, 2017)**

I TRIED pounding on the front door, but no one came. Of course. The security gate is locked tight and won't be opened again until tomorrow morning when old man Parker arrives. Next, I tried prying the door open with a piece of scrap metal but it wouldn't budge. I'm considering bringing down my sleeping bag, lantern, and the rest of my supplies and holing up down here until tomorrow morning. It somehow feels safer here on ground level.

(A chortle of muffled laughter in the background)

Now that I've calmed down, I've given the situation a lot of thought. I can survive just fine until tomorrow morning with-out food and water. I've done it before.

(Another burst of laughter that Livingston obviously doesn't hear)

I just have to keep my wits about me.

(More laughter and then: 'I'm coming, darling. I'm coming.' The voice belongs to a man, deep in tenor and tinged with an Irish accent. A loud, wet cracking sound is followed by guttural cries. The man laughs again and there are several more wet cracking sounds. Livingston takes no notice)

Whether this is all somehow an intricate ruse designed to make a fool of me or truly the work of whatever spirits inhabit the lighthouse, I don't care anymore. I've already got what I came for. The videos and audiotapes I've made are pure gold. More than enough to seal another book deal. Toss in the other things I've witnessed and heard, and we most likely have a movie, as well. It's pay day, and just in time for me. Hell, I don't even have to embellish that much this time around. The only thing I truly wonder about is—

(Livingston gasps)

Get off of me! Get the fuck off of me!

(Frantic footsteps pounding their way up the stairs, finally slowing after a number of minutes. Heavy breathing)

Something grabbed me down there. I felt it on my shoulder...squeezing. Then I watched as a lank of my hair was pulled away from my head. But there was nothing there. My goddam hair was moving by itself.

(Footsteps pick up the pace again)

How in God's name have I not reached the top yet?

(More footsteps)

...one-hundred-and-seventeen, one-hundred-and-eighteen, one-hundred-and-nineteen...

**(Voice recorder entry #29B—
10:27am, Sunday, July 13, 2017)**

...TWO-HUNDRED-and-sixty-six, two-hundred-and-sixty-seven, two-hundred-and-sixty-eight, two-hundred-and-sixty-nine, two-hundred-and-seventy...

Dear God, what is happening?

**(Voice recorder entry #30B—
time unknown, Sunday, July 13, 2017)**

(Note: from this point forward, the voice recorder's time-code is corrupted for reasons unknown, displaying only 0:00 for the remainder of the recordings)

There are things occurring here clearly beyond my comprehension. Forget the hundreds of impossibly extra stairs I just climbed to reach the living quarters. Forget the fact that I witnessed an ancient fishing vessel crash upon the rocks below last night or watched my hair floating in mid-air right in front of my eyes this morning. Forget the cooler full of contaminated water and rotten food. None of that matters.

But the bloody fucking hammer with the initials J.O. carved into its polished wooden handle I just found laying atop my sleeping bag is another story entirely.

Get me the fuck out of here!

**(Voice recorder entry #31B—
time unknown, Sunday, July 13, 2017)**

I'M SITTING with my back against the wall. The lantern is aglow for now, and I can see the entire room and the doorway from this position. But I can't take my eyes off the bloody hammer.

All I have to do is make it until eight o'clock tomorrow morning. I would tell you what time it is now, but my mother-fucking watch has stopped working.

**(Voice recorder entry #32B—
time unknown, Sunday, July 13, 2017)**

HOW IS this storm still raging? How is it possible? It's so dark outside it feels like the end of the world.

**(Voice recorder entry #33B—
time unknown, Sunday, July 13, 2017)**

(Defeated whisper)

I came here for the money. Of course, I did. It's always been about the money.

**(Voice recorder entry #34B—
time unknown, Sunday, July 13, 2017)**

LATE LAST night and the night before, Tommyknockers, Tommyknockers, knocking at the door. I want to go out, don't know if I can, 'cause I'm so afraid of the Tommyknocker man.

**(Voice recorder entry #35B—
time unknown, Sunday, July 13, 2017)**

It shouldn't be night already. It can't be. It wasn't even ten in the morning when I was downstairs at the cooler. There's no way that much time has passed. It's not possible.

**(Voice recorder entry #36B—
time unknown, Sunday, July 13, 2017)**

GET OFF of me! Stop touching me!

**(Voice recorder entry #37B—
time unknown, Sunday, July 13, 2017)**

(Crying)

Someone…*something*…keeps touching my face. I can feel its breath on my neck.

**(Voice recorder entry #38B—
time unknown, Sunday, July 13, 2017)**

(Sobbing)

Please just leave me alone…

**(Voice recorder entry #39B—
time unknown, Sunday, July 13, 2017)**

CAN YOU hear her singing? It's a little girl. She's getting closer.

**(Voice recorder entry #40B—
time unknown, Sunday, July 13, 2017)**

EVERYTHING'S GONNA be okay. Everything's gonna be okay.

**(Voice recorder entry #41B—
time unknown, Sunday, July 13, 2017)**

(THE DEEP Irish voice heard earlier…

'Yes, love, it's done. Each one's nothing but a bloody carcass on a bed sheet. Oh yes, darlin', very bloody.

'What's that? You want this one, too?')

**(Voice recorder entry #42B—
time unknown, Sunday, July 13, 2017)**

THIS IS a bad place. I can feel it whispering inside my head. It wants to show me something…something terrible.

**(Voice recorder entry #43B—
time unknown, Sunday, July 13, 2017)**

(Screaming)

Oh my God, it hurts!

(Sobbing)

Somehow I dozed off and woke up with the most awful pain shooting through my leg. I rolled up my pants leg and found fucking teeth marks! Something bit me while I was sleeping! Oh Jesus, I have to stop the bleeding!

**(Voice recorder entry #44B—
time unknown, Sunday, July 13, 2017)**

(Unintelligible)

**(Voice recorder entry #45B—
time unknown, Sunday, July 13, 2017)**

OUR FATHER who art in heaven, hallowed be thy name, thy kingdom come, thy will be done…

**(Voice recorder entry #46B—
time unknown, Sunday, July 13, 2017)**

(THE FOLLOWING is spoken by Livingston in Hebrew, and has since been translated)

…for rebellion is like the sin of divination, and arrogance like the evil of idolatry. Because I have rejected the word of the Lord, he has rejected me as king.

We know that we are children of God, and that the whole world is under the control of The Evil One.

**(Voice recorder entry #47B—
time unknown, Sunday, July 13, 2017)**

(Frantic footsteps)

I'm going out on the catwalk. It's my last hope.

(The sound of a door opening, then hard wind and rain)

I can't stop the bleeding in my leg. I can't stop the voices. They're getting closer.

(Thunder crashes)

The bloody hammer disappeared from atop my sleeping bag. I hear the echo of heavy footsteps on the stairway. That means he's coming for me now. Joseph O'Leary is still here. He never left. None of them did. If I can only make it until morning, I can—

OFFICIAL POLICE REPORT

FILE #173449-C-34
DATE: July 15, 2017
REPORTING OFFICER(S): Sgt. Carl Blevins; Sgt. Reginald Scales

At 8:47am on Monday, July 14, 2017, the Harper's Cove Police Department received a phone call from Mr. Ronald Parker, age eighty-one, reporting a missing person and summoning them to the Widow's Point Lighthouse.

Sgt. Scales and I arrived at the lighthouse grounds at approximately 8:59am. Mr. Parker greeted us at the security gate and directed us to park next to a red Ford pick-up and a gray Mercedes sedan.

Mr. Parker showed us identification and explained that the Mercedes belonged to a male in his mid-forties named Thomas Livingston. According to Mr. Parker, Mr. Livingston, a well-known author, had rented the lighthouse from Mr. Parker's company for the purpose of paranormal research. The dates of the agreement ran from Friday evening, July 11 to Monday morning, July 14. Mr. Parker was contracted to return to the Widow's Point Lighthouse at precisely 8am on Monday to unlock the front door and escort Mr. Livingston from the property.

Pursuant to this agreement, Mr. Parker claimed that he arrived on Monday morning at approximately 7:50am and waited inside his truck until 8am. At that time, he unlocked the front door and called out for Mr. Livingston. When there was no response, he returned to his truck for a flashlight and entered the lighthouse.

On the lower level, he found Mr. Livingston's cooler still mostly full of food and water. He also noticed a puddle of dried vomit nearby on the floor.

After repeatedly calling out to Mr. Livingston and receiving no response, Mr. Parker climbed the spiral staircase to the lighthouse's living quarters. There he found a blood-soaked sleeping bag, a video camera, a lantern, and several other items belonging to Mr. Livingston. He also noticed a series of strange symbols had been scrawled on the walls in what appeared to be blood.

Before returning to the lower level, Mr. Parker searched the catwalk for Mr. Livingston. He found no sign of him, save for a Sony tape recorder located on the metal walkway. Mr. Parker did not touch the recorder and immediately returned to his truck where he called authorities using his cellphone.

After Sgt. Scales and I finished interviewing Mr. Parker, we searched the lighthouse in tandem. Failing to locate Mr. Livingston, we proceeded to search his unlocked vehicle—where we discovered numerous prescription pill bottles, as well as a loaded handgun, all of which have been logged into Evidence—before searching the surrounding grounds and woods.

At 9:31am, I summoned the Crime Lab, and Sgt. Scales and I began establishing a perimeter.

As of today, thirty-one (31) items have been logged into Evidence, including the video camera and audio recorder. Additional analysis of the digital files found within the camera and dozens of audio files is underway.

Weather conditions remain sunny and clear, and additional searching of the lighthouse grounds is currently underway.

Sgt. Carl Blevins
Badge 3B71925

(Written with Billy Chizmar)

MY FATHER AND
ELLERY QUEEN'S
MYSTERY MAGAZINE

grew up in a family of readers. Three older sisters and an older brother, their choice of reading material ranging from the classics and poetry to Stephen King and Sidney Sheldon. Mom loved her Agatha Christies and *Reader's Digest* condensed novels. My father was the most voracious reader in the house, and it was his eclectic tastes that most influenced the reader—and writer—I would one day become.

My father enjoyed a wide variety of material. Thick volumes of military history checked out from the local library. Non-fiction books about golf and airplanes and home or car repair. Glossy, oversized travel guides covering an array of exotic destinations, many of which he had visited during his years in the Air Force and many more he one day hoped to visit.

And then there were his favorites: mysteries by the masters,

Lawrence Block and Dick Francis and Robert B. Parker. Spy novels by Robert Ludlum and John le Carre and Frederick Forsyth. Stacks of pulp paperbacks by folks like John D. MacDonald, Charles Williams, David Goodis, and Day Keene (almost all of these novels short and sporting nifty titles and even niftier cover art, so they quickly became my favorites as well), these tattered paperbacks usually acquired from the Swap Shelf located by the front entrance of the library.

But my father saved his deepest affection for his magazines. National Geographic. Popular Mechanics. Life. Newsweek. I remember many summer evenings when he would sit out back on our screened-in porch and snip out his favorite articles and collate them into various binders for further study. I don't know why, but it seemed like a magical process to me, and I was fascinated by the idea.

And then there was the Granddaddy of them all: *Ellery Queen's Mystery Magazine.* I don't ever remember my father cutting out pages from *Ellery Queen's.* For him, I think it would have been like snipping out sections of the bible. Instead, each new issue was quickly read and then neatly collected on a bookshelf in the corner of the den, not far from his favorite reading chair. He never subscribed to *Ellery Queen's* (I never asked, but I suspect it was because he didn't want the mailing label to foul up the front cover). He bought each issue at a local book and magazine shop called Maxine's, and I accompanied him on most of these trips. It was during those car rides that my father first taught me about the history of the magazine and many of its authors. He also told me about his favorite stories and encouraged me to try my hand at my own mystery tales (by then I was writing my own shorts, mostly monster and war adventures, and trying to sell them to my friends). I remember feeling happy and proud that he thought enough of my opinion to share those stories with me and talk to me like a grown-up. I remember feeling the early stirrings of an unbreakable bond that would last us a lifetime.

Years ago, I wrote a Story Note in an early collection of mine that described an idyllic childhood of fishing and hiking and playing baseball with my friends, my father inevitably parked in his car somewhere in the background or perched on the first-base bleachers, the lower half of his face obscured by a worn paperback or the new issue of *Ellery Queen's Mystery Magazine,* his eyes peering over the front cover, watching over me. It was a scene I knew well from my childhood days, and a memory I still hold close to my heart today.

WHEN I was a teenager, I had two favorite bookstores in the town I grew up in. The first was Carol's Used Books, which was housed in a couple of trailers, sandwiched between a Dunkin' Donuts and a pawn shop. I spent hours in that place, and I can still remember the exact layout (mystery and horror straight ahead and to the right), the sagging, carpeted floors, and the comforting smell of old books. Carol's closed a long time ago. A used car lot stands in its place now. But I still have dozens of paperbacks on my bookshelves with the *Carol's Used Books* stamp on the inside front cover, and that's good enough for me.

The second store was called Maxine's Books and Cards, and as luck would have it, Maxine's was located right next door to Frank's Pizza, just about the best pizza shop in the entire world. Maxine's is where I first fell in love with comic books and later discovered Dean Koontz's backlist and books by authors such as Bill Pronzini and Ed Gorman and Joe Lansdale. It's where I bought my first Stephen King paperback and my first copies of *Alfred Hitchcock Mystery Magazine*. It's also where my father and I used to drive together once a month to pick up the brand new issue of *Ellery Queen's Mystery Magazine*. For me, Maxine's was sacred ground.

I never told anyone this—not even my father; some things you just have to keep to yourself—but I always dreamed of seeing one of my own short stories in *Ellery Queen's Mystery Magazine*. It always felt like the Holy Grail of magazines to me—and not just because it was my dad's favorite. It's where the best genre writers contributed their very best work; you never got the feeling the magazine published trunk or throw-away stories. *Ellery Queen's Mystery Magazine* was where the big boys and girls came to play.

Many years later, thanks to Janet Hutchings and Ed Gorman, my dream came true when my story "Like Father, Like Son" appeared in the March 1997 issue of *Ellery Queen's Mystery Magazine*.

I remember being so excited on publication day that I couldn't wait for my contributor copies to arrive in the mail.

Sadly, Maxine's was long closed by then, so I drove to the next town over and picked up a couple copies from a magazine shop. I stopped at my parents' house on the way home and gave a copy to my father. I sat in the den and watched him read my story, a hint of tears in his eyes. That was a good night.

MY FATHER is gone now. Cancer. During his final days, I often sat at his bedside and read to him. On his night table sat books by Ed Gorman and Stephen King, a copy of *Ellery Queen's Mystery Magazine* and a stack of other periodicals. When we weren't reading, we talked about life and the people we loved and good books we had read. I told him how my oldest son was devouring books and comics and starting to write stories of his own. We smiled and laughed and cried a lot. We remembered a lot. Those long weeks were the hardest days of my life, but I wouldn't have traded them for anything in the world.

ALL THESE years later, *Ellery Queen's Mystery Magazine* is still here. A time capsule of fine words and memories. For that, I'm grateful.

THE WITCH

"I hate Halloween."

"You hate everything," I said.

"That's not true."

"Name three things you don't—"

"Pizza."

"That's one."

"Fishing."

"Two."

Frank Logan, bald head, double chin, and wrinkled suit, stared out the passenger window of our unmarked patrol car.

"Stuck at two, aren't you?"

"Well, I was gonna say *you're* the third thing I don't hate but that was before you started with this shit."

I laughed and swung a right onto Pulaski Highway. "So what do you have against Halloween anyway?"

He glanced over at me and I recognized the look immediately: it was his *'Should I really waste my breath explaining this to you?'* look.

After a moment, he decided I was worth the effort and went on. "It's become too damn commercial. I read in the paper last week that Halloween is second to only Christmas when it comes to holiday sales revenue. Christmas, for Chrissake!"

I smiled and changed lanes. Another classic Frank Logan rant coming right up.

"When I was a kid, the only thing anyone spent money on was candy. That's it! We made the decorations for our yards and houses. We made our costumes. I was a hobo the first time I went trick-or-treating. A clown the next year. A baseball player the year after that. All homemade. Didn't spend a penny."

"I can't see you as a clown."

"I was five, Ben. What was your first costume?"

I hesitated. "Umm, I don't remember."

"Sure you do. Everyone remembers their first Halloween costume. It's like a rule, like remembering your first piece of ass."

"I really don't remember."

"Sure you do."

I sighed. "I was Casper, Frank. Good enough?"

"Casper the friendly ghost?"

"No, Casper the angry squirrel."

He arched his eyebrows. "Store bought?"

I turned onto a residential street. Jack O' Lanterns grinned their jagged, orange grins at us from front porches. Tombstones poked out of manicured lawns, piles of fallen leaves heaped in front of them in the shapes of corpses. Ghosts and goblins hung from trees. I saw a cluster of police lights in the distance. It was after ten, so the sidewalks were empty of trick-or-treaters, but I could see a good-sized crowd gathered in the middle of the road ahead.

"Store bought?" Frank asked again. Once he got his teeth into something, he didn't let go. It was what made him such a fine detective.

"Yes, Frank, it was store bought. A cheap plastic mask with eyeholes cut out of it, and one of those elastic bands in the back that pinched your ears and neck. I apologize for violating the spirit of Halloween and promise to make up for it next October. Happy?"

He shrugged his shoulders. "Just a question. No need to get touchy."

I pulled to the curb and parked behind a Sheriff's cruiser, opened the driver's door and got out.

"Westerns," Frank said.

I looked at him over the top of our sedan. "What?"

"I don't hate Westerns. You know, movies."

I closed my car door and started toward the scene.

"That's three, Ben," from behind me. "I win."

"WHATDYA GOT, Lenny?"

Sheriff Deputy Leonard Perkins looked up from the small notebook he was scribbling in and shook his head. "It's a weird one, fellas."

"That's what we hear," Frank said.

Lenny closed his notebook and looked around at the bystanders, a mix of excited children—many still dressed in costume (all of them store bought, I noticed), masks pushed up off their sweaty faces—and worried, tired adults. "Guess it makes sense. Being Halloween and all."

"Don't get him started on Halloween," I said.

Lenny looked at Frank and back to me again, waiting. When neither of us said anything else, he went on. "Deceased is Harold Torre. Forty-six-year-old male. Divorced. No kids. Been in the residence for almost fifteen years. Neighbors say he's quiet and polite. Keeps to himself mostly. Doesn't show up at the block parties or cookouts but is friendly enough if you pass him on the street or see him working out on his lawn. Doesn't have many visitors."

"Occupation?" I asked.

"Owns an insurance company right here in town."

Lenny gestured for us to follow and started across the lawn to the front porch of a well-kept rancher. It looked like every light in the house was on.

"This is how one of the neighborhood kids found him."

Mr. Torre was a man of average height and build. I would guess 5'10 and 165 pounds, although it was difficult to accurately gauge since he was presently sprawled face-down on his front porch, one leg tucked beneath the other. He had dark curly hair and wore eyeglasses. The glasses—old fashioned and metal-framed—were lying on the concrete porch amidst a scattering of Halloween candy and an empty dark blue Tupperware bowl.

"No one saw him go down?" Frank asked.

Lenny shook his head. "No one we've talked to." He gestured to a blonde woman and a little boy waiting in the side yard with another police officer. "Kid walked up on him when he was trick-or-treating, found him like that and ran back to his mom crying. She called 911 from her cell."

Frank grunted. "Kid got his trick, I guess."

"Really, Frank?" I said.

Lenny ignored us. "Had to be quick, though. Lotta trick-or-treaters in this neighborhood. Can't imagine much of a break between 'em."

I nodded, remembering my own childhood Halloween nights. We'd practically sprinted from house to house. "You talk to the mother yet?"

"Emerson did," Lenny said. "And we figured you guys would want to."

"Frank can handle that," I said and held up a hand in Frank's direction to stop what I knew was coming.

"No visible wounds," Lenny continued. "The M.E. had us roll him on his side, but only for a few seconds. Didn't find anything."

"Heart attack?" Frank asked.

"Guess it's possible," Lenny said. "But when you take the note into account, it's…doubtful."

"What note?" I asked.

Lenny looked surprised. "I thought you knew. We found a handwritten note magneted to the refrigerator door."

"A note saying what?" Frank interrupted.

"We bagged it and tagged it. It's in the van right now." He nodded his head in the direction of the crime lab van parked across the street.

"Just give us the short version," Frank said, glancing at me, all business now.

"Note claims that if anything happened to him, his ex-wife was to blame," Lenny said. "Evidently they'd been arguing a lot lately. It's dated a week ago yesterday and signed Harold Torre."

"Interesting," Frank said, a split second before I could mutter the exact same response. I read an article once that claimed police detectives who worked together for long periods of time became almost like twin siblings, reading each other's thoughts and completing each other's sentences. I looked at Frank and really hoped it wasn't true.

Lenny flipped open his notebook and read from it: "Ex-wife is Ramona Ann Torre. Age thirty-nine. Maiden name Ramirez. Residence 237 Tupelo. Over in Aberdeen."

"All that was in the note?" I asked.

"Negative. Just her first name. I dug up the rest waiting on you guys."

Frank slapped him on the shoulder. "That's good work, Deputy."

I backed off the porch and looked at Frank. "You go talk to Mom and I'll track down the M.E. Meet you at the van when we're finished."

Frank gave a nod and started for the side yard.

"There's one more thing, detectives."

Frank and I stopped and looked up at Lenny, who was still standing on the front porch with Mr. Torre's body. The deputy loomed over us, an imposing dark shadow silhouetted in the bright house lights shining behind him.

"What's that?" Frank asked, squinting, impatient now.

"Mr. Torre...in the note..." Lenny lowered his voice to make sure no one else could overhear. "He claims his ex-wife is a witch."

"A witch?" I repeated, unsure I had heard him correctly.

But I had. Lenny nodded his head and said it again, a little louder this time: "A witch."

I looked at Frank. He looked back at me, eyebrows arched. "Happy Halloween, partner," he muttered and walked away to talk to the mom and little boy waiting in the side yard.

"SWEET JESUS, please tell me that's not the house," Frank said, staring out the car window at the spilt-level home on the right side of the road.

"That's not the house, Frank."

The home in question was decorated from yard to rooftop like a haunted house from some Grade B horror film. Gargoyles with glowing red eyes stood watch from the second-story roof. Hideously lifelike zombies lurched amongst the grave markers scattered across the front lawn. Fake spider webs drooped from porch railings and tree branches and roof gutters. A blood-splat-tered corpse, swollen tongue protruding, dangled from a noose hanging from a leaning oak tree. Both sides of the driveway were lined with what had to be at least twenty fat pumpkins, orange flames winking secrets in the cool October breeze and forming a welcoming path for gangs of trick-or-treaters ear-lier in the night. A pair of fog machines hidden behind the shrubbery churned out a hazy backdrop and, even with the car windows closed, we could hear the familiar manic beats of the *Halloween* movie soundtrack.

"Look at that," he scowled as we cruised past. "Must've cost them a thousand bucks. At least!"

"Two-thirty-seven is up here on the left," I said, spotting an unmarked sedan parked at the curb. They had arrived a half-hour earlier, to confirm that Ramona Torres was at home and, in case she was indeed guilty, to make sure she didn't decide to make a run for it before we could get there. The two officers would also serve as back-up in the unlikely event we needed it.

"All that money and for what?" Frank went on. "One stu-pid night. It doesn't make any sense."

"I figure it makes plenty of sense to them, Frank, or why else would they do it?"

He grunted and shook his head in disgust.

I flipped a wave to the undercover officers parked across the street and pulled over to the curb and shut off the engine. "Ready?"

"To go witch hunting?"

I tried not to smile. "That's what the man said."

Frank looked at the tidy house at 237 Tupelo. The porch light was on, but all the windows were dark. Rose bushes lined the front of the house and a birdbath stood in the middle of the lawn. "Doesn't look like a witch lives here to me."

"Let's hope you're right," I said, getting out of the car.

"Bet you twenty bucks it was a heart attack."

"No bet."

"Chicken."

I laughed. "Let's just wait on the Tox report. Remember those kids that spiked their teacher's coffee a few years back and he ended up dead? That happened on Halloween, too, you know."

"I hate Halloween," Frank muttered and slammed the car door.

SHE SURPRISED us by answering the door after the first knock.

Frank and I introduced ourselves and showed her our badges, and she surprised us again by inviting us inside before we could even explain what we were doing there.

We followed her into a candle-lit living room and she motioned for us to take a seat. Frank and I sat side by side on a leather sofa. She settled across from us in a high-backed antique chair. Some kind of incense was burning in the room. It smelled exotic and welcoming. I could almost taste it on my tongue.

Ramona Torres was a big woman, at least two hundred pounds, and she was beautiful. Skin the color of creamy chocolate. Dark lush hair that sparkled in the candlelight and reached halfway down her back. Dark, mysterious eyes that made you want to disappear inside them. She was dressed in a flowing black robe etched with gold border that did nothing to hide her glorious cleavage. I noticed Frank staring and hoped I was being more discreet.

Before either of us could begin to explain our late night appearance at her home, she surprised us a third time. "I've been expecting you."

That woke us up. I felt Frank shift on the sofa next to me. "And why is that, Mrs. Torre?" he asked.

"You've come to tell me that my ex-husband is dead, have you not?"

I nodded. "Unfortunately, yes, we have."

"There is nothing unfortunate about it. The man was a pig."

She smiled when she said this, and I felt the temperature in the room drop. Icy fingers caressed the back of my neck. I shivered. *Jesus, this witch business was getting to me.*

I glanced at Frank, sensing he was feeling the same thing. He sat up on the sofa and leaned forward. "Do you think we could turn on some lights in here, Mrs. Torre?"

"Why not?" She clapped her hands, twice, and an overhead chandelier blinked on, chasing away the shadows in the corners of the room.

"That's better," Frank said, looking around. "Thank you."

I glanced around the room and felt myself relax a little. Mrs. Torre's living room looked exactly like a hundred other living rooms I had sat in before on the job. Shelves lined with books and knick-knacks and framed photographs. A widescreen television attached to the wall above a fancy gas fireplace. A piano in the corner by the window. Big potted plants everywhere.

"So you and Mr. Torre were obviously not on good terms?" Frank asked.

Mrs. Torre laughed. "You could say that. I despised the man."

"If you don't mind me asking," I said. "When and why did you get divorced?"

"I filed for divorce ten months ago. About ten years too late." She crossed her legs, and I noticed that she was wearing sandals. Her toenails were painted bright red. "As for *why*...like I said, Harry was a pig. He lied to me. He cheated on me. He abused me."

"Did you ever report him for abuse, Mrs. Torre?" Frank asked.

"I did not. He never raised a hand to me, detective. The only scars he left were inside my soul."

"But you were happy for a time?" I asked. "In the earlier years of the marriage?"

"Harry was a con man, detective. He made me believe in a marriage, in a life, that wasn't real. It never existed. It took me awhile to figure that out, but still I remained with him. No, I was never really happy. At best, I guess you could say I was...grateful."

"Grateful?" Frank asked, and I could hear him scribbling in his notebook.

"That's right." Mrs. Torre thought for a moment. "I was always different, detective. I never really fit in anywhere or with anyone. Even when I was young, growing up back in Mexico, because of my family, people often whispered about me. Many were even afraid of me."

"What about your family?" Frank asked before I could.

She uncrossed her legs. "We were very poor when I was a young girl, but my mother was a very powerful woman. Known many villages away as a healer, among other things. There were always stories about my mother and her sisters. As long as I could remember."

"What kind of stories?" I asked, clearly captivated with the beautiful woman sitting across from me. She met my gaze with a direct stare of her own, and the room suddenly felt too bright and too warm. I felt drowsy, almost as if I had been drugged, and I struggled to remember if Mrs. Torre had offered us something to drink upon our arrival.

I glanced at Frank and he was staring back at me, and I could tell he was experiencing the same sensation.

"…and of course there were those villagers who accused my mother and her sisters of being *Brujas Negras*…"

I looked back at Mrs. Torre and she was smiling at me again, a tired, sad smile, and then I wasn't looking at her at all…I was no longer in her living room…I was somehow…

…inside a dusty village in a jungle clearing made up of grass and mud huts and there were chickens running wild and ancient women washing clothes in a filthy creek and a dirty little girl with

dark, sweaty skin and wide, beautiful eyes holding the hand of an equally beautiful older woman, standing amidst a crowd of others in front of what looked like a stone altar at the jungle's edge and there was an old man bound to the altar with heavy ropes and the man was naked and bleeding and sobbing, his toothless mouth gasping for air, and there was another beautiful woman towering above him, arms outstretched to the sky, both hands clutching a roughly carved stone dagger dripping with blood and plunging it downward…

"…so, yes, you could say I was grateful, detective. Grateful to be accepted by someone from your world. Someone who appeared to be kind and successful and…normal. It was all I ever wanted when I was a little girl growing up in the jungle. It was my fairy tale." Her voice grew harsh. "But it all turned out to be a lie."

I blinked and I was back in Mrs. Torre's candlelit living room. I no longer felt sleepy or drugged. On the contrary, I felt wide awake and alert. I glanced up at the ceiling, looking for the chandelier, but couldn't make it out in the flickering darkness. I listened as Frank's scribbling reached a frenzied pace, and then it abruptly stopped and the room was silent.

After a moment, Mrs. Torre spoke again: "Aren't either of you going to ask if I killed my ex-husband, detectives?"

I felt a single, icy finger trace a path across my neck and down between my shoulder blades, and then it was gone.

Frank got to his feet first, and I was right behind him. I wasn't scared exactly, but I wanted out of that room, out of that house, and far away from that beautiful, mysterious woman.

"Mrs. Torre," Frank said, his voice much softer than I was accustomed to hearing. "Even if you admitted it, I'm pretty damn sure we could never prove it. Not in any crime lab and not in any court of law…"

"YOU THINK she's a witch?"

"No such thing," I said, merging back onto the interstate. We had been inside Ramona Torre's house for just over a half-hour, but the entire visit was a blur. Exhaustion was the culprit; too many cases, too many late nights.

"*Something* was off about her. You see what she was wearing?"

"She was…*different*, that's for sure."

"You liked her, didn't you?"

I looked at Frank. "You were the one staring at her boobs."

"Kinda hard not to," he said. "Be honest, Ben. What did you think of her?"

I thought about it for a moment before I answered. "I think she's a very beautiful, very sad, very lonely woman."

An SUV suddenly blasted past us in the fast lane, blaring its horn, startling both of us. The driver was laughing and wearing a rubber skeleton mask and his passenger was wearing a Donald Trump mask, complete with fuzzy orange hair. The Donald leaned out the window and flipped us the bird before disappearing down the highway.

"Dumbass kids," I said. "Lucky I don't hit the lights and pull 'em over."

Frank grunted and stared out the car window at the dark countryside. "God, I hate Halloween."

A NIGHTMARE ON ELM LANE

My father and I started digging the day after school ended.

I had just finished the seventh grade at Edgewood Middle School and was looking forward to a summer of fishing, bike riding, and playing Magic the Gathering with my friends. If I was lucky I might even run into Katy McCammon at the creek or the swimming pool and finally summon the courage to ask her out to the movies and to get ice cream. Charlie Mitchell had bet me twenty bucks on the last day of school that it wouldn't happen. I was determined to prove his fat ass wrong, even if it meant crashing and burning with Katy. After all, I would have the entire summer to get over it.

My father had just finished his millionth year of teaching upper-level science at the high school and evidently had other plans for the first week of my summer vacation.

"I'M HOMEEE," I announced and flung my baseball hat on the foyer table.

"Don't let the door—"

The screen door slammed shut behind me.

"—*slam!*" my dad finished from the next room.

I walked into the family room, flashed a sheepish grin at my mother, who was reading a magazine on the sofa, and shrugged at my father, who was kicked back in his recliner watching the Orioles on television. "Sorry...I forgot."

"You forget one more time, you're gonna be sorry," he said, a hint of a smile betraying the tough-man attitude. My dad was a lot of things—a terrible singer in the shower, a horrible driver, often embarrassing in public, an ace Scrabble player— but tough wasn't one of them. My mom always called him a Disney Dad.

I plopped down on the sofa and started taking off my shoes. "Who's winning?"

"Don't ask," my dad grumbled.

I laughed and made a face at my mom. She rolled her eyes. My dad was also a lifelong Orioles fan with, how shall I say this, unusual views regarding baseball managerial strategy. He believed in three-run home runs, double steals, and two out bunts. Sometimes all in the same inning.

"My God, what'd you boys do tonight," my mom asked, wrinkling her nose. "You stink."

"Played whiffle ball at Jimmy's," I shrugged. "Then went down to the park."

"You boys catch any fireflies?"

"Yeah, Mom. We all ran around and chased fireflies and stuffed them in an empty jar. Then we played hide-and-go-seek and tag and did a sing-along. What are we, five years old?"

She swatted me on the shoulder. "Don't be a smart aleck."

I grabbed my arm and pretended to swoon.

She laughed. "Go put your shoes on the back porch and take a shower. You're making my eyes water."

I jumped to my feet and gave her a salute—"Yes, ma'am, Janet, ma'am."—and headed for the kitchen and back door.

My father's voice behind me: "Don't call your mother by her first name."

I opened the back door. "Sorry, Henry, won't happen again."

I heard the squawk of the recliner as my father released the leg rest and got to his feet in the next room. I hurriedly tossed my shoes on the porch, slammed the door, and took off for the back stairs...

...just as my father, all five foot eight and hundred-fifty pounds of him, scrambled into the kitchen, nearly slipping in his socks on the linoleum floor and landing on his ass. "I'll teach you not to backtalk your parents!"

I bounded up the stairs, giggling, and locked myself in the bathroom.

"You're lucky today's the last day of school, you little communist!" my father bellowed from downstairs.

I TOSSED the wet towel on the floor next to my dirty clothes and climbed into bed. The sheets felt cool on my bare legs. I used the remote to click on the ten-inch television on my dresser and found the Orioles game. They were losing 8-3 in the bottom of the seventh. It was going to be another long season.

My dad stepped into the doorway. "Hey, I know tomorrow's your first full day of summer vacation, but I need your help for a few hours."

"Help with what?" I asked, dreading the answer.

"I have a little project for us. Won't take long."

"Oh, boy," I said, remembering the last little project. My dad had come home one afternoon with blueprints for a fancy tree house. We'd spent almost two weeks sawing boards and nailing them into place in the old weeping willow tree in the back yard. When we were finally finished, it looked more like a rickety tree-stand for hunting deer than it did any kind of a tree house, and it had cost my dad over three hundred and fifty bucks in materials.

My father laughed. "Now you sound just like your mother. Get some sleep, Kev. I'll see you in the morning."

I RUBBED sleep from my eyes and walked across the patio to the picnic table tucked in the far corner. There were two shovels and a pick-ax leaning against the table, and a couple pairs of work gloves and a sheet of what looked like complicated directions sitting atop the table.

"Not more blueprints," I grumbled.

"They're instructions, smartie pants," my father said from behind me. "How do you expect to do a job correctly if you don't have instructions to follow?"

I resisted the urge to look over at the weeping willow tree.

"You get enough to eat?"

"Yeah," I grumbled.

He picked up the instructions and work gloves. "Grab those tools and follow me."

I cradled the shovels and pick-ax in my arms and followed him into the back yard. He walked past the back-stop I used for pitching practice, past the two-tier bird bath my mom loved so much, underneath the drooping branches of the weeping willow tree, and stopped just short of the vegetable garden that lined our back fence.

"You can put them down here."

I dropped the tools onto the grass. "Okay, now can you tell me? What's the big surprise?"

My father smiled, spread his arms wide, and turned in a slow circle. "This is where our brand new goldfish pond is going."

"Goldfish pond?" I wasn't sure I had heard him correctly.

"That's right," he said, pointing. "Twelve by six foot pond there, complete with miniature waterfall. Rock garden there.

Couple of nice benches there and there. It'll be a thing of beauty when we're done."

This sounded like a lot of work. "Mom know about this?"

"'Course, she does. Whose idea do you think it was?"

I knew better, but wasn't about to say so. "How long is this gonna take?"

He tossed me a pair of work gloves, started pulling his on. "Don't worry, Kev. I only need your help with digging the hole and laying down the liner. I can handle the rest."

I breathed a sigh of relief. Not to be a jerk about it, but I *was* thirteen years old and it *was* summer vacation. I had a lot of important stuff to do.

"We've got two days to get that done. After that, the pump and circulation kit will be here, couple days after that, the live plants and fish." My dad was grinning like a kid in a candy shop. He got a little nutty about things like this, but I sure loved him.

I slipped on the work gloves and picked up a shovel. "Well, what're we waiting for? Let's get digging."

He slapped me on the back. "That's the spirit."

A COUPLE hours later, Mom brought out glasses of lemonade, and my father and I sat in the shade of the weeping willow and took a much-needed break. We were dripping with sweat, and despite the gloves, we both had blisters on our hands.

"Not bad," my father said, taking a long drink and eyeing our progress.

The kidney-shaped outline of the pond was complete. Chunks of sod and dirt were piled off to the side on sheets of clear plastic. Later, when we were finished digging for the day, we would take turns filling up the wheelbarrow and humping loads to the driveway where we would shovel the dirt into the back of my father's pick-up. I wasn't looking forward to that part of the job.

"How deep do we have to go?" I asked.

"Thirty-six inches from end to end."

I looked at the hole. It was maybe six inches deep in most places.

"Take a few more minutes," my father said, putting on his gloves. "Finish your lemonade."

I watched him pick up a shovel and start digging. I sat there in the shade and drank my lemonade and thought about Charlie and Jimmy and the rest of my friends. They were probably down at Hanson Creek right now fishing. Or playing ball at the park. Or betting quarters on the shooting games at the arcade. Or...

My father slung another shovelful of dirt over his shoulder, grunting with the effort. I finished my lemonade and hurried to his side. I figured I had plenty of time for fun and games later on.

"YOU POOR boys," my mother said, watching us struggle to grip our forks at dinner.

She had made my father's favorite, beef stroganoff, and even though we'd worked up quite an appetite, the blisters on our hands made eating a slow process.

"I told you we're fine, honey," my father said. "Few blisters never hurt anyone."

I stuffed another bite into my mouth and nodded agreement. I felt strangely happy and proud of myself. I felt content.

"Well, maybe you should take a break tomorrow and—"

"No way," I said, my mouth still full. "We need to finish digging, so we're ready for the pump on Thursday."

My father beamed. "That's right."

We finished our stroganoff and wolfed down two slices of chocolate cake each for dessert, then we all moved to the den to watch the start of the Orioles game. I was in bed and snoring by nine-thirty. It was my last peaceful night's sleep.

WE WERE up and digging by eight the next morning, energized by a big breakfast and a good night's rest. Dad brought out a radio, and we listened to callers complaining about the Orioles' lack of pitching, hitting, and coaching for the better part of an hour before switching over to an oldies rock station. We were making decent progress on the hole. I figured we'd be moving dirt right up until dark tonight, but we would definitely finish. We were determined.

By late-morning, my father was working his way in from one side of the hole while I attacked the other side. The plan was to meet in the middle, and then use the tape measure to see how much deeper we needed to go. The work was methodical and mindless, but oddly satisfying.

A Led Zeppelin song was playing on the radio when my shovel hit something solid. I wasn't surprised. So far, we had unearthed about a million rocks of various shapes and sizes, an old toy truck, a rusted-out lid from a Speed Racer lunch box, and a few tangles of copper wire that my father said was probably left over from when the house was first built. I had even found a keychain in the shape of a miniature horseshoe with an old key still attached to it. I'd stashed that in my pocket to show my friends later. Maybe it opened a treasure chest somewhere.

I looked down and saw something small and pale in the dirt. Then, I saw another one. Maybe three inches long.

I lifted my shovel for a closer look — and my breath caught in my throat. I'd never seen one before in real life, but I had seen plenty enough on television to know what I was looking at.

They were bones.

"Umm, hey, dad."

The volume on the radio was loud, so I called again, "Dad, I think you should take a look at this."

This time he heard me and came right over. "What's up, Kev?"

I raised the shovel to give him a better look. He squinted in the morning sun, then reached down and picked up one of the bones. "Huh. Probably the previous owner's dog or cat."

He dropped the bone back onto the shovel and hopped down into the hole next to me. "Where'd you find it?"

I pointed out the spot with the tip of my shoe.

He carefully dug a wide circle around it. "I saw this on a National Geographic special about dinosaurs." He dropped to a knee and started sifting through the dirt with his hands.

"Jurassic Park on Golden Elm Lane," I laughed.

"Bingo," my father said, holding up another bone for me to see.

"Kinda gross, don't you think?"

"Just part of nature, son. You're the horror movie freak, how can you think…" He didn't finish his thought. He knelt there, perfectly still, his shoulders suddenly rigid.

"What's wrong?"

He leaned closer to the dirt.

I tried to see around him. "What'd you find?"

My father stood and turned to me, a strange expression on his face. "Let's take a break and go inside and cool off."

I moved to the left to try to see around him. He moved and blocked me. "Kevin—"

"What is it, Dad?"

He let out a long sigh. "Put your shovel down. Carefully. I'll tell you in the house."

"Tell me now," I begged, laying down the shovel on the grass and peeking behind my father into the hole.

Several slender, pale bones lay atop the pile of dirt.

June sunlight glinted off something shiny encircling one of the bones.

It was a dirty gold ring.

BY DINNERTIME, there were three police cruisers parked in front of the house and a police van parked across the street. The back yard was swarming with officers and detectives. Some of them investigating the hole and bagging evidence, others just standing around, talking.

I sat on the patio and watched everything. All of my friends had stopped by at one point or another, but my mother had shooed them away with the promise that I would call them later that night. Most of them spent the evening texting me and watching from across the street, their bikes parked on the sidewalk.

A police detective had interviewed my father and me, first in the living room, and then again as we showed him what we'd found in the back yard. He'd asked us a lot of the same questions two or three times, almost like he didn't believe us. When the other cops showed up, he quickly finished with us and got to work with the others.

Both my mom and dad must've asked me at least a dozen times throughout the day if I was all right. Each time I reassured them I was fine. The truth was I was more than just fine.

I was excited and anxious to find out even more about what was going on.

I eavesdropped on every conversation I could. I offered policemen drinks and made other excuses to talk to them. I even used the zoom on my phone camera to try to get a glimpse of what was going on over by the hole.

Finally, around the time it started getting dark and two policemen started setting up portable lights, I climbed the weeping willow and perched myself inside my tree house. I couldn't see much from up there, there were too many branches in the way, but I was comfortable enough and could hear a lot better.

Around nine o'clock, I heard a cellphone ring somewhere below me.

"Sharretts," a voice answered, and then there was a long pause. "Make sure you check with Henderson first. He left here fifteen minutes ago."

I recognized the voice now. It was the detective who had interviewed my father and me earlier in the day. He obviously didn't realize I was in the tree above him, listening. I knew this because of what he said next.

"That all depends on what Cap says. I think they're gonna GPR the whole damn back yard in the morning."

Another pause.

"Three skeletal right hands so far."

I realized I was holding my breath.

"That's right. No other remains. Just the hands."

I could hear his footsteps moving away from the tree.

"Someone's checking on that right now. Okay, talk soon," and then there was just the muffled chatter of the policemen below and the soft whisper of a breeze in the weeping willow.

A short time later, I crept down from the tree and went inside. I hurried to the bathroom to pee — I'd been holding it for what felt like forever — and realized that I still had the horseshoe keychain in my pants pocket. I knew I should probably go back outside and give it to the police. It could be important evidence.

Instead, I went to the kitchen and ate a snack and used my phone to look up what GPR stood for: *Ground Penetrating Radar*.

They were going to x-ray the back yard tomorrow. They were looking for bodies.

I WAS too tired to call my friends back that night, so I called first thing the next morning. I started with Jimmy.

"My mom says you can maybe come over tonight, but just you, not the rest of the guys."

"Awesome. My mom said she saw the story on the news last night. They had pictures of your house and everything. Golden Elm Lane is famous!"

I'd watched the same news story this morning during breakfast. It felt weird seeing my house like that. Not a good weird either. It was almost like they were trespassing or something.

"What are they doing now?" Jimmy asked. "They find any more skeletons?"

I walked over to the window and looked outside. "A couple vans showed up a little while ago…"

I told Jimmy what I'd overheard the night before about GPR and how there was a guy in regular street clothes pushing something that looked like one of those portable golf caddies with three wheels back and forth across my yard. A cop in uniform walked alongside him, carrying a clipboard and a fistful of little red flags attached to wire stakes. Every once in a while, they would stop and the cop would take a knee and plant one of the little red flags in the grass, and then they would move on again.

Jimmy was fascinated — "it's just like a freaking movie, man!" — and made me promise to text him a photo from my phone. I told him I would. I didn't say a word about the other thing I'd overheard while sitting in the tree house: about the police finding three right hands. Just like with the keychain, I hadn't even shared that information with my parents yet. I didn't know why, but I'd kept that to myself.

FIRST THING in the morning, the police had asked my parents to make sure everyone stayed clear of the back yard, so I was forced to watch from my bedroom window. I pulled my desk chair close and cracked the window a few inches, but I still couldn't hear much. To make matters worse, the weeping willow blocked a good portion of my view. I was flying blind today.

I sent Jimmy a blurry picture of the cops operating the GPR machine and did my best to keep up with my other friends' text messages. I ate a ham and cheese sandwich and Doritos for lunch and skimmed a couple articles in the new issue of *Gamer's Monthly*. I almost fell asleep twice after lunch and took the fastest bathroom break known to man for fear of missing something important. I counted four red flags sticking out of the ground. No telling how many more there were behind the tree and around the hole we'd dug.

The hours dragged on. I started thinking about sneaking outside for a closer look. I even considered sneaking up into the tree house again. What were they going to do, arrest me?

I had just about convinced myself to go for it, when there was a knock on the door behind me. I turned and both my mom and dad were standing there.

"Hey, Kev," my dad said. "Got a minute?"

They walked into the room and sat on my bed.

"Did they find something else? Did they—"

My dad put his hands out. "Whoa, slow down." He glanced at my mom and continued, "We just finished speaking with one of the detectives, and we thought we'd share with you what he said."

"If anything we say upsets you," my mom said, "just say so and we'll stop."

I looked from my dad to my mom and back to my dad again. "Just tell me!"

"This stays inside the house, Kevin. It's family talk, not for your friends. Got it?"

"Got it," I said, nodding and sitting on the edge of my seat.

"According to the detective, they've found skeletal remains from at least three different people in the back yard."

No duh, I wanted to say.

"They've also marked some additional areas they plan to search later this afternoon. The detective told us the lab ran some tests on the bones we found and they came back as more than twenty years old, so fortunately they know we had nothing to do with this."

I hadn't even thought of that. "Wow, we could have been suspects!" I blurted, putting an immediate frown on my mom's face. Wait until Jimmy heard about that.

"They also pulled property records and discovered that the sole owner before us of 149 Golden Elm Lane was a man by the name of Walter Jenkins. By all accounts, he was a friendly, well-liked man with no complaints against him and no arrest record. He was retired from the Navy and worked at the hardware store in Dayton. He was widowed when he was in his sixties and moved to a nursing home about ten years later. That's when we bought the house and moved in."

"Is he still alive?" I asked, my mind working.

My dad shook his head. "Died six years ago. Didn't have any children and no living relatives nearby."

"So, if he didn't do it...who did?"

"That's what the detectives are trying to figure out, Kev. Detective Sharretts said they might have a few more questions for us in the days to come, but mostly they'll be looking around for folks who knew Mr. Jenkins back when he lived here."

"You know some of the world's most famous serial killers were normal and friendly on the outside, right?" I asked, remembering some of the books I'd read. "They weren't all weirdos like Dahmer and Gacy and—"

"You hush now," my mom interrupted, getting up from the bed. "No more talk about serial killers. Get yourself washed up and help us prepare dinner."

"But, Mom…" I whined, looking at my dad for help.

He stood up from the bed. "You heard your mother, Kev. Let's go."

So much for help. I groaned and followed them downstairs.

THAT NIGHT, I dreamed Walter Jenkins was chasing me.

The house was dark, and Jenkins was old and wrinkled, but incredibly fast and strong. No matter where I ran or hid, he kept finding me. He had a hideous grin and an evil laugh and a long, wicked-looking knife. He wanted my right hand.

Terrified and cornered, I crept into the basement.

"Come out, come out, wherever you are," he called in a gravely, sing-song voice.

I sat perfectly still in the space between the washer and dryer, afraid to breathe. I had piled several dirty towels on top of me. I couldn't see a thing.

"I know you're down here," he said, and I could hear the shuffle of footsteps getting closer.

"C'mon now, Kev, I'm not going to hurt you." The footsteps stopped right in front of me. I felt a whisper of cool air as one of the towels was removed from on top of me.

"I promise I won't hurt you."

Another towel gone.

"I'm just gonna kill you!" The last towel was snatched away, and I saw that evil grin and long, shiny blade slashing—

—and that's when I woke up in my dark bedroom, sweaty sheets clenched in one hand, my other hand the only thing stopping the scream from escaping my mouth.

"DUDE, YOU'RE like a celebrity," Doug said. "Everyone's talking about you."

Charlie rolled his eyes. "I wouldn't go that far."

"Don't be a douchebag," Jimmy said and punched Charlie in the shoulder. "You're just jealous."

"The day I'm jealous of gay boy Kevin here is the day you get to bang my sister."

"Already banged her," Jimmy said, pushing off on his bike. "And your mom, too."

Charlie's chubby face went red. He jumped on his bike and started chasing Jimmy down the trail. "Take it back! Take it back!"

Jimmy just laughed and kept on peddling.

It felt good to be with my friends again, instead of locked up inside the house. The police had left a couple days ago, and even the news crews had stopped coming around.

"So they have no idea how they got there?" Doug asked for at least the fifth time that morning.

I shook my head. "It's a big mystery."

"You mean a nightmare," he said, and then his eyes flashed wide. "A nightmare on Elm Lane!" He hooked his hands into claws and started slashing at me. "Maybe Freddy Krueger did it!"

I laughed and pushed him away.

"My dad says they should check out the folks who own the house in back of you," Doug said, still giggling.

"Police already did that. The current owners and the previous two owners."

"And?"

"And nothing, I guess."

Doug grunted and looked around for Jimmy and Charlie. "It's hot as piss. Wanna go get a Slurpee?"

"Sure."

Doug put his fingers to his mouth and whistled. Thirty seconds later, we heard a returning whistle from deep in the woods. A few minutes after that, Jimmy and Charlie came racing down the trail, both of them red-faced and sweating. We all set out for 7-Eleven.

THE FOUR of us sat on the curb outside the store and drank our Slurpees and opened our packs of baseball cards. Charlie and Doug got into an argument about who was a better third baseman, Manny Machado or Kris Bryant, and that turned into a pebble fight until Charlie plunked Doug in the eye. Jimmy and I were content to sit back and watch the spectacle and drink our Slurpees in silence.

A car pulled into a parking spot nearby, but none of us paid it any attention.

"Hey there, boys," a voice called. "Hot enough for you?"

We all looked up. Mr. Barnett from down the street was leaning out his car window, the stub of a cigar poking from his mouth. It smelled like cat shit.

"Sure is," Jimmy answered.

Mr. Barnett looked at me. "Kevin, you're quite the celebrity these days, aren't you?"

Doug gave Charlie a smug look: *I told you so.*

"I dunno about that, Mr. Barnett."

"I saw you and your dad on the news a couple times, walking around in the background. Pretty exciting stuff, huh?"

I nodded, but didn't say anything. Mr. Barnett was the first grown-up to use the word exciting to describe everything that had happened. Of course, all us kids thought it was exciting and cool, but the only words I'd heard other grown-ups use were horrible and terrifying and dreadful. But Mr. Barnett was like that. He wasn't like the other adults I knew. He always drank too much at the neighborhood block parties and shot off too many fireworks on the Fourth of July and my mom was always complaining that he was breaking the speed limit on our street.

"Sooo…the police find anything else that hasn't made the news or the papers?"

"My parents aren't really telling me much," I said. "They're afraid I'll have nightmares."

Mr. Barnett's face tightened, and I could tell he didn't believe me. "So they found the remains of three hands, and that's it?"

I nodded again, worried my voice would betray me.

"You know I asked my father about the guy who used to live in your house," he continued, "and my father knew him."

Now he had my attention. "He did?"

"Said he was a nice enough fella but kept to himself. Said he even had a photograph of him somewhere, from an old Veteran's Day parade."

I thought about telling Mr. Barnett that he should have his father call the detectives, but I didn't. I had finished my Slurpee and just wanted to get out of there.

"Well, boys, I better run. Kevin, Jimmy, tell your folks I said hello. Looking forward to the cookout on the Fourth."

"Yes, sir," Jimmy said.

I waved as he pulled away.

We all got up, tossed our trash into the can, and mounted our bikes.

"That was weird," Doug said.

Jimmy shook his head. *"He's* weird."

"No, that's not what I meant. He pulled up and talked to us and left without even going into the store."

Jimmy thought about it for a moment and shrugged. I thought about it the whole way home.

THAT NIGHT, I heard something in the back yard.

A thunderstorm had rolled in after dinner, dumping nearly an inch of rain and dropping the temperature by twenty degrees. My mom had opened all the upstairs windows, and I had fallen asleep earlier to a chorus of crickets and bullfrogs.

But something else woke me up.

I wasn't sure if I had dreamt or imagined it, but I got out of bed and went to the window.

The back yard was cloaked in darkness, the weeping willow a towering shadow against an even darker backdrop. A lonely bullfrog croaked somewhere in the weeds and I could hear the muffled barking of a dog from the next block over.

I was just about to return to bed when I saw it: a shadow breaking away and moving independent of the other shadows around it. The shadow was in the shape of a person.

And then I heard it, the same sound that had woken me earlier: a *thump* followed by another *thump*, and then the sound of two feet landing on soggy grass.

Someone had just climbed over the fence in the back yard and jumped to the other side.

I SAT on the front porch and watched the sanitation guys emptying our trash cans into the back of their truck. I wondered if they ever found anything valuable in the garbage. It seemed like such a cool job.

I hadn't told anyone about what I'd seen and heard the night before. First of all, I wasn't one hundred percent sure I hadn't dreamt the whole damn thing. My head was still fuzzy. Second of all, I didn't want to worry my parents. They were tense enough with everything that was going on. I'd even heard my mom after dinner last night blame my dad for picking that spot for the goldfish pond.

The street was quiet today. No police had come by the house for almost a week, and the news people hadn't been by in even longer. It had been an exciting adventure while it lasted, but I was glad life was getting back to normal.

"Caught you daydreaming, didn't I?"

I looked up and saw our mailman, Mr. DeMarco's, smiling face.

I laughed. "Guilty as charged."

He stepped past me onto the porch, stuffed some mail into the box, and plopped down next to me on the stoop.

"I'm getting too old for this job." He took a handkerchief out of his pocket and wiped the sweat from his face. As usual, I caught a faint whiff of his cologne. It was the same stuff my father used to wear. Blue Velvet or something like that. He looked over at me. "You doing okay, partner?"

Mr. DeMarco had been asking me that ever since it all happened. He said finding dead folks in your back yard was no

joking matter, and I shouldn't hide my feelings if I was struggling. Mr. DeMarco was cool like that. All us kids loved him.
He was old, had to be at least sixty, but he would still toss his
mailbag under a tree some days and play whiffle ball or kick ball
with us. Other times, he'd treat us all to fudgesicles if the ice
cream man was making his rounds.

"I'm doing good," I said.

"Any plans for today?" He glanced up at blue sky. "Looks
like it's gonna be a good one."

"We're going fishing down at the creek. Just waiting on
Jimmy to finish mowing his lawn."

He got to his feet with a groan. "Now that's a great way to
spend a day like today. Even if they ain't biting."

"Oh, they'll be biting all right," I said, grinning. "We've got
our secret bait."

He squinted at me. "Lemme guess…cheese balls?"

"How'd the heck you know?!"

Mr. DeMarco tilted his head back and laughed. It was a
good, happy sound.

"I know because that's exactly what my friends and me used
for bait in that exact same creek fifty years ago! Those fatty carp
love cheese balls!"

I laughed.

"As a matter of fact," he said, face turning serious. "I told that
police detective pretty much the same thing when he asked. Me and
my friends used to run this neighborhood just like you and yours.
Fishing, kick the can, racing our go-karts down Golden Elm."

I imagined Mr. DeMarco cruising down the road in a go-kart. Then, I thought of something I'd never thought of before.

"Did you and your friends know Walter Jenkins?"

Mr. DeMarco nodded. "Sure did. Even raked his leaves and cleaned his gutters once or twice. Me and Kenny Crawford, God rest his soul. Told the detective that, too."

"What was he like?" I asked.

"He was a good man, Kevin. Don't you listen to any of the rumors going 'round." He paused, thinking for a moment. "Mr. Jenkins reminded me a lot of my own father. That's how highly I thought of him."

I nodded and was about to respond — when a loud whistle sounded from somewhere down the street.

I whistled back and jumped to my feet. "Gotta go, Mr. DeMarco."

"Summer awaits, Kev. Those carp won't wait forever!"

LATER THAT night, I sat by my bedroom window and watched over the back yard. After nearly two hours of seeing and hearing nothing out of the ordinary, I returned to my bed and was asleep within minutes. I didn't have any bad dreams that night.

TWO AMAZING things occurred later in the week.

The first happened on Thursday morning while I was eating breakfast on the back patio with my mom. My phone buzzed in my pocket. I went to take it out and my mom said, "Uh uh, no phones at the table, remember?"

I put my hands out proclaiming my innocence. "I was just gonna turn off the ringer. Geez."

"Don't you geez me, mister."

I smiled and switched off the ringer on my phone — and saw the text.

I thought I was going to faint right on top of my plate of French toast.

The text wasn't from Jimmy or Charlie, as I had expected.

The text was from Katy McCammon.

Kevin, I'm having a pool party this Sunday at 2. You should come. Lemme know. Katy ☺

I placed my phone beside my plate and read the text a second and third time from the corner of my eye. Then, I broke the world speed record for eating French toast and dumped my dishes in the kitchen sink. I yelled goodbye to my mom and ran down Golden Elm Lane as fast as I could to show Jimmy.

The second amazing occurrence happened on Friday evening, just before dinner. My dad and I were watching a Seinfeld re-run when the phone rang. My mother picked up in the other room. A moment later, she came in with the cordless phone pressed against her chest.

"It's Detective Sharretts," she said in a low voice, handing the phone to my father.

"Hello?" My father mostly listened, every once in awhile punctuating the conversation with an "uh huh" or a "no kidding" or an "okay."

After several minutes of this, he finally hung up. "Well, that was interesting."

Stone faced, he walked back to his reading chair and sat down. Turned up the volume on the television. Stared silently at the screen.

My mother *("Honeyyy!")* and I *("Dadddd!")* erupted at the same time.

He cracked up laughing.

"Tell us what he said!" I begged.

It took another thirty seconds for my father's giggling to wind down, then he filled us in. "Detective Martin said they have a person of interest in custody."

My mother clasped her hands together. "Thank God."

"A former resident of Dayton who moved away a long time ago," my father continued. "Evidently he admitted to everything. The detectives are going over his story to make sure it all adds up, but Detective Sharretts thinks it will. In the meantime, they at least have him on a weapons charge, so he's not going anywhere..."

I HAD a hard time falling asleep on Saturday night — I kept telling myself: *In fifteen hours, you'll be looking at Katy McCammon in a bikini; in fourteen hours, you'll be sitting in Katy's back yard with all the cool kids; in thirteen hours…* — so I found an old movie to watch on television. When the credits rolled at one a.m., my eyes were finally getting drowsy.

That's when I heard the footsteps. Not outside in the yard, but inside the house this time.

I held my breath — and heard it again.

A creak on the stairs. Getting closer.

My entire body broke out in cold sweat.

It's just Mom coming back from getting a drink of water, I thought. *She has trouble sleeping.* But I knew better. My mom hadn't woken in the middle of the night in forever, not since she'd started taking sleeping pills. And forget about my father, he slept like a bear in hibernation.

Another creak and the whisper of a footstep on hardwood floor. Someone moving slow and stealthily. Someone creeping.

The house was silent for the next minute or two, and I was just beginning to believe I'd imagined the whole thing, when I heard a quiet *thump* from down the hallway, from the direction of my parents' room. And then I heard a second *thump*. Like something heavy hitting the floor.

I snatched my cellphone from the end table next to my bed and pulled the covers up over my head like I used to do when I was a little kid and afraid of the monster that lived inside my closet. I punched in the security code and keyed in 911, but I didn't press SEND.

My bedroom door creaked open.

Even underneath the blanket, I could hear someone in the room breathing.

Something unnamable — no, it had a name; it was *terror* — stopped me from pushing SEND, stopped me from leaping to my feet and trying to flee.

It's Walter Jenkins and he has a knife.

My heart was beating so hard that I couldn't hear the footsteps shuffling closer. I couldn't hear the breathing growing more labored.

But nothing was wrong with my nose — and that's when I smelled it.

The faint scent of cologne. Blue Velvet or Blue Ice or whatever the hell it was called.

Now I knew who'd buried the hands in my back yard all those years ago.

Now I knew whom the keychain belonged to.

He wanted it back.

DIRTY
COPPERS

1

t was one of those nights when I just couldn't help it—I wanted
to hump her, and I was ashamed of myself as usual.

Heather Neely's husband was a copper who had been
kidnapped by a gang of thugs called the Marauders. They'd
held him hostage for sixteen days until the coppers finally gave
in and released two Marauder gang members. The thing was,
these two were supposed to be executed on YOU ASKED FOR
IT, that holo show where they do some pretty outrageous stuff,
including letting five-year-olds execute baddies.

Anyway, the Marauders got their punks back, and the coppers got Bob Neely back. Sort of, anyway.

The Marauders had cut out both of his eyes, all of his nose,
and sliced off a decent chunk of his tongue for good measure.
The eye thing was kind of ironic, couple years ago Heather

having lost one of her own eyes to one of those attack dogs the genetics labs sell to the criminal underground.

The docs did everything they could for Bob Neely but even given modern medicine there are limits. Especially with psychological damage as severe as his.

So now Neely sits in a dark room at home. He has withdrawn completely from what we call reality. Vegetable is the word we're talking here.

So I do all I can for the poor bastard. Couple times a week, I bang his wife.

"YOU GOT any money?" Heather Neely asked.

"Not much," I said. "Why? You runnin' short again?"

"Yeah, kinda." She looked over at me. "Maybe it's time for the gorilla mask."

I nodded. I needed some extra credits myself.

Now before you get all uppity about this very delicate subject we're about to discuss, just remember one thing. You take that forty-seven percent inflation rate we've got, and you couple that with the new budget cut-backs imposed on coppers, and you consider that most of us are married with families, and maybe you can understand why we don the gorilla mask so damn often.

I said, "It's my turn to be the robber."

"The hell it is. We flipped for it last time, remember? This time it's *my* turn."

"Broads."

"Yeah, and what would you do without us?"

Before we got a chance to pick a location, let alone put on the gorilla mask, we got a call about a very bad accident.

Two hover cars had collided over a slum area, and not only had the cars fallen to earth, their fiery debris had set three houses on fire. It was a mess.

We headed east and five minutes later we spotted an orange-yellow glow on the horizon. Even when we were still up in the air, and angling down for a landing, you could hear little kids screaming in the burning houses.

The cliché is that coppers joke this stuff away. That's never worked for me. I see this kind of shit…I want to get sick and then I want to kill somebody. Like the undoubtedly doped-up hover car driver who caused the accident.

This kind of thing was happening every goddamn day. That's why hover car operator licenses were so hard to come by. The law tried to give only the most trustworthy people licenses. But, hell, since when has the law been perfect?

The holo people were already there and they were having a wonderful time. A little girl — no older than three-years-old — came screaming out of one of the burning houses, her hair and arms and legs dripping with fire. Next door, a naked woman dangled from an upstairs window ledge. This was all great video for the evening network holos.

Neely nudged me in the side and said, "I get the mask tonight." She slipped me the shooter. "You get the gun."

A shooter is what folks used to call a throw-down gun. A weapon that couldn't be traced to anybody. Cops like Neely and I carry them all the time.

The scene was even uglier from the ground. I couldn't handle it. I spent most of my time searching the crowd, trying to find the driver responsible for all this.

The occupants of the first car were white-haired people, old and obviously married. The woman had a gash across her forehead. The man looked dazed. Neither of them looked badly hurt.

Took me about fifteen minutes to find the other guy, what with the crowd and all the holo reporters. He was sitting on a porch stoop, barking into the communicator on his wrist. The accident had left his shiny new mesh clothes a little grubby but nothing could detract from the pure patrician arrogance of him.

I kicked the communicator from his wrist.

"Hey!" he said.

"Up."

"What?"

"Get up. On your feet."

"Do you have any idea who you're talking to?"

"No, and I don't give a rat's ass, either. You know how many people you killed tonight, motherfucker? You see that little girl back there on fire?"

I grabbed his arm and jabbed the sensor needle deep into his wrist.

He screamed. Sensor needles hurt like a bitch. Especially when you use them like weapons.

"This is illegal."

"No shit?" I said. "I guess I better start reading the rule book, huh?"

The sensor needle, just as I'd suspected it would, gave me a reading of five points plus. Off the fucking charts. The indicated drug was stardust, which explained why he'd been able to compose himself so quickly. Stardust fades when any kind of trauma is involved. A guy can look clean and sober and still have a lot of that shit running through his veins.

"Come on, we're going out back," I said.

"What?"

"Between these houses here."

"I'm not going anywhere with you. That was my shyster I was talking to, and he said he'd come right over."

"He did, huh?"

I grabbed the guy by the back of his neck and shoved him between the houses.

Even with the fire and black smoke filling the air, you could smell the stench of the ghetto here. Hell, you could practically taste it. Hot night like this, it was all a copper could do to avoid upchucking. This was one of those neighborhoods where even the little kids carry pieces, and where every family has two or three mutated pit bulls. Mean, blood-thirsty dogs. And they still get robbed all the time.

I got him to the alley and said, "You believe in God?"

"What?"

"I asked if you believed in God."

"No. Why?"

"Good. Then this'll go faster."

"What the hell are you talking about?"

"If you said you believed in God, then I would've given you time to say a couple of prayers. Now I ain't gonna give you any time at all."

"You son-of-a-bitch. You let me go and you let me go right now—"

I brought the shooter up and blew away half his head. It came apart in two large bloody chunks that landed wetly on the gravel behind me. Roving dogs would feast on the pieces later.

I checked over my shoulder for witnesses. No one. Nothing moved.

I wiped the shooter down clean, taking out a can of WIPE, which destroys even microscopic evidence, and then set the piece in his hand.

Sumbitch was feeling so guilty about what he did tonight, he took a shooter and killed himself. Poor noble bastard.

That would be my story. Sure, his shyster would piss and moan about it but unless the dead guy had heavy political connections, the case would be closed.

Most coppers executed people. The courts were so clogged they couldn't handle much more. So when it was a clear-cut case like this one, why not save everybody a little time and money?

And to be perfectly honest, there are some of these people I don't *mind* executing. Not at all.

I slipped out of the alley and spotted Neely in the crowd.

"How'd it go?" she said.

I shrugged. "You know."

My communicator buzzed. The robot dispatcher spoke so loudly that Neely didn't need to turn on her own communicator. Even above the din of the accident, she could hear just fine. Bots are loud-mouthed obnoxious sons-of-bitches and almost every copper I know would love a chance to execute one of them.

When the message was finished, Neely said, "Jesus, can you believe that?"

"Yeah," I said.

She frowned. "Dead guy. With his wang cut off."

"Wow," I said, smiling and protectively covering my crotch with my hand, "his wang?"

"That's right, smartass," Neely said. "His wang."

2

WE DECIDED it wouldn't take long, so we pulled the robbery on the way over to the cybersex bar.

The Alatians probably didn't think they'd become convenience store clerks when they met up with one of our satellites out near Pluto or wherever the hell it was. Alatians are something else, let me tell you. They're these little bluish gill-guys.

At one time — or so our scientists say — Alatia, which is somewhere way out there in what they used to call the space sea, was a mighty interplanetary empire. But then this mad emperor-type took over the planet and got them into all these wars and used up all their natural resources…so now the Alatians travel the space sea looking for planets where large numbers of them can make a home. Mostly they do low-skill work. Kind of intergalactic immigrants, I guess you'd call them.

Three things you need to know about Alatians:

One: Yes, they have two eyes much like our own, but they also have one in the back of their head, staring out from a bald spot in their ratty orange hair. This third eye never blinks.

Two: They're short. Not midgets, just short. Tallest I've ever seen is about five-one, maybe five-two.

Three: They like old-fashioned country western music. Don't ask my why, hell if I know. But that's why, when you go into one of the stores where they're pulling the graveyard shift, you hear all that twangy bullshit. They even wear t-shirts that say

i ♥ little Jimmy Dickens

and ridiculous stuff like that.

Weird little fuckers, these Alatians, let me tell you.

I put the hover car down in the alley behind the liquor store and as I was doing that, Neely was slipping into her coveralls and gorilla mask.

We have one rule about stick-ups. We never shoot, not even in self-defense. Lot of coppers, they don't draw that line, so an Alatian hassles them a little bit, they blow him away. But not us. It's not that we like Alatians so much, it's just that you kill somebody, there's always an investigation, because there are so many anti-copper political groups out there. A guy you want to execute, that's one thing, worth the risk. But one of those little blue bastards? Uh, uh. Not worth risking your career over.

"Smush ee uck," Neely said.

"I can't understand you."

She lifted the gorilla mask and said, "I said 'Wish me luck.'"

"Oh. Yeah. Luck, Neely."

She pulled the mask down and got out of the car.

She was gone five, six minutes.

Then she came running out to the hover car. I had the door open, waiting.

When we were up in the air, she said, still out of breath, her face glistening from sweat, "You know what he did?"

"The Alatian?"

"Yeah."

"How would I know what he did? I wasn't there, remember?"

"He defecated."

"Huh?"

"Crapped his pants."

"Oh."

"'Oh.' You woulda been in there with me and smelled it, you wouldn't just be sayin' 'Oh,' believe me."

"How much?"

"Could you give me a minute, Mulligan? Christ, I haven't even had time to open the bag."

She opened the bag and counted.

"Not bad," she said. "Five thousand nekars."

"Wow."

"I always get more than you do."

"Bullshit," I said.

"Bullshit? Who got six thousand nekars that time at that Alatian dance club?"

"Once, you lucked out."

"Once," she said, shaking her head. "You just can't admit that a broad is a better robber than you are. That's all."

I was going to say something but the thing was, right now I wasn't worried about my ego. I was thinking of the two months overdue rent my share of the robbery credits was going to pay.

"You did good, Neely."

"Thanks."

"But it was still my turn to be the robber."

"Right, Mulligan," she said. "Right."

COUPLE NIGHTS ago one of the newsies was wondering aloud on the holo why so much violence took place in the middle-class cybersex parlors.

Proving once again that newsies don't know shit.

What he was really asking was: how come rich guys weren't getting killed?

Real simple.

Rich guys can afford to keep all their diversions and perversions at home. But for most people who want cybersex, it means going out to the bars. And renting the full-body data suits the wealthy have hanging in their closets at home.

Of course, it took the rich folks to discover that cybersex is even better if you do it in conjunction with hormones that are laced with steroids. These days, the people who go to the bars don't just get hooked on sex. They get hooked on the drugs, as well.

Until three months ago, when the killings started, about the worst calls we ever got around here were to stop crazed cybersexers from running down the middle of the street with their genitals exposed. Men and women alike. Hell, sometimes, I'd swear the gals like cybersex even more than the men.

The thing is the cybersex bars start to take their toll mentally on the people who use them. After a while it fucks with their heads in a bad way. So, from time to time, there's a lot of violence. And of the nasty variety.

When we got there, there were maybe two hundred people out on the street, most of them glassy-eyed cybersexers. Over by the alley, a naked guy was bopping a naked girl against a signpost. Nobody seemed to notice.

The dead guy was on the sidewalk, being sprayed head to toe to keep everything intact. It was like coating him with plastic.

There were at least twenty coppers and twice as many newsies. The huge sign out front kept flashing on and off:

CYBERSEX BOOTHS!
CUM THREE TIMES AN HOUR GUARANTEED!

The whole thing reminded me of one of those old holos where they show Times Square on New Year's Eve. People and lights and noise everywhere.

Neely said, "I can't figure out why guys get into this stuff when the real thing's so easy to get."

I said, "It's never been all that easy for me to get."

"That's because you don't know how to treat women, Mulligan. We want a little romance once in a while. The real thing, you know? You're strictly belching, scratching, farting, and coming."

I felt my face start to get warm.

"My wife seemed to like me all right," I said.

She smiled. "You're a nice guy, Mulligan, it's just you got no class."

Then the detectives were all over us, asking us questions about the previous murder here four nights ago, which we'd covered.

It was the usual boring shit, all this Q&A crap, the homicide boys and girls very spiffy in their shiny black jumpsuits and styled hair. Never mind that they weren't very smart and were even more arrogant than the newsies. I suppose these were the role models Neely had in mind when she told me I had no class.

HALF AN hour later, I was wandering around outside the cybersex place asking questions of my own. A hover car with another uniformed officer had beaten us here by fifteen minutes, and I found him a little ways down the street. He was young, too young, and was intimidated by the fact that I wore the insignia of Kop5, meaning I could double as a homicide dick when necessary. So could Neely. Given the publicity these cybersex murders were getting on the holos, the administration needed every homicide dick it could find.

"So, as far as you know, there weren't any witnesses?"

"No sir," said the freckle-faced kid.

"Who found the body?"

"One of the rovers. Inside."

"You get her name?"

"Yeah. Gwen Fordham."

"She in there now?"

"I guess so."

"You guess so?"

He looked embarrassed. "I shoulda told her to stick around, huh?"

"Hell, yes, you shoulda."

"I'll be more careful next time."

He looked like he was going to cry.

"Hey, kid, it's all right. We all fuck up once in a while."

"It was pretty stupid, not making sure she hung around."

"I get the time some day, I'll tell you all the stupid things I've done over the years."

He smiled.

NEELY WAS already inside, showing around the holo she'd just snapped of the corpse, trying to see if anybody knew him or had seen him earlier in the evening.

When I walked in, she was talking to this big red-headed guy who wasn't being much help at all. His nose had been broken a couple of times. So had most of his knuckles.

He leaned against the tall, tubular booth he'd been using. He seemed very protective of it, as if somebody might try to steal it from him.

"So you knew him?" Neely said.

"Didn't say I knew him. Said I *saw* him."

"Tonight?"

"Tonight and a lot of other nights."

"He was a regular?"

"Yeah."

"And that would make you a regular, too?"

Neely always jabs people when she interviews them. Says jabbing them lets them know who the boss is.

"Yeah, I'm a regular. So what? I'm single, I work hard, I can spend my fucking credits any way I want to. Free country, you know."

I tried to hide my smile. Seemed like maybe Neely had finally met her match in the surly department.

"You ever see him arguing with anybody?"

He shrugged. "You know how steroids affect some people. He argued with a lot of people. So do I. Doesn't mean anything."

"You see him argue with anybody tonight?"

"One of the rovers, I guess."

"What'd she look like?"

"Short, blonde hair, nice ass."

"You see her around here now?"

The guy's eyes scanned the first floor of the cybersex bar. The tubular virtual reality booths ran twenty-five deep on each side of the wide floor. In the middle was a bar and curtained fuck booths where, if you wanted actual sex with an actual woman, you could have it. If you had the money. The women in here were called rovers because they roved around all four noisy floors of this place. Every few minutes, you'd hear somebody screaming in one of the booths. Ecstasy. The women screamed just slightly louder than the men.

"Yeah, there she is," the guy said.

He pointed to a blonde rover standing at the bar. A very intense black man was talking to her.

"We'll go pay her a visit," Neely said, and started to turn away.

"Hey," the big guy said.

Neely turned back to him.

"You're about the rudest fucking copper I ever ran into," he said.

Neely smiled. "You should meet my sister some time."

WHEN WE walked up, the black man was saying, "So I thought what we'd do is both of us, we'd drop some magenta and then you'd get in the booth with me—"

"Are you crazy?" the blonde said. She was topless and wore tight red shorts with a slitted section over the crotch. "They'd fire me in a minute."

"And then," I said, putting my hands on the black man's shoulder, "the coppers would bust your ass."

For one thing, taking a rover into a VR booth is against the law. Especially when they're mixing drugs, the guys in the booth can get pretty violent. VR lets you take out all your sado-masochistic impulses without getting hurt. But you have a rover in there, you start to confuse reality with VR. A while back, a cybersexer snuck a rover into a booth one night and got so excited he ripped her apart with his bare hands. When he got done with her, she was just piles of hot bloody flesh.

For a second thing, magenta is the kind of drug that lands you in prison. Strictly verboten. About thirty percent of all homicides in the city are committed by people stoned on magenta.

The black man turned and looked at me. "We were having a private conversation, this lady and I."

"And she was being smart enough to turn you down," I said. I nodded to the booths. "Why don't you go have yourself a nice, legal time tonight?"

The black man, who was wearing one of those trendy aqua tunics, made a face at the rover and then made a face at me. And then pushed past us, and vanished into the crowd.

"He's all right," the rover said. "His old lady dumped him a couple weeks ago. He's just looking for kicks to help ease the pain."

Neely pushed the holo in her face.

While the rover checked out the holo, I checked out her breasts. They were small and perfectly shaped. You'd think that bare breasts would lose their appeal when they were constantly exposed this way. Not with me. I felt a painful stirring in my groin.

"That's him," the rover said to Neely.

"Him?" Neely said.

"Yeah. He was real drunk and raisin' hell earlier tonight."

"Anything in particular he was raisin' hell about?" Neely said.

"Something with one of the girls."

"Which girl?"

"I'm not sure."

"You work here and you're not sure?"

"Never saw her before. Figured she just started tonight. Lot of times the boss'll meet somebody and just put her on the floor without telling us."

"You describe her?"

The rover shrugged nice, silken white shoulders. "Dark hair. Early twenties maybe. Real good body. Nice high-riding tits."

"Plastic?"

The rover shook her head. "Didn't touch 'em but looked like the real thing to me."

Jesus, she was making my mouth water.

"You have any idea what they were arguing about?"

"Not really. But he grabbed her by the wrist and shoved her against one of the booths."

"Lot of people notice, you think?" Neely said.

"We were pretty busy in here. People packing the booths. I don't think many people saw."

"Where's your boss?"

"Right over there."

She pointed out a man dressed in a black evening-wear jumpsuit.

"The guy with one arm?" I said.

The rover nodded. "Used to be a copper just like you two. But he got in a bad accident. Hover car took him up with his arm caught in the door." She smiled and shrugged her shoulders. "I think he likes this job a lot better anyway."

His name was Phil Anders. He had nose diamonds, ear diamonds, teeth diamonds. And his perfectly shaved head gleamed even more than his diamonds.

He was leaning over the bar talking to his bartender about something secret. He knew we were waiting to talk with him, but he wasn't going to give us the courtesy of wrapping things up quickly. I watched the light bounce off the back of his smooth head as it bobbed up and down as he spoke. From where I was standing he looked like the world's biggest woodpecker.

Then, abruptly, he came over, following his big white slab of a hand. He had a grip that could crush iron. He wanted me to know who was in charge here.

"That's the kind of shit I always hated about being a copper," he said, laughing in a deep baritone. "Some asshole like myself keeps you waiting just to prove how important he is."

I said, "The dead guy outside—"

"Yeah," he frowned. "Just the kind of publicity I need, right?"

I said, "One of your people says the dead guy had an argument with one of your rovers."

"Oh yeah? Which rover?"

"She said she guessed it was a new one. Probably one you just put on the floor tonight."

"I didn't put anybody new on the floor tonight."

I described her to Anders just the way she'd been described to us.

He shook his head. "No way. I've never hired anybody for this place who looks like that."

"You sure?"

"Positive."

"That's strange, then."

"Very strange," Anders said. He looked, and probably was, very upset. "I don't want some chick preying on my customers. You fuckers better do something about it."

"We'll do everything we can, Mr. Anders," I said. I figured the "mister" might calm him down a little.

It didn't. "You mean, you'll do everything you can in between sticking up liquor stores and pawn shops and executing people and selling little boys and girls to international pedophile rings." He smiled icily all the time he spoke.

Neely smiled right back at him. "You seem to know the drill pretty well, Mr. Anders."

He laughed. "How do you think I got enough credits to buy this place? By saving my copper's salary?"

"Just one thing," I said. "We don't deal kids under any circumstances. Never have and never will."

"Yeah, and we kill anybody we *catch* dealing kids," Neeley said.

"Just so you know the facts," I said.

He could see we were pissed and we must have impressed him at least a little bit because suddenly he didn't look half as sparkly or tough or swaggering.

He said, "Well, do the best you can, okay? I'd really appreciate it."

Then he walked back over to the bar and resumed his conversation with the bartender.

Neely and I drifted back toward the front of the club. It took awhile to get there; there were people everywhere. We were ten feet from the door when we heard the scream.

This was no scream of ecstasy, either.

3

TWO COPPERS were trying to restrain her and doing a pretty bad job of it.

She was a small, fine-boned, blonde woman who was just now starting to go gray. She was all feet and elbows and fists; that's why they were having such a hard time restraining her.

What she wanted to do, apparently, was get to the man on the sidewalk. The dead man. You see that a lot, the bereaved just wanting to touch the deceased. The problem is the crime scene. You let anybody touch anything, especially the corpse, and you've violated the scene pretty seriously. Later on, a shyster could kill you with this in court, especially if you get an android judge. There's no way to get to those bastards—they don't care about chicks or dope or money. And there's no way to blackmail them, either. All the fuckers care about is justice.

I pushed through the crowd. Walked over to the woman. Took out my shooter and put it next to the temple on the right side of her head.

You could hear the people gasp all at once.

It got very quiet, very fast.

Was a copper going to blast this woman right out in public?

I turned the little indicator on the side of my shooter to T and blasted away. The public thinks that all shooters can do is kill people. They don't know that the T stands for tranquilizer. You zap someone with a little T-juice, and they calm right down.

It worked like a charm. A minute or two later, the coppers were able to let the woman go.

I walked her down the street, out of the nimbus of holo lights, away from the whispering crowd, and she sat on a bus bench and we talked.

About halfway through the interview, Neely joined us. We sat on either side of the woman.

Her name was Eileen Bridges. Her husband's name was Bob. He'd been a physician's assistant. He'd been coming to the cybersex bar for the past eight months. She hadn't liked the idea at first, she said, but she gradually got used to it. At least he wasn't going out with real women. And this way there was no threat of disease. Or falling in love.

"So you really didn't mind him coming here?" Neely said.

Eileen Bridges had apparently depleted her reserve of tears. All she had left were sharp little sniffles. "Well, I didn't, you know, *like* it."

"Did you ever argue about it?"

"Sure. Sometimes."

"Did he ever hit you?" I said.

"You mean because of the steroids and everything?" Eileen Bridges said.

"Right," I said.

"No. I mean, I know they can make people act kind of crazy but Bobby was able to handle it. He was pretty much of a doctor himself. The doc he worked for was a junkie and Bobby pretty much had to do all the work, anyway."

Neely asked her more questions. I sat back and looked at all the hover cars trying to sneak into the air space above the cyber-sex parlor. The traffic was heavy and slow-moving. The sky was crawling with coppers and the beams of the giant searchlights were criss-crossing the sky. It all reminded me of the old holos about Hollywood, the difference being that old Hollywood hadn't been divided into four sectors that were constantly at war, two of the sectors being pretty much the exclusive property of drug gangs.

Neely said, "How about enemies?"

"Everybody liked Bobby."

"Everybody?"

"Well, you know."

"Mrs. Bridges, do me a favor, all right?"

"All right."

"Knock off the bullshit."

"What're you *talking* about?"

"I'm talking about this nice little act you're putting on for Officer Mulligan and me."

"What 'nice little act'?"

Neely took a deep breath. "According to you, your husband was just a nice normal guy who went to the cybersex parlors as a kind of boyish prank. Right?"

"Right."

"And also according to you, your husband was a wonderful guy who everybody liked and respected. Right?"

"Right."

"Well, Mrs. Bridges, I hate to be the bearer of bad tidings, but I just got a feed on my communicator." Neely tapped her wrist communicator dramatically. "Your husband has a record. Two recent charges. First one is for beating up a hooker. Second one is for having sex in the middle of a supper club."

"I didn't say he was perfect."

"What I'm getting at, Mrs. Bridges, is a guy who beats up hookers is not the sort of guy everybody would like. Beating up a hooker means he had a bad temper, and having a bad temper means he had enemies. So let's just knock off the bull-shit, all right, and get down to it. Who were your husband's enemies?"

Eileen Bridges turned and looked at me with real panic in her eyes. She was a nice, gentle little woman and not used to Neely's sort of harshness.

I just shrugged, indicating that Neely was in charge here.

"Well…I guess Doctor Graves."

"Doctor Graves?"

"Bobby's boss."

"His boss was an enemy?"

"Well, it was because of the party."

"What party?"

"Oh, last year at holiday time, the medical clinic where Bobby worked put on this big party. I couldn't go. I had the flu. And Bobby…well, it didn't really mean anything. He got drunk was all. It really *didn't* mean anything."

"What didn't mean anything, Mrs. Bridges?"

"When he had sex with Doctor Graves' wife. On the desk in Doctor Graves' office, I mean."

"Did Doctor Graves find out about this?"

"Oh, yes. He walked in when it was still going on."

"And he didn't fire Bobby?"

"He said that would be too easy."

"Doctor Graves said it would be too easy?"

"Right."

"So what did Doctor Graves do?"

"He just started making Bobby's life hell for him. Kept writing up disciplinary reports and things like that all the time. You know, all that stuff gets fed into the big computers and it stays on your permanent record. What he was doing, Doctor Graves I mean, was slowly destroying Bobby's career."

"Why didn't Bobby quit?"

"Couldn't afford to."

"All right. How about any other enemies?"

"Sandy Lane."

"Sandy?"

"This nurse he worked with."

"What happened with Sandy?"

"Oh, you know, they had a little thing."

"Sex?"

"Uh-huh."

"How long did it last?"

"According to Bobby, just a few nights. According to her, it was more like four months."

"How'd you find out about it?"

"Sandy."

"Sandy told you?"

"Uh-huh. And to my face. I was at the supermarket one day, getting out of my car, and there she was. She just came right up to me and said, 'Your husband and I are in love and we plan to get married.'"

"And what did you say?"

"What *could* I say? I felt kind of embarrassed for both of us, so I just ran inside the supermarket."

"And you confronted Bobby later?"

"Oh, no."

"You didn't confront Bobby?"

"It had happened before. Women coming up to me like that. Bobby had a lot of these little affairs. They didn't mean anything." Eileen Bridges shook her head. "They really didn't. They were just sex. They weren't real love. The kind Bobby had for me, I mean."

While she was talking, I saw the teenage girl start walking toward us. She wore a tan jumpsuit that flattered her dark hair and long, lovely face. The closer she got, the more I saw the resemblance. She was Eileen Bridges' daughter. Had to be.

"Oh, honey," Eileen said when she saw her. To Neely, "It's my daughter, Melissa."

She got up off the bench and ran to her.

"How'd you find out about this, honey?" Eileen said.

"I was over at Cindy's watching the holo. It was on the news. So I took a skybus down here."

She looked stricken, she seemed so sad. Eileen took her hand and brought her over and introduced us.

Eileen Bridges wouldn't let go of her. Kept giving her motherly little hugs and combing her long, shiny hair with her fingers. And wiping the tears from Melissa's face.

Melissa raised her gaze every half-minute or so and looked at the man sprawled on the sidewalk, the sheet over him.

"I wonder if he'll get cold, lying there like that," Melissa said. She sounded dreamy. Shock victims usually do. "Maybe they should put a heavier blanket on him."

Eileen Bridges looked at Neely and said, "I'd like to take her home."

Neely nodded her assent.

We sat there on the bench and watched them walk away and disappear into the thinning crowd.

Then we went back to work.

The next hour was spent cleaning up odds and ends and checking with all the other coppers on the scene.

Afterwards, we sat in the hover car for another half-hour while Neely typed out the prelim on the car's computer. I spent the time looking up the names and addresses of the two people — boss Graves and girlfriend Sandy Lane — Mrs. Bridges had given us. I then checked them out for criminal records. None. Economic profiles indicated that Graves was well off, with no heavy debt. Sandy Lane wasn't so lucky. A working girl, she'd had to refinance her debt load twice and was on the brink of refinancing it a third time.

When Neely finished with the prelim, she punched off the computer and dusted her hands off and said, "Done and done." Neely spends a lot of her time watching old Laurel and Hardy holos.

Then we shot up into the air and headed back to the station. Time for beddy-bye.

Neely's funny after a murder. You never know which way she's going to go. Murder can make her really horned up or it can make her frigid as hell.

Tonight was the former. She slid her hand across my thigh and said, "You feel like putting into Bradhill down there?"

Bradhill is a park.

I smiled. "Only if you're willing to pay me. My services come pretty high."

"Then fuck you. Forget it."

Murder can also do *that* to Neely. Make her quick to anger.

"Hey, I was kidding. Jesus, you couldn't tell I was kidding?"

"Maybe I'm not in the mood to kid."

"You're in the mood to fool around but you're not in the mood to kid?" I said.

"I didn't know the two necessarily went together."

I sighed. "I'm sorry, all right?"

Her hands were folded over her sweet breasts and she was staring out the window with tears in her eyes. You think the Sphinx is a mystery, you should try Neely some time.

"Let's just forget it for tonight, all right?" she said, her voice soft now.

"Great," I said. Then: "Look, I could really use it tonight. And I think you could, too."

She didn't say anything.

"Neely? You hear what I said? I said I could really use it tonight. And I think you could, too."

I could barely catch her nod. It was a dinky tiny little thing but it was there and I saw it and I put the hover car down near the lake that takes up the northernmost part of the park.

After I killed the rocket, we sat there for a long while not saying anything. Just listening to the night sounds.

I took her hand and held it.

"Let's just do it, all right," she said. "And get it over with." She looked over at me. "You don't need to hold my hand or tell me I'm pretty or special or any of that stuff tonight, okay, Mulligan? You know it's bullshit and I know it's bullshit so why even bother?"

Ah, the language of love.

I suggested we get out of the car, use the blanket I keep on hand for official gonadic emergencies. But she didn't even want to do that tonight.

She slipped out of her uniform with surprising ease, given the confines of the hover car, and then told me to move over to her seat, and then she unzipped me and when I was good and hard, she slid herself down me, like she was sliding down a pole.

Neely has a juicy thirty-eight-year-old body and it's always like getting a gift from the gods. She gives herself up to sex in a way I can only envy. Even when I'm going at it hot and heavy,

I can still hear mosquitos buzzing and feel breezes on my bare bottom and I get ideas about cases I'm working on.

Not Neely. She's a pounder and a screamer and a sweater. I'm like that only at the very end.

I always think of coming as almost like dying and being reborn again because, when you think about it, those two-and-a-half seconds of orgasm are a kind of blissful death, and then you're rejuvenated, and for at least a small amount of time you feel optimistic and happy and at peace. A whole bunch of happy-face little cells bouncing around and applauding their little asses off.

I've never had a bad orgasm and tonight wasn't any exception.

After she'd pummeled me while she was coming, she slumped against me, sort of tucking her face into my shoulder, and said, "I'm depressed."

"How come?"

She gave a little shrug.

"You ever feel guilty about boppin' me all the time?" I said.

She lifted her face and looked at me. "No. My old man's a sweet guy and I love him to death but he's a dud in the sack."

The docs had had her try to make love to her husband a few times, thinking that maybe sex would jar him from his self-imposed prison. No suck luck.

She said, "Well, yeah. Maybe a little. Guilty, I mean. I wouldn't want my daughter to think I'm a slut or anything."

"I just wish you'd be happy once. You know, after we do it."

"It's your ego."

"What's my ego?" I said.

"You think that because I'm not happy, you haven't satisfied me. But you have. I always come and I always feel good."

"About coming you feel good?"

"Yeah," she said. "In fact, about coming I feel *real* good."

"But not about anything else?"

"Not about anything that concerns you."

"Oh."

"See."

"See what?"

"That's what I mean. The way you said 'Oh.'"

"The way I said 'Oh?'"

"Yeah. Like you're all hurt inside and stuff."

"Well, maybe I *am* all hurt inside."

"It's just your ego, Mulligan. Take my word for it. You want me to fall in love with you. But I'm not going for it. No offense."

"Yeah. No offense."

"See."

"See what?"

"You said 'No offense' just the way you said 'Oh.'"

"All hurt inside?"

"Right."

"Because you won't fall in love with me?"

"Right."

I was smart enough to keep my mouth shut the rest of the night.

4

IT TOOK twenty-four hours to catch up with Doctor Graves, and thirty-two to find Sandy Lane.

Doctor William Graves III, as he was referred to in the tri-D letters on his doorway, practiced medicine in an eyrie one-hundred-and-three floors above the ground. I assume he didn't have many patients who suffered from vertigo.

As we stepped off the elevator, Neely whistled. "Wow. He must do all right for himself."

And she wasn't kidding.

Graves had the entire floor and he obviously spent a lot of cash designing and decorating it. Everything was bright and relentlessly cheery. Cute little tunes with syncopated rhythms played low in the background while a very appealing scent of something fresh and outdoorsy was spritzed on the air.

The red-haired receptionist looked sexy in her white nurse's outfit. But not too sexy. Young but not too young. Intelligent but not too intelligent.

"I'm afraid you'll have to give the doctor a few minutes," she said. "He just got in."

I checked the chrono on the wall. "At eleven thirty-seven in the morning he just got in?"

"He was in San Diego last night. His rocket landed just about half-an-hour ago. He came straight here."

Well, Graves seemed to be covered with an alibi. Didn't surprise me. And I emphasize "seemed." A lot of alibis disintegrate on closer inspection.

"No problem. We'll wait," I said.

"He was a very nice guy," the receptionist said.

"Bobby?"

She nodded.

I wondered just how nice she thought he was. Ole Bobby got around a bit. I wondered if maybe he'd ever met up with the red-haired receptionist in a dark conference room.

"IT'S TERRIBLE," Doctor Graves said when we were escorted into his private office. "Just terrible."

He said this even before he offered a handshake.

"He was the best physician's assistant I ever had."

After we were seated, I spent a long moment staring out the window that covered half a wall. This high up, you felt very close to the rockets that were constantly blasting off from the port ten miles to the east. Their flames were vivid against the bright blue sky.

Neely wasn't up for any testimonial dinners that Graves was going to visit upon his old friend Bobby Bridges. She got right to it.

"I believe he had an affair with your wife, Doctor Graves. Isn't that true?"

Graves was a precise, somewhat nervous, middle-aged man in a blue medical tunic. He needed to lose twenty pounds and he needed to get a smaller pair of black horn-rimmed glasses. This pair covered his face.

"My wife and I had some troubles in our marriage," Graves said. "But they've long since been worked out."

Neely said, "But he *did* sleep with your wife?"

"He did."

"And you were angry about it?"

"Wasn't I supposed to be angry?"

"You *were* angry," Neely said. "That's what I'm trying to ascertain here."

"I was angry. Yes."

"Very angry?"

"*Very* angry, if you insist."

"You tried to destroy his career."

"Who told you that?"

I said, "You were in San Diego last night?"

"Yes. I went to see my brother."

"And you stayed at his house?" I said.

"No. He was suddenly called out of town on business. So I stayed in a hotel."

"Which hotel?" I said.

"The Ravenhurst."

"Do you have your credit receipts?"

"I gave all that to Joan when I came in."

"Joan," I said, "is the red-head?"

"Yes."

"When was the last time you saw Mr. Bridges?" Neely said.

He shrugged. "Uhh…a year or so, I suppose."

"Where was that?" she said.

"A medical conference in Boston. It dealt with subjects that concerned assistants as well as physicians."

"Did you speak to him?" Neely said.

"No."

"Did he speak to you?" I said.

"No."

"When," Neely said, "was the last time your wife saw Mr. Bridges?"

"Two years at least. More than that, most likely."

"You're sure of that?"

He looked uncomfortable. A little embarrassed. "She was the one who wanted to reconcile. Not me. I felt she'd humiliated me enough. So she volunteered to have Byreum injections every three months."

Byreum was the technical word for truth juice. Nobody lies under Byreum. And I mean nobody. But the big problem is that ninety percent of all people are allergic to the stuff. A small percentage have such a bad reaction that they find themselves growing hair on their tongue, thanks to a fungus-like growth resulting from the drug. So now they give you a test first and if you show any allergic reaction at all, the drug isn't administered. That allergic aspect makes it pretty much useless for police work. Besides, all sorts of lawsuits could result from giving it to the wrong people.

"You give her the injections?" Neely said.

"Yes."

"And so for at least two years—"

"And so for at least two years now," Doctor William Graves III said, "I can assure you that my wife has been faithful."

"How about you?" I said.

"Me?"

"Have you been faithful?"

"I don't see what my being faithful has to do with it."

"Just trying to figure out if you go to cybersex bars."

"Hardly. I mean, I don't think my patients would be very comfortable if they thought I was shooting up on steroids three or four nights a week."

"So you've never been inside a cybersex bar?"

"Once or twice," he said.

"When was this?" Neely said.

"Five or six years ago. When they first came around. It was the novelty. I wanted to see what they were like."

"Are you allergic to Byreum, Doctor Graves?"

He smiled. "Yes, I am. Were you going to give me an injection if I said I wasn't?"

"Something like that," she said.

He checked his wall chrono. "Listen, I've got a full load of patients today. I really need to get back to it."

He stood up and shook our hands again. "It was a terrible way for him to die, wasn't it? Do you...do you suppose he was still alive when they...cleaved it off?"

He was praying that Bridges *had* been alive, praying that it *had* taken him a long, painful time to die.

"I wouldn't know," I said.

He nodded his head and left us.

The receptionist gave us all the good doctor's credit receipts from last night.

We took copies of them with us, and left.

5

JUST AFTER flashing my ID and being admitted to my apartment, I heard the moans from my daughter's bedroom, and knew that she was at it again.

My first impulse was to go in there and break up some furniture. Actually, what I wanted to do was break her up like so much kindling. But what the hell. She was my daughter and she'd been forced to have me as a father.

I didn't knock. I just pushed into her room.

She was already in the process, so she wasn't even remotely aware of my presence.

She lay naked on the bed, her body covered with a myriad of tattoo symbols of the various causes she'd joined over her sixteen years. She was down to ninety pounds, which is way too thin for a girl of five-six. Her ribs looked like they belonged on an abandoned dog.

I got a blanket and covered her up as well as I could. Her skin was death cold.

The snake was at least three-fourths of the way in her mouth, so I knew better than to try to get it out. Most junkies go into shock when you try and yank the snake out.

The snakes are something we owe to those little bastards, the Alatians, who brought them along with them. You swallow the little black devils and they give you an extraordinary high, one far more powerful than any earth drug. By the time the snake has passed through your digestive tract, and come out your other end, you've absorbed all the poison in it and that's what makes you high. The snake is pretty much dead by that time, so you just pitch the twelve-inch black thing into the Destroy chute.

And then, when you wake up, you go buy yourself another snake.

Ellie had been hooked for seven months now. I'd had to stick up several liquor stores to do it, but I managed to get her into one of those trendy detox places. She ran away after three days. Lost her place on the waiting list. And they kept all the money, of course.

I watched the tail of the snake wriggle between her lips. And disappear. I watched her throat choke down the last of the alien beast.

And then Ellie was completely still except for an occasional tiny whimpering sound.

I went out into the kitchen and put my head down on the table and cried.

I do that sometimes. Just can't help it. It all gets to be so fucking much that I sometimes envy what Rossiter did. Just put his shooter in his mouth and got it over with.

Rossiter used to be my partner. Helluva good copper and a good friend. Married to a real nice lady, three kids, a house down by the river. But it wasn't enough. He was always so goddamn sad. Always talking about the past like it was where he belonged. He'd ride alongside me and blather on and on about when there were rolling meadows as far as the eye could see and real farms where farmers grew corn and wheat and vegetables. And the cities weren't like this back then, he'd say. Sure, there was violence. There had always been violence. But as recently as forty, fifty years ago, you could still walk down most city streets and not get blasted. Hell, they even used to decorate the streets for Christmas and other holidays. And then he'd pull out some old book and show me the pictures and really get himself worked up.

He used to cry in front of me. One minute he was fine, the next he was leaking all over the inside of the car. I always used to get embarrassed. I could just see Neely if I started crying in front of her.

I sat there at the kitchen table and thought of Rossiter this way and it made my heart ache and I cried so hard I thought maybe I would puke. Actually puking didn't sound all that bad an idea. Purgation. Maybe that's what I needed. Purgation.

Then I slept. Right there at the kitchen table with my head down. Just drifted off.

Dreamed of Rossiter and his pasture land. Dreamed of a trip my father took me on when I was just a boy. To the last of the remaining wilderness up in Wisconsin. Most beautiful land I'd ever seen. Went fishing there for two days. Never smelled anything as good as that fresh air in the morning. Never saw water that clear or sunlight that bright and clean. Not even sex was as good as that feeling.

Then I was with my wife again and she was alive and we were cuddling in bed and she was telling me how much she loved me and I was crying then, too, except this time I was crying because I was so happy. My wife was the most perfect human being I'd ever known. Full of laughter and easy smiles. I used to bring her gifts three, four times a week—

"Dad." Then: "Dad."

When I woke up, Ellie was standing there. She had her nose rings and tongue rings and ear rings and nipple rings all in place. She'd sprayed her hair pink. She was getting ready to go out. That was the only thing about the wriggle highs, as they were called. They only lasted about an hour.

"Dad."

I pawed sleep from my face.

"You headed back to school?" I said.

She frowned. "God, Dad, you mean you haven't figured it out yet?"

"Figured what out, honey?"

No matter how pissed off I get with her, I never forget that she's my daughter and that I love her.

"I quit school two months ago."

"Oh, Ellie."

"It's boring, Dad."

"You shoulda told me."

"You shoulda been able to figure it out. I mean, I'm around the apartment an awful lot during the day, aren't I?"

"I guess that's a good point."

"And I haven't been asking you for any school money."

"Yeah, that's another good point."

I reached over and took her hand.

"So what're you doing during the day?"

For the first time, she looked a little nervous. "Oh, this and that."

"This and that?"

"Yeah, you know, a little of one thing, a little of another."

"Aw, kiddo. Don't try to bullshit the old man. Now tell me what you're up to."

She shrugged her sweet little shoulders. "Dancing."

"Dancing?"

"In a club."

"A club?"

"You know, a gyration club."

"Aw, shit."

"Well, it's not like I'm *screwing* anybody or anything."

Vibrating clubs, in case you don't know, is kind of the cut-rate version of cybersex. Naked gals put these vibrating implements on their fingers and then they sit on your lap and squirm around until you come.

"I want you to quit," I said.

"No way."

"You know what your mother would say if she knew?"

Ellie smirked at me. "Yeah? Well maybe you don't know everything about Mom you think you do."

"Meaning what exactly?"

She shrugged again. "Never mind."

She turned and started away.

I grabbed her slender wrist. "Meaning what exactly?"

She sighed, looked uncomfortable. "Meaning that you idealize her too much."

"She was about as perfect as a person could get."

"No, she wasn't, Dad."

I saw the pity in her eyes and it scared me. She really knew something I didn't.

I repeated myself. "Meaning what exactly?"

She sighed. "You don't want to hear this, Dad."

"Yes, I do."

"Please, Dad. Please don't make me say it."

"You said she wasn't perfect — meaning what exactly?"

She sighed again. "Meaning she had boyfriends on the side."

"Oh, bullshit."

"She did, Dad. She even brought some of them up here. One day I came home from school early and I caught her in bed with one of them. Couple days later, he tried to hit on me."

But I wasn't listening anymore. I was just deaf, dumb, and blind. Nothing got through.

Boyfriends.

I thought about Neely's husband sitting in that wheelchair, totally insensate to everything that was going on around him.

And you know what? I felt a kind of envy of him.

Then my head was down on the table again and I was crying and then Ellie was rubbing my neck, and then she was crying too and saying over and over, "I'm sorry, Dad. I shouldn't have told ya. I'm so sorry…"

6

THAT AFTERNOON, the precinct was busy. There'd been a meat riot in one of the western sectors, meat riots being the name the newsies gave to large groups of people with guns raiding supermarkets. I always felt sorry for the starving people, and I took no pleasure in killing them. Some coppers loved this kind of shit — target practice, they called it — but I always tried to avoid this particular duty.

Neely poked my arm and said, "Look."

On the computer screen was a listing of all the sex crimes committed in the city over the past four years.

Under the sub-heading of "Genital Mutilation," we found the number "6" listed.

Six such cases.

Unfortunately, every last one of them involved females. Not a single male in sight.

We next ran backgrounders on all the owners of the cyber-sex parlors, see if maybe they were involved in some sort of illicit activities that Bobby Bridges might have stumbled into. But nothing. For cybersex owners, they were some clean living sons-of-bitches.

We decided to go see Sandy Lane.

"SO YOU never stalked him?"

"No."

"Or harassed him at work?"

"No."

"Or threatened to kill his wife?"

"No."

"Or threatened to kill him?"

"No."

Neely, who had been asking the questions, smiled. "Well, if you didn't do any of those things, Ms. Lane, then Bobby Bridges had quite an imagination."

"He thought I was in love with him."

"And you weren't?"

"Are you kidding? He was just some pushy little guy who thought he was a stud."

"I see."

"Do you know what Byreum is, Ms. Lane?" I said.

"Sure. That truth stuff."

"Right."

"What about it?"

"We'd like to give you an injection," I said.

"Right here?"

"Right."

"Right now?"

"Right."

DIRTY COPPERS | 221

"No."

"You're refusing?" I said.

She nodded. "I want a shyster."

"No problem. You're free to tri-phone him so we can see and hear the whole process."

We'd been at Sandy Lane's place for half-an-hour, a crumbling ancient home right on the edge of a very violent sector. The home had been divided into apartments. She lived in the back, on the second floor.

Chemicals had bleached her hair and whitened her teeth and filled out her breasts and tanned her skin and blued her eyes. She wore a fluffy red robe and matching red slippers that for some reason looked sort of sad on her big flat feet.

She rolled her eyes and said, "I guess I kinda did have the hots for him for a little while."

"I see," I said.

"But I never threatened to kill him."

"All right."

"Or her."

"Okay."

"And I didn't stalk him, either."

"Oh?"

"I'd just kinda show up in places where he was once in a while."

"Ah."

"And a coupla times I probably waited for him in parking lots. At bars, I mean."

"Umm-hmm."

"But I never *stalked him* stalked him if you know what I mean."

I decided to try an old police trick that still worked from time to time.

"We have an eyewitness who says he saw you talking to Bobby at the cybersex parlor the night he died."

"That's a lie."

I nodded to Neely. "You got that Byreum injection ready?"

She held up the hypo.

"All right, all right," Sandy Lane said. "I was there. And I *did* talk to him."

"Talk?"

"Yeah, and that's all, too. I didn't cut off his dick." She looked right at Neely. "Though, believe me, I sure wouldn't have *minded* doing it. He was a son-of-a-bitch. A real son-of-a-bitch."

Then she started crying so hard that I had to sit her down in a chair and Neely had to go get her a glass of water.

7

LATER IN the afternoon, we took Sandy Lane down to the precinct where we took full-length holo shots of her. We then brought in the eyewitness who said he'd seen somebody standing by Bobby Bridges' body the night of the murder. But he couldn't positively ID her. He said maybe, that was the best he could do for us. Maybe.

After the eyewitness left, we spent an hour more with the Lane woman. We collected all the samples we could — blood, tissue, hair, the works — hoping it would be useful later on. Then we let her go. No way we could hold her, given the little we had.

Later that night, an hour or so into our patrol, Neely said, "How about Davis?"

"The holo store guy?"

"Right. He's three months out."

"Maybe we should wait a little longer."

She shook her head. "Mulligan, I don't know about you, but *I* need the money."

"Yeah, I guess I do, too."

"He makes more than we do," she said.

"Yeah, I guess you're right."

So we put the hover car down in Sector 6 and paid a visit to Block 5, Intersection 7. This six-block area is ours for protection purposes. You know how it works. We take no responsibility for any of the robberies or killings that go on in the area. What the store owners are paying for is protection from us busing in hardcores. That's how coppers keep getting their protection money. Buncha store owners start to slide a little on the monthly payments, you just fill up a ground bus with a bunch of dregs and bring them in for a few days. The store owners are only too glad to see them go. Glad enough to pay you off.

We walked in and Neely said, "You owe us three months protection money."

Davis said, "My wife's dying of cancer."

Neely said, "According to you, she's been dying for eight years. Now where's your money, asshole?"

Neely could be a real bitch when she wanted to.

IN THE hover car, Neely said, "Something wrong?"

"I was just thinking about his wife. Her being sick and all."

"He doesn't have a wife."

"He doesn't?"

"Huh-uh. I checked. He's gay. He lives with some guy."

"Well, maybe his boyfriend's sick."

"You want your share of these credits or not?"

"Sure."

After a while she said, "What's wrong?"

"Huh?"

"I said what's wrong? You're not talking tonight. Usually I can't get you to shut up."

I looked over at her. "You know what I just found out?"

"What?"

"My wife?"

"Yeah."

"She had boyfriends."

"You just found that out?"

"You mean you knew about it?"

"Sure. A lot of coppers were punchin' her ticket, Mulligan. A lot of them."

"Jesus."

"Sorry."

"I wanna throw up."

"That's just how my husband would feel if he ever found out about you and me. Sometimes I think my daughter suspects."

"How come?" I said.

"Just little hints. She caught me putting perfume on one night before we went out on patrol. She thought that was real odd. Told me so."

"You knew and you didn't tell me, Neely?"

"I figured you knew, Mulligan. A guy should know things like that about his wife."

"There were a *lot* of them, you said?"

"Well, a 'lot' is one of those relative words. But quite a few, yeah."

"Jesus, I can't believe it."

"Well, I'm sorry, Mulligan, but it's not the worst thing that could happen to a guy."

"Oh, yeah, what could be worse than finding out that your wife's been unfaithful?"

"Well," she said, "getting your dick cut off, for one thing."

AN HOUR later, one of the robot dispatchers pressed the emergency signaler and I picked up.

"Yeah?"

"A man named Epperson wants to talk to you."

"He's probably a bill collector. Tell him to fuck off."

"He says this is about the Bridges case."

"Better take it," Neely said.

So I took it: "Yeah?"

"I want to turn somebody in."

"Yeah?"

"Son-of-a-bitch told me he was going to pay me two hundred credits then he stiffs me and pays me a hundred."

"Who're we talking about here, pal?"

"Graves. Doctor Graves."

I bent over and checked the recorder. Everything was being kept for posterity.

"He paid you to do what?"

"Dress up like him and take a rocket to San Diego."

"While he was doing what?"

"You'd have to ask him. I was just going up to his office when I saw you and your partner there. After he stiffed me, I decided to call you."

"We'll need an official statement from you," I said.

"You'll get it, the son-of-a-bitch."

GRAVES' APARTMENT was on the 118th floor, even higher up than his office. The elevator was silent and fast.

A chunky man with a day's growth of beard greeted us at the door. He wore the money-green suit of all shysters. After the Shyster Massacre, in which more than sixty thousand attorneys were killed in one day of fighting, the federal government decided to make them an endangered species. Now there were huge fines for even hassling them. The most you could do was spit at them. They wore the green suits for identification...and for protection.

"My client admits that he *considered* killing Mr. Bridges the other night," the shyster said, "but he got cold feet at the last minute."

"Where is your client now?" Neely said.

"Resting."

"From what?" I said.

"Ever since he found out that Mr. Epperson talked to you, my client has been in a deep depression. He was appalled to find out that Mr. Epperson — a life-long friend — had betrayed him in this way. My client has almost no faith in humanity left at all."

"The poor dear," Neely said.

"We want to talk to him," I said. "Now."

The shyster was about to object when my communicator started braying.

I put it on silent mode and pressed it against my ear so only I could hear.

After I was done with the message, I put my arm back at my side and said, "You just lucked out, asshole."

"I did?" the shyster said.

"Yeah. Somebody else confessed to the crime."

"They did?" Neely said.

8

THERE WERE six cars hovering around the apartment house when we got there. A small crowd of onlookers had gathered below in the alley. They were bathed in red neon from the emergency lights.

A window had been opened on the appropriate floor. We pulled right up and stepped into the building without using the elevator.

A number of coppers stood around the apartment door.

"Where's Mrs. Bridges?" I asked.

"Inside. With her daughter and the Chief."

Neely and I went in and stood in the dining room while the Chief concluded his questioning of Mrs. Bridges, who sat next to him on the couch.

"So after you killed him, you did what?"

"I, uh, ran into the alley and got rid of the murder weapon."

"What did you do with it?"

"Threw it in the river."

"How much blood did you have on you?"

"Not very much. I was very careful."

The Chief, a prim, gray-haired woman who just happens to be the mayor's aunt, looked at Neely and me and said, "Then you saw these two?"

"Yes."

"And they questioned you?"

"Yes."

The Chief stood up. "You'll sign the confession, Mrs. Bridges?"

"Yes."

The Chief didn't say anything for a moment and I sensed something was wrong.

Eileen Bridges said, "Am I going to the precinct?"

"Yes," the Chief said.

"What'll happen to my daughter?"

"She can stay with me," a pretty blonde girl said. She walked out of the shadows in the hallway.

"Thank you, Cindy," Eileen Bridges said.

Cindy…Melissa had been at her house watching the holo while her mother was downtown murdering her father.

The Chief looked at Neely and me. "You two have any questions for her?"

"Nope," I said.

Neely shook her head.

"Can I go put some things in an overnight case?" Eileen Bridges said.

She looked drawn and tired. Her loose gray dress and messy hair didn't help the impression any.

The Chief nodded.

When Eileen was gone, the Chief said, "It just doesn't feel right."

"What doesn't?" I said.

"The confession," she said.

"Why not?"

"I'm not sure."

I smiled. "I can't believe you're going to turn down a confession."

She smiled back, looking natty in her pressed gray uniform with all the medals on the chest. "I'm being crazy, aren't I? Case like this, the most important thing is to wrap it up quickly, restore public confidence."

I looked out the window. The newsies were hovering out there now, trying to get video by shooting through the windows.

The Chief went over and started closing curtains.

Melissa came over, her face puffy from crying. "Can I go in and help my mom?"

"Sure, honey," I said.

"Nice kid," Neely said, after Melissa had gone.

"Yeah," I said. "She sure is."

I went over to where her friend Cindy was sitting on the arm of a chair. I couldn't help but wish that my daughter dressed and behaved more like this girl instead of her viddy rockers.

"Here's my ID number," I said, handing her a small card. "Things get rough for you with Melissa, just let me know. We've got different ways to help."

"Thank you," Cindy said. Then: "She used to be over at my house all the time. This'll sort of be like old home week. She hasn't been there for almost a year."

"Well, you need help, you remember my card."

"Thank you, officer."

"You're welcome."

I walked back to Neely and she said, "You hitting on her?"

"Very funny."

"She's cute. I wouldn't blame you."

"Yeah, and she's probably all of fifteen."

We heard the crying then, great gasping sobs, mother and daughter in the bedroom.

A minute later, the Chief led Eileen and Melissa out of the bedroom.

"You want to take Mrs. Bridges out to the hover car?" the Chief asked one of the uniformed guys.

The uniform nodded and then took a step toward Mrs. Bridges and that was when I remembered what Cindy had just said.

"Wait a minute," I said to the Chief. "I think you're arresting the wrong person."

"What the hell are you talking about, Mulligan?" the Chief said. I had the impression she didn't exactly think I was a class act.

I looked at Cindy. "Didn't you say it'd been almost a year since Melissa had been to your house?"

Cindy glanced at Melissa. She clearly didn't want to get her friend into any trouble. But just as clearly she wasn't sure how to handle this moment. "Uh, yeah."

"And Melissa," I said, "didn't you say the other night that you'd been over at Cindy's watching holos when you saw the news about your father?"

"Don't say anything, don't say anything at all," Eileen Bridges said.

She put out her hands and said, "Take me to the police station right now. That's what you were going to do, and I demand that you do it."

But the Chief had eyes and ears only for me. "What the hell are you talking about, Mulligan?"

"Dammit!" Mrs. Bridges said. "Take me to the police station!"

"Oh, Mom, shut up!" Melissa said.

And then took her mother in her arms, and the two of them began weeping.

"THAT WAS pretty good, Mulligan."

"Thanks, Neely."

"Maybe the Chief will give you a blowjob or something."

"Uh-huh."

"Seriously, she was real impressed."

"Uh-huh. Let's see if it makes any difference in my next paycheck."

She yawned. "God, am I tired." She looked over at me. Smiled. "You want to fool around, Mulligan?"

"Not tonight, I guess."

"You should be celebrating. You're gonna be a hero. At least for a couple of days."

"You shoulda told me, you know."

"Told you what?"

"You know, about my wife running around."

"Oh, man, Mulligan give it a rest, will ya. She's dead, so what difference does it make?"

BUT IT did make a difference so after the shift was over, I took a ground bus out to the cemetery and knelt down in front of my wife's gravestone and just kinda talked to her about it.

I don't know how you coulda done it to me, babe. I never stepped out on you even once. And believe me, I had plenty of chances...well, maybe not plenty. But I had a few anyway.

I sat there for a long time and thought about breakfasts in bed and walks in the moonlight and holding hands in a darkened movie theater. I thought about bike rides in the park and shopping trips to the square and so many other things I would never experience again.

And then I started crying, right there in the broad morning daylight, and this old bastard who was also talking to some dead person looked over at me and shook his head and fixed me with a steely eye.

"It's a bitch when they're dead, ain't it?" he said. "You're never sure if they're hearing you or not."

(Written with Ed Gorman)

MISCHIEF

Jim Hall was finishing up a phone call when Warwick poked his head into the office.

"Wait till you hear what—"

Jim held up a finger, silencing Warwick, and said goodbye to the councilwoman on the other end of the line. She had a loud, grating voice and he was glad to be rid of her.

"Sorry about that. What's up, boss?"

Warwick glanced around the office and made a face. "This place is a pigsty." He was five-four, weighed a Snickers bar away from two hundred pounds, and seemed in perpetual need of a haircut and a mustache trim. His employees called him The Walrus, but never to his face. This discretion was based on kindness, not fear. Warwick was well liked by his staff.

"You say that every time you come in here."

"Because it's true." Warwick moved a stack of file folders from a chair onto the floor. He sat down and wiped his hands on the front of his pink golf shirt. "It's fucking disgusting."

Jim scribbled a follow-up question for the councilwoman on a notepad before he could forget it. *Definitely an email,* he thought. *No more phone calls.* He looked up at Warwick. "It's not disgusting, it's just…cluttered."

"Your mind is cluttered."

"Yes, it is, and you pay me to write the news, not to clean house, so what's up? You looked excited when you first graced me with your presence."

"I *am* excited."

"Tell me."

"I'm trying." He looked around the room again. "It's hard to concentrate."

Jim sighed. "Just tell me."

His boss leaned forward and smiled. That was another thing: Warwick had braces. The clear kind that were supposed to be invisible but weren't. Add them to his cherub face and big brown eyes and overall shaggy demeanor, and he looked a lot like your typical high school sophomore.

"You remember that series you wrote about the Inner Harbor murders?"

"Sure." Jim picked up a pen and started fidgeting. *Click. Click. Click.*

"Didn't make us many fans in the police department, but the readers ate it up."

Jim nodded. He remembered. *Click. Click. Click.*

"Well, someone else—someone pretty interesting—just recently got their hands on it, and I think it's safe to say you have a new number one fan."

Click. Click. Click. "Tell me." Warwick was a natural born storyteller and loved to drag things out. Jim was used to his dramatic flourishes.

"Does the name Lester Billings mean anything to you?"

Jim dropped the pen onto his desk and sat up. "The Aquarius guy?"

Warwick's smile got bigger. "One and the same."

"What about him?"

"He read your series and loved it."

"And?"

"He wants to meet you."

Jim got up from behind the desk, heart starting to pound in his chest. "When?"

"As soon as it can be arranged. His attorney is calling me back later this afternoon."

"Jesus."

Warwick rubbed his hands together. "You just won the lottery, Jim."

"All these years, he's never talked to the press."

"Nope."

Jim started pacing, his mind working. "Is he still in Pennsylvania?"

Warwick nodded. "Pittsburgh."

"He's gotta be...what, in his sixties by now?"

"Sixty-seven." Warwick stood up and offered his hand. "Congratulations, Jim. You deserve this."

Jim skipped the handshake and went in for a hug. "Thank you, boss." He slapped Warwick on the back. "Thank you."

LESTER EVERETT Billings. White male. Devoted husband. Father of two lovely daughters. College educated. Local business owner. Avid fly fisherman. Volunteer volleyball coach. By all accounts, a good family man, neighbor, co-worker, and friend.

And one of the most prolific serial killers in modern history.

A resident of Hanover, Pennsylvania, from the time he graduated with honors from college in 1972 to the day he was arrested for the murder of Susan Blake in March of 2007, Billings eventually confessed to killing nearly twenty other people between the years of 1990 and 2007.

His victims ranged from the ages of sixteen to fifty-three. Eleven females and eight males. Sixteen Caucasian. One African-American. One Asian. One American Indian. The murders occurred in his home state of Pennsylvania, as well as Maryland, Delaware, New Jersey, Virginia, and West Virginia. Fourteen had been strangled to death. Four had been bludgeoned. One had been stabbed over thirty times.

It was soon discovered that the only common trait shared by all of Lester Billings' victims was the time of year they celebrated their birthdays. All nineteen were born between January 19 and February 18, falling under the eleventh astrological sign of Aquarius.

The press immediately dubbed Lester Billings "The Aquarius Killer" and his black-and-white face—as well as the faces of his victims—dominated television news reports and the front page of dozens of periodicals for the remainder of 2007. Even after the trial in April of 2008, in which Billings was sentenced to nineteen consecutive life terms in the Pittsburgh Maximum Security Penitentiary, articles still appeared with some regularity, all rehashing the same spattering of well-worn facts and details, featuring the same somber photographs and posing the same unanswered questions.

And plenty of questions remained. Despite Lester Billings' apparent eagerness to confess to the killings—one of the detectives is on record as saying, "It seemed like a weight had been lifted off of him. You could see it in his eyes when he finally stopped talking."—Billings refused to reveal many additional details to the police. He gave them names and dates and, in some cases, where they could locate the remains of his victims, but he never once spoke to his motives or why he started killing in the first place. Even more frustrating to the investigating detectives, he never once addressed why he'd chosen victims who were born under the sign of Aquarius. They may have had the killer in custody, but the mind behind the monster remained a mystery.

Billings' wife (Clarice) and daughters (Mary and Nancy) were shocked and understandably horrified by the arrest and resulting revelations. They secluded themselves at a relative's house in northern Maryland where they refused to talk to anyone except the police. Several nights after the news broke, a *People* magazine reporter was arrested outside the relative's house after attempting to take photographs through a den window.

Without additional details to report, the press resorted to interviewing the townspeople of Hanover (although almost all of Billings' close friends and co-workers refused to comment) and, as a result, rumors ran rampant. Billings was innocent and being framed by the police. Billings was a Satanist and his victims were fireside sacrifices to the Devil. Billings was a cannibal and the police had discovered a freezer full of human remains in his garage. Billings was one half of a two-man death squad and the police were still actively hunting for his accomplice.

Clarice Billings eventually returned to Hanover but only for a brief period. She divorced her husband six months after the trial and moved to South Carolina to be closer to her younger sister. She eventually remarried and died of lung cancer in 2012. Mary and Nancy Billings moved out of state and changed their names. Their current whereabouts are unknown.

As the years passed, Lester Billings continued to refuse all press inquiries and lived a life of quiet solitude behind bars. The guards said he mostly kept to himself. Folks didn't bother him and he didn't bother them. He liked to read paperback novels and exercise out in the yard.

The last published photograph of Lester Billings—taken in 2010—showed a slight, middle-aged man with close-cropped hair and thick eyeglasses. In the photo, Billings looked tired and harmless and completely unremarkable. He could be the guy you passed on the street every day on your way to lunch, the guy trying to sell you insurance out of his downtown office—which, incidentally, is exactly who Lester Billings was until his infamous arrest in 2007.

"YOU NERVOUS?" Warwick asked.

Jim shook his head and continued paging through his notebook. "I'm good."

"Liar."

Jim laughed and flipped another page. "Okay, maybe just a little."

It was Thursday morning, exactly seventy-two hours after Lester Billings' attorney first contacted Warwick at the newspaper office. The three of them were waiting inside a drab holding room at the Pittsburgh Maximum Security Penitentiary. There were four chairs and a small wooden table in the room. The walls were painted the color of spoiled milk. Billings' attorney, a bulldog of a man named Hector Coltrane, huddled in the corner having an animated conversation with someone on his cellphone. Warwick, dressed in his best suit, paced back and forth in front of Jim, who sat at the table.

"Why does he get to keep his phone when we had to give ours up at security?"

"No idea, boss."

Warwick stopped pacing. "You sure you have all your questions ready?"

He looked up from his notebook. "No. I don't. I thought I would just wing it."

Warwick's shoulders slumped. "Okay, I'm sorry. I'm just anxious, okay."

"You're not even going to be in the room with us."

"I know, I know." He ran fingers through his tangled mass of hair. "I just wish you had more than ninety minutes."

A deep voice from behind them: "My client wishes the same…"

They turned to find Billings' attorney standing there, his cellphone pocketed.

"…but that's all the State will allow for now. I've petitioned them for additional meetings. If all goes smoothly today, we could find ourselves back here as soon as next month."

Warwick vigorously nodded his head. "I'm sure everything will go smoothly. Won't it, Jim?"

Jim closed his notebook and got to his feet. "No photographs. No touching. No passing Mr. Billings objects of any kind." He pulled a mini-recorder from the pocket of his sports coat. "I'm allowed this and this," he said, holding up his notebook with his other hand, "and I have exactly ninety minutes in the room with him. Not a minute longer."

Hector Coltrane grinned. His teeth were very straight and very white. "Sounds like you've got the ground rules down pat."

"I've done my homework, Mr. Coltrane. I'm ready to do this." Warwick beamed at him like a proud father.

"Shouldn't be much longer now," the attorney said, checking his wristwatch.

As if on cue, the door to the holding room opened and a uniformed guard stepped inside. "He's ready for you, gentlemen."

Mr. Coltrane touched Jim on the elbow and guided him toward the door. "I'll walk with you as far as the next security checkpoint, but that's as far as I go today."

"Got it."

"Once you're in the room, I'll return here to wait with Mr. Warwick. A guard will escort you back when you're finished."

"Sounds good."

Warwick stepped forward, hand extended. "Good luck, Jim."

Jim shook his hand and held it for a few extra seconds. "Thanks, boss, I can use all the luck I can get." He gave his editor a wink and let go of his hand. "I'll see you in an hour and a half."

HE COULDN'T take his eyes off of Lester Billings. He knew he was staring, knew he should look away, but couldn't help himself.

The guard had escorted Jim into the room and pointed out the trio of cameras attached to the walls. He'd explained that they would be watching and could be inside the room within five seconds if anything went wrong, and then he'd left them alone, closing the door behind him.

Jim had opened his notebook, the sound of rustling paper startlingly loud in the silence, taken a deep breath, and looked up at the killer. His first thought had been: *he looks nothing like his pictures.* Billings' head was shaved bald and his cheeks were pitted and sunken. He had a homemade tattoo—about the size of a half-dollar—of something Jim couldn't quite make out on the right side of his neck. Billings also wasn't wearing glasses and he had the greenest eyes Jim had ever seen.

It was those eyes that he couldn't stop staring at now. He'd never seen anything like them. They were mesmerizing.

"Ready when you are, Mr. Hall."

Billings' voice was soft, pleasing, and the sound of it snapped Jim out of his daze. He fumbled the mini-recorder out of his coat pocket, pressed the RECORD button, and placed it on the table in front of him. He noticed his hand was shaking.

"I…I figured we would begin with the death of Susan Blake in 2007 and your subsequent arrest, then jump back to the very beginning…when all of this started for you."

Billings slowly nodded his head. "Very well."

Jim opened his notebook, glanced at the first page, and said, "Susan Blake. Age thirty-four. Legal secretary from Gettysburg. She disappeared after work on Thursday, February 4, 2007. Her body was discovered in a shallow stream three days later on Sunday, February 7. A month later, you were arrested for her murder. Can you tell me what happened?"

Billings leaned forward and rested his elbows on the table. "I was in Gettysburg that Thursday afternoon on business, as the detectives were later able to ascertain, and purely by chance Susan and I crossed paths during her lunch break. One of my longtime employees had a birthday coming up later in the month, so I stopped at one of those Hallmark stores, the ones that sell greeting cards and all sorts of other holiday paraphernalia. While I was waiting in line, the cashier greeted another customer, Susan, by name and asked her how her birthday dinner the previous night had gone. After the cashier rung up my purchase, I stole a glance at Susan and knew she was the one."

"'The one,'" I repeated. "What do you mean by that?"

"I mean that she was perfect and I had to have her."

Jim stared at Billings' right hand as the older man rubbed at an invisible spot on the table. His fingers were long and knobby. They looked arthritic but strong. Jim knew that Susan Blake had been strangled to death by those fingers. "What happened next?"

"I waited for her in the parking lot and followed her to her office building. Then I called my wife to tell her another meeting had been added to my schedule and not to hold dinner. I sat in my truck and waited for the work day to end. When Susan came out, I took her right there in the parking lot."

"You killed her in the parking lot?"

Quick shake of the head. "No. I rendered her unconscious and took her with me. I killed her later that night parked by the woods."

"The police report indicated that Susan Blake was not sexually assaulted. She was also one of your few victims not physically tortured and mutilated. What did you do between the time you knocked her unconscious and the time you killed her?"

"We talked."

"What did you talk about?"

"Life. Death. The in-between."

"Can you elaborate?"

"In truth, I did most of the talking. She cried a lot and begged for her life." Billings sighed. "It didn't work."

Jim felt his face flush and glanced at his notebook to break eye contact. "You mentioned your wife. There was a lot of speculation initially in the media regarding whether she had any suspicions or perhaps was even aware of your...activities. Can you comment on that?"

"Clarice was a lovely woman and a wonderful wife and mother, but she was not particularly bright. She knew nothing."

"Okay, let's talk about the arrest for a moment. Did you know the police were investigating you ahead of time or was it a surprise?"

He started rubbing the imaginary spot on the table again. "It was a surprising turn of events, to say the least. I had somehow missed the security cameras. I'd always been very careful and that evening had been no different. I had checked for cameras, I remember doing so, but I'd just missed them. It was a law office, for Christsake, I should've known better."

Jim turned to the next page in his notebook and glanced at his handwritten notes. "According to off-the-record statements made by multiple detectives assigned to the case, your confessions to the other murders came as a complete shock to them. They had solely brought you in for the murder of Susan Blake. You were not under suspicion or investigation for any additional crimes at that time. What made you decide to confess to the murders of eighteen people when the police had no clue?"

"It was time."

"What does that mean?"

"It means that I was tired, Mr. Hall. It was time."

Jim nodded as if this vague response made sense. "Okay, let's go back in time. According to police records, your first victim was Allen Sheets of Burnside, Pennsylvania. You admitted to killing him in the summer of 1990, and you were forty years old at the time. Why Allen Sheets and why then?"

"My office insured Mr. Sheets' company, and I had the distinct displeasure of meeting with him on several occasions. He was a vile creature, as disingenuous as any man I'd ever done business with. I took great pleasure in killing him."

"You killed Allen Sheets because he was a bad person?"

Billings' lips twitched—*was that the hint of a smile?* "Not at all. I killed Allen Sheets because I had no other choice."

"And why did you have no other choice?"

"Keep asking me your questions from that notebook and you'll find out soon enough."

"Okay...I've done considerable research about mass killers and most begin at an early age by torturing small animals and fantasizing about killing or mutilating humans. Was this the case for you and you simply waited until later in life to explore this dark fascination? Or did something happen in 1990 that somehow gave birth to these feelings?"

"Something happened." Billings started rubbing the invisible spot, this time using the thumb on his left hand.

"What was it? What happened in your life to turn a law-abiding family man into a mass killer at the age of forty?"

He stopped rubbing the table and crossed his arms. "Did you know I was an orphan…just like you?"

Jim's mouth dropped open. "How did you—"

Billings smiled and it wasn't a pretty sight. His teeth were chipped and gray. "You're not the only one who has done their homework, Mr. Hall."

Jim started to say something but nothing came out.

"It's a familiar story, as I'm sure you can attest to yourself. I lived in seven different households by the time I turned eighteen. More often than not, these homes were lacking in basic redeeming qualities, if not outright abusive. When I became of legal age, I set off and made my own way. Earned a scholarship to college. Made good grades and got a business degree. Even managed to stay out of Vietnam when most boys my age were shipped off and killed there. It wasn't easy and it wasn't always pretty, but I got it done, and I did it all with a sense of purpose and dignity. I look back on those years now with more than a little amazement. I was a decent young man making his way in the world with literally *no one* by my side. Until I met Clarice."

"When did you first meet your wife?"

"Year after I graduated. I was working as a clerk at a bank in Philadelphia and she came in one morning to open a savings account. It was love at first sight, for the both of us."

"How long until you married?"

"We married the next year. We didn't want to wait that long, but she had promised her parents." Billings shifted in his chair. "The point I'm trying to make with all this is that I came from nothing and nowhere, with no one at my side, until I met my wife. As a boy, I drifted through life, house to house, school to school, anchorless. But I was still a decent person, Mr. Hall. Do you understand what I'm trying to say?"

Jim nodded. "So what happened in 1990?"

Billings sighed and for the first time, Jim sensed reluctance in the man. He stared down at his notebook and waited for Billings to continue. After a long moment, he did.

"I've never been much of a hunter, Mr. Hall. Despite living in southern Pennsylvania where hunting season rules most men's—and plenty of women's—spring and fall calendars. I gravitated to fishing instead. It's quiet and peaceful and is best enjoyed in solitude. Those are all good things in my mind. I was fishing the day it happened. I had hiked almost a mile into Codorus State Park. There was an isolated cove I used to fish up near the north end. Bass, crappie, perch, pickerel… you name it, and I'd caught it in that cove. It was my secret spot. My church, Clarice liked to joke. On that day, I was tired and sunburnt and decided to try a different route on the way back to my truck, hoping for a shortcut. Only it didn't turn out that way and I ended up getting lost. While I was stumbling around in the woods, I came upon a clearing and the remnants of what appeared to be a small house. Nothing structural left, just a scattering of rotten timber and rusted nails and what remained of a crumbled stone chimney. And there was an old well."

Billings uncrossed his arms and starting rubbing at the spot. Jim watched his thumb move back and forth, back and forth. He didn't think the old man was aware he was doing it.

"The witch grass was up over my knees in one part of the clearing and I almost walked right into the well before I spotted it. If I had, you and me wouldn't be having this conversation right now, and Allen Sheets and Susan Drake might still be alive. The well was old and very, very deep. I tested the ground around it with the tip of my boot, and then I got down on my hands and knees and looked into it. Black as midnight and a rotten smell, like something had taken its last breath deep in its depths, something big, a deer probably.

"Next thing I did was gather up an armful of rocks from the ruins of the house, nothing too hefty, ones about the size of my fist. I got back down on my hands and knees, crawled to the edge of the well again and dropped them in. I dropped four rocks, one after the other, waiting a little time between each, and never heard a thing. Not a splash, a thud, nothing. After the last of the rocks was gone, I got to my feet and was ready to head off when I heard the voice inside the well speak to me."

"You heard *what*?" The words were out of Jim's mouth before he could swallow them.

Billings stopped rubbing the imaginary spot and locked eyes with him. Once again, he was startled by the power of the old man's stare. "You can believe me or not. I honestly don't give a damn. But you asked me what happened and I aim to tell you."

"Please continue," he said. "I'm sorry I interrupted."

Billings eased back in his chair. "The sun was setting by then and whatever curiosity had wormed its way into my brain regarding that old well had vanished with the day's heat. I got started for the tree line, already thinking about the cold beer I was going to have when I finally got my butt home, when I heard the voice call out from behind me clear as can be: 'Come back.'

"I stopped and turned around, a shiver running its way down my spine just like a character from one of Clarice's old spooky movies. I stood there, nice and quiet, listening, scanning the clearing for a visitor. No one there. I'd just started to turn to leave when the voice came again: 'Come back.'

"This time I'd heard where the voice was coming from. I crept up close to that old well and peered down into the darkness. 'Hello,' I said, feeling more frightened than foolish. 'Someone down there?'

"'I need your help, Lester.'"

Jim leaned closer, his elbows sliding across the table, his chin resting on his crossed hands. His eyes were wide and enchanted. He looked like a young boy at his first afternoon matinee.

"When I heard my name the chill spread from my spine to the rest of my body. For a second, I saw sparks at the edge of my vision and thought I might faint, but then the feeling passed, and I mustered the courage to speak again.

"'What…what do you want?' I asked, my shaky voice betraying what little courage I had found.

"The answer came right away, louder this time: *'Mischief.'*

"I wasn't sure I'd heard correctly, but before I could say anything else, the voice came again: *'It'll be fun, Lester. Help me.'*"

"What did the voice sound like?" Jim asked.

"It was a child's voice. That's all I remember. Later, I thought about it a lot and tried to recall if it was male or female or…something else. But I couldn't. All I remember is that it was a child's voice."

"What happened next?"

"What happened next is I woke up."

"You woke up? Wait a minute, it was all a dream? None of this ever—"

Billings put his hands up. "Whoa, whoa. Slow down a minute. Every word I just told you is true and every word happened exactly the way I just told it. That's not what I mean. What I mean is that's the last thing I remember: standing there by that old well as the sun disappeared over the treetops and listening to that voice tell me it wanted to get into some mischief. Next thing I knew I was laying on the cold ground with moonlight shining down on my face and it was almost midnight."

"Jesus."

Billings shook his head. "Wasn't Jesus out in that old well, that's for certain. Anyway, I picked myself up and grabbed my fishing pole and tackle box from where I'd left them, and I got myself out of there as fast as my legs would carry me. By the time I found my truck and got home it was almost one in the morning and Clarice was sitting up in the living room with our next-door neighbor, sick with worry. She scolded me something good and told me that she'd been set on calling the police if I hadn't come home in the next fifteen minutes.

"The next morning I woke with a fever that stuck with me for every bit of two weeks. No matter what the doc fed me, it wouldn't go away. I lost ten pounds I couldn't afford to lose and suffered the worst nightmares of my life. When the fever finally broke and Clarice nursed me back to my feet, I only had one thing on my mind, Mr. Hall, and it wasn't getting back to work at the office and it wasn't getting back to work in the bedroom. It was…"

He locked on Jim with those intense green eyes: "Mischief."

Jim started to respond, when a loud voice erupted from a hidden speaker: "FIVE MINUTE WARNING, MR. HALL. YOU HAVE FIVE MINUTES REMAINING."

"What were the nightmares about?" he asked, ignoring the interruption. "Do you remember?"

Billings leaned across the table, close enough so that Jim could smell the cherry cough drop on his breath. "We only have a few minutes, so what do you say you let me do the rest of the talking?"

Jim nodded his agreement.

"Good, now listen very carefully. There's another body, Mr. Hall. Number twenty. I haven't told the police, I haven't told my attorney, I haven't told anyone…until now."

His eyes widened. "What...what do you want me to do?"

"Tell Hector to inform the police that I will only reveal the details to you. No one else. If they allow us another meeting, I'll give you a name and a location."

"I'll tell him as soon as I leave here." He closed his notebook and placed the mini-recorder on top of it, double-checking to make sure it was still recording.

Billings reached his hand across the table and Jim surprised himself by shaking it. "I'll do my best to—"

"PHYSICAL CONTACT IS STRICTLY PROHIBITED," squawked the hidden loudspeaker.

Startled, Jim tried to jerk his hand back, but Billings held tight, pulling him closer. He could hear the door being flung open behind him. Billings' fingernails dug into his palm, and for one horrific moment, he thought the old man was going to kiss him. Instead, Billings leaned even closer and whispered, "His name is Ornias."

Then Jim's hand was free and one guard was pulling him toward the door while a second guard stood in front of a smiling Lester Billings.

"Wait...what did you say?" Jim called over his shoulder.

"His name is Ornias. Time to do some more homework, Mr. Hall."

BOTH MEN said their goodbyes to Hector Coltrane in the parking lot. The attorney had listened to Jim's story about a twentieth victim and immediately called someone on his cell-phone. When he finished with the short conversation, the three men walked out of the prison together with plans to meet again the following afternoon.

Warwick climbed behind the wheel of his leased Audi. Jim got into the passenger seat. They closed their doors in perfect synchronicity and sat there in silence. Finally, Warwick looked over at Jim and said, "Jesus Christ. What just happened in there?"

Jim shook his head and let out a breath. "I...I don't even know."

"You know what this means?" When Jim failed to answer right away, Warwick went on. "You could get a book deal out of this. Hell, a film deal isn't out of the question, depending on what happens next."

"My head is still spinning."

"I bet it is." Warwick started the car and pulled up to the security gate. "You okay? You look a little...odd."

"I'm fine. Just overwhelmed."

"You want to grab some dinner, do a little pre-game strategy before we meet with Hector tomorrow?"

"Thanks, but I think I'm just gonna go home and order delivery. I need to transcribe the tape." He patted his jacket pocket to make sure the mini-recorder was safe and sound.

"Good idea. Get that shit down on paper while it's still fresh." A uniformed guard waved them through the gate. Warwick flipped a pudgy hand in his direction and steered into traffic. "Think you can have something ready for Sunday's edition?"

"Of course I can. But let's wait and see what Hector has to say tomorrow."

"Another good idea." Warwick snapped his fingers. "Hey, you know who would love this story? Remember Carlos Vargas, the young guy we ran that article about last month? Turned a couple of food trucks into a successful chain of restaurants and then went to Hollywood and became a big-time producer? I bet he would…"

Jim stared out the passenger window at the blur of fast food joints and strip malls and tuned out the sound of Warwick's voice. His boss was excited, and when he got excited he didn't shut up. Not that Jim blamed the guy. He was pretty damn excited himself. But he was also a bit uneasy about the whole thing. It felt wrong somehow to benefit from a situation such as this. It felt *ghoulish*.

Jim glanced down at his right hand, rubbed a finger against the small abrasion on his palm where Billings had pressed his fingernail into him. There was a tiny streak of faded blood there. He wiped his hand on his pant leg with a shudder of disgust and looked out the window again.

JIM TOSSED the pizza crust back into the grease-stained box and returned his attention to his laptop screen. He'd transcribed the tape as soon as he'd walked through the door, even before he'd ordered a large pepperoni and a side salad from the Italian restaurant down the street. He knew there was software that would handle transcription, but he didn't trust it.

While he ate, he'd researched the mysterious name that Lester Billings had revealed at the end of their interview: *Ornias*.

Now, he read over the notes that he'd summarized into a separate document:

According to The Encyclopedia of Angels *by Rosemary Guiley, Ornias was a fallen angel, who along with many other demons, had been bound by King Solomon to build his temple. He was described as a very troublesome demon who inhabited the constellation Aquarius and enjoyed strangling people born under the sign of Aquarius. Ornias had various abilities attributed to him, including the gift of prophecy, body transference, shape-shifting, and causing physical pain with a mere touch. He was considered mischievous, almost impish (were it not for the hideous acts attributed to him), and he was also well known for playing games with his victims.*

Jim stared at the screen. An icicle of unease tickled the back of his neck as the words echoed inside his head:

Fourteen of Lester Billings' victims had been strangled to death.

It was soon discovered that the only common trait shared by all of Lester Billings' victims was the time of year they celebrated their birthdays. All nineteen were born between January 19 and February 18, falling under the eleventh astrological sign of Aquarius.

"When the fever finally broke and Clarice nursed me back to my feet, I only had one thing on my mind, Mr. Hall, and it wasn't getting back to work at the office and it wasn't getting back to work in the bedroom. It was…

"Mischief."

He picked up a pen from the coffee table in front of him and wrote down eight words on a blank sheet of paper in his notebook: LESTER BILLINGS. THE OLD WELL. DEMON. POSSESSION. ORNIAS.

He started to close the notebook, then hesitated and scribbled a ninth word and underlined it: MISCHIEF.

Jim stared at the word for a moment, then left the notebook open on the coffee table and went upstairs to take a shower.

THAT NIGHT, he dreamed he was lost in the woods.

Bathed in moonlight from a cloudless night sky and staggering through a thicket of decaying trees, the bare branches clawing at his face, scratching his arms and hands. A thin branch reached out and slapped at his cheek, drawing blood. He could taste the warmth of it on his lips. He staggered out of the thicket into a small clearing and dropped to his knees, sobbing, chest heaving. A small cabin stood in the distance, the front windows flickering with the dim glow of a burning fire. A finger of gray smoke curled from the stone chimney.

Something in the basement of his brain warned him to stay away, to turn around and flee in the direction he had come from. But he was exhausted and ignored it.

He scrambled to his feet and set off toward the cabin. An owl hooted somewhere in the treetops and lit off, the sound of its flapping wings very loud in the shadowy silence. Startled, Jim slowed his pace and glanced around the clearing. The night was windless. Nothing else was moving. He started to turn around to resume his way to the cabin, when he saw it. Tucked away in the far corner of the clearing: a stone well.

Without thinking, Jim changed direction and headed for the well. He broke into a fast jog. His heart was hammering. Something was drawing him there. In that moment, he realized what had been bothering him. He could've sworn he'd been here before. That he'd spent time here within this clearing and seen this cabin—and most definitely, this stone well—many times before. He just couldn't remember when.

He reached the well and rested both his hands on the rough stone, catching his breath. The opening yawned at him like a hungry, dark mouth. He leaned closer to peer deeper into the darkness—as a skeletal corpse hand reached up over the edge and latched onto his right hand.

He gasped in terror and tried to jerk it back, but the thing in the well wouldn't let go.

A nightmare face emerged. Black holes for eyes. Decaying flesh hanging on pale exposed skull. Maggots squirming from the dark, wet socket of a toothless mouth.

Jim screamed, but gagging quickly drowned out the scream, as the creature's foul stench flooded his nostrils. He tried again to yank his hand back, and this time, it worked. He broke the corpse's grip and went sprawling onto his back in the clearing—

He woke in his darkened bedroom, gasping for breath. He flung the sweat-soaked sheet off him and sat up in bed. Once his eyes adjusted, he glanced down at his right hand. The Band-Aid he'd put on earlier was missing. A trickle of fresh blood marked his palm.

JIM HELD the door open for an elderly couple and hurried inside the crowded Starbucks. The weather report had called for sunny skies and moderate temperatures, so of course it had started raining just before dawn. Distracted and still shaken from his nightmare, he had rushed out of his condo this morning without an umbrella. Now, a widening puddle spread on the floor at his feet while he waited in line for his daily cappuccino.

He paid the cashier, ignoring her dirty look (she must be in charge of cleaning the floor, he thought), and someone tapped him on the shoulder. He turned to find a beautiful blonde woman he'd never seen before. Dressed in a stylish business suit and heels, she was carrying a folded-up umbrella.

"Here," she said, holding out a stack of napkins. "I think you need these more than I do." She smiled and Jim stood there and couldn't think of a single clever thing to say.

"Thanks," he finally mumbled, taking the napkins. She smelled so good, it made his head spin. He wanted to ask her what perfume she was wearing; he wanted to ask her right then and there for her phone number. Instead, he mopped at his dripping face and neck with the napkins and tossed them into a nearby trashcan.

"I've seen you here before," she said. "You're a writer of some kind, right?"

Jim nodded, still in disbelief that she was talking to him. "I write news and features for the *Sun* paper."

Her eyebrows went up. "Impressive."

"You might not think that if you saw my paycheck." *Jesus,* he thought. *What a stupid thing to say.*

She laughed. "Wow, honest *and* humble. A rare combination these days."

"Must be because I'm a Sagittarius." *A Sagittarius? Where the hell did* that *come from?*

The blonde stuck out her hand. "I'm Terry, by the way. And I'm a Taurus. You know what they say about Tauruses."

Jim didn't have a clue what they said about Tauruses and didn't care. He shook her hand, feeling the warmth of her skin against the cut on his palm. "I'm…Jim. Nice to meet you."

AS JIM Hall walked into the conference room at half past one, Warwick and Hector Coltrane were already seated and waiting for him.

"Sorry, I'm late," he said, taking a seat and placing his notebook and a manila file folder on the table in front of him. "Phone call went long."

Hector waved away the apology. Warwick took a sip from his coffee mug. "No worries," he said, "the two of us had a lot to talk about."

"Have you heard from Rick yet?" Rick was the head of legal affairs for the *Baltimore Sun.* If he didn't sign off on a second meeting, there would be no article for this Sunday's newspaper.

"Spoke with him twice in the past hour," Warwick said, grinning like a schoolboy. "We're good to go."

"Excellent."

"I reviewed the notes you sent over," Hector said. "I'm impressed."

Jim shrugged. "I just asked the questions. Your client did all of the talking."

"Perhaps," Hector said, "but there was a reason Mr. Billings chose you. I didn't quite understand his decision initially. Now, I believe I do."

"Well, thank you," Jim said, and started rubbing at something on the table with his thumb.

"I'm waiting for a return call from a Detective Cavanaugh," Hector continued. "Evidently, he's the only detective still active that worked on the initial investigation."

"He's the one I'll be talking to?" Jim asked, and returned his attention to whatever he was trying to scrub off the table.

"I'm sure there will be plenty of others, but I figured he was a good place to start."

Warwick put down his notes and craned his neck to see what Jim was doing. *Had he spilled something on the table?*

He noticed Jim was wearing a Band-Aid on his hand. *Was he bleeding?*

As if he could read his mind, Jim looked up at Warwick and smiled. He stopped rubbing his finger against the table. "Does it bother you that you were born under the sign of Aquarius, boss? With everything that's going on?"

Warwick started to respond, but hesitated. *What an odd question to ask.* Warwick glanced at Hector and he could tell by the surprised look on the older man's face that he was thinking the same thing.

"Not really," Warwick finally answered, wondering why he'd never noticed before how green Jim's eyes were. The way the writer was staring at him, grinning, made Warwick very uncomfortable. He tried to cover it with a fake smile. "I stopped being afraid of the boogeyman a long time ago."

Hector laughed and opened his leather portfolio, ready to get down to business.

The odd grin slowly faded from Jim's face, but he continued to stare at his boss. Warwick looked away first and gazed down at his notes. Hector asked him a question about the Sunday edition deadline and he answered, then quickly looked back at his notes again.

It didn't matter. He could still feel Jim Hall's green eyes on him.

THE MAN IN THE BLACK SWEATER

The beer was gone. The fire was dying. A chill had crept into the autumn night air.

"What's the worst thing you've ever done?"

The boy in the red hat spoke up first. He was drunk.

"I killed someone once. A hit and run. I was speeding and it was an accident, but I could have maybe saved the girl's life if I had called for help. Instead I got back into my car and left her there."

The man in the black sweater slid the knife out of his pants pocket. After three long years, he had found him.

ODD NUMBERS

Six ninety-three...six ninety-four...six ninety-five.

I stop in front of the Redbox machine and tap the toe of my right shoe against the bottom of the unit. Three times. Not two times and not four times. Always three.

I live three blocks from the corner of Hanson and Cherry Streets, which is where the local Rite Aid is located. The Redbox machine is tucked against the front left wall of the squat, brick building. Exactly six-hundred-and-ninety-five steps from the front door of my house. It's another nineteen steps to reach the automatic doors leading inside the Rite Aid, but I'm not venturing inside today. I'm just here for a movie.

I scan the selection of new titles and settle on an action-thriller. Friends find it strange that I like these kinds of movies, but I do. Handguns and head-butts and things that go boom; escapism at its very best. I find I can shut off my mind for a couple hours and just let myself be entertained.

I slide my credit card back into my wallet, my wallet back into my pants pocket. I wait for the machine to spit out my movie and when it does, I grab it and turn to head for home—

One...

—and almost knock Old Lady Reeves right off her feet.

"I'm so sorry," I sputter, steadying her by one frail shoulder. I notice the dark brown wig she's wearing has been nudged slightly off-center, but I don't mention it.

My eighty-three-year-old next-door neighbor readjusts the purse on her arm and smiles up at me. "It's okay, honey. I shouldn't have snuck up on you like that." She glances at the movie in my hand. "Anything good?"

I show her the title and she wrinkles her nose. "Not much of a story, but lots of gunfights and boobs. You'll love it."

I crack up laughing, and she does the same—and the sound of our laughter in the cool autumn air does my heart good. I know I need to laugh more often.

"You want a ride home?" she asks. "I'll only be a few minutes inside."

"Thanks, but I'm enjoying the fresh air."

She straightens her purse again and starts shuffling toward the entrance. "Stop by tonight around dinnertime if you're hungry. Making beef stroganoff."

My eyes widen. "That's not fair! You know I'm on a diet!"

Her voice takes on a teasing tone, and I want to chase her down and hug her. "I know no such thing, Mr. Bryant. I only know that I'll be setting the table at six sharp. One plate or two, it's all the same to me."

I groan. "I'll be there."

"Very well. Dinner for two then," she says over her shoulder, and I watch the electric doors swallow her away.

"Dinner for two," I mutter to myself, smile fading, thinking: *Even number. Bad luck.*

I head for home, counting inside my head as I go.

One...two...three...four...

I'VE ALWAYS liked numbers—and counting things.

It started many years ago when I was a child. I can remember spending hours alone in my bedroom with my baseball card collection. Counting. Organizing. Memorizing batting averages and fielding percentages and earned run averages. And my coin collection; mostly just wheatie-pennies and buffalo head nickels, but I was obsessed with it for a number of years. My father always used to tell me: *only a coin's physical condition is more important than the number printed on it.* Even then, I liked the simplicity of that statement.

My natural love of numbers made school easy for me. I was always good at math. Formulas just made a weird sort of sense. The numbers were almost like letters, the complex equations like words that linked to form sentences. Doing math was kind of like reading for me. I remember telling the middle school counselor that one day and she just looked at me like I was talking gibberish. I never went back and talked to her again after that.

But it wasn't just math that it helped me with. When you get down to it, history is really just remembering stories and dates and all sorts of other kinds of numbers—the sizes of armies and navies, the dates of invasions and the anniversaries of events ranging from independence to assassination. English is merely more of the same, and poetry is nothing but numbers if you look at it in a certain light. Poetic formulas and patterns and iambic pentameters and weak syllables and so on. Even Einstein is known to have said, "Pure mathematics is, in its way, the poetry of logical ideas."

Being good at numbers helped me get good grades, but it did so much more than that. It made other students acknowledge my existence and it made my teachers proud of me. It also made my mother smile that beautiful smile of hers and made her love me more.

That's how it started.

Two twenty-three…two twenty-four…two twenty-five…

THE THING with odd numbers didn't start until later when I got into high school. I don't why it sprung to life when it did—there was no single catalyst, no one moment in time that I can remember—and I don't know why it has become such an important part of my life. But it has.

For the past thirty years, when I lock my door at night or when I leave the house, I always check the doorknob three times to make sure it's locked. Always three—never two and never four. When I brush my teeth in the morning and at night, I always brush fifty-five strokes. Never less, never more. When I set my alarm clock, I never set it for a flat time such as 6am I always set it for 6:03am or 6:33am. When I fill up my gas tank, I always stop at an odd number. If my tank is full and the meter reads $58.46, I sneakily squirt fifty-four cents of gas into a nearby drain or right onto the pavement.

Yes, I know there is medicine for this type of thing. I tried many different kinds for many different years, and none of them made the numbers inside my head disappear. So I've learned to live with them. In fact, I've learned to cherish them. They may extend the amount of time it takes me to travel from Point A to Point B, and they may clog my head at times with a spider-web of criss-crossing and hop-scotching patterns and formulas (a lot like math or poetry in that regard), but they also make my life more interesting and remind me of a time when life was happier and simpler and a whole lot safer.

Five fifty-five…five fifty-six…five fifty-seven…

WHEN I was a junior in high school, I volunteered to keep game stats for the basketball and baseball teams. I enjoyed watching the games from the bench and was a natural at keeping records.

The coaches couldn't lavish enough praise on my detailed game reports and over time even the players learned to tolerate my presence. By the time I was a senior, one or two of them even grew to like me.

At the Varsity Basketball banquet, team captains Frankie Johnstone and Dennis Smith—who would both be killed later that year in a head-on collision with a snowplow—called me up to the podium and presented me with an honorary Edgewood Rams jersey. My last name was stitched along the top of the back of the jersey, just like the real players, and centered underneath was the number 33.

I had never told anyone—not even my mother—that my favorite number was 33, but they had somehow known. I remember staring at myself wearing that jersey in my bedroom mirror night after night once my parents had gone to sleep. I still have it. It's hanging upstairs in my bedroom closet right now.

If 33 is my all-time favorite number, then 24 is my all-time least favorite. The biggest bully on both the basketball and baseball teams wore number 24. Riley Evander. As dumb as he was mean, and he was plenty mean.

And then there's this: my mother died on February 24. A heart attack while carrying in bags of groceries from the car. February, the second month of the year, the only month with twenty-eight days (two more even numbers for you) is an awful month. Nothing but filthy gray skies and ice-slicked highways and a hollow, aching loneliness. The number 24 is a bad number. It's evil, like bananas and mushrooms.

Six seventy-five…six seventy-six…six seventy-seven…

"*SIX NINETY-THREE…six ninety-four…six ninety-five.*"

No one can hear me, so I speak the final three numbers aloud as I mount the front porch of my house and reach for the doorknob.

Before I can check the door, a car horn blares behind me on the street. I look and return a wave to my occasional poker buddy, Tim King, who lives on the next block. He toots a good-bye—three short bleats, thank you very much—and disappears down the street.

My mind immediately catalogues and calculates the incident without prompting or warning. Old Lady Reeves. John Wagner. Tim King. That's three "hellos" on the way home. At six hundred and ninety-five steps, that's an average of one hello per every two hundred and thirty-one steps. And a little change left over. Odd numbers all. Good.

I turn back to the house and tap my right shoe against the base of the door three times, while at the same time trying the doorknob three times before sliding my key into the lock.

All is well, so I step into the foyer and close the door behind me, once again checking it three times to make sure it's locked. Then, I go into the kitchen and grab a bottle of water from the fridge and stand in front of the big bay window, drinking my water and staring outside at the back yard. There's a scattering of fallen twigs that need picking up and leaves that need to be raked, but I decide to watch my movie before it's time to head next door for dinner. It's Sunday, after all.

I start for the family room.

One…two…three…

MY ALARM goes off at 6:33am Monday morning. It takes me just over a half-hour to shower (eleven steps from bedside to bathroom) and dress and fix myself a cup of coffee and a breakfast sandwich. I lock the front door at 7:05am and check it three times. Seventeen steps from the front porch to my car parked in the driveway. All is well.

The drive to work usually takes anywhere from twenty-five to forty-five minutes, depending on traffic. It takes exactly twenty-nine minutes today. During the first twenty-seven of those twenty-nine minutes, I listen to seven songs from the Elton John Greatest Hits CD in my car. The last two minutes I drive in silence. I never like to reach my destination in the middle of a song. It's bad luck.

When I pull into the Bender & Price Electronics employee parking lot at 7:37am, the lot is still mostly empty. I flip a wave to Henry at the front gate, steer around a gaping pothole marked by a pair of orange traffic cones, then turn left into the second aisle. I swing my car into parking spot number 33. I turn off the engine and allow myself a smile. It's going to be a good day.

I WASH the dinner dishes by hand and leave them on the counter to dry. Then I wipe my hands with the towel hanging under the sink, triple-check the oven is turned off, and walk over to the bay window. Nine steps.

Today hadn't turned out to be a good day, after all. Still no word on the possible promotion. Still not a hint of recognition from the pretty new redhead in Accounting. And a flat tire on the way home.

I notice a pair of cardinals fluttering in and out of the bird-feeder out back and decide it's time for a refill. That usually cheers me up. My mother loved bird-watching when I was a boy, and she taught me volumes about the various species and their habits.

I open an overhead cabinet, take out a brand new bag of bird-seed, and head downstairs to the back door. Twenty-seven steps.

Once outside, I zip up my jacket against the evening chill and count my steps as I make my way to the weeping willow tree that umbrellas the back portion of my yard.

Eleven…twelve…thirteen…

Somewhere in the neighborhood a car backfires and I can hear the hollow thumps of a basketball bouncing on a nearby driveway.

Nineteen…twenty…twenty-one…

The cardinals sense my approach and take off with a silent flap of scarlet wings.

Twenty-five…twenty-six…twenty-seven…

Two houses down and across the street, I hear Mrs. Cavanaugh calling in her boys for dinner. It's a lonely, somber sound.

Thirty-three…thirty-four…thirty-five…thirty-six.

I stop abruptly at the base of the tree. Frowning, I quickly look back over my shoulder at the house. The kitchen light is on; otherwise the house is cloaked in darkness.

Thirty-six steps.

Instead of the usual thirty-seven.

Something is wrong.

WORK THE next day passes in a fast-forward blur of spread- and balance-sheets. Still no news about my promotion and still not even a sideways glance from the pretty redhead.

Earlier in the morning, when I pull into the employee lot fifteen minutes early, I find a red pick-up truck parked in my spot and have to settle for number thirty-five. I don't know it then, but it's a sign of things to come.

Now, after a thankfully uneventful drive home and a half-hearted attempt at dinner, I find myself standing just outside the back door to my house, staring at the towering weeping willow tree. I can stall no longer. I start walking.

One…two…three…

Deep breath. I'm sure it's nothing. Just think of something happy.

Seventeen…eighteen…nineteen…

Probably just took bigger steps yesterday. It's happened before, hasn't it?

Twenty-five…twenty-six…twenty-seven…

I never take bigger steps, and I know it.

Thirty-one…thirty-two…thirty-three…thirty-four.

My heart feels like it's going to burst out of my chest.

Thirty-four steps.

Two fewer than yesterday.

Three fewer than *all* the days before.

Shuddering, I look back over my shoulder—and I *know*.

The tree is getting closer to the house.

THE ALARM clock goes off at 6:33am—but I'm already awake. I have been for hours. I reach over and turn it off and swivel my feet off the bed onto the cold floor.

I sit there for a long moment, massaging my temple, trying to think away the dream.

I usually dream in formulas or equations. Floating numbers, like dust motes in a sun-splashed July bedroom, that somehow weave and vortex in and out of focus to eventually link and form a perfectly perfect pattern.

But this dream is different…

The tree is closer. Almost halfway across the yard now. Close enough to bend over with a creak of ancient wood and reach out with one long gnarled and twisted arm, its dry bark scraping against my bedroom window like skeletal fingers clawing to get in…

HUMP DAY at the office, and nothing is going right.

Not only have I not heard another word about my phantom promotion, I think the vice-president avoided me this morning. In fact, I'm sure of it. I spotted him earlier in the break-room (thirty-one steps from my corner office to the break-room), but when I started to walk over to make small-talk about the upcoming Seahawks game, he ditched me and ducked out the back door.

And then there's Cynthia, the redhead from Accounting. She finally noticed me this morning—oh, she noticed me all right—but only because I tripped in my hurry to chase down the VP and sloshed my glass of orange juice all over the front of her expensive sweater. I apologized several times, but I could tell she stopped hearing me after the first time. I could also tell by the disgusted look on her face that there would no second chance to make a decent impression.

I have a bad feeling, and my bad feelings are usually right.

I had one the night Frankie and Dennis got flattened by the snow-plow during my senior year in high school.

I had one the day the Edgewood Senior Citizens' Hall burned down and seven people died.

I had one the night I lost my father.

And I had a very bad feeling the day my mother passed away. It's the numbers.

I mentioned before that numbers are like letters to me; complex equations and formulas are like simple words and sentences.

And they are everywhere.

The world is filled with numbers. You see them everywhere you turn. License plates and billboards. Newspapers and magazines. Televisions and cellphones and computers and books.

To most people numbers are just so much more eye-candy or mind-clutter. But, to me, they form patterns and pictures inside my mind. To me, they make perfect sense, and I often find it difficult to understand how others fail to detect and decipher them with the same ease and simplicity.

I might see a total of seventy-seven numbers on license plates on my way to the grocery store one afternoon. Another two hundred and fifty-three numbers on various cans and cartons and other packaging while at the store. I may check out at register three and pay a total of $147.47 for my purchases. On the way home, I may stop at a total of five traffic lights and three stop signs.

These numbers mean nothing to the average person. Random and overwhelming and meaningless. But, to me, they tell a story. Sometimes a good story; often times not so good. Sometimes they act as a warning.

I wish I could leave work early today, but I know I can't do that. Not with the promotion on the table and the stack of work on my desk.

Instead, I stare straight ahead and try to focus on the numbers on my computer screen.

But only the odd numbers.

...*NINE*...*TEN*...*eleven.*

I let go of the breath I'm holding in.

Eleven steps from bedside to bathroom.

At least *something* has remained the same.

Yesterday, I reached my car in the driveway in sixteen-and-a-half steps—instead of seventeen.

The day before, I strolled from my office to the break-room for a refill on my coffee, and it took thirty-two steps—instead of thirty-one.

On the way back to my office, I took thirty-two-and-a-half steps. I locked my office door and wept at my desk while my coffee went cold.

It's been a week since the VP ditched me and I spilled orange juice on the redhead's sweater. I look at my reflection in the mirror and can see the toll that stress and lack of sleep have taken. My face is gaunt and pale, my eyes sunken and red.

My world has gone mad, and I can't begin to determine why. *Have I done something different after all these years? Have I done something wrong?*

I slip off my pajamas and step into the shower.

Once again, I search my mind and try to retrace my actions in pursuit of an answer—but there is nothing to find other than the obvious. It all started with the tree. That damn tree.

I'm not a foolish man. I know what the psychiatrists would say. I've heard it all before.

Two simple words: Childhood Trauma.

I was nine the night I was attacked by the tree.

I don't remember why the tree always bothered me so much. There was nothing particularly menacing or frightening about it. It was an old oak. The tallest tree in the yard of my youth. Sure, it leaned a little toward the house I grew up in, and its branches obscured most of the view from my second-floor bedroom. But it was just an ugly old tree. I remember my mother sending me outside to read Encyclopedia Brown and Hardy Boys books under its cooling shade and to play marbles in the grass amongst its ancient roots.

And I remember having nightmares about it. Unsettling dreams that were eerily similar to the dreams I was experiencing now.

My mother blamed the comic books I read and the Creature Double Features I loved to watch on television on Saturday afternoons and my overactive imagination for the dreams. My father just told me to stop being such a big baby and a sissy. After the third or fourth time I had the nightmare, he angrily forbade me from watching any more scary movies. But he worked at the plant most Saturdays, so my mother let me watch them any way. In fact, she usually joined me. The two of us cuddled beneath a blanket on the sofa, lights dim, bowl of buttered popcorn on our laps.

Mom was wonderful like that. She would always surprise me with fun adventures—like night fishing at the quarry or the time she pretended the electricity was out all weekend and we lived by candlelight until it was Monday and time for school again—and she always made me feel "special" instead of "different." That was her favorite word for me—*special.*

My father, on the other hand, told me directly to my face that something was wrong with me. That I wasn't special, that I wasn't even *normal* like all the other neighborhood kids. I guess that's why he left us the summer I turned sixteen. He got in his truck one Thursday evening and drove away for a night shift at the plant and never came home again.

My mother spent a lot of time trying to convince me that it wasn't my fault—that they'd had a lot of "grown-up issues" and we were better off for his departure—but your father up and leaving is a hard thing to make peace with. At any age.

I turn off the shower and stand there naked and shivering, silently counting to thirty-three, back in the present now, and afraid of where the day will take me.

As I carefully step out of the shower and reach for a towel, my mind betrays me—and I am nine years old again. Lying in the dark in my childhood bedroom. Surrounded by my books and model airplanes and superhero posters.

I have just awakened from another nightmare and am counting the plastic models hanging from kite-string from the ceiling in an effort to calm my thumping heart. I have just reached the number eight (a British Spitfire dive-bombing my bookshelf) when I hear a stealthy scratching noise at the window.

I have just enough time to glance at the window and make out one spidery, claw-like tree branch gently caressing the glass before the window explodes inward in a shower of broken shards. The claw-branch lunges into the room, grasping for me...

I scream and my parents come running.

My mother rushes to my bedside, face stricken, taking me in her arms, asking, "Are you okay, honey? Are you hurt?"

My father just stands there in the middle of my bedroom, staring at the shattered window, mouth hanging open. Finally, he turns to me with a cold expression. "What the hell did you do, boy?"

MONTHS LATER, fed up with my continuing night terrors, my father would try to blame the movie *Poltergeist* for my bad dreams and a summer thunderstorm for the broken window.

But I knew better. I had never seen that movie—still haven't for what should be obvious reasons—and, in case my memory had somehow failed me, I checked the weather charts: there was no storm that night. The night skies were clear, the temperature mild, and the wind light and from the northwest.

There was no storm.

THE WALK from my front porch to my car in the driveway takes sixteen steps—another half-step fewer than yesterday. My drive to work takes twenty-four minutes and four seconds. It's never taken fewer than twenty-five minutes before.

None of this surprises me anymore.

Tonight is the real test.

...TWENTY-ONE...twenty-two...twenty-three...

I find myself consciously trying to take smaller steps across the grassy back yard, but my body doesn't allow it.

...twenty-seven...twenty-eight...twenty-nine.

Jesus, it feels like I just started walking.

Twenty-nine steps from back door to weeping willow—this feels like a waking nightmare.

I immediately start back for the house, but instead of counting, I unclip the cellphone from my belt and, with trembling hands, call the number I programmed into my phone earlier today.

Two rings (pick up, dammit!) and a man's voice answers: "Freeman Tree Service, how can we help you?"

"I have an emergency. I need a tree cut down. Right away."

"Okay, sir. Is the tree presenting a danger to your home or place of business?"

"No. I mean yes. It is."

"Okay, I'm gonna need to get some info from you to start. Address, telephone number, some details about the tree's location."

"Anything you need. I just need it down by tomorrow at the latest."

I hear a shuffling of papers at the other end of the phone. "Sir, our schedule is currently running at least two days out, so Friday afternoon is gonna be the earliest we can get a crew out to you…"

FRIDAY AFTERNOON is too far away. I know that, but there's nothing I can do.

I glance at the red glowing numbers on my bedside alarm clock. 3:47am. I'm exhausted, but sleep doesn't come easy these days. At the most, I'm getting three, maybe three-and-a-half hours a night.

4:03am. Maybe I should try another sleeping pill.

4:24am. God, I hate that number.

I toss and turn in bed, trying to think happy thoughts: my mother laughing while she shows me how to knot a necktie in the hallway mirror; the two of us sitting in the bleachers at Camden Yards, drinking lemonade and counting the advertising banners that decorate the upper deck; my bright red Edgewood Rams jersey hanging in the closet.

The pleasant memories work their magic, and I'm just about to doze off when I hear a scratching noise coming from the bedroom window. Too scared to open my eyes and look, I hold my breath and listen...and it comes again. Louder this time.

I pinch my leg to make sure I'm not asleep.

I'm not—and sleep doesn't come at all tonight.

FOR THE first time in nearly two decades of employment at Bender and Price Electronics, I leave work early.

By two in the afternoon, I can take it no longer, so I call Personnel and tell them I feel feverish and nauseous and I need to go home. The nice lady on the phone tells me something must be going around the office and she hopes I feel better.

I'm afraid to count the steps from my office to the parking lot, so I don't. Nor do I time my drive home.

It's just past three in the afternoon, and once again I'm standing in front of the bay window in my kitchen, staring out at the weeping willow tree.

There's no reason to walk outside and count my steps. Not anymore. The tree has moved past the shed on the left side of the yard and the birdbath that stands just a dozen or so yards from the back door. It's a wonder its branches aren't pressing against the back of the house, trying to smother it.

I turn my back to the window and close my eyes in thought. After a moment, I open them and retreat to the family room for a drink.

AN HOUR and three drinks later, I stumble upstairs to the bedroom bathroom. I don't look out any windows along the way and I don't count my steps.

The house phone rings—and I almost spill my drink when I try to balance it on the edge of the sink.

The house phone rings again. I ignore it.

I open the medicine cabinet.

The phone rings a third time and the answering machine picks up. After a silent beat, I can hear a man's voice coming from downstairs in the kitchen:

"Mason, it's Charlie Griffin. Sorry to hear you're out sick. I have some good news that should make you feel better, though. You got the promotion. You're our new Director of Sales. I apologize for it taking so long, but we needed to hear back from corporate and you know how that goes. Anyway, feel better, buddy. We'll celebrate next week with lunch."

BUT I don't hear any of this—just a muffled mish-mash of indecipherable words from downstairs—because the bathroom door is closed and I'm too busy counting pills as they spill from the tilted bottle into my sweaty palm.

...thirty...thirty-one...thirty-two...thirty-three.

Thirty-three. My lucky number.

I flick the first three pills into my mouth like breath mints—and swallow them with a gulp of bourbon.

I savor the burn and stare into the mirror and swallow three more.

I don't think about the tree or my father or how big the world is.

I swallow three more pills.

I don't even think about my mother's smile or her sweet laughter or how soft her hands feel when she holds me.

Three more.

Instead, I think about the red number thirty-three jersey hanging in my closet—and I wish I had put it on before I started this.

Three more pills, and the image in the mirror ripples like pond water that has just swallowed a stone.

Still more pills and another gulp of bourbon, and I realize I've lost count. It doesn't matter.

I picture the jersey in my hands and wish I could run my fingers along the stitching of my name one last time.

Three more pills.

The image in the mirror blurs, and then coalesces into that of a pale teenager, a bright red jersey hanging loosely on his skinny frame. The boy in the mirror is smiling.

I recognize that self-conscious smile and, with the numbness spreading up my legs, I gulp down three more pills. Old Lady Reeves is going to be so sad.

I look away from the mirror and swallow three more pills—and my palm is empty.

I start counting while I wait.

One...two...three...

THE HUNCH

"All I'm saying is that you should consider the idea."

"I did."

"Yeah, for about ten seconds." I sighed. "You need the exercise, Frank."

Frank Logan, bald head, double chin, and wrinkled suit, stared at me from the passenger seat of our unmarked patrol car.

"We're outdoorsmen, Ben. Fishermen. Hunters. We don't play tennis, for Christsake."

"My doctor says it's a great way to lose weight and get fit."

"Your doctor's an asshole."

"Really mature, Frank." I swung a left into the Eastern Precinct parking lot. Flipped a wave at a uniformed cop I knew from my days downtown.

"Can you imagine me walking into a country club? Little white shorts and a polo shirt. I'd rather hump my ex-wife."

"Who said anything about a country club?" I asked, searching for a parking spot close to the station.

"Where else you gonna play tennis?"

I glanced at my partner to see if he was being serious. "There are public courts all over the city, Frank."

He shook his head. "I don't believe that."

"What do you mean you don't believe that? What's not to believe?"

"I'm just saying I've never seen one."

"Jesus Christ, we drive by them every day. Big fences around them so the balls don't—"

"Why you getting so riled up?"

"Admit you've seen them before, Frank. Every damn school has tennis courts. So do most of the parks."

"Those are basketball courts."

I stopped the car in the middle of the parking lot and looked over at him. I could feel my face getting red. I opened my mouth to argue, then thought better of it. "You're the asshole, Frank."

He arched his eyebrows. "Really mature, Ben."

I showed him my middle finger and took my foot off the brake. Frank pointed at an empty spot ahead. "Speaking of assholes, pull in there."

RESERVED FOR SGT T COLLINS was stenciled across the asphalt.

"Where do I know that name?"

"Last month's softball game. The douchebag with the tight uniform and the wife—"

"—with the gigantic fake boobs."

I swung into the parking spot and turned off the engine. We got out and started walking. Halfway across the lot, I said, "You've never hunted in your life, Frank."

"Not true."

"Name one time."

He started walking bow-legged and in a horrible John Wayne drawl: "I hunt bad guys all the time, padna."

I opened the door to the station house and walked inside. "How did this become my life?"

From behind me: "Guess you just got lucky, cowpoke."

CAPTAIN RICKSTAD was waiting for us in the hallway. He shook our hands and got right to business. "You guys get a chance to look over the file I emailed?"

I nodded. "He sure looks like your guy."

"I think so, too," Rickstad said, and then hesitated. "But just wait until you talk to him, something's a little off about the whole thing. I can't put my finger on it."

"You worried he might be clean?" Frank asked.

Rickstad shrugged. "That's why I called you guys."

"What's wrong with Henderson?" I asked. "He's good in the box." I had worked with Charlie Henderson for a year before we both made detective. He was a solid cop.

"Salmon fishing in Canada with his son."

"Lucky guy."

"Tell me about it. He's not back until next week. That leaves me with Burton and Burton's an asshole."

I looked at my partner. "There's a lot of that going around."

Frank stared innocently back at me.

Rickstad gestured down the hall. "You guys want coffee? Water?"

"I'm good."

Frank shook his head. "Give me a minute to drain the dragon and we'll get started."

WHILE FRANK hit the restroom, I sat and studied the bank of video monitors that displayed various angles of the interrogation room across the hallway.

A man sat alone in the room, arms crossed on the table in front of him, head resting atop his arms. He hadn't moved since I started watching. He could have been asleep.

According to the police report, the suspect's name was Harold Rutherford II. With a name like that you would have expected him to be the trust-fund son of a wealthy corporate tycoon or at the very least a successful businessman himself, not a junior college English instructor.

Rutherford, age forty-three, was five feet and ten inches tall, weighed one hundred and eighty-five pounds, had black hair and brown eyes. He wore contact lenses or glasses, depending on the day. He was married to Rose Marie Rutherford, age forty-two, his high school sweetheart. She worked at a down-town florist shop. Rutherford and his wife had no children.

Rutherford belonged to a monthly book club at the college and was well known at several local libraries. He collected old stamps and did most of his buying and selling online. He was a private man and not very active in his neighborhood. According to several of his neighbors, the only time they saw Rutherford was when he was walking to and from his car in the driveway or mow-ing his lawn. He wasn't considered unfriendly, merely elusive.

Rutherford took medication for allergies, blood pressure, and anxiety and saw a psychiatrist twice a month. He claimed to suffer from pedophobia, the fear of children, which is especially pertinent considering the crime he is suspected of committing.

Based on information gathered during the investigation, Rutherford had been taken into custody for questioning with-out incident this morning at his home on Canterbury Lane. He refused legal counsel. Search warrants for his home and auto-mobile were currently being served.

I SLAMMED the door to the interrogation room, and Rutherford jerked his head off the desk and sat up. Behind his dark-framed glasses, his eyes were red and swollen. He had been crying at some point.

"My name is Detective Crawford and this is my partner, Detective Logan."

We sat down across from him. Rutherford took off his glasses and rubbed at his eyes with a fist. Up close, he looked exactly how I pictured a community college English instructor to look like.

"This interview is being recorded by video," I continued. "Do you understand that, Mr. Rutherford?"

He nodded.

"I need you to respond verbally."

"Yes," he answered, not much louder than a whisper. "I understand."

"You also understand that you are not under arrest at this time?"

"Yes."

"And you understand that you have turned down your right to have legal counsel present for this interview?"

"Yes. I've done nothing wrong."

Frank placed a manila file folder on the table, opened it and shuffled some papers around. Looking down at the folder, he asked, "You reside at 1920 Canterbury Lane, is that right?"

"Yes, sir."

"How long have you and your wife lived there?"

"Since I started working at the college. A little over eight years now."

"And you like it there?"

Rutherford shrugged. "It's fine I guess."

"Any problems during those eight years?"

"Problems?" He looked confused.

"With your neighbors. Any disputes? Feuds? Incidents?"

THE HUNCH | 297

"Oh, no, not at all. We…mostly keep to ourselves."

"How are you feeling today, Mr. Rutherford?" I asked.

"I…I'm not well. I think I'm coming down with a bug of some sort. Or maybe a sinus infection."

"I understand you've called out of work the last few days."

His eyes flickered, clearly surprised. "Yes…yes, I have."

Frank looked up at him. "Do you know why you're here, Mr. Rutherford?"

"I…they think I had something to do with that missing kid."

"Bobby Evans," I said. "The kid's name is Bobby Evans."

Rutherford didn't say anything, so I went on. "Robert Thomas Evans. Age twelve. Lives with his parents and younger sister at 1046 Canterbury Lane. That's right at the end of your block. Do you know Bobby, Mr. Rutherford?"

He shook his head. "No."

"Seen him around the neighborhood? Walking down the sidewalk? Riding his bike past your house?"

Rutherford glanced up at the camera mounted to the wall in the far corner of the room. "Probably. Many children live on our street."

"Never met Bobby before?"

"Once. He knocked on the door and asked if we needed someone to rake the leaves in our front yard."

"When was this, him knocking on your door?"

"I'm not exactly sure. Maybe two weeks ago."

Frank leaned an elbow on the table. "And what did you say to Bobby when he asked about raking your leaves?"

"My wife…she did most of the talking. I don't do well… with kids."

Frank leaned closer. "Explain what that means: *I don't do well with kids.*"

Rutherford took a deep breath. Looked down at the table. "I suffer from a rare condition known as pedophobia. Most of the literature neatly sums it up as the fear of children. But it's more than that. At least for me. Fear is certainly a significant factor, but my primary symptoms are extreme aversion and crippling tension. If exposed to children for any period of time, I experience severe anxiety attacks. I crumble." He glanced up at us, and then quickly back to the table. He was embarrassed.

"How long have you had this condition?" Frank asked.

"It started during my senior year in college."

"So you're fine being around kids one day and the next day…" He left it hanging.

"Unfortunately, that was pretty much the case." Rutherford paused, then continued. "I never had many friends growing up. I was an only child. My mother and I moved around a lot. I was never popular or well-liked. I was the target of frequent bullying all throughout grammar and upper school." He was looking down at the table again. I noticed a small bald spot growing at the center of his head. "My therapist believes my condition stems from those early negative experiences."

"Can you describe the first time you felt this…aversion to children?" Frank asked.

"There was a daycare facility at one end of campus, an ugly brick building for the children of faculty members and older students. I used to see little kids running around on the playground and older kids playing basketball outside the building all the time. I was walking across the quad one day when I spotted a group of children led by one of the daycare workers heading my way. This was a fairly ordinary sight; they often took the kids on little field trips across campus. But that day something felt different. The closer they got, the more anxious I became."

Frank leaned forward in his seat, genuinely fascinated. I kept my eyes on Rutherford.

"At first, it was just an unsettling feeling in my stomach. The same sensation I get whenever I'm on an airplane. Then, as the children drew nearer, I felt it whispering inside my head, that subconscious voice warning me to change direction, to avoid them...growing in volume and intensity as the kids closed to forty yards, thirty, twenty...until the voice was screaming at me to run, to run away as fast as I could. So, that's what I did. Feeling like I was in the middle of a nightmare I had no control over, I dropped my knapsack and fled into some nearby bushes where I dropped to my knees and vomited my breakfast into the weeds."

Rutherford rubbed his eyes again. "It took me nearly fifteen minutes to clean myself up and regain my composure. When I finally returned to the sidewalk, my knapsack was gone. I went to Lost and Found every day for a week, but I never got it back."

"How long was it before the next incident?" I asked.

"It happened again two weeks later at a shopping mall. Then, a few days after that, at the grocery store. That's when I decided to go see a therapist."

"Still seeing the same one after all these years?"

He shook his head. "The first time, I went to see someone on campus. The health clinic was free and I was poor. After I graduated, I found Dr. Mirarchi over in Fallston. Been seeing her ever since."

Frank took his cellphone from his jacket pocket and stared at the screen. He looked up at me and said, "They need us outside for a minute."

I started to get up from my chair, but sat back down again. "Something I'm curious about, Mr. Rutherford. What is the age range of the children you're affected by? Babies? Toddlers? Teenagers? All of the above?"

"My therapist and I examined dozens of incidents and came up with an estimate of children over the age of seven or eight and under the age of fifteen. Of course, it's not an exact science but we feel pretty confident that we're close."

"Bobby Evans falls right in the middle of that age group..." I said, trailing off.

Rutherford nodded. "Exactly. That's my point. I couldn't have tolerated even being close to him."

Frank pushed his chair back and stood up. I followed him out of the room.

RICKSTAD WAS waiting outside in the hallway. A burly plainclothes cop was standing behind him talking on a cell-phone. "Good job getting him started."

Frank nodded. "I almost feel sorry for the guy." He winked, "Almost."

I noticed the sheet of paper in Rickstad's hand. "What you got for us?"

He handed it to me. I studied it for a moment. "Is this what I think it is?"

"They found it in the garage. Hidden inside an old cigar box."

I passed it over to Frank. He scanned the paper and looked up at me. "Oh, boy."

I USED my thumb to slide the sheet of paper across the desk. "What can you tell us about this?"

Rutherford started to reach for it, then pulled his hand back and looked up at me for permission.

"Go ahead. It's a photocopy."

He picked up the paper. His hands were shaking. After a moment, he put it back down. "It's not what it looks like."

"It looks to me like a map," I said. "With a number of houses in your neighborhood marked off. There are also two playgrounds and an elementary and middle school marked off."

Frank tapped the upper right corner of the map. "Can you tell us who lives here, Mr. Rutherford?"

Rutherford leaned closer for a better look, and then sat back again. "That's...the Evans' house."

Frank and I just stared at him.

"I'm telling you, it's...it's not what it looks like. It's three or four years old, from back when my condition was at its worst. My wife and I...we drew this together so I could avoid any unnecessary run-ins. We tried to—"

"Why was it hidden inside your garage?" Frank interrupted.

"It wasn't hidden. I got to the point where I didn't need it anymore, but I was hesitant to throw it away. I didn't want a reminder of that horrible period of my life inside the house where I could see it every day, so I tucked it away out in the garage."

Frank shifted in his chair. "Let's go back and talk a little bit more about your childhood experiences and how you think they contributed to your phobia." His voice was lower now, almost soothing. I had heard it like this before, and I knew he was on to something.

Rutherford looked momentarily confused by the abrupt change of subject, but then you could see relief set in. He cleared his throat. "My father left us the day before my sixth birthday. He was supposed to be out picking up balloons and a birthday cake for my party, but he never came home. When my mother checked the closet and dresser drawers, all my father's clothes and shoes were missing. So were the two big suitcases that were always stored in the cubbyhole under the stairway and the coffee can of emergency cash my mother kept high on a kitchen shelf.

"A couple months later we learned that he had left us for another family, 'a wife and son he could be proud of' he told my mother on the telephone during the one and only occasion they spoke after he left. My mother never shared this information with me, but I had been listening to their conversation on the upstairs extension. My father was a difficult man. Emotionally cold and verbally abusive. He desperately wanted me to share his love of sports, but I was small for my age and more interested in comics and cartoons. I was only six. His favorite word to describe me was wimp. Pathetic was a close second. I had always had suspicions that my father didn't love me at all, that he'd regretted having me as a son—I know how ridiculous that sounds considering everything I just told you—but I was just a little boy and it wasn't until that phone call that I knew it had been true all along. I loathed my father after that, and even though I didn't know the other kid's name, his new son, I loathed him too.

"When I was seven, we lost the house to the bank, and my mother and I moved in with her sister's family in Aberdeen. I hated that arrangement even more. Aunt Charlotte was a hundred pounds overweight and mean as a hornet. My mother used to say that her sister was angry at the world, and I believed it. Aunt Charlotte had a teenaged son named Benny and a nine-year-old daughter named Sandy, and they tortured me from the day we moved in to the day we moved out. You name it, they did it. They nicknamed me Scary Harry, and I hated it. They played dirty tricks on me with only one goal in mind: to publicly humiliate me. Physical and mental bullying. Stealing my toys and books. Scaring me in the middle of the night. And, worst of all, spreading rumors about me in the neighborhood and at school. They lied and told kids that I wet my bed every night; that we had moved in with them because my father had gone to prison for molesting children; that my mother worked nights downtown as a prostitute. Needless to say, after all that, I became even more of a target outside of the house."

Rutherford stopped and looked up at us in a daze. "Am I talking too much? You probably didn't want all these details..."

"You're doing great," Frank said in that calming voice. He placed the file he'd been going through down on the table. "What happened next?"

Rutherford's shoulders relaxed a little more. This time, he looked directly at Frank as he spoke. "The summer I was nine, my mother got a factory job and we moved to a two bedroom apartment in Darby. For a while everything was better. My mother's job was going well and she'd even started singing silly songs again while she washed the dinner dishes. It was a small thing, I know, but not to nine-year-old me. To that kid, it meant she was building a home again, she was happy again. Her singing meant...hope. I also relished not having my cousins around and being brand new in town, which meant I was largely invisible, and which was considerably better than being known as Scary Harry."

Rutherford sighed and for a moment I thought he might start crying. He cleared his throat and continued: "Then summer ended and I went to yet another elementary school, and everything changed again. It was like I had a target printed on my forehead: THIS PATHETIC WIMP WON'T FIGHT BACK. PICK ON HIM ALL YOU WANT. Even without my cousins there to stir up trouble, it was worse than ever before. I got picked on before school, during classes when the teachers weren't looking, during lunch and recess, after school on my walk home. I couldn't understand why it kept happening. I started having nightmares. My mother told me it was because I was small for my age and soft spoken, but that didn't make sense to me. There were other kids even smaller than me and they didn't get bullied every day."

He reached up and wiped at his eyes, and this time his fingers came away damp. "Couple years later, my mother got laid off and we had to move again. I started middle school in a new town and the whole miserable pattern started once again."

Tears were streaming down his cheeks now and the last couple of words came out in a muffled sob. Frank reached into his jacket pocket and handed Rutherford a folded handkerchief. That was new; I had never seen Frank offer his handkerchief to a suspect before.

"Thank you," Rutherford blubbered, wiping his face. He started to hand the handkerchief back, but Frank put up his hands.

"Keep it. I have a drawer full at home."

Rutherford pulled it back and wiped at his dripping nose.

"I'll tell you what, Mr. Rutherford. Why don't we step out for a second, give you some time to compose yourself. We'll grab some waters for all of us, then come back in and wrap this up. Sound good?"

Rutherford nodded his head and said in a small voice that could have belonged to a ten-year-old, "Okay, sounds good."

AS SOON as the door was closed, I asked, "What have you got, Frank?"

I had worked with Frank Logan for almost ten years now, and I knew when he was zeroing in on a suspect. Most of the time, we knew what the other was thinking. Today wasn't one of those days.

He opened the file folder he was carrying and handed me the sheet of paper on top just as Rickstad walked up carrying three bottles of water.

"What have you got?" Rickstad asked, echoing my question.

Frank looked at him, then back at me. "A hunch." He gestured to the paper I was holding. "Halfway down the page. Read what two of Rutherford's neighbors had to say about Bobby Evans."

I read the witness accounts twice and handed the paper to Rickstad. He read it, then looked up at Frank and made a grunting sound. "Seems like a reach to me."

Frank shrugged. "Like I said, it's just a hunch. But I think it's a good one. We need to push him."

Rickstad handed back the report. "Which one of you is gonna do the pushing?"

Before I could say anything, Frank answered, "I will."

I WALKED into the interview room alone and sat down without a word. Frank came in a moment later, carrying all three bottles of water. He placed a bottle on the table in front of me and handed one to our suspect.

"Thank you," Rutherford said and immediately uncapped the bottle and took a drink. His face was all cleaned up. Frank's handkerchief was nowhere in sight.

"Can I ask you something?" Frank said in that same soothing voice.

"Sure."

He sat down. "Why did you refuse legal counsel?"

Rutherford's face brightened. "Because I haven't done anything wrong. If I'm innocent why do I need an attorney?"

"You'd be surprised how many folks don't agree with that reasoning," I said. "Most people make the call just to protect themselves."

"Nothing to protect," Rutherford said.

I opened the file and pretended to read. "You've suffered from pedophobia for just over twenty years now. Have your reactions to children remained consistent throughout all those years or have they varied at different times?"

"I'm not sure I understand the question."

I closed the file. "I mean have you always reacted in the manner in which you described earlier? Fleeing the scene? Anxiety attacks? Severe emotional distress?"

"Oh, yes, I have. The severity has varied. Like I told you, I experienced a particularly rough time of it for three or four years, but medication helped plateau that out."

"What was the worst reaction you ever experienced?"

Rutherford looked over at Frank, then back to me again, deciding how much he was going to tell us. He decided to go all-in. "When I was in my late thirties, when my condition was at its worst, I had an incident while on vacation. I fainted and urinated in my shorts. It happened on a public beach in front of dozens of people."

"Ever react with anger? Violence?"

Rutherford vigorously shook his head. "No, never."

I stared hard at him. "You're sure?"

"I'm positive," he answered and looked away.

Then it was Frank's turn.

"We appreciate you sharing as much as you have, Mr. Rutherford. I know this hasn't been easy."

"I'm just trying to help."

"And we appreciate that, don't we, Ben?" He looked at me and I nodded.

"We're almost finished here. I just have a couple more questions."

"Okay." Rutherford took another drink of water.

Frank made him wait almost a full minute, staring down at the open file folder, and then he said, "The investigating officers talked to some of your neighbors. Do you know a Joanne Cavanaugh and a Henry Straub?"

"Sure. Joanne lives across the street from us and Henry lives down the block."

"You like them?"

"I...don't really know them very well."

"Let me read you something, Mr. Rutherford. This first statement is from Henry Straub."

Rutherford suddenly looked nervous again. He started tapping his finger on the table.

Frank picked up the report and started reading. "'Rich Evans is a good guy. He plays in our poker group and we golf together maybe two or three times a month. But his boy, Bobby, is another story. That little shit needs to be taken out to the woodshed and taught some manners. He came around the house a couple weeks ago and asked if we needed our leaves raked. I told him no thanks and you know what the brat said to me? He said, 'C'mon, Mr. Straub, you know your wimpy ass ain't going to rake them yourself.' I couldn't believe it. I told him I was going to tell his father, and he flicked me the bird and called me a 'pussy' under his breath. I slammed the door on him and started to call Rich, but my wife stopped me. Told me I needed to cool down first. I never did get around to calling him.'"

Rutherford sat up. "You think Henry Straub had something to do with Bobby's disappearance?"

Frank shook his head. "We checked him out first thing. Bobby's been missing for just short of seventy-two hours. Mr. Straub was at the Grand Canyon vacationing with his family from last Saturday until their return yesterday evening."

Frank looked down at the report again. "This next statement is from Joanne Cavanaugh. 'Bobby Evans was a bully. I witnessed it time and time again. Whether he and the other children were riding bikes or playing whiffle ball or tag. He was bigger than all the other kids and he liked to throw his weight around. He was always teasing the other children and calling them names. I can't repeat most of the words he used, but douchebag and wimp were two of his favorites.'"

Frank stopped reading and looked up at Rutherford. His eyes glinted like razorblades in the fluorescent light. "Your wife wasn't home the day Bobby Evans came to your house, was she?" The soothing voice was gone. "She was working at the florist shop when Bobby knocked on your door." Frank shook his head in disgust. "Don't even think about lying to me."

"Wha…what…?" Rutherford stammered, his face going pale.

"Did he call you a pussy, Harold?" Frank slammed the file folder down on the table, scattering papers across the floor. "Or did he call you a wimp like all those other kids used to?"

Frank was yelling now. Thick veins bulged on his forehead and neck. "Did he make fun of you, Scary Harry? Is that what happened? He teased you and made you his bitch and you finally lost your temper?"

Frank got to his feet and Rutherford slid his chair away from the table, cringing behind it, trying to make himself as small as possible. He looked like a terrified child.

"C'mon, you little wimp," Frank taunted, walking around the table. "For once in your pitiful life stop being such a baby."

I reached out to stop him, but I was too late. Frank jerked his arm away and towered over a moaning Rutherford. He sneered and lowered his voice: "Your father was right about you, Harold, you're nothing but a pathetic wimp."

Something in Harold Rutherford's face changed then. I was staring right at him, and I saw it happen, and I still can't tell you exactly what it was. The slant of his lips maybe. The shape of his eyes. The color of his skin. I honestly have no idea. But, I'm telling you, in that moment, he became someone else.

Rutherford lunged to his feet and stood nose to nose with Frank. "You want to know what happened to that snot-nosed little brat?" he hissed. "You want to know where I put him when I was done with him?"

I moved between Rutherford and the door, and snuck a glance at the camera mounted on the wall in the corner of the room. I hoped Rickstad was watching.

Frank didn't give an inch. He remained very still. "What did you do to him, Harold?"

Rutherford smirked. "Want me to draw you a map, Detective?" A moment ago, he'd sounded like a whimpering child. Now, he sounded insane and angry and very dangerous.

Frank didn't budge. "Tell me what happened."

"'Tell me what happened! Tell me what happened!'" Rutherford laughed and sat back down in the chair and crossed his legs. "If you say so, Detective. But you better grab your pen and paper. There were a lot of them."

Stunned, I found my voice. "A lot of what?"

Rutherford looked over at me. "What do you know, he speaks!" He barked with laughter.

Frank took a step forward. "Tell us what you did with—"

"You can find Bobby Evans—or what's left of him—in the culvert behind the old car wash. And, as a matter of fact, Detective, he *did* call me a pussy and I *did* lose my temper. I lost my temper big time." Rutherford giggled.

"*What's left of him…*" I repeated, unsure I'd heard him correctly.

"That's right. I kept his head, Detective. For proof."

"Proof?" Frank blurted.

"I'm sure your investigators have discovered the key to my storage unit by now. Take a look for yourself. I assure you the skulls are unlike any you've ever seen before."

"What in the hell are you talking—"

"They're not human, Detective. They're monsters. Every last one of them. Go on and take a look. You'll see."

"How many others?" I asked, my voice sounding far away.

"I still remember their names, believe it or not." He uncrossed his legs and grinned up at us. "Carlos Sanchez. Peter Block. Randy Matthews. Johnny McClernan. Doug Stiner. Katy Lotz. Frankie Stoner…"

"YOU HUNGRY?" Frank asked as I drove out of the station house parking lot three hours later.

"I could eat."

"How about the diner on Fourth?"

I turned left on Martin Lurther King Boulevard and merged into traffic. We drove across town in silence. The sky rumbled and raindrops spattered the windshield. I turned on the wipers.

Frank finally broke the quiet. "Guy like that…nine victims."

I nodded. "We've seen it before."

"I dunno. This guy was…different."

I glanced at my partner. "You kind of liked him, didn't you? In the beginning, I mean."

Frank ignored the question. "Rickstad talked to his psychiatrist. She said it was too early to know for sure, but it sounded like his condition caused him to split—that's the word she used—into two different personalities. The first personality the victim. The second one the protector."

"What do *you* think?"

Frank stared out the rain-streaked window. Just when I thought he wasn't going to respond, he said, "Hell, I don't know what to think. It sounds like a whole lotta bullshit, but what do I know?"

The diner swam into view up ahead. I hit the turn signal. "I need coffee."

"I need a bucket of Coke and two servings of biscuits and gravy."

I turned in. There was an empty parking spot by the door. I pulled in and turned off the car. "You really need to improve your diet, Frank. And start exercising more."

"Don't start with me, Ben."

"You want to live long enough to see your kid graduate from college, don't you?"

"My kid's a moron."

He had a point. Rain drummed a soothing rhythm on the hood of the patrol car. "Tennis, Frank. Just give it a try. We can play doubles."

He scowled at me. "You didn't just say that."

We got out of the car and walked inside.

ROSES AND RAINDROPS

Another child was killed yesterday…

And probably right around the time that it happened, I was sitting alone on my screened-in back porch, eating dinner and watching the storm break. A bowl of cabbage soup and a cheese sandwich cut into four neat squares. Too tired to even make it to the dining room table. I'm getting to be an old fart, can barely leave the damn house anymore. This weather makes me feel even worse, but I stayed out just the same and watched until the clouds drifted away. There might not be too many left for me. Not too much of *anything* left for me, so I like to see all I can.

It wasn't a big one. Not as far as storms go. Us folks here in Aberdeen, Virginia have seen much worse. I'd barely finished my soup and started on my sandwich when I noticed the wind letting up. Sure enough, a half-hour later, the rain slowed to a drizzle and the scattered line of baby evergreens along the north fence straightened their shoulders and relaxed, while tiny water-falls cascaded down onto their lower branches.

There hadn't been much thunder or lightning this time around either. Nothing special or impressive about this storm. Just a steady, depressing downpour; the kind that creeps through the walls of your house and seeps right into your bones; the kind that makes you want to crawl into bed and pull up the covers even though it's barely five in the afternoon.

So, no, it wasn't a big storm, especially not for Aberdeen. Lasted barely a handful of hours, and then went on its merry way up north toward our Yankee neighbors in Maryland. A lot of folks probably thought—*hoped*—we had gotten lucky this time. Escaped without harm. But a lot of folks 'round here are damned fools.

We didn't get lucky.

ANOTHER CHILD was killed yesterday...

This is how it happened *this* time. At least, this is what Pecker Robbins overheard down at the Texaco station. Now, I know what they'll say about ol' Pecker. That he listens to Alex Jones and believes George Bush and Barack Obama are teaming up to send in United Nations soldiers to take away his hunting rifle. Far as I know, Bush spends his days on a ranch somewhere in Texas. And Obama? Well, I don't much care for him either, but the man has been in office eight years now and not yet has anybody shown up at Pecker's door and demanded his guns. So, I reckon he's wrong on that.

But not on this.

The call came in to police dispatch as the storm was winding down. Megan Bradley's husband, Jerry, told police that they had locked their daughter, Kassie, in her upstairs bedroom, soon as the storm first arrived.

Just to be safe, you understand.

Megan had unlocked the bedroom door shortly after six o'clock to serve Kassie her dinner and discovered the girl was missing. The frantic mother checked the bathroom, underneath the bed, and inside the walk-in closet before noticing the curtains fluttering in the breeze. The bedroom window was open.

According to Pecker (who heard it from one of the responding officers), Megan called out for her husband—quietly at first, then shrieking with panic. At the sound of her voice, Jerry bounded up the stairs and stopped in the doorway, following his wife's wide-eyed gaze to the billowing curtains. Without a word, the couple—maybe gaining strength from each other's presence—moved forward together. Moved slowly, I reckon.

I imagine their footsteps made whispering sounds on the plush carpet. Knowing that a story is only as good as the details, Pecker recounted to me how the officer had described Kassie's bedroom. If I close my eyes, I can picture those poor parents inching past the pink-canopied bed, the neat desk with the laptop computer, her bookshelves lined with soccer trophies and those Harry Potter books.

They stopped in front of the open window. I'll bet the rain was louder there. Jerry reached out and pushed aside the soaked curtains—

—and there on the drenched windowsill, they found a single red rose petal.

According to Pecker, that was when Megan fainted.

About an hour later, after the storm had ended, one of the responding officers found Kassie's remains in the Bradley's south meadow. Her tiny torso slit wide open from her neck right down to below her belly button. To no one's surprise, her eyes and ears were missing, as were her fingers and toes.

And, of course, just like all the times that had come before, they found—clinched between her crooked, little teeth—a single blood-red rose.

ANOTHER CHILD *was killed yesterday…*

I know this whole business must sound strange to an outsider, but us folks here in Aberdeen have grown used to the storms and their deadly consequences. Over the years, we've learned to fear and loathe the storms with all our hearts, but we've also learned to accept them as part of our town's undeniable heritage.

Believe it or not, it doesn't get talked about much anymore. Times are tough the world over, and people around here know that. They also know that Aberdeen has somehow remained untouched by many of the problems that plague today's society. We don't have drugs or poverty. Our schools are safe. The churches are full on Sunday. Property taxes stay pretty low. There are no terrorists training out in our cornfields. Hell, other than when the storms come, there's no crime to speak of. Maybe some teenagers driving too fast, or somebody getting drunk and starting a fight. Maybe some mischief come Halloween night. But that's small stuff. Folks here recognize that Aberdeen has somehow remained a prosperous place to run a business, to raise a family and put a roof over your head and three squares on the table every day. For a lot of folks, that's all that matters.

If you've got those things, you might tend to look the other way so that you can hold onto them. You might make excuses, become forgetful. You might even pretend.

For years, I wasn't one of those people. I often wondered to myself—worried to myself—about the small town I'd been born and raised in. Why had we been cursed to live in such fear? Why had none of us went and asked for outside help to solve this terrible mystery?

Although I never had any children of my own to worry about—my Jenny couldn't have kids and it never mattered a lick to me, no sir—the questions troubled me on many a long and restless night.

Until nine years ago, almost to this very day, when—completely by accident—I stumbled upon the answer.

It was the hottest summer I could remember—and believe me, I've seen a lot of hot summers—but by no means the driest.

The storms hit us something fierce that year, and a half-dozen children were dead by mid-August.

I was still working at the mill then, putting in my ten hours a day and collecting a legitimate paycheck. I miss those days. You spend your life looking forward to retirement, and then, when it comes, you spend the rest of your days wishing you could go back to work. Life is tricky that way.

I remember it was a Thursday, just before quitting time, and Teddy Jenkins, the mill foreman, came into the shop and asked me to make a special delivery for him. He was all secretive about it. Whispered so the other workers wouldn't hear him. He said it was important and he would have done it himself, but he had an anniversary dinner planned with his wife and there was no way in hell he could miss it (if you'd ever set eyes on Teddy's wife, Mabel, you know he was telling the truth). Anyway, Teddy finished with a hearty pat on my back and said I was the only man he could trust to do the job right.

The whole thing struck me as a little strange—Teddy wasn't exactly the complimenting kind, and if there's one thing folks in Aberdeen can all agree on, it's that he didn't trust *anyone*— but I needed the overtime, so I obliged. Also, looking back, I reckon he'd played to my ego a bit. Sneaky bastard.

I helped Teddy load my pick-up with a dozen sacks of mulch, another two dozen sacks of planting soil, and a stack of heavy two-by-fours. The bed sank a good few inches, and I wondered if my shocks would hold, but they did. Then he lowered his voice again—even though there was no one else around—and gave me directions to the house I was to deliver to. When he was finished, he made me repeat them. Twice.

I had never seen Teddy act like this before. Usually, he was loud and obnoxious and full of bluster. As I climbed into my truck, I looked at his expression and realized something.

He was scared.

It was in his voice and his eyes and the way he moved. Teddy Jenkins was downright terrified of something.

"Listen here," he growled, coming up to my driver's side window. "Drop the goods right there in front of the porch and be on your way without delay. These people pay good money and always on time. In return, I deliver their purchases and respect their privacy. You do the same. Understand?"

Puzzled and unsettled, I nodded my agreement and was on my way.

The evening was hot and sticky. The roads I was driving were rutted dirt, and bounced me around like I was riding on a rollercoaster at the State Fair. I waved to a little boy carrying a fishing pole on my way out of town, but the little prick didn't so much as wave back. I just shook my head at him and kept on going. The truck radio was broken, so I had a lot of time to think during the drive, and my thoughts were dominated by Teddy's bizarre behavior. I decided there had to be a simple explanation to the whole thing. Just had to be patient and wait and see for myself.

I was heading west and deeper into the thick woodlands of the valley. I'd hunted the valley more times than I could count but always further south where the interstate ran. Same with fishing; the Hanson River held some of the finest small-mouth bass in the state, but all the best spots were located to the south. Dead west was a whole lot of dark forest and scrub brush. Despite having lived there all my life, it was new territory for me.

After ninety minutes of jostling around on those old dirt roads, I finally spotted the bent-over weeping willow with the red cross painted on its trunk just like Teddy had described. I turned left into a weed-choked driveway that wound its way through a tunnel of trees. The overhanging branches blocked out the sky, casting enough shadow that I had to turn on the headlights. The trees seemed to swallow the road, and I rolled up my window to keep the branches from slapping at my arm.

I followed that dark, leafy tunnel for what had to be nearly a mile and had just about convinced myself that it was never going to end when it abruptly did just that — and I found myself in the sun again, squinting at a modest, nicely kept log cabin perched in the middle of a gently sloping, grassy hollow. I looked around but didn't see anyone outside. There were no cars out front. I parked by the porch, as Teddy had directed, and got out.

"Hello?" I called, stretching.

There was no reply. I noticed then how quiet it was. Not even the whir of crickets or the chirp of birds in the surrounding woods. Only thing I heard was the ticking of my cooling engine.

Feeling unsettled, I lowered the truck bed and started unloading the planks of wood and sacks of mulch and soil. I glanced at the house as I worked, searching for a face in a window or any sign of movement. Nothing. I found myself working faster. I wondered who the hell these people were, and why they lived way out here in the middle of nowhere, without even a Walmart nearby. I mean, there's living in the country, and then there's living in the *country*. Aberdeen is surrounded by farms and hunting cabins. But this? This was something else.

When I'd finished unloading, I decided to wait until I got home to sweep out the bed of my truck; no small decision for a man of my stubborn nature and work habits. But that unsettled feeling in my stomach had grown into a full-fledged case of the willies by then, and I just wanted to get the hell out of there.

I hopped in the driver's seat and put the key in the ignition—and then it hit me.

I had to pee.

If there's any single urge stronger than curiosity—or even fear—in a man of my age, it's the urge to piss. Like my Daddy used to say: *when you gotta, you gotta.*

I glanced back at the dark mouth of the tree tunnel, and decided I better get it over with right then and there. I've always said it was politer to piss in a man's backyard than his front, so I started around back. By that point, I'd pretty much convinced myself there was nobody home.

I rounded the corner. Cords of firewood were stacked eight feet high along the side of the house. Unusual, considering it was still summertime. I kept walking.

The back yard—it was more meadow than yard; a good three acres of trees had recently been cleared and stumps pulled up—was impressive. I stared in wonder, thinking: *it would have taken a work crew a full week and a ton of equipment to do that much clearing. How did they get the equipment back here?*

I had just about reached the tree line and was going for my zipper when I heard a sound behind me. Faint laughter. Coming from the house.

I forgot all about my need to pee. Forgot about Teddy's warning to respect their privacy, as well. I wanted to know what the hell was going on here. I quickly worked my way toward the back of the house. Without thinking, I edged closer and crouched down below a window. I heard more giggles. Clearer now. It sounded like a woman. Unable to resist, I inched up and peered over the windowsill.

And pissed right in my pants.

Piled on several plates in the middle of a big wooden table were mounds of glistening body parts—blood-splattered ears, fingers, toes. And internal organs, too—long, slippery ropes of intestines and plump, shiny brown bags that were either livers or kidneys. I've field dressed enough deer in my time to know what organs look like. But these didn't belong to no deer. The stench was revolting, even muted through the wall. It reeked of foulness and sweetness at the same time—an electric tang not unlike the way a thunderstorm smells when it comes rolling in across the hills.

A wrinkled old couple danced around the cramped dining room, cackling with glee, pausing only to gorge themselves with more mouthfuls of dripping morsels.

The old man said something I couldn't quite hear, and the woman laughed again, mouth open wide, revealing perfectly straight rows of white—albeit gore-stained—teeth. They had to be dentures. A woman that age? But no, they were her real teeth. If they weren't, then she had access to the greatest cosmetic dentist of all time. But it wasn't just her teeth that threw me. Her eyes, two brilliant blue sparks, twinkled like those of a teenaged girl in love.

The old man skipped like a little boy into the next room and returned with a stained brown package. He unraveled it across the table revealing four human hearts.

The woman's eyes widened. She snatched one of the organs and bit into it like a ripe peach, twisting her head back and forth like it was a particularly tough piece of beef jerky. Blood dripped from her fingers and chin.

The old man tilted his head and smiled lovingly as he watched her chew. It was that gesture that finally broke me. Of all the repulsive sights in that charnel house, it was that smile—and the adoration behind it—that scared me the most.

I turned and ran. I'm not ashamed to admit it. I made it about twenty yards before falling to the ground and puking. Stones and briars jabbed at my knees and palms, but I barely noticed.

I pushed myself up and started running again, and that's when I saw another patch of trees had been cleared on the opposite side of the house—and row after row of stunning, bright red roses growing in the carefully manicured dark earth. I stumbled to a halt and stood there shaking. The piss on my pants leg began to turn cold.

The old man inside that house had cleared the trees and stacked the firewood by himself; maybe the old woman had even helped. It wasn't Teddy Jenkins. It wasn't anyone from town. There was never a work crew up there. The old man and woman had cleared the trees themselves. They were old and wrinkled on the outside but eternally young and strong on the inside, where it counted.

They weren't human.

They couldn't be.

They were monsters.

Immortal monsters draining the lives from our helpless children to somehow replenish their own.

Standing there at the edge of that garden, staring out over the dozens of flowers destined for innocent victims, frozen with fear and revulsion, it was too much. I got dizzy and my ears began to ring. Willing myself not to faint, I ran like hell, jumped into my truck, and barreled through that dark tunnel of trees without slowing.

Indeed, I didn't so much as tap the brake pedal until I was out of that valley and back across the Aberdeen town limits.

And I've never been back there since.

ANOTHER CHILD was killed yesterday…

I've never spoken a word about that day to anyone. I had a gut feeling—and gut feelings are usually right—that Teddy knew exactly what the hell was going on at that house. All of it. That would certainly explain his odd behavior that day. I never got the chance to ask him because he dropped dead not long after. Heart attack, down at the VFW. Fell right off his barstool and cracked his head open during the middle of the Redskins game.

Nowadays, when I think about it, it almost feels like a dream. It feels like it happened a long time ago, when I was a younger man, but in the grand scheme of my life, it wasn't. And yet, that dreamlike feeling remains. As does my confusion. They say wisdom comes with age, but I've yet to gain an understanding of what I saw that day.

I don't know how long they've been up there, the old man and woman. Maybe forever. Maybe they were here before us. I don't know how it all started or when or even why. And I don't understand a damn thing about those awful roses. Maybe the old woman feels remorse for the killings and leaves the roses as tribute or remembrance; or maybe they enjoy the killings and the rose is simply a macabre calling card.

And there's one more thing that really puzzles me on those lonely, sleepless nights when I find myself staring at the ceiling and wondering about this town I call my home and these people I call my neighbors.

I wonder about the storms.

I don't know, and that makes me angry and frustrated. I just can't make sense of them.

But then again, I can't do much of anything these days. Even need help getting to the shithouse when my arthritis gets cranky. Growing old? I don't recommend it. Friends and loved ones go off and die, leaving you lonely. Everything hurts, physically and emotionally.

Sometimes, when I sit on the back porch and watch the storms roll through and wait to hear if it's happened again, I can't help but remember how gracefully the old man moved across the floor; the gleam in the old woman's crystal blue eyes, and how they stared at each other with such youthful love. It would be nice to feel that again. To feel anything, other than the aches in my joints and the loneliness in my heart. To dance again. To laugh. To have energy again.

To have an appetite.

And more and more every day, while I sit here alone waiting to die, rubbing my aching hands together, watching the children pass without so much as a wave hello anymore, I am tempted to somehow get back to that house again—and ask that old couple to let me join them.

(Written with Brian Keene)

STEPHEN KING AT 70
A TRIBUTE
TO THE
GUNSLINGER

The most important things are the hardest to say…
because words diminish them.

—The Body

HOW DO you say a proper thank you to the man who handed
you the key? How do you when words aren't enough?

Fiction is the truth inside the lie.

—IT

I WAS a sophomore in high school the first time I met Stephen
King. It was October of 1981 and my English teacher, a lovely
man named Richard Gallagher, showed up for class one afternoon with a stack of photocopies in his arms. He asked several

330 | RICHARD CHIZMAR

students to pass them out and announced that we would be spending the next couple of days reading a short story he had recently stumbled upon in an obscure magazine.

The story was a nasty little shocker called "The Monkey" by an author I had never heard of, and initially I was just thrilled to have the opportunity to read the word "fart" out loud in class (that's pretty much a rule, by the way; all fifteen-year-old boys love to talk about farts). But the deeper we got into the story, the more I realized that something else—something far more significant—was happening.

By the time we'd finished reading and discussing "The Monkey," my path was crystal clear. It was as if a secret door had been opened and I had caught a glimpse of my future in the landscape beyond. I knew I wanted to spend my life doing to others what this Stephen King fellow had just done to me: he'd somehow managed to make the real world around me disappear and replaced it with a fairy tale. A dark and frightening fairy tale, to be sure, but that's exactly what the whole experience felt like to me: it felt like *magic*.

> Sometimes when you're young, you have moments
> of such happiness, you think you're living on
> someplace magical like Atlantis must have been.
> Then we grow up and our hearts break into two.
> **—Hearts in Atlantis**

YOU FORGET when you're young. The world is too big, the sky too bright, the days and nights filled with too many possibilities. So you go where the wind carries you, and you forget. Sometimes even magic slips away.

> Books are a uniquely portable magic.
>
> —*On Writing*

FAST FORWARD five more years: it's 1986 and I'm in the middle of my junior year of college. And I'm completely lost.

Despite the transformative experience of reading "The Monkey," I've not spent the past five years creating my own form of literary magic. Instead, I've devoted my days to playing college lacrosse and attending countless parties and even managing to take in the occasional class or two (if it wasn't raining). I was majoring in business and the year before I'd been named an All-American midfielder, and it felt like I was holding the world in the palm of my hand.

And then everything changed.

Shortly into the new season, I injured my ankle and re-injured my knee, and before I knew what was happening I was out of the game. For good. I spent the dark days that followed sitting alone in my apartment, drifting aimlessly around campus, dragging myself to physical therapy appointments, and trying desperately to find something—anything—to feel happy about.

And then one day, while wandering around the mall to waste time, I bumped into an old friend—and my world turned upside down again.

I remember stopping in front of the bookstore and staring at the biggest display of books I had ever seen. There had to be at least fifty copies stacked in a spiraling tower. The cover art grabbed my attention first: a cracked gray sidewalk and a paper boat gliding down a rain-filled gutter, and my God, that sharp green claw reaching up out of the sewer grate. Then my eyes moved to the bright red title: *IT.* And the author's name above: STEPHEN KING.

I grabbed a copy from the top of the tower, savoring its weight in my hands. I opened the book to the first page and scanned the opening sentence:

> The terror, which would not end for another twenty-eight years—if it ever did end—began, so far as I know or can tell, with a boat made from a sheet of newspaper floating down a gutter swollen with rain.

I felt a familiar stirring in my heart. The whispery kiss of a resurfacing memory. I stood there, transfixed, and read to the bottom of the page, and then the next page, and the one after that. The bookstore disappeared. The world disappeared. I was no longer standing in a shopping mall in Maryland. Suddenly, I was walking the stormy streets of Derry, Maine with Georgie Denbrough at my side and Pennywise the Dancing Clown waiting for us down below.

Pennywise was terrifying and grotesque, and he wanted me to float with him down there in the dark sewers of Derry.

But I didn't care.
I was home again.

The place where you made your stand never mattered.
Only that you were there…and still on your feet.

                                                    —*The Stand*

TO THIS day, I believe that *IT* saved the life of a very lost and confused young man. At the very least it carved the path for my writing and editing career, and gave me something to dream about again.

I spent two weeks devouring the novel, savoring those final hundred pages, rationing my daily page count because I didn't want the story to end.

And, along the way, I rediscovered the magic.

Shortly after I finished reading *IT*, I landed a part-time gig at the college newspaper writing Sports and Feature articles. I didn't have a clue what I was doing, but that didn't matter. I learned as I went. Rediscovering the magic had given me courage I didn't know I possessed. Within a few months, I was writing and submitting my own short stories to small press magazines. The rejection letters piled in, but so did the acceptances (okay, they didn't so much as pile in as much as *trickle*, but those scattered acceptances were more than enough to keep me going). I remember driving away from the post office one winter morning, a publisher's check for $25 sitting on the passenger seat beside me, and thinking: *I'm a writer. I'm a writer. I'm a writer.* The words echoing inside my head the whole way home.

I was twenty-one years old.

Six months later, I started *Cemetery Dance* magazine.

It's been my life ever since.

> Amateurs sit and wait for inspiration,
> the rest of us just get up and go to work.
>
> **—On Writing**

THE DEBUT issue of *Cemetery Dance* magazine was published in December of 1988.

In late 1989, a small envelope postmarked Bangor, Maine showed up in my P.O. Box. I opened it and found a promotional blurb for *Cemetery Dance*. It was signed Stephen King. I stared at the letter for a long time, thinking: *I'm not dreaming, am I?*

Two years later, a thick manila envelope arrived in that same P.O. Box. Inside, a brand new short story called "Chattery Teeth" by Stephen King. Once my heart recovered from the shock, I hurried down the hallway of our apartment to show my wife, Kara. There were smiles and whoops of joy. And there were tears—from both of us. She understood. She knew.

> Hope is a good thing, maybe the best of things,
> and no good thing ever dies.
>
> **—Rita Hayworth and**
> **the Shawshank Redemption**

FAST FORWARD again. It's 1996. I'm thirty years old, and the doctor has just told me that the cancer I beat six months earlier has come back. It's in both of my lungs, my liver, my stomach, and my lymph nodes. I'm staring at twelve weeks of chemotherapy and 50/50 odds of surviving.

My family and friends rally around me. Phone calls. Visits. Cards.

Late one night not long after, the fax machine in my office buzzes: a lengthy handwritten letter from Stephen King. He'd heard that the cancer had returned and wanted me to know that he was thinking about me. He wanted me to know that he believed I could beat it.

I'm still here.

And I still have that letter.

> Life was such a wheel…and it always, at the end,
> came round to the same place again.
>   —*The Stand*

I COULD tell you a hundred more stories like these. Each one of them a priceless jewel from a treasure chest of dreams-come-true.

I could tell you what it felt like when the manuscript for *From A Buick 8* showed up at my office (talk about a Monday morning surprise!) with a note explaining that Stephen wanted to know if I would be interested in publishing a limited edition.

I could tell you what it felt like when Stephen and his agent extraordinaire, Chuck Verrill, sent me a novella called *Blockade*

Billy, and the three of us shocked the publishing world with a secret-release Stephen King hardcover to mark the start of baseball season.

I could tell you what it felt like to collaborate on *Gwendy's Button Box,* and how when a reporter asked me if working on the book with Stephen King was a dream come true, my answer was honest and direct: "I've been a dreamer my entire life, but I never dreamed this big."

I could even talk about how a surprise business relationship grew into a surprise friendship as the years passed. Thousands of emails and texts exchanged. The occasional baseball game or movie premiere. Rarely talking about writing, business even less. My favorite conversations centering on our families, our dogs, the people and books and movies we most admire. How I often find myself asking for advice and guidance, not just professionally, but as a father of two boys of my own. And how Steve listens with a generous and patient ear, and usually knows the words I most need to hear.

Finally, I could tell you about the endless kindnesses that Steve has blessed my family and me with. Laughter shared with Billy and Noah across a dinner table. A voice cameo in a Billy-directed student film. Countless opportunities for all of us to chase our dreams. And much more.

> The most important things are the hardest
> to say…because words diminish them.
> —*The Body*

THERE IS a brief scene near the end of the movie, *Tombstone*, which I think about often. It's my favorite moment in the film, and I can't think of any other scene in any other movie that better encompasses my own personal view of friendship and loyalty.

> Turkey Creek Johnson: Why you doin' this, Doc?
> Doc Holliday: Because Wyatt Earp is my friend.
> Turkey Creek Johnson: Friend? Hell, I got lots of friends.
> Doc Holliday: I don't.

I'll tell you a secret: I don't either.

I'm the kind of guy who surrounds himself with a very small group of trusted friends, most of them I've known since the long ago days of childhood. A *ka-tet,* if you will.

I'm blessed and grateful beyond words that Steve King is one of those friends. People often ask me what he is like in "real life" (their words, not mine). I usually respond briefly and protectively. I simply say that he's smart and kind and funny as hell. And that's all true.

But he's more than that.

He's the most talented and generous man I know.

Happy 70th, Steve.

May there be many more.

I love you, brother.

THE ASSOCIATION

Harold Peterson stood at the top of his driveway, hands on his hips, staring into the open garage. He frowned. Dozens of cardboard boxes, stacked three and four high, filled every available inch of it. Several in the front row were marked: LIVING ROOM, BEDROOM #1, KITCHEN.

"Trying to figure out a good excuse so you can get out of unpacking?"

Harold turned to find his wife, Lily, standing behind him. He smiled and glanced up at the summer sky. "It *is* an awfully nice day. Think maybe I'll play a round of golf first and get to work on this mess later."

Lily walked close and wrapped her arms around her husband, snuggling her face against his shoulder. "Think again, mister."

Harold laughed and hugged her back.

"Besides, you don't even play golf," she said.

"Can't think of a better day to start."

Lily giggled and swatted him on the butt.

They stood there in each other's arms, not talking for a moment, just staring at their new home.

Finally, Lily broke the silence. "I can't believe it's ours."

"I can't believe how much crap we had crammed into a two-bedroom condo."

Lily shrugged. "We lived there for eight years. What did you expect?"

Harold leaned down and kissed his wife on the forehead. "I expect us to live here happily ever after."

THEY CARRIED and unpacked boxes the rest of the morning. Harold focused on the upstairs bedrooms and basement. Every time he came upon a box marked BOOKS, he whined like a teenager. Lily worked on the living room, bathrooms, and kitchen. The only time she complained was when she stubbed her toe against one of the front stairs.

By noon, they were both drenched in sweat and starving. Harold called for lunch delivery from a local pizza shop that the realtor had recommended and they ate on the front porch.

"I think we're making good progress," Lily said in between bites of her chicken pita.

"I do, too," Harold answered, showing her a mouthful of cheesesteak sub, a gob of melted cheese dripping onto his t-shirt.

"Oh my God, stop it," Lily scolded, wiping at his shirt. "What will the neighbors think?"

They had always been this way: Lily, the earnest one, the nurturer. Harold, the mischievous joker, rarely serious, seldom acting his age, always putting a smile on everyone's face.

They'd met at a party during their senior year at the University of Virginia. Lily had been an English major with designs on teaching and maybe one day writing a novel or two. Harold had followed in his father's footsteps and earned a degree in finance. A job at his family's brokerage firm was awaiting him after graduation.

Despite their parents' protests and offers to help, they'd lived in an apartment the first eighteen months after their spring wedding and saved every cent they earned. They'd used the money to buy a two-bedroom condominium in the city and lived there for almost eight years before feeling secure enough to start house hunting in the suburbs.

Two months ago, they'd found their dream house here on Brooks Road in the exclusive community of Broadview. Three days ago, they'd moved in.

They were content and happy, excited about the future, and in the early stages of talking about starting a family.

They were sure this was the house where they would grow old together.

"UGH, MY entire body feels like a punching bag." Lily turned off the light in the bathroom and walked stiffly into the bedroom.

Harold patted the empty half of the bed beside him. "Climb in and I'll give you a massage."

Lily eased herself in with a groan. Harold scooted over and started rubbing her neck and shoulders.

"Oh my God," she moaned. "That feels so good."

For the next twenty minutes, Harold worked his fingers over every inch of her body, right down to the bottoms of her feet. When he was finished, Lily was rag-doll limp and nearly asleep. "Thank you," she mumbled. A minute later, she was snoring.

Harold watched the rise and fall of her chest for a moment, thinking how lucky he was. How lucky they both were to have found each other. Then he reached over to the nightstand for the remote control to turn off the television. It wasn't there.

He looked around the room and spotted the remote sitting next to his wallet on top of the dresser. Sighing, he swung his legs out of bed and quietly walked across the room. He grabbed the remote and was about to return to bed when something outside the window caught his attention. He leaned closer, careful to remain hidden behind the curtains.

Someone was standing in the middle of the street, staring up at the house.

Between the darkness and a tangle of overhanging tree branches, Harold couldn't make out whether it was a man or woman. All he could see was the still figure of someone standing there, watching. He was about to go downstairs and investigate further when the shadowy figure turned and started slowly walking away.

Harold watched the person disappear down the street and then climbed back into bed. He clicked the remote to turn off the television and lay there in the darkness, thinking about what he'd just seen. He wondered how long the person had been out there watching the house before he'd walked by the window and noticed him. Harold felt unnerved and was certain that sleep would be a long time coming, but within minutes of turning off the television, he was snoring even louder than his wife.

DESPITE THE uneasiness he'd felt the night before, Harold was too busy the next morning to even think about the mysterious figure he'd seen standing in front of the house.

It had been Lily's idea to paint the third upstairs bedroom before hauling in the contents of what would become their joint office. Harold had gone along with it—mostly because she'd been so excited and he didn't have the heart to tell her no—but now he regretted it. He was exhausted and covered in baby blue paint.

Lily giggled and used a wet-wipe to rub at the splotches of paint streaking his cheeks and nose. "You look cute, honey."

"I look like a goddamn Smurf," he grumbled.

"Hold still and stop being such a baby."

"I'm not a baby, you're a baby."

Lily used the corner of the wet-wipe to dab away a spot of paint from Harold's chin and tossed it into a nearby waste-basket. "There, you big baby, I'm all finished."

Harold gave her a pouty look and glanced out the upstairs window. Outside, a red-and-white mail Jeep was just pulling away from the curb in front of the house. "I have an idea," he said, looking back at her.

"Oh, boy, here we go."

"No, I'm serious. We're almost done up here. Why don't you finish painting and I'll go downstairs and whip us up some lunch? How does BLTs and iced tea sound?"

Lily started to protest, but stopped herself. "Okay, it's a deal."

Harold didn't hesitate. He yanked off his paint-spattered t-shirt and headed out of the room. Before he reached the hall-way, he heard from behind him, "You big baby." Harold grinned and started downstairs.

But instead of going to the kitchen, he hit the bottom of the stairs and headed out the front door and down the driveway. A couple of shirtless kids cruised past laughing on skateboards. A man across the street was mowing his lawn. He saw Harold and flipped him a friendly wave. Harold returned the gesture just as he reached the mailbox. He opened it and pulled out a stack of what looked like junk-mail and closed it again. He was halfway up the driveway when he noticed a thin piece of pink paper—a pink-slip—with the words FIRST WARNING printed boldly across the top.

Harold stopped walking. He stood there in the driveway and read the notice from top to bottom, then he read it again.

It was a form letter from the Broadview Homeowners' Association explaining that they were in breach of contract. In a blank space near the top of the form, someone had filled in their address and near the bottom of the form, that same person had handwritten: FAILURE TO PROPERLY STORE TRASH AND REFUSE. SEE CLAUSE 14B FOR ADDITIONAL INFORMATION.

Harold looked up at the big pile of empty cardboard boxes sitting at the top of the driveway. Were they serious?

"I DIDN'T even know we *had* a neighborhood association," Harold said, shoveling in another bite of lasagna.

Lily pushed her salad plate aside. "I did. We had to pay our first year's dues at closing. Weren't you even listening to the realtor?"

He shrugged. "Only about where to sign all those damn papers."

Harold had shown Lily the warning notice during lunch that afternoon. Surprisingly, her mood had immediately darkened and she'd stewed about it the rest of the day while they'd unpacked and arranged books on the built-in shelves in the living room. It wasn't like her to act this way. She had a temper, but she was always the reasonable one.

"Where do they get off telling us what to do?" she asked.

"I'm right there with you, baby, but isn't that what home-owners' associations do? They make up a bunch of dumb rules for people to follow?"

"But to give us a warning our first week here? And for a bunch of stupid cardboard boxes?"

Harold shrugged. "I guess they're pretty strict."

She put down her fork and picked up the pink-slip. "Not strict, ridiculous."

"Ridiculous," he agreed, nodding.

"Clause 14B," she said. She'd found the homeowners' association rules online earlier in the afternoon and looked it up. "So we should have broken down the boxes and stored them alongside the house until trash day. Big flippin' deal. They weren't even out there for twenty-four hours. Who in the world would have complained about that?"

Harold thought about the dark figure standing in the street the night before and decided not to say anything to Lily. She was upset enough. He leaned over and refilled her wine glass. "It really is okay, baby. We just have to forget about it. We'll probably never hear from the stupid homeowners' association again."

BUT HE was wrong.

Two weeks later, another pink-slip showed up in the mailbox. Lily found it when she returned home from her afternoon run, and she was livid.

"Look at this," she said, waving the notice in Harold's face when he walked in the door that evening from work. "Another warning!"

"What did we do wrong this time?" Harold took the pink-slip from her and read it standing in the foyer. "Second and final warning. Improper lawn ornament/decoration? What in the hell are they talking about?"

Lily snatched the notice away. "They're talking about our bird bath, Harold."

"Our ... You're kidding me?"

"I wish I was. Evidently, all plastic lawn ornaments are forbidden. Only concrete, sandstone, marble and copper are acceptable. Do you know what that means?"

"No pink flamingoes for the front yard?"

Lily flashed him a stern look. "It means someone was snooping in our back yard."

Harold thought about it and nodded. "You're right. With the tree-line, you can't see the bird bath from the street and you definitely can't see it from either of our neighbors' yards."

"Even if someone had spotted it from a distance, no way they could tell it was made of plastic. Someone had to have snuck into the back yard and checked it out from up close."

"All right, now this whole thing's getting creepy."

"Tell me about it." Harold walked into the living room and dropped his briefcase on the floor next to his reading chair. "Tell you what, I'm gonna make some phone calls tonight after dinner and look into this."

LILY HEARD footsteps in the hallway and looked up from her book. "So what did you find out?"

Harold walked into the bedroom, rubbing his temple. He looked tired and perplexed.

"Not a whole lot, I'm afraid." He sat down on the edge of the bed. "First, I tried calling the number printed on the home-owners' association notice. An answering machine picked up and said to leave a message after the beep. Only there wasn't any beep. I called back three more times and got the same thing."

"That's strange."

"Then, I called Nancy Williams, the agent who sold us the house. She was…pretty vague. She said she didn't know much about the homeowners' association but had never heard any complaints. She went on and on about how exclusive Broadview was—the best schools, low crime, very little turnover—and then she suggested we ask some of the neighbors about the association."

"Duh. Why didn't we think of that?"

"Probably because we don't really know anyone around here yet." Harold started to say something else, but hesitated.

"What's wrong?" Lily asked, scooting closer.

Harold looked up at her. "I think she was lying."

"Who? Nancy?"

He nodded. "I'm sure of it, actually. She sounded nervous and, near the end of the call, she just about jumped out of her skin trying to change the subject."

"That doesn't sound like Nancy."

"That's what I'm saying. As soon as I mentioned the home-owners' association, it was like a switch had been thrown. Even before I told her about our problems with them."

Lily thought about it for a moment. "Then I guess we have to talk to the neighbors."

"I guess we do."

THEY CAREFULLY planned it out in advance. Lily would talk to Mrs. Cavanaugh next door and Harold would talk to Chuck Noonan across the street. Mrs. Cavanaugh was a widow in her late sixties, a friendly woman who was often seen outside tending the rose garden in her front yard. Chuck Noonan was barrel-chested and tattooed, and married to the skinniest woman Lily and Harold had ever seen. At least once a week, he would slip on a colorful tank-top and big, clunky headphones, and hop on a noisy riding mower to cut his lawn.

The plan was simple: they would wait until they spotted Mrs. Cavanaugh or Chuck Noonan working outside, and then they would swoop in for a stealthy interrogation. "Make it quick," Harold quipped. "Get in and get out."

As luck would have it, that next Saturday afternoon, both Lily and Harold got the opportunity at the exact same time. As they turned left onto Brooks Road and approached their house on the way home from the grocery store, they saw both Mrs. Cavanaugh and Chuck Noonan outside in their respective yards.

Lily and Harold quickly unloaded the bags of groceries into the kitchen. Before heading off, they fist-bumped in the foyer and kissed each other for luck.

"I HOPE you don't mind the interruption," Lily said, keeping her voice low so as to not startle the older woman. "I just had to walk over and tell you how lovely your roses are."

Mrs. Cavanaugh looked up from the thorny branch she was pruning and smiled. "That's so very kind of you to say." She dropped the shears into the pocket of her vest and slipped off her gardening gloves. "Do you garden, dear?"

Lily shook her head. "I never have, but I would like to learn one day. Maybe once we get settled in next door you can give me some tips on how to get started."

"I would be delighted to." Mrs. Cavanaugh glanced next door. "How are you and your husband liking the neighborhood so far?"

Bingo, Lily thought. *There's my way in.*

"Oh, we love it here. Everyone's been so nice and friendly, and the house is wonderful."

The older woman beamed. "Our family moved here in 1983, and my husband and I knew it was our forever home from the first night we spent in it. It's a fine place to raise a family and grow old." Mrs. Cavanaugh winked. "Trust me, I know all about the growing old part."

"Goodness, you're not old at all, Mrs. Cavanaugh." Lily placed an affectionate hand on the older woman's arm. "Just look at you out here with all these beautiful roses. And didn't I see you taking a walk the other afternoon?"

"Well, I do try."

"Can I ask you something, Mrs. Cavanaugh?"

"Sure, honey, anything you want."

Lily lowered her voice a notch. "Can you tell me anything about the neighborhood homeowners' association?"

The warm smile on Mrs. Cavanaugh's face faltered. It was just for a split second, and then the smile was back, but Lily saw the whole thing.

"Why...why do you ask?"

Lily shrugged in an effort to look casual. "I was just wondering. The other day I was going over the papers from our settlement and I noticed the fee for the homeowners' association."

Now it was the older woman's turn to lower her voice. "I really don't know much about the association. My Ronald handled all that business. What I can tell you is that, according to longtime gossip, only the original founders of the Broadview neighborhood and their offspring are allowed to be board members, and they take their duties seriously. *Very* seriously. My husband kept a printed copy of the bylaws in his den, and he knew most of it by memory."

"The whole thing sounds kind of mysterious," Lily said and smiled.

Mrs. Cavanaugh surprised her by nodding in agreement. "I suppose it is, dear. I suppose it is."

"Any idea why?"

"Not even a clue. It's just always been that way." The older woman sighed and glanced nervously at her house. "I'm feeling a little bushed now, dear. I think I'll head inside for a nap. Thank you so much for stopping by to say hello."

Lily waved after her. "Thank you for the lovely chat. Hopefully we can do it again sometime soon."

HAROLD WALKED across the street and waited on the sidewalk while Chuck Noonan finished mowing his side yard. When he cut the final strip and turned the corner into the front yard, Harold gave him a wave and gestured: *do you have a minute?*

Chuck waved back and steered in Harold's direction. It took him maybe thirty seconds to reach the sidewalk. He cut the engine, and the mower burped black exhaust and went mercifully quiet. Chuck stood up and stretched. The vinyl seat and his Grateful Dead tank-top were both soaked in sweat. "What's up, Harry?"

Harold didn't bother to correct him. To guys like Chuck Noonan, he would always be a Harry. "Couple things, actually. First, I wanted to tell you that I'm having a poker game in a week or two. Just some friends from the office. Thought you might be interested in joining us."

Chuck hopped down from the mower, grinning. "You're damn right I'm interested. Bunch of rich accountants like you, I'll make a bundle."

"I'm actually a broker. I handle—"

Chuck waved him off. "Accountant, broker, same thing." He slapped Harold on the back. "Anyway, it's damn nice of you to invite me. I'll be there with beer and chips for the whole gang."

"Thanks, I'll let you know the date once we set it."

"You said there was a couple things. What else you need?"

Harold glanced across the street and saw Lily talking to Mrs. Cavanaugh by her rose garden.

"… to Harry, Earth to Harry."

He blinked and looked back at Chuck. "Sorry about that. Caught me wool-gathering." He cleared his throat. "The other thing wasn't anything terribly important. I was just wondering what you could tell me about the homeowners' association around here."

Chuck's face clouded over. The smile disappeared and his eyes went dark. "Why you asking about the association? You in some kind of trouble?"

Harold stepped back involuntarily. "No, no, nothing like that. I was just curious."

Chuck waggled a sausage finger in Harold's face. "Bullshit. Tell me why you're asking or I'm done here."

"I…I…"

Chuck lowered his hand and glanced around the neighborhood. "You got a warning, didn't you?"

Harold was at a loss for words, caught completely off guard by his neighbor's odd reaction. He didn't know why, but he blurted the truth. "Yeah," he said, nodding, "I got a warning."

Chuck took a deep breath and lowered his head. His entire torso jiggled with the effort. "I fuckin' knew it." He looked up and the sausage finger flashed in front of Harold's face again. "Listen to me, neighbor, and listen to me good. I'm only saying this once. Read the bylaws and obey them to the word. Don't get any more warnings, but if you do, pay the fine and keep your nose clean after you do."

Chuck turned and climbed onto his riding mower. He fired the engine and it roared to life with another loud burp of black exhaust. Without a backward glance, Chuck Noonan swung a U-turn and drove away.

"SO THAT was a big fat waste of time. We're no better off now than before we started this whole thing." They were sitting across from each other at the kitchen table. Lazy afternoon sunlight slanted through the window above the sink. Springsteen's "Jungle Land" played softly from a radio sitting on the counter.

They'd taken turns recounting their side of the story, Lily first, then Harold. When they were finished, Lily had poured them each a big glass of red wine. They'd needed it.

"I wouldn't say that," Lily said. "We know a little something about the origins of the association now. And we definitely know that everyone else around here is just as weirded out about it as we are."

"Chuck Noonan was *scared*."

Lily nodded. "I think Mrs. Cavanaugh was, too. I felt bad for bringing it up."

"So what do we do next?"

Lily didn't have an answer.

TWO DAYS later, in the middle of a busy Monday morning, Lily was carrying a load of clean laundry up from the basement when she heard a noise coming from the back of the house. She paused at the top of the basement stairs and listened. After a moment, she heard it again. A stealthy scraping noise, like someone was trying to pry open the sliding glass door or one of the ground-level windows.

She placed the laundry basket on the floor and tip-toed into the kitchen to look for her cellphone. It wasn't on the counter and it wasn't on the table. She remembered then that she had left it in the basement on top of the drying table. She was just about to head downstairs when she heard the scraping sound again. Closer this time.

She grabbed a dirty pan from the sink and crept to the entryway leading into the dining room. Taking a deep breath, she steeled herself and peeked around the corner.

A dark shadow shifted in the far window and quickly disappeared.

Lily stood there, heart pounding in her chest and hands shaking. She wasn't sure if it had been a trick of the sunlight or her imagination or something else. All she knew was that one second she thought she'd seen something at the window, and the next it was gone.

She dropped the pan with a clatter and scampered back into the basement to get her phone. Once she had it tucked safely in the palm of her hand, and 911 was dialed, and her finger was resting directly above the SEND button, she carefully approached the window again.

There was no one there.

She quickly checked the other ground-level windows.

Once again, she found nothing out of the ordinary.

She was almost convinced the whole thing had just been her stupid imagination when she reached the sliding glass door that led to the back deck.

She had wiped the glass door clean not an hour earlier with Windex and a roll of paper towels. It had been spotless when she had finished.

Now, it was covered in greasy fingerprints.

Lily retreated to the kitchen and called Harold at the office.

HAROLD LAY in the dark and listened to the slow rhythm of his wife's breathing. Sleep had been a long time coming tonight.

He'd cancelled two meetings and come home early from the office that afternoon after Lily had called him in a state of panic. He'd spent the next hour searching the house and back yard until she'd felt secure they were alone and safe. They'd talked about calling the police, but ultimately decided against it. The lock to the sliding door appeared untouched, as did all of the windows. What exactly were they going to report—a glass smudger?

Harold thought about when he had pulled into the driveway earlier that afternoon. Chuck Noonan had been walking across his front lawn toward his pick-up truck. Harold had tooted the car horn and waved. Chuck had completely ignored him, gotten into his truck and driven away without any kind of acknowledgement.

What the hell is going on here? Harold thought. *Everything was so perfect just a month ago.*

Harold reached over to the nightstand for the remote control and his eyes caught on the bedroom window. He considered it for a moment, then quietly got out of bed and walked to the window. He used a finger to part the curtains and peered outside.

The yard and street were bathed in moonlight. Everything looked still and silent.

Harold stared out the window for several minutes longer and was about to return to bed when he saw it—a dark shadow shifted and then detached itself from the thick trunk of an oak tree in the front yard. And started slowly walking down the street.

Harold didn't hesitate this time. He took off out of the bedroom and down the stairs. He hurriedly unlocked the deadbolt on the front door, flung it open and ran across the lawn and out into the street. The only sound in the night was his bare feet slapping against the cool concrete. He ran to the south end of Brooks Road, where it intersected with Tupelo Avenue. Looked in both directions.

There was no one in sight.

He jogged back the way he had come, passing his house on the right, and didn't stop until he hit the four-way intersection at the end of the block.

Once again, the street and lawns were empty.

Harold started walking back to the house, trying to catch his breath, when he remembered the front door. He had left it wide open in his haste.

What if…?

He started jogging.

He rounded the bend in front of Mrs. Cavanaugh's and saw someone standing on the porch of his house. He took off sprinting.

The person frantically waved and started toward him, and Harold realized it was Lily. She had woken up and was probably confused and terrified.

He met her halfway across the lawn.

"Are you okay?" she asked, her voice shaky. "What happened?"

"Someone was watching the house. I chased after him, but he got away."

Lily smacked him hard on the shoulder. "Don't ever do that again, you hear me?"

Harold rubbed the tender spot. "Ow, that hurt."

"Promise me, you dumbass."

He put up his hands. "Okay, okay, I promise."

They started back to the house when Harold had a thought—a very bad thought. "Hold on, let me check something."

"What?"

Harold didn't answer. He hurried to the mailbox and opened it. He reached inside and pulled out a pink slip of paper.

"No fucking way," Lily said.

"FIRST OFFENSE: failure to utilize clearly marked trash receptacle for recyclable matter."

"You've got to be kidding me," Lily interrupted. "We recycle, it's just not marked!"

"See clause 23A for additional details. Amount of fine: $5,000 ..."

Lily gasped and sat up on the sofa beside Harold.

"...payable within five business days of this notice."

"We're not paying." Lily got up and started pacing back and forth across the living room. "We'll hire a lawyer if we have to, but we're not paying those bastards one penny."

"Lawyers cost money, too."

She stopped and stared at Harold, her eyes burning with anger. "So you think we should just pay it?"

"I'm not saying that. All I'm saying is that lawyers are expensive and homeowners' associations usually have deep pockets. Fighting them could be costly."

"Yeah, and how do you think they get those deep pockets? By ripping off honest people like us."

"I have an idea." Harold held up the pink slip of paper. "We're supposed to mail a check to the P.O. Box listed on the notice." He got up from the sofa and walked to the small writing desk tucked in the corner of the living room. He grabbed a pen and scribbled something along the bottom of the notice. "Why don't we mail this instead?" He handed the pink-slip to Lily.

"'We would like to discuss this matter with you as soon as possible. Please contact us at 410-679-2928. Sincerely, Harold and Lily Anderson.'" She looked up at her husband. "*This* is your plan?"

Harold shrugged. "At the very least it might buy us some time. And, who knows, maybe we can talk some sense into these people."

"They don't exactly strike me as reasonable folks."

Harold put his hand on Lily's shoulder. Gave her a reassuring squeeze. "C'mon, honey, what do we have to lose?"

THEY GOT their answer two days later in the middle of breakfast.

Harold was skimming the *Sports* section of the newspaper and Lily was pouring a glass of fresh-squeezed orange juice when someone pounded on the front door. Harold jumped in his seat. Lily squealed and dropped the half-filled glass onto the kitchen floor, where it shattered into dozens of sticky pieces.

"What the hell was that?" Harold asked, getting up from the table and heading for the front door.

Lily tip-toed around the mess on the floor. "Wait for me."

Once they reached the foyer, Harold leaned close to the door and looked out the peep-hole. He started to unlock the deadbolt and Lily stopped him. "Be careful."

"It's okay, there's no one out there." He opened the door.

The front porch was empty.

He walked out and looked in both directions. A dog was barking somewhere down the street, but there was no one in sight.

"Honey…"

Harold turned to find Lily standing behind him on the porch. She was pointing to a pink slip of paper fluttering in the morning breeze. Someone had used a hammer to nail it into the door just above the peep-hole. The carved wood around the paper was dented and scarred.

Harold ripped the note off the door and read aloud:

"'Reminder: remit payment within 72 hours of this notice or your fine will be doubled.'" He stared at the pink-slip for a moment, and then handed it to his wife. "I guess we got our answer. Check it out."

Lily read the handwriting at the bottom of the note. "*'We have nothing to talk about, Mr. Anderson. Pay the fine or suffer the consequences.'* Jesus."

"I don't think Jesus wrote that," Harold said.

Lily gave him a look and Harold lowered his head. She stepped back into the foyer and reappeared a few seconds later with the car keys in her hand.

"Where are you going?" Harold asked.

"*We're* going to the post office." She headed for her car in the driveway. "Get in."

LILY BRAKED hard at a red light and looked in the rearview mirror. "I don't think anyone is following us."

"Following us?" Harold glanced back over his shoulder. "What are you talking about?"

The light turned green and Lily hit the gas. "There was a black truck behind us for a while. I thought it might be tailing us."

"Don't you think that's a little paranoid?"

"Someone just hammered a fucking nail into our front door, Harold. I don't think much of anything qualifies as paranoid anymore."

"Slow down, honey."

Lily hit the horn and swerved around a red Jeep. The teen-aged girl behind the wheel stuck her arm out the window and flicked them the bird.

"Please slow down."

The traffic light ahead turned yellow. They had plenty of time to stop, but instead Lily accelerated through the intersection.

"And you just ran a red light."

"I've had enough of their bullshit."

Harold braced his hand against the dashboard as they changed lanes again and bounced through the next intersection. "And I think we just got air."

Two blocks later, Lily finally slowed and swung into the post office parking lot. She turned off the engine and reached into the back seat for her purse. She pulled out a black magic marker and an envelope.

"C'mon," she said, climbing out of the car.

"What are you gonna do?" Harold asked, following behind like a puppy.

"You'll see."

They walked inside to one of the tall packing tables. She uncapped the magic marker and scrawled the P.O. Box address on the front of the envelope. Then she printed along the bottom of the pink slip of paper in big capital letters:

FUCK YOU AND YOUR STUPID FINE!

&

FUCK YOU AND YOUR STUPID RULES!

"Lil, honey, you think that's a good idea?"

Lily ignored him. She folded the slip of pink paper and stuffed it inside the envelope and sealed it. She walked over to the stamp vending machine and inserted a handful of coins. The machine spat out a single stamp, which Lily licked and affixed to the top right corner of the envelope. Then, she dropped it into the mail slot and turned around and left.

They drove home in silence.

"WINE OR lemonade?"

Harold looked up from the magazine he was reading and smiled. "Lemonade, please."

"Coming right up." Lily poked her head back inside the house, leaving Harold alone on the deck.

The last couple days had been strained between the two of them and Harold didn't even fully understand why. He knew it had something to do with the damn homeowners' association, but he didn't know what he had done wrong. In the end, he'd decided to leave the final decision up to Lily: write a check or call a lawyer. She had until tomorrow to decide.

He'd been surprised and relieved earlier this evening when Lily had greeted him at the door after work with a hug and a kiss. They'd both been relaxed and talkative during dinner, and he was hopeful that they were out of their funk for good.

"Here you go." Lily walked onto the deck and handed him a tall ice-filled glass.

"Thanks, honey."

She sat down in the chair next to him and sipped from her own lemonade. "It's so pretty out here in the evenings."

"You just missed a bunch of deer down by the tree-line."

"Any babies?"

"Not that I saw."

"Last night, there was a whole family down there."

Harold lifted his glass and took a drink. "Ahh, that's good."

"What do you think about a vegetable garden next spring?"

"I think vegetable gardens are a lot of work…" He saw the disappointed look on Lily's face. "…but I think we should do it. It'll be fun."

Lily rested her head on Harold's shoulder. They sat there and watched the sun drop below the horizon, and then they went inside and straight to bed.

HAROLD FINISHED drying off and tossed his wet towel over the shower door. "Well, that was pretty spectacular, if I do say so myself."

Lily smiled at her husband through a mouthful of toothpaste.

Harold couldn't remember the last time they had started making love in bed and finished up in the shower. Things were definitely looking up. He scooted past his wife and walked naked into the bedroom.

"Honey, do you know where the Tylenol is?" Lily walked out of the bathroom wearing only her robe. It was untied at the waist and Harold could see her wet skin glistening. He felt himself stir again.

"Hang on." Harold searched the cluttered mess on top of the dresser until he found a bottle of Tylenol. He handed it to her. "Headache?"

She grimaced. "Bad one."

"Maybe it was all that screaming you just did."

"Ha ha, funny."

Lily took a bottle of water from the nightstand and swallowed three of the pills. She crawled into bed and pulled the covers up to her chest. Her head was pounding and she was starting to feel nauseous. She closed her eyes.

Harold climbed in next to her and turned off the light. "I love you, Lily."

Softly, from the darkness beside him: "Love you more, baby."

A SHORT time later, the sound of Lily vomiting woke Harold. He sat up to help her and was immediately struck by a wave of nausea and dizziness. His vision blurred and his head felt like it had been set on fire. He looked over at his wife. She was struggling to lift herself out of a puddle of vomit. Her eyes were wide and helpless. He tried to reach out to her, but his arm wouldn't work. His head slumped back onto his pillow. He lay there in agony and watched his wife die. A few minutes later, he joined her.

A LONE ambulance cruised down Brooks Road, dark and silent, like a shark prowling night waters. It backed into the driveway of 1920 and cut the engine. Two men got out and were met at the front door by a tall, dark figure. They talked for a moment, and the two men wheeled a stretcher into the house.

A short time later, they reappeared with a body on the stretcher. They loaded it into the rear of the ambulance, its back doors yawning open like a hungry mouth, and then returned to the house with the empty stretcher.

A few minutes later, they reappeared again, wheeling another body. They loaded it into the ambulance and closed the doors and drove away.

Not long after that, the front door of 1920 Brooks Road opened and the dark figure emerged. He crossed the front lawn and started slowly walking down the center of the street until the night swallowed him.

CHUCK NOONAN stood on the sidewalk the next morning and stared across the street at 1920 Brooks Road. All the windows along the front of the house were open, the curtains billowing in the July breeze.

Chuck was about to go back inside to watch the rest of *Good Morning America*—Garth Brooks was a guest today and

Chuck wanted to hear him sing his new single—when a car slowed and pulled to the curb beside him.

"Morning, Mrs. Cavanaugh. How you feeling these days?"

"Oh, fair to middling, fair to middling." She glanced at the house across the street and frowned. "It's a shame, isn't it?"

Chuck thought about poker night with a bunch of rich accountants and nodded his head. "That it is, Mrs. Cavanaugh."

"Carbon monoxide again?"

"That's the look of it."

"Wonder who will move in next?"

"Your guess is as good as mine."

"Well, have a lovely day, Mr. Noonan. Time to tend to my roses."

"You, too. Don't stay out in this sun for too long."

Mrs. Cavanaugh waved goodbye and drove away. Chuck Noonan watched her pull into her driveway, and then headed back inside, hoping he hadn't missed Garth Brooks.

THE SCULPTOR

"How's it going, Alex?"

"Don't ask, Marcus, you don't want to know. Give me the usual."

"Still can't work?" Marcus said as he scooped ice into a glass and poured the bourbon.

Alex shook his head. "Nine months."

He lifted the glass to his lips, intending to sip. Instead, he finished it off in a couple of swallows and placed the glass back on the bar. "Keep 'em coming."

It was a dark little hotel bar called the Black Diamond in Alex's neighborhood, with shiny mahogany and backlit hanging plants. Not especially stylish, but comfortable and quiet. He loathed the sound of people having fun when he was miserable. Twinkling piano music came from the corner, where a lovely Asian woman was seated at the old piano.

"She's new," Alex said. "It's nice. I like it."

Marcus smiled. "She plays a lot of the old stuff I love, she's good, and I told her she's welcome here anytime." He leaned his hands on the bar, arms spread, a rotund black man with a bald crown and a lot of salt in his pepper fringe. "Sorry about the work, man. Must be tough to run out of ideas."

"No, it's not that." He knocked back another drink and Marcus poured. "The ideas are still there, the urge is — no, the *need* to sculpt is still there. But I've…I don't know, somehow I've lost my connection to it, or something. But it's still in there, squirming and clawing. Trying to get out." He lifted the glass. "That's why this has become such a good friend." He took a sip.

Marcus's eyes darkened with worry. "You sure you're okay? You know, I don't close tonight. You slow down on that drinking, we can go out when I get off, have a few together."

He shook his head, then finished the drink. "I wouldn't do that to you, Marcus. I'm not good company for anybody tonight. I'm better off alone."

"Well, if you change your mind, you've got my number."

Alex tapped a finger on the edge of the glass. "Pour me another."

ALEX JERKED awake and sat up clumsily in bed, in the dark, with the feeling that thick tentacles were wrapped around his legs. He was merely tangled in the covers and a little sweaty, even though it was a chilly night. He had been awakened by a noise.

It was a scratching sound, but it stopped the moment he sat up, if it had been there at all. He listened to the night's silence, wondering if he had dreamed it. It was probably Sophie, his Siamese cat. She often had bursts of energy at night and ran through the place as if pursued. He lay back and rested his head on the pillow. He had been quite drunk when he'd gone to bed earlier that night, so drunk he couldn't remember going to bed at all, and his head was still thick, his stomach still queasy.

The sound came again, louder this time, a harsh scraping sound, as if something heavy were being moved in increments over the floor. Something much heavier than Sophie. It came from the direction of his studio down the hall.

Alex rose up again, extracted his legs from the clutching covers, and sat on the edge of the bed. Although he normally slept in the nude, he found he was still wearing his boxers.

He lived in an ancient, remodeled warehouse that consisted of four separate rooms and an enormous open studio space. It was cold and drafty that night, so he stood, took his robe from a chair beside the nightstand, and slipped it on as he stepped into a pair of old flip-flops. He swayed for a moment and almost sat on the bed again because he was still drunk and not too steady on his feet. Instead, he headed for the door and stopped when he heard the sound again.

Fully awake now, the fact that someone else was in the house cut through his alcoholic haze like a razor and made him feel an inner chill unrelated to the room's temperature. He turned back to the nightstand, opened the top drawer, and removed the loaded .38 pistol he kept there.

He opened the bedroom door, leaned out, and looked in both directions. The hall was empty. The soft light he always left on over the stove fell through the open kitchen doorway. He saw no one, no sign of anyone. Stepping out of the doorway, he turned left and started toward the closed studio door at the end of the hall, his flip-flops slapping softly against his heels as he walked. Drunkenness gone now, vaporized by a sudden surge of fear, Alex felt hyper-alert. A bead of sweat trickled down his temple and his heartbeat increased as the door of the studio grew larger in his view.

The terrible scraping noise came again and Alex froze, fist clenched on the butt of the gun.

Losing my reason for living wasn't enough, he thought. *I needed a home invasion to top it all off. Maybe he's armed and he'll end it for me, get the whole damned thing over with.*

He started forward again.

TWO WEEKS after his thirty-second birthday, Alexander Lynn Cason made the jump from the ripped-bluejeans, long-haired, unemployed freak world of sidewalk sculptors to the highly respected and deliriously lucrative world of the *artiste*. His award-winning black-granite statue of two Vietnam infantry grunts lifting a wounded comrade to the outstretched arms of a Huey helicopter medic had allowed his foot to slip firmly in between the success threshold and the constantly slamming door of rejection.

More significant work followed, and before he had time to catch his breath, he was being featured in dozens of art publications and was even covered by pieces in *Time* and *Newsweek*.

Four years later, in a festive, televised ceremony in the nation's capital, Alex celebrated the pinnacle of his new career when, during the traditional Fourth of July ceremony, his eighteen-foot statue of George Washington was unveiled in front of the Washington Monument, and Alex captured the heart of a patriotic America.

The big-ticket commissions continued to pour in and he was able to choose his work more selectively. Over the next four years, he worked just twice — a bust for a Harvard Law School library and an eccentric billionaire's life-size sculpture of George Armstrong Custer making his last stand at the Little Bighorn, both of which earned him enough money to focus on personal projects in his home studio for a while. These creations were not for sale and were rarely even shown to the public. They simply kept his skills, vision, and soul happy and content.

Until nine months ago, when the troubles began.

Initially, he began having problems concentrating on his work. His usually sharp and clear vision felt blurred and sluggish. Then, slowly, his ability to sculpt abandoned him a piece at a time. It was like parts of his body falling off. He was quickly, systematically stripped of the skills that allowed him to create and the inspiration that brought those skills to life. He was suddenly a novice once again, all of his experience vanished as if it had never been, replaced by feelings of self-doubt and a sense of crippling inadequacy.

At first, he thought a part of him had died, but that was not accurate. As he had explained to Marcus, his favorite bartender, the thing inside of him that was released when he created something special was still there, still alive and squirming. But it was trapped. Somewhere deep inside him, it was bound and writhing and suffocating, in a tight cocoon.

Alex told no one. He had no family and no close friends, only acquaintances. Marcus was the closest thing he had to a real friend. Alex had learned at an early age not to trust easily—from his parents. They were textbook alcoholics, never physically abusive, but always neglectful. The three words he remembered most clearly from his childhood were not "I love you." Instead, they were a cold and dismissive: "Not my problem."

So, he had told no one of his troubles. He had even kept it from his agent and his manager and let all calls go to voicemail. After a while, he stopped checking his messages and email, and he never answered his door. He was completely alone with his suffering.

The previous evening, he had tried one final time to find his muse and create something. *Anything.* For two hours, he'd worked with a block of clay, searching for the *thing* hidden inside, waiting for the spark of inspiration that would find it. The inspiration did not come and the block of clay yielded nothing.

And yet, inside of Alex, it still squirmed.

Frustrated, he had gone for a walk through the park, along the canal, then hit some bars on the way home, an activity he had been engaging in with increasing frequency over the past six weeks. His last memory before being awakened in bed was of one of those bars. He could not even remember which one it was. Only that he had vomited in a toilet stall in a filthy bathroom.

He wanted—*needed*—to sedate that thing inside him, make it stop writhing, but before he could accomplish that, he had sedated himself into a blackout. It had not been the first time and he feared it would not be the last. His work had been his life, but that life seemed to be over now. Drinking helped to numb the pain of his loss. Drinking helped him forget.

ALEX TURNED the knob, pushed the door open, and looked into the silent, mineshaft-black darkness of his studio. The gun felt heavy in his right hand as he aimed it into the darkness. He reached his left hand over it, found the two light switches just inside, and flipped them up.

The sudden brightness blinded him, and he shielded his eyes with his forearm. After taking a moment to adjust, he lowered his arm and saw it. The gun forgotten at the end of his suddenly limp arm, he whispered, "What the hell?"

Centered in the middle of his studio was an enormous block of rough, uncut granite of exquisite quality. He estimated it was ten feet tall, eight feet wide.

He lowered his eyes to the rough grooves in the wood floor forming a path that extended three feet from the granite, then stopped. It was as if the slab had been lowered onto the floor from above, or had somehow risen up through the floor from below, then had been pushed or dragged for three feet to the center of the studio.

That was the sound he had heard. But how had the slab been moved? And by whom? It would have to have been a *team* of people with the appropriate equipment. He looked around the room slowly. There were no hiding places in his studio; it was a vast, open space, quite well-lit, and there was no one in it.

Something brushed softly against his bare calves and he reflexively leaped forward into the studio with a startled yelp. He spun around to see Sophie sitting in the doorway cleaning her face after a midnight snack. She stood and stared at him from the doorway for a moment, then turned and padded back down the hall, her tail a bouncing question mark.

Alex turned to the enormous block of granite — he was closer to it, now — as frantic warnings tumbled through his head. *Get out of here, leave, just turn around and go, because something's wrong here, something's very wrong.* Closing his eyes tightly, he thought, *I'm still drunk. That's all. This isn't happening.*

When he opened his eyes, the stone was still there. He walked closer, reached out a trembling hand to touch it, and then abruptly pulled it back. *Not yet,* he thought without knowing why.

Alex took a few more steps until he was only inches from the stone. Narrowing his eyes slightly, he closely examined the surface. It was perfect, the finest granite he had ever seen. He yearned to touch it. But still, he did not.

How did it get here? And why?

He stepped around the slab and walked to the row of windows along the wall beyond. He raised the blinds on one of them and looked out into the night, trying to understand the presence of the enormous block of granite. There was no one outside, the narrow street which the window looked upon was deserted, with only the dim glow of a single streetlight cutting through the darkness.

Turning away from the window, he began to pace, eyes never leaving the block of stone. Minutes passed. An alien, unfamiliar sensation rose slowly within him. Sweat rose on his forehead and upper lip in tiny glistening gems. His body trembled as if he had come down with a fever, and his pacing slowed to a stop as he began to feel unsteady on his feet. He wondered vaguely if he was getting sick.

He wanted to touch the stone, feel it against his skin. He already could feel the rough edges against his palms in his mind. He wanted to hammer away at it, cut into it. The warning voice came again: *No, don't do it, get out of the studio, lock it, and have someone come haul it off!* But he was distracted by the sudden awareness of his own heart beating, of his blood rushing through his veins.

He hurried to one of his work tables, placed the gun on it, and flung open a wide drawer. Inside were his hammers and chisels. Quickly, before he could change his mind, he snatched up one of each and turned back to the granite.

It stood there, a great monolith of pale stone. Waiting for him.

He took a step forward, then stopped, and turned back to the work table. Among the tools and jars, he spotted a half-full pint of bourbon that he had left there recently. He put his tools down, picked up the bottle, unscrewed the cap, and took several long, sloppy gulps, nearly emptying it before placing it back onto the table.

He wiped his lips with the back of his hand and approached the block of stone, putting both tools in his left hand. When he reached out this time, he did not pull back. Instead, he softly placed his right palm against the rock. Immediately, he felt a surge of warm energy rush from the stone into his hand and throughout the rest of his body, a tingling that traveled through his arms, down his torso, and into his genitals. As his penis swelled, his mind was hit by a raging storm of ideas and emotions that swirled and coalesced, then moved with an inaudible hum downward through his arms and into his hands, where it burned for release. Something else in him swelled, as well, something at his very center. The part of him that was truly Alex experienced something familiar, something that happened often when he was working and being creative: the growing awareness of something bigger than himself that was coming *from* himself.

His hand slowly caressed the granite, as if the rough, hard surface were the velvety skin of a forbidden lover. He closed his eyes and felt the stone throughout his entire body, with all of his nerves.

The room began to spin, slowly at first, then faster. When he opened his eyes, it was still spinning. Everything in the room

— the row of windows, the overhead lights, the tables — melted together into a swirling, kaleidoscopic blur around him. Only his hand and the stone remained stationary before him.

Run! Now! Before it's too late!

He switched the hammer to his right hand, placed the tip of the chisel against the granite, and did not move for a while. Then he brought the hammer down and a jagged chunk dropped to the floor with a thud. He struck again and another piece of stone fell away.

Soon, he was hammering at a feverish pace, only vaguely aware of his blurry surroundings as they spun around him, as if in a trance, locked away in some deep part of his mind with nothing more than a narrow tunnel of vision focused on the stone and chisel. As the tunnel gradually narrowed and everything darkened, it occurred to him that it was just like the old days, back when he worked tirelessly, creating intensely. But that was not true. It was not like the old days. It was better. It had never been so easy.

ALEX WOKE on the floor in his underwear, shivering in the cold, gray, morning light shining through the one window with raised blinds. He lay amid powdery dust and chunks of chipped stone, head pounding, feeling like he had a knife buried to the hilt in his neck.

He groaned as he lifted himself groggily off the floor onto his hands and knees. He turned his head and squinted at the digital clock on one of the tables. It was 1:11 in the afternoon. That meant he had been lying on the studio floor for — he did not know when he had fallen asleep, only that it had been dark. He could not remember falling asleep or what he was doing at the time. Or anything else, for that matter.

He groaned and muttered curses as he struggled to his feet, punished by his aching muscles for every movement. As he pushed himself to his feet, a sharp, stabbing in his right hand almost made him fall to the floor again. Once standing, he examined his hand and found that the end of his thumb was purple and swollen and had blood caked around the nail. In the meaty pad of his thumb there was a small, red pinprick.

Alex tried to remember injuring his thumb, but as before, he could remember nothing about what he had been doing before going to sleep. Looking down at his thumb, he saw the rubble of sculpting all around his feet. Tossed beyond it was his robe in a pile on the floor.

Then he remembered.

He turned around and faced the granite, looked at what he had done, and staggered backward, muttering, "Jesus Christ." He stepped back further, gawking at his work with a slack jaw and wide eyes.

I couldn't have done this. Not this much detail. Not with just a hammer and chisel. Not in one night.

"Impossible," he whispered.

But there was no other explanation. He looked around on the floor and spotted the hammer and chisel lying among ash-colored dust and chunks of stone. He found his flip-flops nearby and slipped his feet into them, then turned to the granite again.

Although he had no memory of it, Alex somehow had carved the lower portion of the slab. Two thick, powerful legs had been chiseled out of the granite from just below the waist to the ankles. He had finished neither the body from the waist up nor the feet, nor the gap between the legs. Hanging on each side of the legs was the lower half of a muscular arm. But the limbs were not those of a human being.

The arms and legs were covered with tiny scales that appeared to come to sharp points. Each scale had been carefully chiseled out of the stone. The scales gave way to a smoother texture around the wrist and on the hands — if they could be called hands. They more closely resembled claws, with seven long, slender fingers from which curved deadly talons.

Alex spotted a crimson smear on one of the pale talons and leaned close to inspect it. *That's what I cut myself on last night,* he thought, looking down at his injured thumb.

He crouched to look at the legs. They were like tree trunks, with smaller scales than the arms. They stopped at the ankles and ended in the base of the block of granite.

Standing unsteadily, he rubbed the back of his aching neck and surveyed his work. While he was glad that the muse had returned to him last night, something about it did not sit right with him. He still did not know where the granite had come from.

As he turned, he spotted the pint of bourbon on the table. *Aha*, he thought as he headed for the shower. *That stuff really kicked my ass last night.*

AFTER A long, hot shower, some coffee, a hard-boiled egg, and half of an English muffin, Alex returned to the studio feeling refreshed by the cleansing and invigorated by last night's accomplishment. He turned on some Prokofiev and settled into his work environment, looking forward to experiencing the same fervor that obviously had driven him last night.

But when he picked up his hammer and chisel, they felt foreign in his hands, useless objects with which he had no connection. He placed the chisel against the stone and poised his hammer to fall, but he felt nothing. The urge to strike with the hammer, penetrate the stone, and cut and shape it into something it was not before, was simply not there. It felt like trying to eat when he was not hungry. The need was absent, and it was not, he had found, something that he could summon on command. Not anymore.

His hands fell to his sides, loosely clutching the useless tools. Head slumped forward, he looked down at his work from the previous night and yearned to do more. But he knew it was not going to happen now.

He left the studio, put on his coat, and went walking. He strolled along the canal, through the park, bought a bag of bread crusts to feed the ducks. As he left the park a short time later, he glanced across the street at the old hotel that housed the Black Diamond, his favorite little bar, where Marcus poured the drinks and now a woman made pleasant music on the piano. Passing the hotel as he proceeded down the street, he found himself in the crosswalk at the end of the block, and then he walked back the other way on the opposite side of the street.

He decided he would try to work again that night. When it was dark. Maybe that would help. And maybe a few drinks would help, too. They certainly had not slowed him down last night. He still couldn't believe what he had accomplished in one night.

He passed the entrance to the Sherman Hotel and went directly through the door to the Black Diamond and headed for the bar.

"Alex," Marcus nodded as he approached. "The usual?"

"The usual." He perched himself on a stool, took a handful of beer nuts from the bowl on the bar. "No music?"

"She comes in around five. Everything okay?"

"Yeah. Why?"

Marcus poured. "You don't mind my saying, you look like hell."

"Oh, yeah. That."

"Hung over from last night?"

"Partly that, partly exhaustion. I was up until...well, all night long, I guess. Working."

"Hey, congrats, man, you're getting some work done."

"More than that. The work is…I don't know, I woke up in the studio and—"

"You slept in your studio?"

"Well, I don't know if I curled up on the floor or just passed out, but that's where I woke up. And when I saw what I'd done…how *much* I'd done…in just one night…"

"What was it?"

Frowning down at the glass of amber, he shrugged. "I…I'm not sure. It's not done yet." He took a swallow of his drink.

Marcus stared at him for a moment, then asked, "You sure you're okay?"

"Yeah, sure. Why'd you ask again?"

"Because you look kind of, I don't know…*lost*. Like some abandoned kid, or something, I don't know."

Alex nodded slowly. "Funny you should say that. That's exactly how I feel when I can't work."

HE STOPPED at a few bars on the walk home, the same bars he had visited the previous night before returning to his studio and becoming an artist again. Maybe he could recapture it, whatever *it* was, and make some progress on that…thing.

Throughout his walk, while talking to Marcus, and drinking in bars, his mind kept returning to what he had created, to those sharp scales and enormous, seven-fingered hands with their menacing talons. It had not been derived from any of the images that had been occupying his mind as possible projects. It did not look like anything that had emerged from his imagination. People who knew his work probably would guess that it was not his at all.

And yet, he had sculpted it.

Alex walked home slowly because a part of him did not want to see the unfinished sculpture again.

It's not too late! Don't go back! Go to a hotel, somewhere, anywhere. But don't go back home.

And yet, his hands were twitching to get back to work.

THE BLINDS on the window at the far end of the row were still up and the rectangle in the studio wall framed a segment of the night. The studio was silent until Alex, who lay on his side with his body curled in a childlike posture around the base of the granite, awoke with a scream and scrambled to his feet. He stumbled around for a moment before he realized where he was. He went to the window and stared out at the darkness, thinking, at first, that it was still night. But a narrow strip of murky light began to glow in the eastern sky. Dawn was coming. He turned around and looked at his work, walked slowly toward it, and stopped a few feet in front of it, head tilted back. What he saw twisted something inside his gut.

The creature had been fully revealed and towered over Alex. His ladder leaned against one side of it. He had no memory of moving the ladder or climbing it, but obviously he had because there it was, and obviously he had been busy because there the creature stood, not quite complete yet — for one thing, its feet remained trapped inside the uncarved base of the stone — but exposed.

Two thick horns, like the horns of a great ram, curled from the sides of its head, and a short, squat horn sprouted from each of its broad, muscular shoulders. The creature seemed to be pulling its shoulders back, elbows bent at its sides, enormous, claw-like hands open as if ready to reach out. Its head was tilted downward so that the eyes, which seemed to be smiling, looked directly at Alex. Its nose was flat and stubby, with exposed nostrils above its most terrifying feature — an impossibly wide, lipless mouth open just enough to reveal the many jagged, protuberant fangs inside, and curled enough to form a subtle, cold smirk.

It was the best work he had ever done, and might very well turn out to be the finest work of his lifetime. But he had no memory of doing it, only aching muscles in his arms, back, and legs. The thing chilled his blood.

Alex turned and headed for the door to get something to drink and perhaps wash his face to clear his head, when he heard a sound that made him stop and listen.

Grinding. The gritty sound of stones grinding together.

He turned and made a whimpering sound when he saw that the statue's head had turned toward him. It was still watching him. A deep moan worked its way out of him.

The creature cocked its head as it stared at him and the movement left shimmering trails, lingering images of the head that blurred together as it moved. It reminded Alex of the time he had tried acid in college, but there was no comfort in that because he knew he was not on acid now, just as he knew that he had created that thing with his own hands.

The grinding sound continued as the creature moved its jaw back and forth, trying it out, experimenting, as the large, reptilian eyes blinked, as the scoop-like hands flexed their long fingers. Then it turned to him again and began moving its mouth as if speaking, the lipless rims touching briefly, the black tongue making quick movements of articulation.

Alex made a hoarse sound of protest because he did not want to see what he was seeing, and he *certainly* did not want the thing to speak.

He heard nothing. But he *felt* things. He had thoughts that were not his own and felt the need to get Sophie. It was, quite suddenly, the most important thing in the world to him, finding Sophie, holding her to him.

The statue was forgotten instantly as he turned and hurried out of the studio and down the hall, calling the cat's name and making kissing sounds with his lips. He ducked into the bathroom, but the cat was not there. Nor was she in the kitchen, where her food and water bowls were kept. He found her curled up on his bed asleep.

"There you are, Sophie," he said as he scooped her up in his arms and held her close. She lifted her head and blinked her sleepy eyes as he carried her back down the hall. He felt immensely relieved to have found her as he carried her into the studio, stroking her as he spoke quiet nonsense until she was plucked away from him so quickly that she did not have a chance to make a sound.

Alex cried out in shock and lifted his head to see the creature bite down on the Siamese cat. He felt warm blood spatter his face.

He turned away, sickened, and as he began to walk in a frantic, confused circle in the studio, he found he could not stop screaming.

THE FOLLOWING day, Alex found himself walking briskly and with purpose along the canal, the diamond patterns in the chain-link fence along the waterway flying by him in a blur. It was a gray, chilly day and it felt like rain. There was someplace he needed to be. He had no idea where, only that it was important that he get there. As he walked, he took his phone from his pocket and checked the time. Eight minutes before three.

He suddenly cut to the right, leaving the sidewalk to cross Canal Street, then he started down Chester Street, which joined Canal at a T intersection. On the first block, he passed a convenience store, a strip mall, and an apartment complex, and on the next he passed a few small homes with front lawns and driveways. The moment he saw the school up ahead, he knew it was his destination.

The Chester Street School was a red brick building with a narrow strip of lawn along the sidewalk in front and an American flag on a pole at the entrance to the path that led to front steps. As he approached, he saw no children in front of the school and knew he would have to wait a few minutes, and with that knowledge came the startling shock of realization: *It had sent him to get a child.*

Yesterday, it had made him scour the neighborhood for cats and small dogs. The creature had enjoyed Sophie and wanted more of the same. But after a day of those treats, it wanted something bigger. Something better.

Ever since it had awakened, it had been telling Alex to finish it. The words were not spoken aloud. The creature's abominable mouth moved in that blurry, acid-trip way and the words formed inside Alex's head in his own voice.

"Finish me, Alex. Finish me now."

There was plenty of detail work left to do, enough to keep him busy on the creature between feedings. Enough to keep it silent. But the feet remained unfinished, still locked in the solid, flat base of granite block. When it told him to finish, Alex knew it was referring to its feet. It wanted to walk. To be free.

What have I done? Alex thought as he stood staring at the school across the street. *What have I created?*

There was a fenced-in playground beside the school, empty now, the monkey bars and jungle gym and sliding board standing like the skeletal remains of exotic creatures in the gray light.

He checked his phone again. The school bell would ring in four minutes. A moment later, the double doors in front would open and swarms of children would spill down the steps and over the front path.

Alex stepped off the sidewalk to cross the street, thinking, *I can't do this, I can't, there's no way.* But he moved forward, unable to stop himself. No, *afraid* to stop himself. If he tried to walk away, would the creature know? Did it have some kind of connection with him even five blocks away? And, if so, what would it do if he tried to resist? He was afraid to find out.

On the sidewalk, he strolled along the fence in front of the school trying to appear no different than any other pedestrian. But inside he felt increasingly sick now that he understood why he was there.

Was this now his life? Fetching food for that thing? Keeping busy with touch-ups to avoid giving it feet so it couldn't walk free? Acting on its every whim?

The muted pealing of a bell came from the school.

The dogs and cats had been bad enough. Especially Sophie. Poor Sophie. He missed her so much.

You're going insane.

Alex kept his eyes on the double doors at the school's entrance.

Stop it now while you still can. Before you're a gibbering maniac.

The doors opened and children poured out of the building, down the broad steps.

Before you become a killer.

The children hurried down the path toward the sidewalk. *Go! Now! Run!*

With a cry of panic lodged in his throat, Alex turned and ran. He braced himself for an explosion of the creature's anger inside his head, but it didn't come. Maybe he was too far away. Maybe the connection didn't extend very far, maybe not even beyond the studio.

The Black Diamond was just a few blocks over. He wondered if Marcus would be there at such an early hour.

Alex ran faster as it began to rain.

HE ENTERED the Black Diamond, soaking wet, as Marcus wiped down the bar. When Marcus looked up and saw Alex hurrying toward him, out of breath, water dripping from his hair and down his face, he stopped wiping and said, "What the hell happened to you?"

Alex bumped into the bar and nearly knocked over one of the stools as he panted for breath.

"Calm down, take a seat," Marcus said.

He perched himself unsteadily on a stool with both arms resting on the bar. Suddenly overcome with emotion, he struggled not to cry.

"You're not gonna believe me, Marcus," he said. "You'll think I'm crazy."

"Let me get you a drink."

He put a glass of bourbon in front of Alex, who picked it up with a trembling hand and gulped it down. He thumped the glass onto the bar and stared at it a moment, thinking. Marcus would never believe what he had to say. Alex needed to *show* it to him.

"You have to come with me," he said.

"What? Where?"

"You've got to come to my place. I'll show you. If I tell you, you're gonna think I've lost my mind."

"I just got here and started my shift," Marcus said. "I can't take off now."

"Look, you've got to, because…because…"

His shoulders began shaking with sobs before he could get it under control and he lowered his head.

"Jesus, Alex, what's going on?"

He took a deep, steadying breath and lifted his head, looked at Marcus. "You're the closest thing I've got to a real friend in this town. You've got to help me. And to do that, you've got to come to the studio and see what…what I've done."

Marcus nodded slowly. "Okay…yeah…look, I'll ask Jerry to come out of the office and work the bar for an hour and we'll take off. Okay?"

Alex nodded and wiped the tears from his face.

ALEX DID not speak on the way to his place because he knew how crazy everything would sound. Marcus had an umbrella, but Alex hardly noticed the rain as he walked, then jogged, then walked again, while Marcus struggled to keep up.

Once inside, he took Marcus to the kitchen, where Alex removed his dripping coat and hung it on the back of a chair. Marcus did the same, and they sat at the table to catch their breath from the walk.

"Earlier in the week, I heard a sound in the middle of the night," Alex said. "At first, I thought it was the cat. But it turned out to be a huge block of granite in my studio. It wasn't there when I'd gone to bed, but it was there in the middle of the night all of a sudden, out of nowhere."

"Someone brought a block of granite — "

"Not just a block. It's at least ten feet high. It's huge."

"Then it must weigh — but where did it come from?"

"I don't know."

"You're saying someone brought it into your studio and just left it there? For no reason? That's crazy."

"See what I mean? Well, I went to work on it. The thing I — the *piece* that I did, it's…it's in there now. That's what I want to show you."

"Okay. Then why are we sitting in the kitchen?"

Alex leaned toward him and whispered, "Because I'm afraid of it."

Marcus looked at him silently for a moment, his face tense with concern. Then he said, "If I go in there with you, will you promise me something?"

"What?"

"When we're done in there, if I think you need to get some help — I'm just saying, you know, if I think you need to see a doctor, something like that — you'll do it. Deal?"

Alex was surprised by the flush of embarrassment he felt in his face as he nodded. "Yeah, I know, like I said, you'd think I was crazy if I told you everything first." He stood. "Let me show you."

They went down the hall to the closed door of the studio. As he unlocked it, Alex said, "One thing, and it's very important." He turned to look over his shoulder at Marcus. "If I say run, you run. Understand? You just get the hell out of here as fast as you can. Do you hear me?"

Keeping his face neutral, Marcus nodded.

Once in the studio, Alex heard Marcus gasp when he saw it.

The enormous figure stood in the original position in which Alex had carved it, but now the front of the pale creature was drenched in a crimson apron of blood that cascaded down from the chin and over the front of the body, dribbling in streams down the neck and throat, covering the belly and thighs. The tremendous hands were splashed with it, as was the base in which the creature's feet were still trapped.

"Jesus Christ, Alex, what have you done?"

"I told you, I went to work on the granite and—"

"No, the blood, all this *blood*."

"Oh, yeah. That. That's from the animals."

Marcus turned to him. "Animals?"

"Cats, small dogs. That's what I was afraid to tell you. See, this thing—"

Marcus squinted at him as if Alex suddenly had gone out of focus. "You've been sacrificing animals to this—"

"No, no, *no*. I *fed* them to him. I mean, he made me. He sent me out to get them. He…I don't know how…he gets inside my head and makes me…he makes me do things."

No longer squinting, Marcus looked hard at Alex as he slowly took a step backward, then another. "You're serious about this, Alex?"

"Yes! I'm telling you, it had me hunting for children earlier today. It wanted me to bring it a *child*. But I went to you instead. I didn't know what else to do."

Taking another step back, Marcus said, "You have to get help, Alex. Okay? You need to see somebody right away. You promised me you would, right?"

"Marcus, you've got to believe me. This thing, it's, I don't know, it's a—"

"Listen to me, Alex. This thing?" He reached up and placed a hand on the creature's stone arm. "It's a statue. That's all. It can't—"

Marcus screamed as he was lifted off the floor, but by then, it was too late. The creature had wrapped its enormous paw around Marcus's neck and lifted him to its widening mouth. It bit into Marcus's throat and neck as if it were biting into a ripe apple.

Alex whimpered as Marcus's legs kicked and jittered. He slapped his hands over his eyes, but still heard the jagged, gargling screams, so he stuffed his hands over his ears and clenched his eyes shut. His head filled with the sound of his own sobs.

LATER, ONCE the studio was silent except for the slow, gentle dripping of blood from the statue, Alex picked up his hammer and chisel. He did not want to think about what he was doing because he was afraid he would think himself out of doing it, and he *had* to do it.

He imagined living the rest of his life the way he had lived the last few days and knew that he would rather die. If he had the courage to end it himself, he would, but he did not believe himself capable of it. Looking at the bloody claws at the end of his sculpture's muscular, scaly arms, he suspected it would not be a problem for the creature.

The studio reeked of blood and human waste, and Alex used his foot to nudge aside the remaining pieces of his friend, Marcus. They left gory smears on the floor. He crouched before the statue and placed the tip of the chisel against the granite base.

"You're finishing me." It was Alex's own voice inside his head, but they were the creature's words.

"Yes," he said out loud.

"You're freeing me."

"Yes."

"Are you afraid?"

"No. Yes. I am. Of course I am. But I can't live like this."

The room began to spin in a blur all around him, but his eyes remained focused on the rock. The sounds of the hammer striking the chisel and the chisel cutting into the stone filled his head until they were so loud they would have drowned out the creature if it had spoken. But it remained silent as Alex worked, waiting patiently for its freedom. His focus became so intense that everything rushed together in the center of his field of vision and he was swallowed by blackness.

HE ROSE slowly from the blackness, then emerged like a corpse bobbing to the surface of a still lake. Before opening his eyes, he wondered if he was still alive.

He was, once again, lying face-down on the cold floor of his studio, muscles aching. It was colder than usual, bitingly cold. Pushing himself slowly to his knees, he wondered *why* he was still alive and suspected he had lost consciousness before finishing the job. He stood, swayed dizzily for a bit, then turned around.

The statue was gone.

He quickly looked all around the studio and his eyes fell on the great hole in the wall that had once been the last window in the row, the one with the blinds up. It was gone, as was most of the window next to it, and cold night air filled the studio.

The creature had let him live and had, like some kind of phantom, disappeared into the night.

But it might come back.

That thought quickly cleared up the grogginess in his head and he left the studio, hurried down the hall, went into his bedroom, and flipped on the light. He pulled a large suitcase from the closet, flopped it onto the bed, and opened it. He quickly rummaged through his drawers and closet, stuffing clothes into the suitcase.

When it was full, he forced the suitcase closed, took all the money from his wall safe, grabbed his coat in the kitchen on the way out, and left.

Outside, he walked. He had no idea where he was going, only that he was going *away*. If it came back, he would not be there.

What if it doesn't come back?

Not my problem.

He picked up his pace.

What if it stays out there? You know what it's doing.

Not my problem.

You know *it's hurting people. Killing them. Shedding their blood. Bathing in it.*

At the next corner, he stopped and watched for a cab, started waving at the first one he saw. He focused on the three words, like a mantra.

Not my problem. Not my problem. Not my problem.

(written with Ray Garton)

MURDER HOUSE

Screenplay by

Richard Chizmar & Billy Chizmar

FADE IN:

1   INT. CAR - MOVING - NIGHT   1

Two people drive down a dark, isolated road. JANE is the
driver. RICK is her passenger.

>   RICK
>   We really doing this?

>   JANE
>   You're damn right we are. It's a
>   once in a lifetime opportunity.

The CAR slows and we see a large FARMHOUSE looming in the
darkness on the right side of the road.

Jane exhales.

>   JANE
>   There it is. Murder House.

>   RICK
>   I don't know about this.

CUT TO:

2   EXT. FRONT PORCH - NIGHT   2

We watch as the car slows and swings into the driveway.

3   INT. CAR - NIGHT   3

The car drifts past the front porch - and a DARK FIGURE
emerges from the shadows.

>   RICK
>   (startled)
>   Jesus Christ.

Jane laughs. This whole thing is obviously her idea.

>   RICK
>   Who's this guy again?

Jane parks behind a cool CLASSIC CAR and turns off the
engine.

>   JANE
>   The real estate agent's son. Come
>   on.

She grabs a VIDEO CAMERA from the back seat and gets out. Rick follows her out...

4   EXT. DRIVEWAY - NIGHT   4

...and SLAMS the car door. Jane gives him a look and leads the way.

As they approach the porch, the car's headlights blink out.

                         CRAIG
                   (from the shadows on the
                    porch)
                You're late.

                         JANE
                Yeah, sorry 'bout that. Had to stop
                for gas. Craig, this is Rick.

Craig ignores the introduction.

                         CRAIG
                You bring the money?

Jane pulls an ENVELOPE from her back pocket.

                         JANE
                Right here.

She hands it over. Craig opens the envelope and slowly counts the BILLS. Stuffs it into his pant's pocket and comes back out with a KEY RING.

Starts to unlock the door.

                         CRAIG
                You've got two hours.

He JIGGLES the DOORKNOB a few times, and then really leans into it.

The door finally SCREECHES open.

He holds it for them. Jane and Rick step inside...

5   INT. FOYER - NIGHT   5

...and turn around to look at Craig, who remains on the porch, SILHOUETTED in the doorway.

3.

                    CRAIG
          Make sure you lock up when you're
          done.

                    RICK
          You're not coming with us?

                    CRAIG
          That wasn't part of the deal.

Now it's Rick's turn to give Jane a look.

                    CRAIG
          I'll drive by in a couple hours.
          Your car better be gone.

Before either of them can reply, he closes the door in their
faces.

Rick turns on his FLASHLIGHT. Shines it on his face.

                    RICK
          Super nice guy. Really glad I got a
          chance to meet him.

                    JANE
          He's all right. Nervous, that's
          all.

                    RICK
               (looking around)
          That makes two of us.

Rick walks over and tries a LIGHT SWITCH. Nothing.

                    RICK
          Of course.

                    JANE
          The house has been on the market
          for three years. What did you
          expect?

Jane unslings the VIDEO CAMERA from over her shoulder and
turns it on.

WE IMMEDIATELY SEE HER NIGHT-VISION POV AS SHE BEGINS TO
SLOWLY PAN AROUND THE FOYER AND THEN UP AND DOWN THE WINDING
STAIRCASE.

The house is empty. No furniture. No paintings on the wall.
Empty and silent.

4.

                    JANE (O.S.)
          My name is Jane Sharretts.

GOES CLOSE ON RICK'S FACE

                    JANE (O.S.)
          The wide-eyed gentleman
          accompanying me tonight is Rick
          Thompson. It's a few minutes past
          midnight on March 9, 1978, and we
          are standing just inside the
          doorway of 1930 Hanson Road,
          otherwise known as the infamous
          Murder House.

Jane clicks off the camera and smiles.

CUT AWAY FROM CAMERA POV

                    JANE
          This is going to be bitchin.

                    RICK
          I don't know about this.

                    JANE
          Stop being such a pussy.

                    RICK
          I'm not a pussy.

                    JANE
          Then stop being such a buzzkill.
          We're gonna make a killing with
          this footage.

                    RICK
          I thought you promised not to sell
          it anywhere?

                    JANE
          I just paid the guy a hundred
          bucks, Rick. You really think I'm
          not going to sell this?

Rick doesn't answer.

Jane starts walking further into the house. Rick stays close
on her heels.

5.

                    JANE
          Come on, let's do this.

                                        CUT TO:

6   INT. KITCHEN - NIGHT   6

THE CAMERA TURNS ON AND ONCE AGAIN WE SEE WHAT THE CAMERA
LENS SEES: AN OLD WOODEN DOOR.

                    JANE (O.S.)
          The family knew the killer, and the
          killer knew the house. He entered
          quietly through the side door that
          fateful night. It was late, almost
          midnight, and he must have thought
          everyone would be upstairs
          sleeping.

THE CAMERA SLOWLY PANS AROUND THE ROOM. WE SEE AN EMPTY
KITCHEN WITH A FIREPLACE. CAMERA GOES CLOSE ON THE
REFRIGERATOR.

                    JANE (O.S.)
          What he didn't expect was for Frank
          Cavanaugh to be suffering from
          insomnia and looking for a midnight
          snack.

THE CAMERA POV SLOWLY SWINGS AROUND THE ISLAND AND FOCUSES ON
THE FLOOR IN FRONT OF THE SINK.

                    JANE (O.S.)
          The killer stabbed Frank more than
          a dozen times and then sliced his
          throat to make sure the job was
          done properly. He left a trail of
          boot prints in a spreading puddle
          of blood as he headed for the
          stairs and the rest of the family.

THE CAMERA POV PANS AROUND THE ROOM AGAIN, BUT THIS TIME ON
THE MANTLE OF THE KITCHEN FIREPLACE THERE IS A DAGGER.

Jane and Rick take no notice of this and exit the room.

7   INT. DINING ROOM/FAMILY ROOM - NIGHT   7

THE CAMERA SLOWLY PANS AS WE WALK THROUGH A PAIR OF DARK, EMPTY ROOMS.

We hear the ECHO of our footsteps, the CREAKING of the hardwood floors and the howl of the WIND outside.

We also see a LOWER CABINET DOOR swing open by itself behind them - but Jane and Rick do not notice.

> JANE (O.S.)
> He crept carefully through the
> family room and dining room before
> entering the foyer.

8   INT. FOYER - NIGHT   8

> JANE (O.S.)
> It was here that he encountered
> Joanna Cavanaugh coming down the
> stairs dressed in a nightgown. At
> the time, she was eight and a half
> months pregnant.

THE CAMERA PANS BACK UP THE WINDING STAIRWAY.

> JANE (O.S.)
> Joanna must have been as confused
> as she was afraid. She knew the man
> standing in front of her. She liked
> him and trusted him. Perhaps she
> even began to approach him, but
> then she saw the blood splattered
> all over his shirt and face. So
> then she ran.

Off-screen FOOTSTEPS as the camera works its way up the stairs.

> JANE (O.S.)
> The killer caught her halfway up
> the stairway. He stabbed her nine
> times in the back, twice in the
> buttocks, and once in the back of
> her skull. A waterfall of blood
> cascaded down the hardwood stairs.

Somewhere in the house, a door SLAMS.

THE CAMERA POV JERKS ABRUPTLY.

> RICK (O.S.)
> What the fuck was that?

THE CAMERA STEADIES AND FOCUSES ON A FRIGHTENED RICK AT THE
BOTTOM OF THE STAIRS.

> JANE (O.S.)
> I don't know but I hope we got it
> on video.

The sound of SHUFFLING from above. Rick looks up in panic.

> RICK
> There's someone else in the house.

> JANE (O.S.)
> No. No one's been in here for—

Rick runs up and blocks the lens with his hand.

> RICK (O.S.)
> Turn the damn camera off.

Rick is pacing back and forth in front of the stairway. Jane
is standing on the bottom step.

The MOONLIGHT casts their SHADOWS clearly along an old
wallpapered wall.

> JANE
> And I'm telling you it was the
> wind. It's an old drafty house.

> RICK
> Then how do you explain the
> footsteps.

> JANE
> (shaking her head)
> You watched the video replay. You
> listened. It sounded like an animal
> scuttling around up there or
> something.

> RICK
> Yeah...or something.

Jane stands and puts her arm around Rick and smiles that
million-dollar smile of hers.

8.

                    JANE
        You can wait down here if you want,
        but if I were you, I'd come along
        for the ride.

She starts up the stairs. Rick watches her for a moment, a
stubborn look on his face - which quickly crumbles.

He hurries after her.

                    RICK
        Wait up.

As they leave, their shadows naturally leave with them.

HOLD ON THE WALLPAPERED WALL AS A THIRD SHADOW STEPS INTO
FRAME.

                                        CUT TO:

9   INT. UPSTAIRS BEDROOM - NIGHT   9

THE CAMERA POV MOVES SLOWLY DOWN A HALLWAY AND ENTERS A DARK
BEDROOM. PANS AROUND.

                    JANE (O.S.)
        Brian Cavanaugh. Twelve-years-old.
        A shortstop on his middle school
        baseball team and a straight A
        student. This was his bedroom.

THE CAMERA FOCUSES ON A CLOSET DOOR.

We move closer and a hand reaches on-screen and opens the
closet.

                    JANE (O.S.)
        The killer found Brian hiding in
        this closet. Was the young boy
        crying? Hysterical? Did he even
        open his eyes when the closet door
        swung open? You would think the
        killer would've had mercy because
        Brian was so young. But you would
        be wrong. Brian was stabbed seven
        times. He took his last breath in
        this closet.

Jane clears her throat. She's tough but this one gets to her.

9.

JANE (O.S.)
And cut.

CUT TO:

10   INT. TOP OF STAIRWAY - NIGHT   10

Jane and Rick are heading back downstairs. Moving slowly by
the light of Rick's flashlight.

RICK
This place is giving me the creeps.

Jane doesn't respond. Deep in thought.

RICK
You really think it's haunted like
everyone says?

JANE
(after a beat)
I think there's a lot of bad energy
in here.

Rick thinks about that, then...

RICK
That got to you back there in the
bedroom, didn't it?

JANE
(nods)
For a minute, yeah. It's pretty
horrible stuff.

RICK
Why do you think people are so
fascinated with all this? Murders?
Killers? Scary stories?

11   INT. FOYER - NIGHT   11

Jane stops at the bottom of the stairway and looks at Rick.

JANE
Oldest story in the book. Good
versus evil.

She starts walking again.

10.

12   INT. HALLWAY - NIGHT   12

        They enter the hallway.

                        JANE
                The world's a fucked-up place, man.
                Evil's all around us. We go through
                our every day lives scared to death
                of being touched by it, so most of
                the time we block it out, pretend
                it doesn't exist. But sometimes we
                can't block it, we can't stop
                thinking about it, and that's where
                this stuff comes in.

13   INT. BASEMENT STAIRS - NIGHT   13

        Jane opens the door to the stairs leading down to the
        basement.

                        JANE
                Scary movies, books, hell, even
                haunted houses on Halloween. When
                people feel the world closing in
                around them, what's better than to
                take a nice safe trip down the
                rabbit hole...and if that rabbit
                hole is soaked in someone's else's
                blood, all the better because it's
                not them, it's not their blood.

14   INT. BASEMENT STAIRWAY - NIGHT   14

        Jane starts down. Rick follows.

        She hesitates and glances up - as a muffled THUMP sounds
        from somewhere in the house.

                        RICK
                You hear something?

                        JANE
                        (shakes head)
                Just the clock ticking. Come on,
                let's do this basement scene and
                wrap it up.

        She starts walking again.

11.

                    RICK
          Oh, goodie. The basement.

                                          CUT TO:

15   INT. BASEMENT - NIGHT   15

CAMERA POV OF A DARK AND CLAUSTROPHOBIC BASEMENT.

Low ceilings. Pitch black corners. Spider webs. This is the
dark heart of the house.

                    JANE (O.S.)
          While the killer was busy with her
          older brother in the closet, ten-
          year-old Christina Cavanaugh—

Something scampers across the floor several feet in front of
the camera - and Rick SCREAMS just off-screen.

                    JANE
          Okay, Mice one, Rick zero.

                    RICK
          I said I was sorry.

                    JANE
          And take two.

CAMERA POV OF THE SAME DARK BASEMENT.

                    JANE (O.S.)
          While the killer was busy with her
          older brother in the closet, ten-
          year-old Christina Cavanaugh fled
          downstairs. If she hadn't most
          likely been in a state of severe
          shock, the young girl quite
          possibly could have run right out
          the front door and escaped to the
          safety of one of her neighbors.

THE CAMERA FOCUSES ON THE MIDDLE OF THE ROOM.

                    JANE (O.S.)
          Instead, she panicked and ran into
          the basement to hide. Trapping
          herself. I can't imagine what it
          must have felt like for her down
          here.

Huddled in the darkness beneath the
pool table. Not able to see even a
few feet in front of her. Hearing
the killer's heavy footsteps
circling above, then echoing as
they climbed down the old wooden
stairs, getting closer, and closer.

THE CAMERA POV PULLS BACK.

                JANE (O.S.)
The killer dragged her out from
beneath the pool table. She fought
him, her fingernails raking the
flesh from his face, clawing at his
eyes. But, in the end, it didn't
matter. The killer stabbed
Christina Cavanaugh a single time,
directly through her heart.

Shuffling footsteps right behind the camera, and then a
shaky voice mere inches away.

                RICK (O.S.)
Okay, cut. Great job. Let's get the
fuck outta here.

As they turn to leave, the beam of Rick's flashlight sweeps
across the room - and we catch just a glimpse of a DARK
FIGURE in silhouette.

Jane and Rick do not see this.

They head upstairs.

                        CUT TO:

16   INT. FOYER - NIGHT   16

Rick is holding the video camera, trying to focus on Jane,
who is standing in front of the doorway.

                RICK
I wish we had a tripod.

                JANE
It's fine. Doesn't have to be
perfect. It'll give it some of that
cool wiggle-and-jiggle.

           RICK
        (shivers)
I swear it's getting colder in
here.

CAMERA POV AS IT ADJUSTS FOCUS ON JOHN.

           RICK (O.S.)
Wait. Can I say action?

           JANE
        (tired)
Really?

           RICK (O.S.)
Yes, really. Anddd...action.

Jane's face brightens and she comes to life.

She pulls out an OLD FAMILY PHOTO and holds it up to the
camera: the smiling faces of the Cavanaugh family.

           JANE
When news of the murders became
public, the entire town of Edgewood
mourned the loss of the Cavanaugh
family. They were well known and
well loved.

Beat.

           JANE
But when the identity of their
killer was revealed, the town found
itself in a state of utter shock
and disbelief.

Jane steps closer to the camera and takes out a SECOND PHOTO:
a middle-aged man.

           JANE
Francis Lawrence had lived in
Edgewood, Maryland for more than
two decades. He was forty-nine
years old and one of the small
town's most respected citizens. He
was a little league baseball coach
and a member of the volunteer fire
department. He was also the priest
of the town's only Catholic church,
which the Cavanaugh family had
dutifully attended.

14.

Jane steps closer and gestures to the top of the stairway landing.

> JANE
> When the police, summoned by a concerned neighbor, arrived at 1930 Hanson Road the morning after the massacre, they entered through the front door and were greeted by the still-swaying body of Father Lawrence. Sometime after committing the murders, he had slipped a noose over his head, tied the rope off on the upstairs banister, and jumped.

Jane gestures upstairs again.

> JANE
> He'd left a note pinned to the floor by the murder weapon explaining that the Cavanaugh family had been communing with the devil. Nothing more, nothing less. The dagger he'd used to kill the Cavanaugh family was later determined to be over 500 years old. No one knows where he got it.

Jane glances around the house, gives her most thoughtful look to the camera.

> JANE
> For months, investigators searched for answers. But they found none. The autopsy failed to reveal any abnormalities in Francis Lawrence's brain. The endless interviews uncovered nothing remotely troubling or unusual in his life.

Jane takes a deep breath, composes herself.

> JANE
> Thirteen months after the murders, a young family from Virginia moved into 1930 Hanson Road. After only six weeks, they moved out. They claimed to have heard strange voices and noises from all throughout the house. Water faucets, televisions, and lights would mysteriously turn on and off.

> One night, the wife awoke from a
> vivid nightmare grasping at her
> neck. She was hysterical. In the
> light of the next morning, she
> discovered a strange bruise
> encircling her neck, almost as if a
> noose had been tightened there
> while she'd been sleeping. The next
> family who moved in fared slightly
> better. They lasted four months
> before fleeing the home.

Jane saves her most dramatic expression for last.

> JANE
> Every town has a haunted house
> located within its borders. If not
> haunted by things unseen and
> unknown, then a place borne of
> violent tragedy. Some of these
> houses become legendary and enter
> the national conscience. The
> Amityville Horror in upstate New
> York comes to mind. Tonight is the
> five year anniversary of the
> Cavanaugh family massacre, and I am
> Jane Sharretts coming to you live
> from the belly of the beast in
> Edgewood, Maryland - 1930 Hanson
> Road - the Murder House.

While Jane monologues - unseen by both of them - a HOODED
FIGURE exits a SMALL DOOR in the background and stands
motionless for a few moments, staring into the lens of the
camera. The Hooded Figure leaves as Jane finishes her story.

> CUT TO:

17   INT. FOYER - NIGHT - LATER   17

Jane is putting the lens cap on the video camera.

> JANE
> You sure we shouldn't do another
> take?

> RICK
> I'm sure. You nailed it.

> JANE
> Translation: I'm a big pussy and
> just want to get out of here.

16.

                    RICK
          Translation: you're a fucking
          princess and I just wanna get out
          of here.

Jane laughs and glances around the foyer.

                    JANE
          I left the camera bag in the
          kitchen.

She walks out and Rick, of course, scurries to catch up.

                                        CUT TO:

18   INT. KITCHEN - NIGHT   18

They enter and Jane grabs the CAMERA BAG from the island.
Stuffs the VIDEO CAMERA inside and zips it closed. Yawns.

                    JANE
          Let's rock and roll.

Rick starts to turn around - and stops in his tracks. Eyes
wide. Staring at the side door, which is slowly opening in
front of his eyes.

                    RICK
                 (whispers)
          Jane.

Jane keeps walking.

                    RICK
                 (louder)
          Jane.

Jane stops and turns around.

                    JANE
          What now?

                    RICK
          The door.

Jane takes the flashlight from Rick, walks closer and shines
the light on the door - and we see that it is standing ajar.

She reaches for the doorknob...

                    RICK
          Don't touch it!

17.

...and closes the door. She turns back to her friend.

                    JANE
          Calm down. I'm sure there's a
          reasonable explanation.

                    RICK
          And I'm sure I don't give a shit.

He takes the FLASHLIGHT back from Jane and heads for the
foyer.

                    RICK
          I'm getting out of here.

This time it's Jane's turn to follow.

                                        CUT TO:

19   INT. FOYER - NIGHT   19

Jane is struggling to keep up.

                    JANE
          Dude, slow down.

Rick jerks to a stop and Jane slams into him.

Dozens of BURNING CANDLES line the foyer walls and stairway.

They both stare up at the second floor banister - where a
NOOSE is hanging.

                    JANE
                (under his breath)
          What the fuck?

Rick swings around and grabs Jane by her arm.

                    RICK
          You did this!

                    JANE
          What? No! Think about it, I was
          never alone. Not even for a minute.

                    RICK
          Then it's the guy who let us in.

                    JANE
          Craig? Why would he—

> RICK
> I don't know! Because he's a dick?

Jane slowly removes Rick's hands from her arm. Looks up at the noose again. Thinking. Now they're both scared.

> JANE
> I swear I'm not pranking you, man.
> I don't think it's Craig either.

> RICK
> Then what the hell's going on?

> JANE
> I don't know.

We watch from behind as Jane cautiously approaches the front door, glancing up at the noose as she passes beneath it.

She reaches out a hand and we think she's going to try the doorknob, but then we go CLOSE ON HER HAND - and see the DAGGER sticking out of the door, as she yanks it out.

Jane slowly turns around and Rick sees the dagger in her hand.

> RICK
> What are-? Where did that come
> from?

Jane starts walking toward him, a blank expression on her face.

Rick starts to back away.

Jane walks closer, closer - and then she takes both hands and PLUNGES the DAGGER into her own stomach.

Bent over, grunting, she pulls the knife out and, snarling, she staggers forward to stab Rick.

Rick turns to flee...

...and SLAMS right into FRANK CAVANAUGH, who is wearing a black robe with the hood down so we can see his face clearly.

Frank smiles and reaches for Rick's neck.

Rick turns and runs for the stairway.

Rick flees up the stairs, flashlight held in front of him.

19.

As Rick reaches the second floor landing, all three bedroom
doors SLAM SHUT simultaneously.

Rick bolts down the hallway, pulls open the attic door and
climbs up the narrow stairway.

Rick enters the attic and stops in his tracks.

THREE HOODED FIGURES sit in a triangle around a PENTAGRAM
drawn on the attic floor.

BURNING CANDLES everywhere.

An OLD WOODEN CRIB sits at the head of the pentagram.

Off Rick's terrified face and the sound of a BABY CRYING, we

                                        CUT TO: BLACK

                                        FADE IN:

20   EXT. COUNTRYSIDE - MORNING   20

We see rolling hills and fields in the morning sunlight.

                                        CUT TO:

21   INT. CAR - MOVING - MORNING   21

Craig pulls into the driveway and sees Jane's car parked
exactly where it had been the night before.

                    CRAIG
            Mother. Fucker.

                                        CUT TO:

22   EXT. HOUSE - MORNING   22

Craig climbs out of the car and SLAMS the door. He walks
onto the porch and takes out his KEY RING. Unlocks the door.

                    CRAIG
            You two have one minute to get out
            of here or I'm calling...

His angry voice fades - as he yanks open the door and sees
something in the foyer that the camera can't see.

                    CRAIG
            ...the cops.

20.

We close on his shocked face and...

                              CUT TO: BLACK

END CREDITS

THE CUSTER FILES

The handwritten letters, journal entries, and notes excerpted below are from the personal collection of esteemed historian Ronald Bakewell. The papers were discovered after Bakewell's recent death and assembled into the narrative that follows by Bakewell's longtime associate, Byron McClernan. They have not been made available to the public until now. In an effort to provide clarity, minor editing has been done to the language, and spelling and punctuation errors have been corrected.

(Personal letter—Private George E. Adams, Seventh Cavalry—June 21, 1876)

Dear Father and Mother,

I miss you both desperately but believe you would be very proud of your youngest son. I have learned so much during my time here and the men I ride with are of the finest caliber. I am proud to serve by their side and pray I will distinguish myself in battle, as so many others in the Seventh have done before me. Lieutenant Colonel Custer is a larger than life figure. He reminds me of Grandpa Frank at times, with his booming voice and ability to make the tallest of tales seem believable. The men admire and fear him in equal measure. Some believe him to be aloof, even cruel, but I find him charming and confident, and would follow him anywhere...

(Journal entry—Corporal John J. Callahan, Seventh Cavalry—June 21, 1876)

...and because of this strategy it has been long days of riding and short nights of rest. It is no wonder the men are so tired. Still, I have heard few complaints and witnessed even fewer moments of weakness amongst the men. We have been trained well and know the routine. I have little doubt the campaign will be successful.

Oh how I wish you were here with me, my darling Wanda, sitting beside me on this dark prairie, staring up at the magnificent night sky, counting the stars and playing our wishing game. My first wish upon a star tonight would be for our precious baby Genevieve to grow up to find happiness and good health. My second would be for you and me to build that cabin by the lake we always dreamed of, to grow old together, and watch our grandchildren play at our feet. One day, soon, I promise you…

(Personal letter—Private George Eiseman, Seventh Cavalry—June 22, 1876)

I hate it. The men are filthy. Fighting, cursing, farting, burping, shitting, pissing. They are no better than the horses that carry them. The officers offer meager improvement, bullies and barbarians to a man. The days are endless, the mess tastes like buffalo droppings, and there is not a single aspect of this dreadful land I can give praise to. I hate it here.

(Journal entry—Lt. Col. George Armstrong Custer, Seventh Cavalry June 23, 1876)

…therefore I can only describe it as a feeling of being set free after a long imprisonment. Imagine an eagle taking flight for the first time after enduring a lengthy injury to one of its wings, a grizzly bear healed of its hindquarter wound and returning to the fast hunt. That is akin to what being on campaign feels like for me. I was born to lead men in the field. I was born to chase glory. I sit here on my cot inside my tent, writing by the light of a single lantern, and I am at absolute peace with but one corner of my heart left incomplete. I will return to your arms soon, my dearest Libbie, and we shall once again sit upon the porch at Fort Lincoln, sip your splendid tea, and doze to the setting sun. Sleep now, as shall I. More tomorrow, my Rosebud.

(Journal entry—Corporal John Foley, Seventh Cavalry— June 23, 1876)

I believe the men feel it, feel *something*, even if the officers continue to turn a blind eye. First, there was the missing food supplies. The cooking staff was publically scolded for being careless but the matter was never investigated further. Unusual to say the least. Reno is the most detail-oriented officer I have ever served under. Then there was the captured scout from two nights ago. Reno insisted that he was Lakota, while Tom Custer and Benteen argued that he was Cheyenne. Well, then why did my old friend Sergeant Perkins tell me confidentially that the scout was of neither tribe? That he was some new breed he had never seen before. Wild, feral, with the strangest markings on his pony Perkins had ever seen. Eyes the color of blackest night. Skin paler than many white men. And then there are the rumors of how the scout had bitten two men during his capture. Both soldiers now quarantined in Sick Hall. Finally, there is the matter of so many other men falling ill. Why are there so many? And why all the secrecy surrounding their illnesses? I am not a man of superstition, but it is beginning to feel as though this campaign has been cursed.

(Personal letter—Captain Thomas Custer, Seventh Cavalry—June 23, 1876)

...but I imagine we will just have to wait and see. Terry and Gibbon are out there if we need them. The same should be said of Crook, but I believe he would be a tad slow in coming to our aid, even if summoned. (That was a joke. I think. I hope.)

George is clear-headed and affable thus far into the march, if a bit more subdued than his usual nature. One of the Crow scouts asked me yesterday, a look of sincere concern etched across his brown face, why George had cut his long yellow hair. He was convinced that it was bad luck for him to have done so before battle. I could only chuckle when brother Boston chimed in and responded with that crooked grin of his, "Come now, haven't you ever heard of 'Custer Luck'? The only kind of luck George has is of the good variety. The man was practically born with a horse shoe up his rear end."

I will write again, old friend, when time and temperament allow. In the meantime, light a cigar for me next time you sit down at the chessboard. Tell Charlie I said to break a leg.

Yours truly,
Tom Custer

(Personal letter—Sergeant Robert H. Hughes, Seventh Cavalry—June 23, 1876)

Something is wrong here. It began as an underlying feeling of unease—the past few nights have been too quiet; where have the night creatures gone? Even the crickets and frogs remain silent—but it has since grown into something else entirely. I have the most dreadful feeling.

(Journal entry—Corporal George H. King, Seventh Cavalry—June 24, 1876)

I was on the way back from my morning smoke when I overheard Curley and Bloody Knife talking to some of the officers. The hairs on the back of my neck stood up as I listened to them report, "Big camp. Many lodges, many fires burning. Too many braves to count." I pulled Bloody Knife aside later in the day and asked for more details. His eyes told me everything else I needed to hear. "Must wait for more men. Bigger guns. Yellow Hair is brave but will not listen." Bloody Knife's voice was solemn, his eyes anxious. I have never seen him act in such a manner. He told me he is praying to the Great Spirit for a vision to be sent to Custer in his sleep. I'm not holding my breath. I'm not sure the bastard ever sleeps.

(Personal letter—Sergeant Jeremiah Finley, Seventh Cavalry—June 24, 1876)

We lost another two men last night. Their rifles and packs and horses remain, but they have otherwise vanished. This brings the total to nineteen missing. Desertions are rare for the Seventh, this level of frequency unheard of. Who leaves all of their personal belongings and sets off on foot in the middle of this inhospitable terrain? It makes little sense. We have doubled the guard and still no one has seen or heard anything out of the ordinary. To the contrary, the nights have been unnaturally quiet and still. We long-marched almost eighty miles today and with good reason, I figure. We better hurry and catch up with Crazy Horse or there won't be enough of us left to fight...

(Personal letter—Captain Thomas Custer, Seventh Cavalry—June 24, 1876)

...which is perhaps a stroke of profound good fortune, as we should be close enough to engage the enemy within a day, two at the most. Once again, George has managed to accomplish what many others before him could not. His unbridled energy this campaign is only matched by his fierce determination to defeat the legendary Crazy Horse on the field of battle. I asked him during this morning's ride if he would be satisfied with Crazy Horse's surrender. He appeared shocked and rather dismayed at such a proposition. His response? "Sitting Bull, yes. Crazy Horse…I want to destroy."

(Journal entry—Private William Moodie, Seventh Cavalry—June 24, 1876)

They're lying and for the life of me, I cannot figure out why. There is no way in hell I'm believing that Elmer deserted. And without his horse? His gun? His lucky squirrel tail? I don't believe it. He would just as soon run out of here without any trousers and boots on than leave without his lucky squirrel tail and carbine. Private Elmer Babcock is a lot of things—a shitty poker player at the top of that list—but he ain't no goddamn deserter. You couldn't find a more loyal soldier anywhere.

(Journal entry—Private James Brightfield, Seventh Cavalry—June 24, 1876)

I know what I saw and I know what I heard. I was standing guard post on the northern perimeter of camp. It was after midnight when I heard one of the men crying out in the dark. A quick, muffled bark, and then silence. At first I thought maybe my ears were playing tricks on me—there shouldn't have been anyone out there beyond the safety of the firelight—but then I heard the sucking sounds. A wet smacking, slurping noise like a starved animal feasting on its kill. It was then I knew it wasn't an Indian. They may be savages, but they move like the wind. I mustered my courage, and with my rifle pointed in front of me, I went to investigate. I freely admit that I made as much noise as I could manage with the hopes that whatever was doing the feasting would soon be frightened away by my approach. Thirty or so yards outside of camp I found it: a wide circle of blood. Splashed on the grass. Soaked into the dirt. And a scrap of blood-stained cloth that looked like it came from an undershirt. I stood there scanning the shadows and had the strangest sensation that something was watching me. Looking over my shoulder the entire time, I hurried back to camp and reported what I had found to my Sergeant. He thanked me and promised to relay the information to the Captain. It was only later that I realized something odd: Sarge hadn't looked the least bit surprised when I had told him my story. I find that rather unsettling. Sarge also made me swear not to repeat any of the details to the other men. Not that I would have anyway. Who would ever believe such a tale?

(Journal entry—Lt. Col. George Armstrong Custer, Seventh Cavalry—June 25, 1876)

The scouts have returned. Today is the day. I will not wait for Terry or Gibbon. I will not wait for more guns. We will surround and attack the village on my command. Reno will approach from the south, Benteen on my far flank. The scouts are uneasy, as are many of the officers, but I remain supremely confident. I believe the savages will see our dust coming, will hear the thunder of our horses, and they will flee. There is not an enemy walking this earth that can defeat the Seventh.

(Personal letter—Captain Frederick Benteen, Seventh Cavalry—June 25, 1876)

The fool! It's already been decided: we attack today. No cannons, no Gatling guns, no reinforcements from General Terry. Custer, once again, the impatient fool. I dared to question the great one's decision to split up the regiment into three, and his only response was typical Custer arrogance: "You have your orders." The men are exhausted. Why not at least allow us another night's rest and to engage at dawn instead of midday? I'm sure we will emerge victorious, of course, but at what cost? Custer is without conscience. He cares only of the newspaper headlines and his own perverse sense of immortality...

(Personal letter—Trumpeter Thomas J. Bucknell, Seventh Cavalry—June 25, 1876)

Dearest Court,

The orders came down just minutes ago. We will attack the village in an hour's time. I've heard rumors of almost a thousand Indians, perhaps more. Please know how much I love and cherish you if I am unable to make it home to your arms. Please know that I tried my very best.

With all my love,
Thomas

P.S. Please give my momma a hug when next you see her.

(Journal entry—Private John Papp, Seventh Cavalry— June 25, 1876)

I overheard my sergeant talking about the camp this morning. Lodges as far as the eye could see. Too many ponies to count. We're all going to die in this valley. Every last one of us.

(Personal letter—Private Andrew J. Moore, Seventh Cavalry—June 25, 1876)

I've never seen so many Indians. May God have mercy on our souls.

(Battlefield note dictated by Lt. Col. George Armstrong Custer to runner, Trumpeter John Martini—June 25, 1876)

Benteen.
Come on. Big village. Be quick. Bring packs.
P.S. Bring packs.

(Personal letter—Corporal Henry M. Cody, Seventh Cavalry—June 25, 1876)

In the event that someone finds this upon my almost certain death…

Bloody Knife is dead. Major Reno is incompetent. He ordered us to retreat and fight on foot in the timber and now we are trapped here and dying. I can hear the dull roar of gunfire in the distance, presumably Custer's companies engaging. We are badly outnumbered and have but one chance at escape. To ride through their lines. Otherwise it will be a massacre. Reno is no longer giving orders. God help us.

Regretfully,
Corp. Henry M. Cody

(Battlefield note given to runner—written by Major Reno, Seventh Cavalry—June 25, 1876)

Need reinforcements. Ammunition. Outnumbered but holding timberline. Something wrong with these savages. Bullets do not stop them. Men are being eaten alive. Chaos. Hurry.

(Personal letter—Captain Otto Hageman, Seventh Cavalry—June 25, 1876)

We are fighting monsters. How do you kill your enemy if they are already dead? They are toying with us now. I saw Custer fall...

(Battlefield note given to runner—written by 1ˢᵗ Sergeant James Butler, Seventh Cavalry—June 25, 1876)

G. Custer is gone. Killed in the first moments of battle. Heavy casualties. Send men and guns. Surrounded.

(Journal entry—Sergeant James T. Riley, Seventh Cavalry—July 1, 1876)

Strict orders have been given by General Terry not to speak of this but I feel as though I must record my thoughts lest my head burst with the horrid reality of what I recently witnessed.

On June 28, my men and I were tasked with burying the bodies of the massacred Seventh Cavalry. It was a dreadful duty, as most of the bodies were bloated and blackened by the sun, and mutilated beyond recognition. Even poor Thomas Custer was not spared the indignity, as his head was crushed flat and he was only identifiable by the crude tattoo located on his left shoulder. As for the legendary George Custer, he was one of the very few that remained without disfigurement. Only his eardrums had been punctured. Perhaps most strangely, he died with a smile on his face, as if he knew his heroic death would cement his legacy once and for all.

As is usual procedure, a casualty count was completed, and it appeared as though a large number of bodies were missing. Perhaps as many as three or four dozen with no explanation. When I questioned the other officers, I was greeted with backs turned, heads held close, and conspiratorial whispers. I am quite certain that one or more of these officers held the answer close to their lips but simply did not feel comfortable sharing that answer with me.

But yet that wasn't the worst of it. Amongst the gruesome mutilations we encountered on that grassy field overlooking the Little Bighorn were crudely amputated arms and legs, disembowelments, sliced off noses and ears and penises, and of course missing scalps to a man. One body inexplicably held one hundred and five arrows. Another was posed with the trooper's severed arms laid out in place of his missing legs, which were never found. But none of these travesties troubled me as deeply as the many throats I came upon that appeared to have been ripped open…no, that's not entirely accurate or truthful…they appeared to have been *chewed* open. And, still stranger, all of these particular corpses were as pale as a winter snowfall. Seemingly drained of every last drop of blood. What kind of savage could inflict such a wound?

(Personal letter discovered after his death—Private Christopher Criddle, Seventh Cavalry—November 19, 1907)

To Whom It May Concern,

I pray this letter is duly noted upon my passing and its contents are taken in the spirit in which they were written—as my absolute truth and atonement.

Most here in Springdale know of me as only an honest storekeeper. No spouse, no family, a handful of unremarkable details regarding my past. Just a solitary man in his later years who loves his books, root beer floats, and the striking of a fair bargain.

What they don't know—and what would certainly come as a shock to each and every one of them—is that in a former life and faraway place I was once a Private in George Custer's famed Seventh Cavalry. It was long ago and I was a very different man then. Young and angry and desperately in need of discipline and acceptance. In short order, the Seventh became my home, and I came to adore everything about that choice of life. Until the Little Bighorn, that is.

Yes, I was with Custer at the Little Bighorn. I knelt no more than ten yards away from him when he was felled by a gunshot to his temple. Minutes later, his brother Thomas went down at my feet and followed George to whatever awaits us all after this world.

But how could this be, you ask? There were no survivors at the battle of the Little Bighorn. The newspapers claim it was a massacre. It was and I did. Survive, that is. Thanks to simple dumb luck and the unexpected aid of one generous soul—whom I will never mention, not even here in my final testimony—I not only was able to survive the battle with only a minor wound to my shoulder, I was also able to disappear, my body and mind after that day incapable of returning to a life of soldiering.

So, yes, I admit I am a deserter. A fugitive at large. Although I am quite certain that no one realizes this fact—not then, and not now. From what I have come to understand, many of my fellow troopers were missing from the field that day. Many others mutilated beyond recognition. Somewhere on that grassy knoll, I am certain there is a wooden cross with my name scrawled upon it.

I, alone, know the details of that day. I saw the Indians stream by the hundreds out of those hidden gullies. I heard a shocked Custer bark his orders and the trumpets blow retreat. I was there when we realized we were cut off and surrounded, when we dismounted to make our final stand. Most of the men fell to arrows and spears and bullets at intermediate range, but as the battle raged, more and more resorted to taking their own lives. The air became filled with gun-smoke and screams. It was hard to hear if any further orders were being given, harder still to see clearly. That's when the creatures came. They crawled on their bellies through the high grass like snakes, their bloody teeth bared, their black eyes unblinking. I watched as trooper after trooper were dragged to the ground with incredible strength…their throats ripped open by razor-sharp teeth…and drained of their blood. I tried to kill the savages but my bullets had no effect on them.

For decades, I was never able to find the proper words to put a name to the monsters I witnessed in that God forsaken valley. And then, several years ago, I heard about an Irish writer by the name of Bram Stoker who had recently published a sensationalistic novel entitled *Dracula*. The book told the story of a night creature who drank the blood of his victims and cursed them to the eternal life of the undead. These creatures were given a name: *vampire*. I was able to acquire a copy of this book a short time ago from one of my contacts in Boston. Stoker's tale was set across the ocean in Europe, a far cry from the dusty plains of the American West, and there were of course many other differences from what I experienced at the Little Bighorn. But there were also a multitude of striking similarities, enough so to convince me that Stoker's book might not be merely a work of fantastic fiction after all.

I've never spoken or written of that fateful day at the Little Bighorn until now, and I will never make mention of it again. If only it was as easy to erase it from my conscience. I dream of them, you see. With their dark, hungry eyes and protruding, razor-sharp teeth. Sometimes, I find myself sketching their hideous faces on the backs of bills of sale while standing at the counter in my store.

When I realize what I am doing, I inevitably crumble these drawings and toss them into the trash bin or watch them burn in the flames of my fireplace at home. But it doesn't matter. The faces always come back to me in my nightmares. I cannot ever forget them. So many mornings I wake up drenched in sweat and terror, my hands clutching my throat, protecting the soft flesh and holding in my screams. Then, I wash myself, and dress, and head to the store, where I greet the townsfolk with a tired smile and a nod of my head and perhaps a few pleasantries. And each time the bell above the door rings, signaling the arrival of a new customer, I glance nervously from whatever task I am performing and pray that I don't see those strange, dark eyes or razor-sharp teeth, that whatever those creatures were, they haven't decided to journey East in their quest for fresh blood.

So, there you have it. My truth. I alone survived the Battle of the Little Bighorn. And on those long and lonely nights when their faces visit my dreams, I wish to God I hadn't.

Sincerely,
C. Criddle

(Personal letter discovered after his passing—Ronald Bakewell—February 9, 2018)

...and so I leave the final decision in your worthy hands, Byron. History is yours for the changing. Or not. No one should judge your either decision. Just remember our old motto from University days: nothing holds more power than the truth.

Yours in admiration and friendship,
Ronald Bakewell

THE LONG WAY HOME

was watering the tomato plants on my balcony and trying to decide whether I should take a shower or go for a run when the phone rang. No one called me these days—except for misguided solicitors a few times a week—so I let the answering machine pick up. It beeped and I heard my mother's voice, sounding much older than the last time I'd heard it: "You need to come home, Charlie. Your father died."

And that was it.

I SAT on the armrest of my rented sofa and played the message. When it was finished, I played it again and listened with my eyes closed. My mother sounded like a stranger. I pictured her standing in the kitchen of the small house I'd grown up in, staring out the window above the sink at the ancient weeping willow tree that bordered our side yard, absently twirling her hair in her fingers, the phone pressed tight against her ear.

The house would be bustling with the news of my father's passing. My brother, Sam, would be there, of course. Aunt Charlotte and Uncle Bobby. The cousins. The Cavanaughs from next door and probably half of the rest of Hanson Road would be coming and going to pay their respects.

Dad was a good man and well liked in our hometown of Salisbury. He was always lending someone a hand. Helping them fix their car or lawn mower or boat, cleaning their gutters, taking down some trees, or repairing a fence. He believed in helping others and being a vital member of the neighborhood. Growing up, he always used to tell me, "We have to try to be part of something bigger than ourselves, Charlie. Whether it's our church or vocation or community, life isn't about taking, it's about giving. We all have a deeper purpose to serve."

It was a lesson I had yet to learn.

NINE MONTHS earlier, on the rainy afternoon I was released from Hagerstown Prison, my mother was waiting for me outside in the parking lot. We stood there for a long time, just looking at each other, hugging and laughing and crying, neither of us saying much of anything. It was the first time we'd seen each other in six years.

She had accepted my monthly collect calls without fail, but my father wouldn't allow her to visit by herself, and he refused to come anywhere near the place. His pride, my mother claimed, but I knew it was something else: shame.

I was supposed to be the golden child. Handsome and popular, with a scholarship to play baseball at the University of Richmond, the future had once looked sky-high for me. Pro scouts had even started to sniff around our games and the local newspaper had crowned me as a "hometown hero" in a front-page article announcing my college decision.

On the other hand, my older brother (by almost two years) was cut from the same swath of cloth that had produced my father. Serious-minded and on the quiet side, Sam kept a much lower profile. Smart and extraordinarily patient, he was a natural tinkerer just like Dad. He excelled in school and, while I had a different girl on my arm every weekend, Sam started dating Jenny Lomax in the tenth grade and never stopped. Despite spending much of his teenage years standing in my shadow, he rarely demonstrated jealousy at the attention his younger brother received. On the contrary, Sam was one of my best friends and biggest fans. Our mother used to call us "thick as thieves."

That was the two of us in a nutshell, the Freeman boys. No one in a million years could have guessed the disparate futures Fate had in store for us just around the bend.

When Sam graduated college at the top of his class and landed a job at a prestigious engineering firm in Washington D.C., no one was the least bit surprised. Not long after, he married his high school sweetheart, and, a year later, Jenny gave birth to their first child. A son named after our father.

I was a different story altogether. I spent most of my freshman year at Richmond recovering from a serious knee injury I'd suffered during Fall Ball and drinking too much. Instead of returning home after the end of spring semester, I shacked up in a run-down off campus apartment with a few of my teammates and spent the summer rehabbing my knee and getting plastered on a nightly basis. By the fall of my sophomore year, I had added cocaine to my rigorous party routine and by spring break—after several warnings and a failed NCAA drug test— I'd been kicked off the baseball team. A certified letter was sent home to my parents and my scholarship was revoked.

A couple months later, I was arrested for the first time.

I DIDN'T own a car, but my downstairs neighbor—a retired concrete worker named Jeremy—had an old pick-up truck he'd been trying to sell for a couple months and for fifty bucks he agreed to let me borrow it for the week. I couldn't afford the fifty, but I didn't have much of a choice. The last thing I wanted to do was take a Greyhound bus home to bury my father.

Home. It felt funny even thinking the word after all this time.

The day after I'd been released from Hagerstown, my parole officer explained that I needed special permission if I wanted to leave the state of Maryland at any time in the next twelve months. The same rule applied to setting up residence and getting a job. I guess the State wanted to keep an eye on me, to make sure I'd been properly reformed.

I wanted as little contact as possible with my drill ser geant of a parole officer and didn't like the idea of asking for special permission or special anything, so I did the first thing that came to mind: I got as far away from my hometown as possible and moved to the westernmost part of the state. A little town named Burtonsville, about forty miles southwest of Cumberland. There wasn't much there, but rent was cheap, people minded their own business, and there was a lumberyard hiring manual labor.

Time passed slowly in Burtonsville. I worked forty to fifty hours a week hauling and cutting timber, went to AA meetings every Thursday night at a local elementary school, and spent a lot of time sitting alone in the dark eating pizza and watching bad movies. I spoke with Mom every other weekend on the telephone, but Dad and the rest of the family were still a no-show. I was mostly fine with that. I didn't have a clue what I would say to any of them.

Despite being there for almost nine months, I hadn't made many new friends in town. I grabbed breakfast at Waffle House from time to time with a couple guys from the lumberyard, but none of us were big talkers. Usually the weather and the Orioles, and they liked to swap hunting and fishing stories. A pretty, blonde waitress from the pizza joint around the corner asked me to the movies about a month ago, but I politely declined. She was a good bit younger than me, and I didn't think I was ready for that anyway.

I wouldn't say I was lonely, but some days were harder than others. If I found myself going stir-crazy or felt my brain starting to get away from me, I either went for a long jog around town or gave my AA sponsor a call. Virgil Marshall sold farm equipment for a living and talked good sense to me and several other recovering alcoholics in Burtonsville. He had the most god-awful handlebar mustache I'd ever seen and told horrible, rambling, filthy jokes, but otherwise he was a good man. He had fought the wars and come out on the other side.

In fact, it was Virgil who had suggested I purchase the half-dozen tomato plants growing in plastic pots on my second-floor balcony. "A small step," he claimed, "toward becoming a responsible caregiver."

I didn't know about all that, but I was a big-time fan of BLTs and was looking forward to harvest time.

Once I had finished listening to my mother's message for a third time, I went into the bedroom and packed jeans, t-shirts, socks, and clean underwear into a knapsack. I didn't own a suit or nice shoes, so I would have to pick something up down the road for the funeral. Probably get a haircut, too. I went down-stairs and talked to Jeremy about his pick-up and he agreed to water my tomatoes while I was away, and then I said my good-bye and hit the road.

I didn't bother calling Mom before I left to ask what had happened or tell her I was coming. My father had been diagnosed with lung cancer almost a year ago. He'd been doing well enough the last time she and I had spoken, but I knew from reading the brochures that things could change in a hurry.

Salisbury was a six-hour-plus drive, longer if any of the mountain roads were being worked on, which happened a lot this time of year according to the local news. There would be plenty of time to think. And remember.

I had spent the past seven years of my life trying to forget, but I had a feeling that wasn't going to work anymore.

HI, MY name is Kyle Thomas. I'm twenty-six years old and I'm an alcoholic.

Some days—even after everything that had happened—I still couldn't believe it was true.

Today wasn't one of those days.

As I pulled onto the interstate—after loading up with gas and an extra-large coffee from Wawa—I did what I often did on those graveyard-quiet, dead-end nights when sleep refused to come: I traveled back in time and tried to figure out what the hell had happened to my life.

First, there was the alcohol. I never drank much in high school. Mom and Dad kept a tight lid on that sort of activity, and I was stone-cold obsessed about training for baseball. My body is a temple and I must treat it as such, and all that happy crappy business.

That all changed when I got to Richmond. Most college students drank to be cool and fit in, or to get laid. A game of beer pong here, a game of flip cup there, maybe the occasional slammer of a night where they go overboard and end up puking in a trashcan. I wasn't one of those people. From the very beginning, I drank to get hammered. Drinking socially just didn't make sense to me. If I wanted to stand around talking and sipping from a frosty mug, I would have sipped lemonade or sweet tea like my mother used to make. But if I was drinking beer, hell, I wanted to drink *all* the beer.

Virgil said some people are just wired that way. The disease is often hereditary, passing down from one generation to the next. Other times it comes clean out of the blue like a Texas tornado and destroys everything in its path. Whatever the reason—and this wasn't an excuse, merely an acceptance—I was one of those people.

Then, there was the cocaine. Despite seeing it around at a few parties during my freshman year, I never touched the stuff. It felt big city and dangerous to me. But then I'd started dating Lexie Sharretts at the start of sophomore year and she turned me on to it. Lexie came from a different world, and I found everything about that world exotic and exciting. Money, fast cars, yacht clubs, I was like a kid in a candy store. I liked cocaine the first time I tried it (Lexie and me in bed in her apartment), loved it the second time, and craved it like oxygen after the third. The drug not only made me feel happy and confident, it made me feel invincible. I wasn't just going to come back stronger and faster than ever before from my knee injury, I was going to have such a blockbuster season that scouts were going to come out of the woodwork and offer me a seven-figure signing bonus to leave college early. Thanks to the cocaine, I was absolutely sure of it.

Finally, there were my grades, or lack thereof. This part wasn't very complicated. I'd simply stopped going to classes. Between training and physical therapy, spending time with Lexie, partying, and waking up hung over every morning, there simply wasn't enough time for studying and homework. After all, I was headed to the big leagues, right? What did I need a degree for?

I RELAXED my grip on the steering wheel and resisted the urge to slam my fist on the dashboard. I knew violence wasn't the answer—unfortunately, only after a lot of first-hand experience—but when I thought about how I had thrown my life away, it wasn't easy. I wanted to break things. I wanted to break myself.

But I had already done that.

Instead, I counted to ten inside my head, rolled down the window, and cranked up the radio. Mick Jagger preached to me about JFK and the devil, and I sang along.

The evening was warm but there was little humidity, rare for August in Maryland, and the air felt good on my face and arms. It was just past six on a Friday but traffic was sparse. Not many people commuted long distance to work out here in the mountains.

For a moment, I tried to picture Lexie Sharretts's face and couldn't. Christ, I couldn't even remember what the girl looked like anymore.

I glanced at the speedometer and eased up on the gas pedal. I wasn't in that much of a hurry and a ticket was the last thing I needed. The idea of walking into another courtroom and facing another judge made me want to puke. I settled in at sixty-five and checked the time again. If all went according to plan, I would roll into Salisbury right around midnight. That seemed fitting somehow.

AFTER I'D been kicked off the baseball team and thrown out of school, I refused to return home to Salisbury. My father called the morning they received the certified letter, and every day after for two weeks. My mother and Sam tried almost as many times. They all threatened to come down and get me and take me home. After awhile, I just stopped answering the phone. None of them had any idea how bad it was. They were patient and kind despite their obvious disappointment and confusion, but it didn't matter. I couldn't do it. I couldn't face them and the rest of the town. I was too embarrassed.

I slept on a ratty sofa at one of my shadier friends' studio apartment and got a job cleaning dishes and clearing tables at a busy restaurant off campus. I still drank every night, sometimes sneaking leftover pitchers from the tables I was supposed to be cleaning, and still did coke when I could afford it, which wasn't very often now that Lexie had dumped me.

A couple months passed and with it the sense of shame lessened enough for me to promise my mother I would come home for an upcoming weekend to help celebrate her birthday. I missed my family and finally felt decent enough to show my face.

But the day before I was scheduled to get on a bus and head to Salisbury, I got into a fight at a downtown bar that resulted in six stitches in my forehead and a broken plate-glass window. I (along with the jackass I'd been fighting) was arrested for disturbing the peace and destruction of property.

Instead of celebrating Mom's birthday that weekend, Sam and my father drove south and bailed me out of jail. I was grateful, but once again, I refused to go home with them. At first, they were livid, all indignant sputtering and shaking heads, but when that didn't work, they begged me. But it didn't matter. I wasn't going. Maybe ever. I was nineteen years old. They couldn't force me to do anything I didn't want to do. I promised my father I wouldn't drink anymore and sent them on their way. It was the best I could manage.

THERE WAS a fire burning somewhere near the highway, and the smoke was stinging my eyes, so I rolled up the truck window and closed the vents. It took about thirty seconds for the interior of the pick-up to feel like a sauna, but I figured I'd outdrive it in another five minutes or so.

The Rolling Stones had given way to David Bowie, Lynyrd Skynyrd, and Johnny Cash. Sam had always loved Johnny Cash, had a big poster of him in his bedroom growing up. He'd even tried to style his hair like Johnny's his senior year in high school. I used to make fun of him, Steady Sam jamming to the Man in Black, the ultimate rebel. My big brother usually just smiled and turned up the volume until he couldn't hear me anymore.

ABOUT A month after I'd been arrested, Sam showed up at the restaurant one evening, sat at a table by the bathroom, ordered himself a steak and baked potato for dinner, and waited there until I finished work.

We took a walk along the river and talked. Well, Sam did most of the talking. I just listened and nodded my head every once in a while.

Sam had done some long-distance detective work and talked to my old roommate and a couple of my former teammates. They'd told him all about Lexie and the partying. I told him that my behavior was my own responsibility and no one else's. Lexie wasn't some kind of blonde she-devil who had corrupted a good old, innocent country boy; I had done that all by myself. As for the partying, I admitted I had let it get out of control, but claimed I had a better handle on it now. All of which was a big fat lie. Hell, I was buzzed that very night from stealing shots from behind the bar, Sam just didn't know it.

After more than an hour of listening to him lecture, I told my big brother I loved him and appreciated the advice, but my feet hurt from working a double-shift and I needed to get some rest.

He asked one last time if I would come home with him, and when I shook my head, he pulled out an envelope from his jacket pocket and handed it to me. I opened it and found seven hundred dollars in cash. "Dad asked me to give it to you. He said to tell you it's not much, but he hopes it helps a little," Sam said, hugging me goodbye. "Maybe you can get your own place. Start taking better care of yourself."

Two hours later, I had spent the entire envelope on cocaine. The coke barely lasted three days, and when it was gone, I was burning so intensely for another hit that I broke into my manager's office at the restaurant and stole the petty cash. The whole thing had been captured by a security camera, and I was arrested later that night.

THE TRUCK window was rolled down again, the temperature dropping into the high seventies as dusk drew near, and I still felt the red-hot rush of shame spread across my face. I'd been a junkie, plain and simple. There was no other word to describe it.

For the past six months I'd been sending money home to my mother every other week to try to make some sort of amends. Each time a payment showed up in the mailbox, she'd call and try to talk me into taking it back ("Buy yourself a cellphone, honey, or some new clothes…") but I refused. It wasn't much, a hundred and fifty here, a buck and a quarter there, but it was the right thing to do. Mom and Dad had wasted so much money on me—fines, court costs, attorney fees—it made my stomach ache just thinking about it.

I spotted a rest stop up ahead and pulled off and parked. I was thirsty and needed to pee something fierce. On the way to the restroom, as I was crossing the parking lot, I watched a father lift his young son into a car seat, buckle him in, and kiss him on the tip of his nose before closing the door.

I swallowed the lump in my throat and kept on walking.

AFTER MY second arrest, I had no choice but to move back home. The restaurant fired me, of course, and my friend had finally had enough and kicked me out of his apartment. Then, there was my father. For the second time in as many months, he made the drive south and bailed me out. But this time his help came with one condition: that I move back to Salisbury, get a job, and keep myself out of trouble.

I had no money, a police record, a forthcoming court date, and no place to live.

So, I went home.

At first, it wasn't so bad. I moved back into my old bedroom and being there seemed to help settle me. My father called in a favor and got me a job laying asphalt with a road crew working the next county over, so I didn't have to worry much about running into any old friends. The closest I came was one afternoon when I spotted my ex-high school History teacher while I was working the flag and directing traffic. I turned my back on her before she could get a good look and she went on her way without recognizing me.

I stayed home at night. No bars, no parties, nothing. I spent most evenings watching the Orioles on television and reading my old comic books.

It wasn't easy, but some nights I forced myself to go downstairs and watch the game with my dad or sit on the screened-in back porch and keep my mom company while she played solitaire. Despite everything I'd done, talking to my mother was still laid-back and comforting. Without putting any pressure on me, she spoke about my future like I still had a chance. "You just have to get your feet back under you," she would always say, with a hopeful smile. "It'll happen, just give it time."

My father wasn't quite so uplifting. He was friendly and supportive enough, but there was a coolness to his words and body language, and he was all about today, never once talking about the future with me. Plans, hopes, dreams— not a word. It was like he believed I had already ruined any chance I had of making something of myself, and now the best I could do was remain invisible and not bring any more disgrace to our family.

When I was growing up, my father would often mow the lawn or tinker around out in the garage until dusk, and then he'd come barreling inside, give my mom a big sweaty kiss, fix a plate of cheese and crackers and pepperoni at the kitchen counter, grab a couple cold beers from the fridge, and he and mom would camp out in front of the television for an hour or two watching their "shows." That all stopped when I came home. I never heard a peep of disagreement from either of them, but they definitely started spending more time apart than together. I still saw Dad snacking on the occasional platter of cheese and crackers, but the absence of those cold beers spoke volumes. Dad had made damn sure not a drop of liquor remained in the house. Not even my mother's favorite wine.

I wish I could say that I had stopped drinking anyway, but that would be a lie. I had purchased a small silver flask from one of the guys on the road crew and had taken to sneaking shots of vodka during lunch breaks and before bedtime. I didn't miss the parties and beer at all. Hard liquor delivered a much better burn.

Sam came home for two weeks during winter break and it was then that I finally understood how deeply I had fractured our family. He greeted the three of us at the front door with a big smile and hugs, and then we went into the kitchen to drink hot chocolate, listen to his stories, and poke fun at his scraggly attempt at a beard. It felt good being all together again, laughing and joking, almost like old times.

After our parents had turned in for the night, I heard a knock at my bedroom door. "Come in," I said, knowing it was my big brother, expecting the good feelings to continue.

I couldn't have been more wrong.

The smile was gone from his face. He eased the door closed behind him and sat on the edge of my bed, his eyes holding not a hint of his previous warmth.

"Don't say anything, just listen," he whispered, waggling a finger in my face, and I could see then he had come to hate me. "When you screw up again, and you *will* screw up again, because that's what fuck-ups do, Mom and Dad are not going to be there for you. I'm not going to let them. You've wasted enough of their savings already."

I started to say something but he cut me off. "Shut up, Charlie. Just shut up. Do you know Mom doesn't go to St. Stephen's anymore because of you, because she couldn't handle the gossip? Do you know Dad was going to cut his hours last year, but instead he's put in for overtime?"

I shook my head, unable to form the words even had I been permitted.

"I'll do my best to keep up the act for Mom and Dad," he continued, "so their holiday isn't ruined like everything else you've spoiled for them, but you need to stay out of my way. I can barely stand the sight of you."

He got up and started for the door, then stopped.

"I know you think this is what they want, you here under the same roof, but the best thing that could happen is for you to go away and never come back again. You broke their damn hearts, Charlie."

I waited for him to slip back into the hallway and close the door, and then I whispered, "I'm sorry" to my empty bedroom.

THE BEST thing that could happen is for you to go away and never come back again...

I moved over into the slow lane and wiped the tears from my face, listening to the horrible words ricocheting around inside my head.

Never come back again...

Almost like a warning.

My heart thundered in my chest as I remembered the details of that night, the sound—the conviction—of my brother's voice, the glint of loathing in his eyes.

Never come back again...

I spotted the neon glow of a Wal-Mart sign in the distance and hit my turn signal for the next exit.

SAM RETURNED to school the first week of January and, as far as I knew, our parents never suspected a thing.

Work was slow—the asphalt crew transformed into a snow removal crew during the winter, and it had been an unseasonably dry couple of months—so I started getting a serious case of cabin fever. To alleviate that dreadful sensation of the walls closing in, I started sneaking out a few nights a week after my parents went to sleep, something I hadn't even resorted to in high school. It was easy. I simply crept down the carpeted hallway and staircase, slipped out the basement door, and walked into town.

I didn't go to local bars or even liquor stores.

Instead, I crept around like a phantom in the night, ducking into shadowy alleyways and behind trees and rows of shrubbery each time headlights swept across the roadway. I glimpsed the glow of television screens in windows and heard muffled conversations beyond closed doors and envied the people living those lives. It was during those late night walks that I truly realized what I had become: an outsider.

Sam came home for a long weekend over Easter break. Once again, he put on the fake smile and phony friendly voice, and Mom and Dad ate it up. The family was back together, that was all they cared about.

There was no closed door, follow-up lecture this time. We both knew it wasn't necessary after the last one.

On the Saturday night before Easter, while we were hauling empty garbage cans up from the curb, Sam confronted me. "I know you've been sneaking out at night."

I was stunned but managed to be defiant. "What in the hell are you talking about?"

"Don't play dumb with me, Charlie. I heard you last night."

"That was the first time," I stuttered, cursing myself for being so stupid.

"You're lying. I talked to Stan Burris. He's seen you at least three or four other nights. Slinking around town like some kind of pervert."

"Stan Burris is a fucking idiot."

"Maybe so, but if you do it again, I'm turning you in."

"To who?" I asked, my voice rising in anger.

He leaned the garbage can against the side of the house and walked inside without answering.

Despite the warning—hell, maybe because of it—I snuck out the very next night. And made the biggest mistake of my life.

IT KILLS me now to admit this, but as the weeks dragged on that winter and my late night wanderings continued, at some point I crossed the line from innocent voyeur to petty thief. I broke into sheds and garages and cars and stole items ranging from purses and wallets to tools and sporting equipment. I kept the cash and sold the rest to a coworker on the road crew who owned a quarter stake in a pawnshop.

To this day, I still don't understand why I did it. Virgil told me once I most likely started breaking the law again because it was what was expected of me at that point. I don't know if he was right or it was just a bunch of self-help mumbo jumbo, but the truth of the matter was: I felt more alive when I was walking the edge.

On Easter night, after a long day of feasting on honey-glazed ham, scalloped potatoes, and green bean casserole, watching home movies, and playing a marathon game of Hearts at the kitchen table, Mom and Dad turned in early at shortly after nine o'clock. Sam followed an hour later. I closed up house and my bedroom door at ten-thirty, and then opened it again and snuck out at fifteen minutes after midnight, extending my middle finger when I tip-toed past Sam's bedroom door.

As I made my way across town, I had the distinct feeling I was being followed, so I doubled back and hid behind a tree, searching the shadows for movement. But I didn't see a thing. Not even a roaming dog or cat. Chalking it up to paranoia and my overactive imagination, I continued on my way until I found an unlocked work truck parked along the curb near the intersection of Broadview Avenue and Tupelo Road.

I eased the passenger door open, quickly switched off the interior light, and was about to lift a silver tool box out of the back seat, when I heard someone call out behind me.

"Hey, what the hell you doing?"

I turned to run, but before I made it more than five or six feet, I was tackled to the ground.

"Fucking punks stealing my shit." The man was large and strong and pissed off. I elbowed him in the head and rolled out of his grasp, started to take off running again, but he grabbed my ankle and held on for dear life.

I spun and tried to kick him away, but he was too fast. He twisted my leg and sprang to his feet, throwing punches as he did. I felt a whoosh of air as the first punch missed my nose by less than an inch, and then a fist glanced off the side of my head and my ear started ringing. I quickly back-pedaled, struggling to stay on my feet, but he kept coming.

"Kill you, motherfucker," he bellowed.

I believed him, too.

He lunged and caught me on the shoulder, and I felt my left arm go numb. He immediately reared back and attacked again. I ducked and he missed, and I instinctively put all my weight behind a wild right-handed haymaker.

I felt my knuckles connect with his jaw and heard two sounds almost simultaneously: the loud crack of bone on bone and the louder crack of his skull hitting the sidewalk.

He lay there on the ground, unmoving. I watched as a dark puddle spread around his head.

I stood there, knowing I was in big trouble, hearing Sam's voice telling me he knew I would screw up again because that's what fuck-ups do, my eyes darting back and forth in the darkness, torn between running away and banging on the front door of the man's house and waking someone to call for help.

And then sirens shattered the night and I saw flashing lights getting closer, closer, and I knew the decision had been made for me.

I SAT in the Wal-Mart parking lot and finished activating the Nokia burner phone I had just purchased, along with two candy bars and a bottle of Gatorade. Then I punched in the numerical code printed on the back of the plastic card and added ninety minutes of airtime. That was more than I would need.

Once I was sure the phone was working, I pulled out of the lot and merged back onto the highway. It was dark now, going on nine o'clock, and the traffic had grown even lighter. I left the radio off.

After a few miles, when I felt ready, I grabbed the phone from the passenger seat and called a number by memory. It rang three times before it was answered.

"Hello? If you're selling something, you need to take a hike."

I laughed. "Dude, you sell tractors."

"I beg your pardon. I am a distinguished merchant of only the finest farm equipment in the land."

"So you're pretty much a used car salesman."

"Your words hurt me, Charlie. Deeply. Now what can I do for you and whose phone are you using? I don't recognize the number."

"I picked up one of those cheap throwaways. I called to tell you that my father died. I'm on my way home as we speak."

The sound of the television in the background went silent and Virgil's voice changed. "Ahh, damn. I'm sorry, kid. You okay?"

I shrugged. "I think so. Lots of thoughts bouncing around inside my head."

"That's normal, Charlie. You and your father had a…complicated relationship."

"You mean I was the black sheep of the family and ruined his life, don't you?"

"That's bullshit. You made mistakes and so did he. You're both too stubborn for your own good."

"Anyway, I just wanted to let you know in case I don't make it back for the meeting next Thursday."

"That's fine. You know you can always attend a meeting at home, if you feel the need. I can look up the details for you if you'd like."

I surprised myself by agreeing, "I'd appreciate that."

"Charlie, you know it's okay to say you called to tell me about your father because we're friends, too, right?"

"Ummm, sure."

"I mean we *are* friends, Charlie. I'm more than just your sponsor."

"I know that."

"Okay, just making sure. I think you need to be reminded that you're a decent person once in a while. Not too often or you'll get a big head, but every once in a while is okay."

"Thanks, Virgil."

"Don't mention it. Now tell me about those thoughts bouncing around your head."

"Ahh, you know, reliving the past, trying to figure out why I did the things I did, the usual."

"Play, rewind, play, rewind, and so on, is that how it goes?"

"You know it."

"Just remember what I always say: The past is the past for a reason. Learn from it and move on. Believe in the good things."

"What good things?"

"Don't start with me, boy."

I smiled. "Yes, sir."

"Let me ask you something before you go, Charlie."

"Shoot."

"Do you remember when you first started coming to meetings in Burtonsville?"

"Of course."

"You remember old lady Henderson?"

"Sure."

"She was an old witch, crotchety and cranky as hell. No one liked her very much, including me."

"I remember."

"Well, you changed all that. You were the new guy but you took the time to talk to her about her family. You didn't let her nasty-ass mouth scare you away. You even fixed her car that one night in the parking lot."

"So what's your point?"

"My point is you didn't have to do any of those things. She was one of those people who made it very hard for others to reach out and help. But you did it anyway."

"Okay."

"My other point is you have a good heart, Charlie Freeman, and that's rarer than you think. You've made your mistakes and paid for them. Accept the fact that other people—other *good* people—also make mistakes. Sometimes big ones. You have to forgive and move on. That big heart of yours will lead you to good things soon enough."

FOR THE second time tonight, I wiped tears from my face. I wasn't much of a crier, never had been, but that goddamn Virgil had a way with words. But it was more than that. I wanted to believe the kind things he said about me so badly it made my heart ache.

I checked the time and was surprised to see that it was nearly ten o'clock already. Another couple hours and I'd be back in Salisbury for the first time in almost seven years. It didn't seem possible, both my long absence and my unplanned home-coming. My father was dead. I was an ex-con. It all felt like a bad dream.

I remembered waking up my father one night when I was probably only seven or eight years old after I'd had a particularly scary nightmare. Instead of being angry at me for interrupting his sleep, he'd taken me into the kitchen and poured a big glass of milk and we'd gone outside into the back yard and sat side-by-side on the picnic table next to Mom's garden.

He put his arm around me and pointed out Mars and Venus in the night sky and showed me how to find the Big Dipper and the North Star. We talked baseball and fishing and monster movies and I asked about the bullfrogs and the crickets that were making so much of a racket that night. Then, and I remember this as clear as if it were yesterday, I asked him about fireflies. What did they do? Where did they come from?

After a long pause, my father looked at me and said, "Well, you know how I told you about frogs and the different purposes they serve?"

I nodded. "They eat insects and bugs, but they also get eaten by fish and snakes."

He pulled me closer. "That's right. Fireflies are a little different. Sometimes I think God creates something special just to remind us that the world is beautiful, that magic still exists."

"Like what?" I asked.

"Well...like the Grand Canyon for instance, or the ocean or the moon," he said, pointing high above our heads. "And fireflies."

"Fireflies are magic?" I said, looking up at him, transfixed.

"I think so, Charlie. I really do." And then he hopped down off the picnic table and headed for the house at a jog. "Stay right there. I want to show you something."

He returned a couple of minutes later with one of Mom's canning jars. "If you don't tell her I poked holes in the lid, I won't."

"What are the holes for?"

He smiled. "Come and see."

I followed my father into the darkness then and he showed me how to catch fireflies with my bare hands, carefully, so as not to harm them. We ran in circles, chasing magic that night, slipping and falling on the wet grass, laughing and yelling under the stars, just the two of us, a father and son dressed in pajamas, best friends, and nothing else mattered in the whole world.

I BLINKED away the memory and reached for the phone again. I had purchased it for a specific reason, and it was time to put it to use.

I punched in the number and half hoped that I had remembered it incorrectly.

My hands were shaking.

I heard a familiar voice and a loud beep.

I left a brief message, my voice strong.

I hung up and glanced at the clock.

Ninety more minutes, and I would be home again.

SALISBURY WAS a working-class town with a population of nearly 20,000 people. But it seemed smaller than that. Divided into a half-dozen slices-of-pie communities by several large farms, the houses were modest and well maintained, the land low-lying and flat and much of it thickly wooded.

I tapped my brakes as I approached the old Pepsi bottling factory and was not the least bit surprised by the lack of change it had undergone. I had worked my first job at the plant—the summer I turned fifteen—hauling cases of empties out of the back of trucks and sorting them onto a conveyor belt. The three-story, white-washed building looked exactly the same as it had when I was a teenager.

Another couple of miles and I slowed again as I drove past the Perdue Farms corporate headquarters. Perdue Chicken was the town's largest employer, providing work for more than 2,000 residents, including my father and Uncle Bobby. Even at this late hour, the parking lot was full and the windows blazed with light, the night shift just getting started.

Everything about the town looked the same to me—the high school, post office, pizza shop, even the gas stations—like I had stepped into a time machine. I guess it shouldn't have shocked me as much as it did, considering it had only been seven years, but for some reason I couldn't put my finger on it did. Seven years felt like a lifetime.

I stopped the truck and stared at the little league field where I had first learned to play baseball. My father had been my first coach. He'd shown me how to field a grounder and lay down a bunt.

On the move again, I crossed over Winter's Run where Sam and I used to fish with our friends for perch and sunnies and catfish, and where we would swim on hot summer days, swinging from an old tire and hurling ourselves into the deepest part of the creek. I remembered when I had landed wrong and cracked my head open on a rock one Fourth of July. Sam had carried me home over his shoulder for almost a mile. Mom had almost fainted when we'd walked in the front door, both of us covered in my blood.

I followed the winding road parallel to the creek for another couple of miles and reached the old wooden Hanson Road Bridge at five minutes before midnight. I pulled to the dirt shoulder and parked and turned off my headlights, and when my eyes adjusted to the darkness, I could just make out the silhouette of a car parked on the opposite side of the bridge. I couldn't tell what make it was or if there was anyone inside, but it didn't matter. I knew whose car it was.

He had gotten my message.

I CLIMBED out of the truck and stood at the mouth of the bridge, searching for movement. I could hear the rush of water flowing over the rocks below, and the familiar smell of creek mud and algae bloom greeted me. High overhead, the breeze shifted and a sliver of moonbeam filtered down through the trees.

I had kissed my first girl standing on this bridge: Carol Burnside. I'd been fourteen years old and head-over-heels in love with my next-door neighbor. Six months later, her family moved to Pennsylvania and I never spoke to her again.

I started walking across the bridge, slowly, eyes scanning, when a voice came from the darkness: "Charlie, is that you?"

I froze. "Sam?"

I heard footsteps on gravel and my big brother walked into view. His hair was cut short and he was wearing a gray suit minus the tie. I was surprised—and annoyed—to realize he looked younger than me.

He smiled nervously. I could tell he didn't know whether to shake my hand or hug me. Instead, he did neither. He just stood there, staring. "It's good to see you. I couldn't believe it when I heard your message."

"It was you," I said, getting right to business. "You followed me that night."

The smile vanished.

"All these years…you must think I'm so fucking stupid."

"I don't think you're stupid, Charlie."

I put a hand up. "Shut up, okay. Just…shut up. It's your turn to listen."

He nodded and looked at the ground.

"That night you came into my room...you told me '*The best thing that could happen is for you to go away and never come back again.*' I thought it was a warning, but it wasn't, was it?" I clenched and unclenched my fists. "It was a *promise.*"

"I didn't know what else to do. You wouldn't listen—"

"You followed me that night," I said. "You were the one who called the police."

"You almost killed a man."

"It was an accident. I was trying to get away."

"I knew you were using again during winter break. I saw the signs and I didn't know what to do."

"I wasn't using!" I screamed in his face, and he jerked back from me, shielding himself with his arm like I was going to hit him.

I wanted to. More than anything. I wanted to choke him and throw him off the damn bridge. "I haven't touched drugs in over seven years, not since that night in college."

"That's great, Charlie. It really is."

"I knew someone was following me. I even doubled back and checked, but I didn't see anyone." My shoulders sagged. "You called the police on your own damn brother."

Sam looked down at his feet again. "I'm sorry."

I laughed then. I couldn't help it. "You're *sorry?*" I held my arms up toward the sky. "Hear that, everyone? He's sorry!"

"Charlie—"

"All these years, not one visit, not even a phone call or a fucking postcard."

He was crying now. "I wrote letters—"

"Bullshit."

"I did. I wrote lots of them…I just couldn't get up the nerve to mail them. I still have them, Charlie. Hidden in my office. You can read them if you want."

"No, thanks," I snarled. I felt the heat rise in my face and my hands curled into fists again. I took a step toward him.

"I don't care what you do to me," he said, holding his ground, "but will you please wait until after the funeral to tell Mom?" He wiped his nose with his suit sleeve. "She's fragile. I don't think she can handle any more right now."

I was trying to decide whether to floor him or tell him to go to hell when Virgil's voice whispered inside my head: *Accept the fact that other people—other* good *people—also make mistakes.*

I hesitated. *Sometimes big ones.*

I lowered my hands. *You have to forgive and move on.*

I turned and started walking away, slowly counting to ten inside my head. *That big heart of yours will lead you to good things soon enough.*

"You won't say anything, right, Charlie?" he called out from behind me, his voice edged with panic.

I waved a hand in his direction, but I didn't turn around and I didn't stop walking until I reached the truck.

I MADE a left on Cherry Avenue and followed the familiar winding curve up over the hill and there it was in the distance.

Home.

My breath caught in my throat and my eyes welled with sudden tears. I quickly wiped them away.

The lights were on in the kitchen, and I could see my mother's favorite rose-covered curtains still hanging in the window.

As I pulled into the driveway, a second light turned on upstairs—in my old bedroom—and I saw a dark shadow flit across the window. My mother was still awake.

I sat inside the truck for a minute, gathering myself, and then I grabbed my knapsack and got out. Crickets whirred in the open fields around me and although I hadn't noticed a single one while I had been driving, dozens—maybe hundreds—of fireflies danced in the night sky, blinking their tiny yellow-green lights.

I turned in a slow circle, eyes wide, mouth hanging open, staring with astonishment. I had never seen such a sight in my entire life.

Sometimes I think God creates something special just to remind us that the world is beautiful, that magic still exists.

I slowly reached out and caught a firefly in the palm of my hand. It blinked a friendly hello to me and fluttered away.

Fireflies are magic?

I walked to the other side of the truck and gazed into the back yard where I could just make out the dark shape of an old picnic table sitting next to Mom's garden.

I think so, Charlie. I really do.

For a fleeting moment, I thought I glimpsed two figures sitting there, and then they were gone.

When I turned back to the house, the front door was standing open and my mother was hurrying down the porch stairs.

I dropped my knapsack and ran to her.

STORY
NOTES

You know the drill, folks.

For those readers who enjoy learning about "the story behind the story," these Notes are for you. So pull up a chair and have a seat, and let's talk a bit. I have a few more secrets I want to tell you.

And if you're one of those readers who would rather just stick to the stories themselves, hey, that's okay, too. Go right ahead and ignore these little afterwords and dive right into that next book on your *To Read* pile. If it's anything like mine, it's about head-high off the floor and tottering.

Finally, regardless of which camp you find yourself in, please wait to read these Story Notes until *after* you have read the stories themselves. There are spoilers lurking in the shadows ahead.

THE MAN BEHIND THE MASK — This story originally appeared on my website (cleverly located at RichardChizmar. com, for the curious among you); this is its first appearance in book form.

I've often wondered what happens to survivors of serial killers after they manage to escape or are rescued. The personal journeys and obstacles they must endure and overcome in order to once again become healthy, functioning human beings in today's society. I've thought a lot about the tornado of emotions they must experience on a daily basis. The guilt and regret; the memories and fears; the hopes and dreams.

"The Man Behind the Mask" is the result of all those dark musings. I like this story a lot, despite its horrific ending. I adore and admire the main character, Jennifer Shea. She certainly deserves a better fate than the one I gave her. As for the story's conclusion, I don't know that I've ever written a more disturbing final act. I shuddered when I first wrote it, and I'm wincing right now just thinking about it.

THE BAD GUYS — This short tale first appeared in *Ellery Queen's Mystery Magazine* (you can read more about my affection for the magazine in the first of two essays, which appear later in this collection). The story itself came very quickly (a single sitting at the keyboard) and, as does much of my fiction, explores the thin line that exists between "the good guys" and "the bad guys." Just as with real life, it's often hard to tell the difference. I thought a lot about my dear old friend, Ed Gorman, as I wrote this story. I sure miss you, Ed.

THE MEEK SHALL INHERIT... — Many of my stories focus on the horrors and dark secrets that lurk in normal, everyday suburban neighborhoods. I've always found "the monster next door" a whole lot more terrifying than vampires or zombies or any other type of supernatural creature. These folks are usually evil and clever as hell, and unless we catch a break and their masks slip, we often never find out the truth about them until it's too late.

"The Meek Shall Inherit..." is an example of too late. The neighborhood in the story is the neighborhood I grew up in. Jimmy and Brian are real life kids that lived on my street. Best friends—brothers—I am still close with today. I hope they forgive me their part in this dark adventure.

SILENT NIGHT — I'm a big kid at heart, and I love the holidays. Halloween, Christmas, Thanksgiving; you name it, and I'm a fan. But I've also—from a very early age—always recognized the darker shadows that permeate these special days. The sense of melancholy and loneliness and despair that often walks hand-in-hand with the joy and celebration. It's simply more difficult for some people to hide the truth—from themselves as well as others—during the holiday season. Just thinking about it breaks my heart.

We are never provided with the main character's name or true identity in this story—both victims of the long ago sacrifice he made in order to protect his family. Throughout, he is only referred to as "the man." Somber and laced with regret, "Silent Night" is a different kind of ghost story.

WIDOW'S POINT — For me, 2017 was the year of the collaboration. First there was *Gwendy's Button Box*, co-written with Stephen King. This coming-of-age novella was a blast to write (understatement of the year), and surprised all of us by landing on the *New York Times* bestseller list for a month and selling all around the world. I'm grateful for every second of the experience and hope to do it again one day.

But, believe it or not, there was a second collaboration that meant even more to me.

When Mark Parker (editor/owner of Scarlet Galleon Publications) asked me to write a horror story involving the sea for his *Fearful Fathoms* anthology, two thoughts came immediately to mind: 1) I want to write about a haunted lighthouse; and 2) I wonder if my son, Billy, would be interested in writing with me.

Billy, eighteen at the time, had already sold several short horror stories and essays to pro-level publications, so I knew the idea of haunted sea tales would appeal to him. But writing alongside his old man? That I wasn't so sure of.

Fortunately, he dug the idea, and we soon set off on our adventure. I sat down and wrote the opening of the story, establishing our main character and the initial history of the Widow's Point Lighthouse. Billy took it from there, lending the story his own unique flavor and helping the characters and setting come to vibrant life. We traded sections back and forth for a couple weeks—added, subtracted, rewrote, polished—and, before we knew it, we had a completed story. We sent it off to Mark Parker and, to our relief, he loved the story and gave it a place of honor in his anthology. It is reprinted here for the first time.

But Billy and I weren't quite finished yet.

"Widow's Point" refused to leave me alone, even after it was published. The history of the lighthouse, the spirits that roamed within its stone walls...they kept lingering in my thoughts, whispering to me, *calling* to me.

One afternoon, I texted Billy and told him I didn't think we were finished with the story, that I believed there was more to tell. To my surprise, he replied that he had been feeling the exact same way. In short order, we decided to expand the story into a full-length novella. The writing came fast and furious. We called it our "everything but the kitchen sink" story (because we giddily crammed just about everything we could think of into the narrative), and had so much fun from start to finish. When we were done, we knew we hadn't reinvented the wheel, but felt we had crafted a compelling and truly unsettling page-turner.

A slim hardcover edition of *Widow's Point* was published in January 2018. To father and son's delight, sales and reviews were strong, and foreign rights were soon sold to numerous countries, including England, Germany, Italy, and Bulgaria. Audio

482 | RICHARD CHIZMAR

rights recently sold here in the States, and a film adaptation is currently in the works. Finally, there are now plans for a prequel and a sequel to *Widow's Point*, and I can't wait to get started.

MY FATHER AND *ELLERY QUEEN'S MYSTERY MAGAZINE* — Not much to say about this one that isn't covered in the original essay. My father was a quiet man. A reader, a thinker, a tinkerer (his garage workshop was a magical place when I was a kid), the hardest working and best man I've ever known. He (along with my mother) supported me every step of the way, even as I ignored my college degree to start a small publishing company at age twenty-one. He was and will always be my hero.

THE WITCH — I've written several stories featuring Frank and Ben, my two favorite police detectives. "Night Call" and "Night Shift" appeared in my last collection, *A Long December*, and two more appear in this one.

For the record, I love Halloween. I love everything about it—the old-fashioned traditions and set pieces, and even all of the modern gaudiness and flash. But I'm a pretty simple guy. Give me some spooky music and homemade decorations, and I'm a happy man. Throw in a pillowcase full of candy to dig through, and a pocket full of candy corn to throw at the cars that drive too fast through my neighborhood on Halloween night, and I'm downright giddy.

A few readers have commented that "The Witch" is almost an anti-Halloween story, but it's truly not intended to be. Frank Logan can be a cranky SOB. I blame him.

A NIGHTMARE ON ELM LANE — As noted earlier, I write a lot about suburban neighborhoods. I grew up in one in the small town of Edgewood, Maryland, and it was a pretty wonderful experience. Think Kevin Arnold and *The Wonder Years*, and you'll get a fairly accurate picture of what it was like for me. My best friends lived right up the street. We walked to school together. Trick-or-treated together. Had more sleepovers than I can count. We spent our summers playing outside all day—whiffle ball, marbles, kick the can, flashlight tag, trading baseball cards, fishing, exploring, shooting BB guns, building forts, throwing crab apples at cars. We had our haunted house (The Myers' House), our grumpy neighbors, our weird neighbors, our bullies, and we even had our wrong side of the tracks.

It was an idyllic place to grow up, but it wasn't perfect.

And I recognized that from a very early age.

Even as a young boy, I scanned the local newspaper (we only had one). I read about the thefts, the assaults, the small town scandals. I saw the burn-outs selling weed outside of the pool hall and noticed the bruises on some of my friends (not my closest friends, thank God, but guys—and girls—from the next street or block over).

I remember walking home by myself many nights and imagining what life was like for the people who lived inside the houses I passed. I saw lights glowing in windows or televisions flickering on dark curtains, and made up stories about the people inside my head.

A lot of these houses hold secrets, I remember thinking. How well do we really know our neighbors? We wave hello to them, beep our car horns as we drive past, maybe share a hot dog and a soda at a neighborhood cook-out, but how well do we *really* know them?

What might they be hiding inside those walls? In their dark basements and dusty attics and locked bedrooms? What might they have buried in their back yards…?

DIRTY COPPERS — I miss Ed Gorman every day, as a friend and mentor and writer. I've written a lot about Ed in the past—both while he was still with us and after he passed away—so I won't repeat myself here. Just know this, if it weren't for Ed, I probably wouldn't be writing and publishing today. He, along with Steve King, are pretty much my guardian angels in this crazy business, and I will always be in their debt.

When I first began to assemble this collection, I realized that I hadn't read "Dirty Coppers" since it was originally published back in 1997. Twenty long years ago. That's a long time for more experienced eyes to look back on a piece of fiction. After two decades, words tend to grow moldy, their vibrancy and clarity lost in a maze of cobwebs. So I had no idea what to expect when I pulled out the manuscript, but the very last thing I would've predicted were tears in my eyes.

The tears didn't come because I had rediscovered that "Dirty Coppers" was a classic piece of sci-fi/noir fiction (trust me, it's not) or because it was a complete embarrassment (it's not that, either). The tears came because, for about an hour on that Sunday evening while I turned the pages, my dear old friend was alive again. Sitting there at my side, reading our story in that deep, sarcastic voice of his, laughing that wonderful gruff laugh of his. Ed Gorman, my guardian angel, teaching me again. Even now.

MISCHIEF — I've always been fascinated with serial killers. How they're made and how they often exist for years—sometimes decades—living among the rest of us without detection. For me, there is nothing more terrifying.

The mysterious clearing that Lester Billings stumbles upon in "Mischief" exists in real life. I was taking a walk one autumn afternoon with my family and in-laws around a lake in Pennsylvania when we decided to take a shortcut back to the car. We ended up getting lost for a short time, and that's when we wandered into the clearing. There was no well and no crumbling building (as there exists in the story), just a stretch of sun-burnt grass and weeds, devoid of any trees and even the barest hint of nature's beauty. None of the others said a word, but

I felt it right away—there was something wrong with the place. I couldn't put my finger on exactly what it was. Something was just *off* about it, and I was relieved to leave it behind us.

I've thought a lot about that clearing over the years—even dreamt about it a time or two—and I guess I always knew that I would write about it one day. Hopefully, that dreadful place is out of my system now and I can forget all about it.

Hopefully, it doesn't work its way into your dreams now.

THE MAN IN THE BLACK SWEATER — Believe it or not, I had never heard of a "drabble" until Kevin Kennedy asked me to write one last year for an anthology he was editing.

"What the hell is a drabble?" I emailed, prepared to turn him down.

"It's a one hundred word story," he answered. "Precisely one hundred words."

Well, hell, that sounded like fun.

"Count me in," I wrote back, and proceeded to not only contribute my own drabble, but a collaboration with my son as well.

And I was right—it ended up being a lot of fun, a nifty little exercise in word economy.

ODD NUMBERS — This is an odd one (no pun intended). As much an in-depth character study as a weird tale, I feel a lot of sympathy for the main character in "Odd Numbers." How could I not? He's such a decent man living a nightmare existence. Whether that nightmare primarily exists inside his head or is indeed reality isn't up to me. In the end, that's your (the reader's) decision to make.

Some people have asked how much of this character is based on me. Fortunately, not that much. I admit I *do* prefer odd numbers over even, and 33 *is* my favorite number (my jersey number from back in my lacrosse days) and 24 my least favorite number, but I swear I've never counted my steps walking to the store, nor do I believe the trees in my back yard are creeping closer to my house. Although, now that I think about it…

THE HUNCH — Another Frank and Ben story. I really enjoy writing about these two middle-aged detectives and their unique perspective on the world around them. In fact, once I knock out a handful of other writing deadlines, I plan to sit down and write a longer piece featuring Frank and Ben. It will serve as the anchor for a mini-collection of Frank and Ben tales coming later this year from Borderlands Press.

Frank and Ben, and their very own book of stories. I think they'd like that idea. Well, at least, I think Ben would. I'm sure Frank would find something to bitch about.

ROSES AND RAINDROPS — Back in the late 1980's— yeah, I know, many of you weren't even alive back then—the horror scene was a happening place. New York publishing was booming and there were horror-specific imprints from TOR and NAL and Zebra and Leisure. Each month brought a wide variety of new horror titles, and themed and un-themed mass-market anthologies overflowed bookstore shelves. You could even still find pro magazines like *The Twilight Zone* and *Omni* at your local newsstand.

But, for me, the small press was where the most vital work was being published in the horror genre. You had a proliferation of quality specialty book publishers (Dark Harvest, Ziesing Books, Underwood-Miller, Donald Grant) and semi-pro mags that were every bit as entertaining—and difficult to sell to—as the big boys. I'm talking about *The Horror Show, Midnight Graffiti, New Blood, Grue, Deathrealm,* and several others. And then there were the really small—but no less enjoyable and devoted—publications like my own *Cemetery Dance* and *Thin Ice* and *Portents* and *Doppelganger* and *Eldritch Tales* and many many more.

If you're starting to get the picture that the late 80's was a great time to be a horror fan and writer, you're right on target.

I was there. I lived—and loved—every minute of it.

I sold my first short story in 1987. I was a twenty-year-old college student at the time. The story was a devil-comes-to-small town, Stephen King imitation, and, after only a handful of rejections, it sold to a California-based publication called *Scifant.*

I remember that was a very good day.

Over the next several years, I racked up dozens and dozens of rejections (from pretty much every pro and semi-pro magazine I mentioned above) and many more sales (to most of the smaller publications I mentioned above and a stack of others, including the elegantly-titled *Festering Brain Sores* magazine).

In addition to *The Horror Show*, the magazine I most wanted to land a story with back in those days was Chris Lacher's *New Blood*. The magazine looked spectacular and Lacher paid professional rates and had published good stories by many of my favorite authors at the time; guys like Ray Garton (his first short fiction sale, I believe) and Bill Relling and Dave Silva. They were graphic tales that didn't flinch from violence or sexuality or even downright deviance. It certainly wasn't my usual fiction flavor, but I was young and energetic and determined to crack the *New Blood* vault—something I finally did, after more than a dozen rejections, in 1990 with a nasty little tale called "Roses and Raindrops."

I remember several things about that special sale:

Chris Lacher offered some wonderful suggestions that made the story better (I still have the marked-up manuscript in my files);

It was my biggest sale to date, and Kara and I celebrated with a steak and shrimp dinner;

I was devastated a short time later when *New Blood* closed its doors before the story could appear within its pages.

For reasons unknown to me then and now, I never submitted "Roses and Raindrops" to anyone else after it was returned to me. For over two decades, it sat in my files. Forgotten.

Until a year or so ago, when I stumbled upon the old, yellowed manuscript—and several others—tucked away in a dusty file at my home office.

Finding and rereading those old stories—written at a time when Cemetery Dance Publications and my marriage and the birth of my boys and so many other life-altering moments weren't even a flicker in my mind—truly felt like taking a ride back in a time machine.

So many amazing memories came rushing over me, and I sat there and let them, remembering my old Apple computer; my dot-matrix printer; my beat-up desk and the first-floor apartment window I used to stare out of when my imagination was really working; the Post Office box I would rush to every afternoon to retrieve my mail; all the rejections; and the acceptances.

It really was a wonderful time to be young and full of dreams.

The first manuscript I pulled out and read that day was "Roses and Raindrops." It was rough around the edges (boy, was it) and very much in the vein of an EC Comics tale (as were most of my early story sales), but it was also something else—it was clearly a product of those heady horror days of the late 80's, and more importantly, it was *fun*. When I finished reading it, I decided I still liked the story quite a bit and immediately considered rewriting it.

I even sat down one afternoon and started. But then I had a change of heart—and a much better idea. I thought: *why don't I send the story to one of the other writers who grew up during that time period and ask them to rewrite it? Someone who was doing the exact same thing I was doing back in the late*

80's—churning out stories and stuffing them in envelopes with return postage and sending them off on their way with a hope and a prayer.

The first person I thought of in regards to "Roses and Raindrops" was Brian Keene. Talk about a guy who has worked in the trenches and paid his dues. I wasn't sure if Brian would be receptive (he's a pretty busy dude), so I was thrilled when he immediately and eagerly agreed to collaborate on the story. He even told me that he'd also been a big fan and had tried to crack *New Blood* magazine for many years himself. Once I'd heard that, I knew I'd made the right choice.

"Roses and Raindrops" (man, I still love that title) was finally published in 2016, paired alongside a second "rescued" short story, as an Apokrupha Press chapbook aptly titled, *Unearthed.*

STEPHEN KING AT 70: A TRIBUTE TO THE GUNSLINGER — Not much to add about this one. When Anthony Breznican, an editor at *Entertainment Weekly*—and a fine author himself; check out his first novel, *Brutal Youth;* it's an amazing book—asked if I would write a birthday tribute to Stephen King, I couldn't say "yes" fast enough.

I didn't mean to get quite so personal in the piece, but I couldn't help it. I love the guy.

THE ASSOCIATION — Yes, I love Bentley Little's novels and short stories (I even helped to adapt one of his tales for cable television—the wonderfully twisted "The Washingtonians" for Showtime's *Masters of Horror*).

And, yes, I know Bentley published a book some years ago called *The Association,* and it involved an evil home association.

So, what in the heck am I doing writing my own evil home association story and calling it "The Association," you ask? Well, that's a fair question. And the only answer I have is: *I couldn't help it.*

I had agreed to write a story for an anthology of anti-authority stories, dark tales that flipped a big, fat middle finger at "the man," and when I sat down to write, this is where my imagination took me.

I loathe everything about home owner associations. I'm sure some of them are well meaning and properly run by kind and logical folks, but I'll be damned if I have found one yet.

THE SCULPTOR — This is the second of two "rescued from the files" short stories published in this collection. I've already written at length about the first one, "Roses and Raindrops," so I'll try to keep this brief:

The second manuscript I slid out of the file that long ago afternoon was a lengthier tale called "The Sculptor." Right away, I remembered that it was my college roommate's favorite story of mine back then, and that it had never sold, despite

STORY NOTES | 493

STORY NOTES | **493**

STORY NOTES | 493

dozens of submissions (so much for my buddy's good taste). To my surprise and delight, I found myself still liking the story. Much like "Roses and Raindrops" it was a simple, fun, throwback horror tale.

And I had the perfect writer in mind to rewrite it: Ray Garton.

Remember when I mentioned earlier that Ray had sold his first-ever short story to *New Blood* magazine? Even at such a young age, Ray was a big deal back then. Still barely twenty years old, his debut novel, *Seductions*, had already been published in mass-market and Garton classics such as *Live Girls* and *Crucifix Autumn* weren't far behind. Ray was a master at writing about everyday folks down on their luck and faced with otherworldly obstacles. I knew he would be perfect for "The Sculptor."

Ray Garton and Brian Keene. I'm immensely grateful to both these guys…not only for years of entertainment and support and friendship, but for answering my calls and agreeing to come out and play with me (and my two stories from a long-ago time).

Both Ray and Brian are better writers than I am, and these two stories show it. The three of us had a blast, and we hope you did, too.

***MURDER HOUSE* SCRIPT** — My family and I recently moved into a restored, two-hundred-year-old farmhouse. The house sits on a nice stretch of land with a pond and lots of towering trees and grassy fields. It's a great place to live and create, and I love everything about it.

Before my family and I moved in, we ("we" meaning a contractor; I'm not so handy with a hammer and nail) did a major renovation of the interior of the house. The old stonework, and original moldings and hardwood floors remained, but much of the rest was made nice and new and shiny.

But before we would allow the contractor to take even a single step inside the house, my son, Billy, and I had the exact same thought: *we* have *to film a horror movie in here. It's old, it's empty, it's creepy as hell at night. It's perfect!*

So, that's what we did.

Billy and I spent a couple days in early January writing a short script that worked for the interior of our new house. We hired a local production company to produce and film the movie. We hired actors. And, over one long weekend just before the start of the new semester (three very long nights and one freezing cold early morning), Billy and I co-directed *Murder House*.

Friends have asked if we felt strange or even nervous filming such a dark and twisted movie in the house we were about to move into, as if our actions could possibly have somehow cursed our new home before we spent even a single night under its roof. I mean I get where they were coming from with the question. The title of the movie, after all, was *Murder House*, and it's not every day you design a huge pentagram inside your attic and surround it with burning candles. But, regardless of their reasoning, Billy and I always just smiled and shook our heads. *No, no, we're not worried.*

Well, maybe just a little bit.

THE CUSTER FILES — I've always loved movies about the Old West. When I was a kid, I often ditched whatever I was doing with friends on hot summer afternoons to run inside and catch a good western on television (I even used to check the *TV Guide* that was inserted into our Sunday morning newspaper ahead of time so I could mark the calendar that was magneted to our refrigerator with upcoming dates and show times). If a good "shoot em up" was scheduled on a school night, I would beg my parents to let me stay up late. And if the movie featured the U.S. Cavalry fighting Indians on the warpath, even better.

In my youthful naiveté (nowadays I root for the Indians in my westerns and in real life, too), my hero was the greatest Indian fighter of all-time, General George Armstrong Custer. I was obsessed with the guy. To me, he was brave and brash and a fearless leader. I watched every film that even mentioned Custer in passing, checked out books about his life from the library, and couldn't even tell you how many history reports I wrote about him for school. I knew dates and places and every other significant detail from Custer's life, and wanted nothing more than to grow up to serve in the Seventh Cavalry.

As the years passed, my obsession—like so many other fascinations from childhood that feel like they will live forever—faded and drifted away to the basement of my brain.

But it never totally left me, and when I was asked earlier this year to write a horror story featuring a real-life historical event, I immediately thought of "Yellow Hair" and the legendary Battle of the Little Big Horn.

"The Custer Files" is my version of what *really* happened on June 25, 1876.

THE LONG WAY HOME — I know people like Charlie Freeman. Broken, unhappy people who have made mistakes and spent the rest of their lives paying for them. Hopeless people who truly believe that they don't deserve good things because of past sins and transgressions. And it breaks my heart.

At times, I've stepped in and tried to help some of these folks with varying degrees of success. Other times, I've just stood by and watched, unable to find the right words to say or the right things to do. It's a terrible, helpless feeling.

I set out in "The Long Way Home" to write a fairly straightforward story about a father and a son and the deep canyon of regret that existed between them, but as is often the case with my fiction, things got a little…complicated.

I like the character of Charlie quite a bit and take solace in the fact that he's only twenty-six years old when this story takes place. There's still plenty of time for that big heart of his to lead him to the "good things."

COPYRIGHT INFORMATION

ABOUT THE AUTHOR

RICHARD CHIZMAR is a *New York Times, USA Today, Wall Street Journal, Washington Post, Amazon,* and *Publishers Weekly* bestselling author.

He is the co-author (with Stephen King) of the bestselling novella, *Gwendy's Button Box* and the founder/publisher of *Cemetery Dance* magazine and the Cemetery Dance Publications book imprint. He has edited more than 35 anthologies and his short fiction has appeared in dozens of publications, including multiple editions of *Ellery Queen's Mystery Magazine* and *The Year's 25 Finest Crime and Mystery Stories*. He has won two World Fantasy awards, four International Horror Guild awards, and the HWA's Board of Trustee's award.

Chizmar (in collaboration with Johnathon Schaech) has also written screenplays and teleplays for United Artists, Sony Screen Gems, Lions Gate, Showtime, NBC, and many other companies. He has adapted the works of many bestselling authors including Stephen King, Peter Straub, and Bentley Little.

Chizmar is also the creator/writer of *Stephen King Revisited*, and his third short story collection, *A Long December*, was published in 2016 by Subterranean Press. With Brian Freeman, Chizmar is co-editor of the acclaimed *Dark Screams* horror anthology series published by Random House imprint, Hydra.

His latest book, *Widow's Point*, a chilling tale about a haunted lighthouse written with his son, Billy Chizmar, is currently being made into a feature film.

Chizmar's work has been translated into more than fifteen languages throughout the world, and he has appeared at numerous conferences as a writing instructor, guest speaker, panelist, and guest of honor.

Please visit the author's website at: Richardchizmar.com